# *The* River Nymph

## ANNE LOVETT

WORDS OF PASSION • ATLANTA

Published by Words of Passion, Atlanta, GA 30097.

Editorial: Nanette Littlestone
Cover and Interior Design: Peter Hildebrandt

ISBN: 978-0-9996579-5-9

Library of Congress Control Number: [new system goes live 5/20/19]

# DEDICATION

~~~~~~~~~~~~

Dedicated to my three aunts, for the roles they played in my life.

# BOOK I

~~~~~~

## Chapter 1

ASHBYVILLE, GEORGIA, AUGUST 1924

Tenny Oakes needed a place to stay the night, a place where nobody could find her. A place where nobody would mind the dried sweat and river water that plastered her washed-out dress to her body, or her damp, battered boots caked with dust.

The sun's orange ball shimmered toward the river, streaking the dusty horizon, and a freight train hooted and clattered across the tracks she'd crossed five minutes earlier, maybe the same train that had taken her brother away.

She shouldered her croker sack and studied the livery stable, where a painted horse's head fixed its jaded eye on her. Back at Weedy Grove, a barn corner might have done, but the streets of this town afforded precious little shelter.

The freshness she'd felt after her dip in the river was gone, but still she was glad for it. The green water had been like a baptism, being born again, and her old life had curled away in the water along with the dirt and shame she'd carried from Weedy Grove. She was never going back. If only Byron hadn't gone. She counted all the bad things that had happened since he'd left.

About to move on, she noticed a rusty-haired young man in a black car having his gas tank filled at the stable's pump. He was looking at her strangely, and she shied away like a rabbit at crackling grass. With her pale towhair and sun-browned face, men tended to stare at her. This stare was different, and she couldn't say why.

She licked her parched lips. She was passing tired, for she'd walked two days. She leaned back against the building and watched a boy about sixteen who was tall, fair, and with a spotty face like her brother Milton come out to meet a buggy that had just driven up.

He had an unfinished, needy look. After the driver had left and the boy had begun to unhitch the horse, she walked over and touched his arm.

"Hsst! Boy!"

"Who you callin' boy?" said the young man.

"Meant no offense."

"What you want, girl?"

She nodded at the stable. "Can I stay here tonight? I'm little and don't take up much room."

"Hell, no," said the boy. "Old man Jones'd be after my hide if he catched you here."

"He wouldn't have to know. I'm real quiet." She bit her lip. What would her sister have done? She lowered her eyelashes and looked up, straight into his washed-blue eyes, and saw his expression change. Just like the men that visited her sister.

His tongue ran over his puckery, sunburned lips. "How do I know you ain't gone mess with these horses? Steal one, maybe?"

She slowed her voice, made it slow like dark sorghum. "I ain't no horse thief. I just come from the country and got nowhere to go till I get a job."

The boy's eyes traveled over her, lingering at the curve of her hip. What a sight she must appear—old work boots, dress so washed-out it was white, one of Ma's old work shirts across her back, and a croker sack over her shoulder. But her teeth were white and strong from chewing cane most of her fourteen and a half years, and her pale hair had been washed clean in the ripples of the river.

He narrowed his eyes. "What's your name?"

"Tenny," she said, lifting her chin.

"Tenny what?"

"Oakes. Like the trees." It was hard to get out the new last name, seeing as she hadn't used it before.

The boy cocked his head at a skeptical angle. "Come on in, Tenny Oakes." He led the big dapple gray into the stable, and Tenny followed into the dim, high space lit by late sunbeams, its straw-covered floor smelling of dung and dust. He pointed the way to a loft and a ladder. "Stay there till I get off work."

"Got anything to eat?"

"A couple of syrup biscuits in my lunch sack. I was just goin' to throw 'em out. Ma packed too much stuff today."

She decided to press her luck. "Got any chocolate? I'm a plumb fool for chocolate."

He looked her up and down again, reckoning. "What would I be doin' with chocolate?"

"You just look like the kind of boy who might have some, that's all." She knew he was watching her. She wiggled her fingers through her pale hair. "Maybe I better look for someplace else."

The boy's eyes flicked around before they settled back on her. "Nah, don't do that." He walked over to the water trough and reached behind it for the canvas sack hidden there. He pulled out half a Hershey bar and held it up. She started toward him, but he closed his fist around the bar and stuffed it into his pocket. "Give it to you later."

"Give me the biscuits now," she said.

He cut his eyes at her, reached back into the sack, and brought out a bundle wrapped in waxed paper. This he handed to her. She tucked it in her own sack and filled Pa's old tin canteen from the water pump. She climbed to the loft and looked down to make sure that he had gone.

Sitting on a bale of hay, she ate the syrup biscuits and turned up the canteen. Then she carefully washed her hands with the last of the water.

A dark cloud of what was to come pushed at her like a mule nudging the small of her back. She knew what she had to do, and it wasn't what she wanted. She thought about ways she might get the chocolate, get a night's sleep in the hay without doing that thing he wanted, but she was tired and her mind wasn't working. She'd get right in her head about this directly, but right now she'd enjoy her full belly.

Worthless, they had called her before she had escaped from them.

As she lay in the hay of Jones's Livery Stable, she knew she was not worthless. She had seen her own reflection in the shallows of the river with the blue sky beyond, and felt her feet on the streets of Ashbyville, her Bible bumping against her back, and knew she'd made it this far for a reason. She'd run away for her sisters and brothers. For her father, who could not save her, who could not even save himself.

She heard the creak of footsteps on the ladder. "Hsst! Girl! You still here?"

She didn't say anything, hoping he would go away, hoping she would not have to do that thing, but his head appeared at the top of the ladder. She could push him off, she could cause trouble, she could run. She only squinted her eyes and breathed in the smell of hay.

He climbed on up, and she didn't get up as he approached her, his pale skin shining with sweat in the last of the light. "Got to hurry before old man Jones comes back." He began to unfasten his canvas trousers.

She looked at the shining ruddy baton parting his shirt-tail, his eager face as though he could not believe his luck. But she was choosing, this time. She would do what she needed to do to survive.

"The chocolate," she said.

He groaned, dug in his pocket, and tossed her the half Hershey bar. It felt cold, and she looked up in surprise. "I've been keeping it in the Coke box," he said.

She stuffed it in her croker sack and lay back on the hay.

It was over quickly, hardly hurt at all, and afterward, the boy warned her as he buttoned his trousers, "You stay quiet up here. Jones'll be by to check on things. Just keep your trap shut, and he won't look up here. And be gone by sunup."

She thought about asking him how you go about finding somebody, but she felt she only had time for one question. "Where can I get work?"

"You better go back where you came from."

"I aim to get work."

He looked at her sideways. "Lots of girls work at the mill."

"What's that?"

"Girl, don't you know nothin'? It's where they take the cotton and spin it into yarn."

Cotton. Seemed she couldn't get away from it. "How do I get there?"

"Down by the river. Head toward the mornin' sun. Ask somebody on the street. Everybody knows where it is."

The boy scurried down the ladder, and she lay back on the hay and ate the chocolate slowly, letting it melt on her tongue. Working in a mill. Well, whatever that was like, it had to be a heap better than working in the fields or on her back. For some reason she thought about the young man at the gas pump. Maybe he'd looked at her, but he hadn't looked at her with lust in his heart, like that boy here. More like . . . like wonderment, and it made her feel all funny inside. And she wanted that feeling to happen again.

# Chapter 2

W as she the naked girl he'd seen at the river? Pete Godwin excused himself from his mother's supper table and walked out to the porch, while the cicadas chirred and lightning bugs rose from the grass. He wanted to think about the girl he'd seen at the gas pump in front of Jones's Livery stable while he was filling up his father's Buick.

The river nymph.

He'd been helping his cousin Gussie set up her camera and tripod to shoot some ducks, and Gussie was under the cloth patiently waiting for the ducks to cooperate while he held the tripod steady. Bored, he glanced across the sluggish Ocmulgee and there she was, a girl with silky, pale hair piled on her head, stepping out from behind a clump of sweet shrub, naked as God made her, and sloping down to the river, carefully, holding onto twisting roots, and gliding into the water.

He caught his breath. Faintly he heard Gussie's shutter click, heard her ask him to hold tight while she changed the plate. He watched the girl as she dove under, swam around, and pulled herself out, her cottony hair now loose, streaming behind her. Pete, in a haze of fascination, couldn't move. Somewhere the river rustled and birds chirped in the trees and August insects filled the air with humming.

A car's roar on the river road behind him startled him out of the trance, and he lost his balance and pitched forward, knocking the tripod and his cousin's precious Graflex to the sand. "What the hell, Pete!" Gussie howled.

Pete's knee ached where he'd landed. He pushed himself up. "Gussie, you all right? Sorry!"

Gussie snatched up her black headcloth and shook it. "You'd better be sorry. What got into you?"

"That car." He pointed to a yellow Pierce-Arrow roadster, backing up the dirt road.

Gussie barely glanced at the car. "You'd better hope my camera's not broken."

The car stopped and the driver looked out. "Hey, folks, I didn't see you. Can I help?"

"We're okay." Pete shoved his hands in his pockets. "Your damn bucket of bolts messed up my cousin's shot."

"My sincere apologies," the man said with a rueful smile. "I've met you, haven't I? Pete Godwin? And your cousin is Miss Pemberton?" He smiled in Gussie's direction.

She gave the interloper her official smile, teeth only. "I need to retrieve my camera."

"Swell. I'll help you look."

The man got out of the car. Nattily dressed in light linen pants and a blue-and-white striped shirt, this jelly bean wasn't out here by the river to fish. He was dressed like a sheik out to impress a girl, but Pete saw no sign of one. He glanced over at Gussie and, to his disgust, saw a glimmer in her eyes.

Pete and the Pierce-Arrow guy fanned out in the underbrush and briars. In just a few minutes the idiot had come up with the Graflex. "Got it! Here you are, Miss Pemberton."

Taking the black box gingerly in her hands, she looked at the man curiously. "I don't believe we've been introduced."

"Ned Fletcher, at your service," he said. "I met Mr. Godwin here at a card party, but he's pretending he doesn't know me."

Pete made a noise and muffled it with a cough. There had been poker and drinking. Just as well Gussie didn't know.

"Humph." Gussie glanced up at Ned Fletcher from under her eyelashes. She turned the camera over in her hands, brushed sand from the bellows, and inspected the lens carefully. "Seems to be in one piece. Still, the shot's ruined."

"I think you clicked the shutter, Gussie," Pete stood his ground, arms akimbo.

She slid her gaze to the stranger. "How did you know my name?"

"Mr. Fletcher is the new mill manager," Pete interrupted. He didn't like the way Gussie was appraising this guy. He was far too old for her, and recently arrived to take the place of young Toby Burkett, who'd been managing Burkett Mills for two years under the direction of his father. Before he drowned in this very same river.

Pete shook his head in denial. God! How could that have happened? Poor Toby.

"I make it my business to know the names of all the beautiful girls," Ned Fletcher was oiling.

Gussie extended her hand. "Pleased to meet you, Mr. Fletcher. Thanks for helping."

Ned Fletcher lifted Gussie's hand and swiped his lips across it. "I have to run," he said. "As it happens, Miss Pemberton, I have a meeting with your father this afternoon. Perhaps we'll meet again."

Gussie watched him go. With a silly smile on her face.

Pete drove her home, noting the yellow Pierce-Arrow parked in the driveway of his uncle's red-brick Georgian house. He'd always liked that house, though now the white columns were peeling and one shutter hung crookedly. If he wasn't so busy at the hospital, he'd offer to fix it for his uncle.

Nobody was prosperous these days with the downturn in cotton. Well, that Fletcher would have his work cut out for him at Burkett Mills, trying to keep that place churning out money now that the Great War was over and the boll weevil was taking its toll.

He headed over to the ball field and watched the last game of the doubleheader against the Augusta Tygers, then he went to the station for the gas. He wanted the car again this evening, because the lovely Miss Swanee Burkett had agreed to go with him to see *The Thief of Baghdad* at the Rose Theatre.

"Hidey there, Little Doc." Abner, in oil-spotted khaki, lifted the hose and fitted it to the Ford's tank. The cylindrical pump clicked, filling the evening dust with the odor of gasoline. Abner patted the car's flank. "Your pop still like this car?"

"Yep," said Pete. "Wish I had a car of my own."

"Got a Chevy I'll sell you," said Abner. "Bought it off that feller Fletcher. Got hisself one of them fancy cars."

"A Pierce-Arrow?" Pete wondered how Fletcher could afford it. Did he have family money?

"You bet. He's a single fella and wants a car to squire around the ladies. Why, back in my day it was near impossible to get one by theirselves. They always had to haul along a little brother or sister, even when you was out walkin'. . ."

That damned Fletcher. The last time Pete had taken Swanee Burkett out for a drive and a sundae, all she'd done was chatter on about "Daddy's new mill manager." Learned the business up North, he did, and came highly recommended, she'd told him. Pete didn't want to be bored rigid with that kind of talk this evening.

Ned Fletcher could never really take Toby Burkett's place. Suicide? Didn't seem right. Toby had everything. But who would gain from his death? Maybe Ned Fletcher, but he hadn't even been in town then.

Ned Fletcher, with his slick manners and Valentino face, was no Toby. Valentino, yes, but for the scars. Some said he'd gotten a face full of shrapnel in France, but Pete doubted Ned Fletcher was any kind of hero.

Pete especially didn't like the way Gussie had looked at that sheik. Lost in thought, he almost missed seeing the pale-haired girl in the washed-out dress, wearing workboots, making her way in the fading daylight.

She gazed around at the streets and the shops as though she was searching for something. She stopped to talk to a boy who was unhitching a horse at Abner's livery stable, and Pete got a good look at her face.

It was the elfin face of a child, rounded, big-eyed, with a little pointed chin, but this child's face was tough and tanned, as though she had spent long hours in the sun. Too striking to be called pretty, the face struck Pete with its odd beauty, its determined expression. He guessed her to be about fourteen or so.

Was this his river nymph? The hair looked the same. That expanding feeling of wonder he'd had at the river flowed back. He kept his eyes on her until she disappeared into the livery stable with the boy. He shook his head. He'd better forget about her. Too young, just a girl, really, yet she had eyes like an old soul.

Abner, who had not ceased talking, never noticed the girl, and Pete didn't think it worth mentioning. He paid Abner for the gas and drove home, yet he couldn't quite forget that face. It had seen suffering, he thought, and that was a look he was beginning to know only too well.

Gussie, in contrast, had never known misfortune. A flapper, seventeen years old, and all her charmed life had been just swell, except for the trouble she made for herself.

After Pete had let her off at her door, Gussie strolled into the hall and leaned her tripod against the wall. She tugged off her tam and hung it on the hat stand, noting the Panama she'd seen on Ned Fletcher, and then she glanced toward her father's closed study door.

She'd take her equipment to the basement darkroom and then come upstairs when she heard the study door open. Ned Fletcher intrigued her. He had an air of mystery, an air of adventure. So what if Pete didn't like him? Pete didn't know everything.

Just as she picked up her tripod, someone rapped at the front door. Huffing in exasperation, she flung it open to see a young man with too much untidy brown hair looking down on her. Carrying a law book. A student.

"Good afternoon, miss," he said. "Is the judge available?"

"My father's busy right now. You'd better come back later."

"But we have an appointment." The student gestured at the tripod in her hand and the bulky camera case on her shoulder. "May I help you carry that somewhere?"

"No, thank you." She set the equipment back in the corner. How could she get rid of him?

"I don't mind waiting, Miss Pemberton," the young man said. "Maybe you'd tell him Henry Benedict is here?"

"He has a visitor." This fellow wasn't bad-looking for a student. She indicated a small bench in the hall. "Sit here, please."

The library door burst open and Ned Fletcher stalked out. Her father's voice boomed, "Good day to you, sir!"

This time she really noticed him. Late twenties, maybe, his deep brown hair slicked back with pomade, his mustache well-groomed. His hazel eyes met hers and he smiled. "We meet again, Miss Pemberton." He took the Panama off the hat stand, clapped it on his head, and adjusted it to a jaunty angle.

So dapper, yet his nose might once have been broken, and a scar crossed his chin. "Thank you again, Mr. Fletcher, for finding my camera. Good-bye."

"My pleasure." He touched his hat and let himself out, glancing back, still smiling. The door closed with a soft click.

How she must have looked to him! Dusty, sweaty clothes, curls whipped into frizz by the wind! She hoped he was amused. But this Henry Benedict person was now heading toward her father's door! She caught his arm. "Wait. I need to see Papa before you go in."

"I've come all this way on my bicycle," he said. "You're here all the time."

Earnest green eyes met hers. She ought to give in, but she had an important mission. "I won't be a minute." She slipped past him and hurried into the familiar scent of pipe tobacco and leather. Papa's face was flushed and his white hair stood up as though judgely hands had run through it. His mustache twitched.

"Papa, I . . ."

He waved her words aside. "Augusta, that damn fool wants to buy Arcadia."

Gussie eased the door closed behind her. "What? Does he think he can grow cotton when everybody else is growing broke?"

"I promised your grandfather on his deathbed I wouldn't sell. That bounder Fletcher knew I have no sons to take it over, and that Amelia's boy is going into medicine."

She walked to her father's chair, stood behind it, and rested her hands on his shoulders. "Dear Papa," she said. "I don't blame you for being furious. That Fletcher man has some nerve."

"Furious? Who said I was furious?"

Gussie glanced at the row of Georgia Code books on the shelf behind the desk. One was askew, which meant he'd taken out the bottle behind it for a nip. "If you say so, Papa."

The judge picked up his pipe and began to stuff tobacco into it. "He was probing to see if I needed the money more than the land. Sneaky cuss. Thought I'd sell cheap." He struck a match to the pipe.

Gussie's mother had been forced to economize ever since cotton had started its long slide downward. The farm that her grandfather had left them wasn't profitable now, especially since Papa and Aunt Amelia had to pay someone to manage it.

Not only was it hard keeping up appearances, it was hard to keep anything to yourself in this burg. New York, the place where everybody was having fun, shimmered like a mirage on a hot road. She could spread her wings with nobody to tell her to act like a lady.

Judge Pemberton drew on his pipe before speaking again. "We'll keep Arcadia come hell or high water. There's nothing like the land. We'll get by. Your mama doesn't go in for frippery and society like some folks."

Gussie's heart sank. She liked frippery and society. If she was going to become a photographer, she had to get out and mix with people, make contacts.

Especially at the upcoming social event of the season. "Papa, we will be going to the birthday party, won't we? Everybody who's anybody will be there."

Judge Pemberton raised his eyebrows. "Oh, worried about that, are you? Suppose we've got to go, for political reasons." He winked. "Worried about a new frock? I'll speak to your mama. Now what have you been up to this afternoon, racketing around with young Pete?"

"I was out taking pictures, Papa. I got a few good ones. And the funniest thing happened . . ."

The front door slammed, echoing in the hall. "Here's your mama back with my automobile," said the judge, winking at Gussie. "I'm going out to the ball park to clear that scalawag's ugly mug out of my head."

Gussie's mother stormed in. Her faded red-gold hair was coming out of its pins, and her afternoon dress, a rumpled cotton print, looked a bit worse for wear.

"Sorry to interrupt, darlings. Mac, your student, Henry Benedict, is here to see you. He says he's been waiting a good while." The judge smacked his forehead with the heel of his hand. "Clean forgot about young Benedict! I promised him a little time. Humph. I wanted to go catch that second game of the doubleheader. I guess I'll just have to take him with me."

The judge rose, grabbed his seersucker coat and his pipe, and kissed his wife's cheek. "I'll leave you two."

Gussie felt her mother's eyes on her. The front door closed, and now her mother spoke. "I wish you'd come with me next Sunday. I'd like you to meet the girls I'm working with."

Gussie pursed her lips. "Mama, my photography is important."

"Every single Sunday? Can't you spare some time to help others?"

Gussie sank into her father's walnut swivel chair, swinging it back and forth. "Do you think they'd let me take their pictures?"

"That isn't nice, Augusta."

Gussie bit her lip, thinking of the new frock she wanted. "But the pictures could go to the paper for a story. Maybe it would keep more girls from getting into trouble."

"What! It would embarrass them no end."

"But maybe it would make other girls think twice. I'd be doing a public service, and that's what you want me to do."

Gussie's mother sighed. "What I'd like to embarrass is the boys that got them into this. Do you realize the boys—or men—usually get off scot free? Sometimes the girls' families throw them out. Tell them they're bringing shame to the family. Usually their biggest sin is looking for the love they're not getting at home."

Gussie considered. "Well, maybe I could just do a portrait from the neck up. Make them look pretty. But not today," she pleaded. "Tonight I'll help you address those postcards for your women's rights lecture. I'll take flyers around town on my bicycle."

Belinda looked at her suspiciously for a moment. "You must want something, chickadee."

Gussie widened her eyes. "Me? Want something? Oh, no, Mama." She'd wait until the right time to beg for that new dress. One with fringe on it, so she could shimmy.

"We'll see," Belinda said. "Now you can put that clutter in the hall away."

"Yes, Mama."

She hurried out to the hall and lugged the heavy camera and equipment down to the basement darkroom. She'd develop the plates later, because right now her head was full of the swell cotillion which kicked off Swanee's coming-out this year. Maybe Senator Vincent would come. After all, his son was paying court to Swanee, and she knew Swanee's father was all for the match.

Maybe the Lieutenant Governor would come. Not the Governor! Papa hated the Governor. She wished she could take her camera so she could sell the shots of the bigwigs to the *Ashbyville Clarion*. Her shoulders slumped. She knew Papa would never permit her to take a camera to a social occasion.

Hanging her tripod on its wall hook, she stared at the bottles of chemicals on the shelf. She wondered idly if she'd captured an image of the naked girl and if anyone would want to buy it. It'd be blurred, most likely. She stowed the camera case.

Who was the girl? Where was she going? She and Pete had talked about it on the way home. He'd said that because of her tanned legs and arms and face, she must be a runaway farm girl. Leaving her home and making her way to the big city.

What a girl! That's what Gussie wanted to do, except she wanted to run away to New York, where all the fun was. Jazz, cocktails, parties— maybe she could get a job with a magazine!

She didn't want to be like Mama or her sisters. Mama was always doing good, and that was fine if you wanted to stay in a town like Ash- byville. In fact, her mother would have stopped that river girl and tried to help her.

Well, maybe that girl didn't want to be helped. Maybe she had the right to find her own way. Like Gussie wanted to find her own way. It was hellacious, being the youngest. Anna was married and Jessie was a teacher, but people just patted Gussie on the head and told her how cute she looked. Maybe that river girl wanted to prove she could make her own way.

# Chapter 3

Tenny left the livery stable just as the sun crept over the horizon, drawing early-morning mist into a dewy peach-colored sky. As the boy had told her, she followed the streets toward the gathering brightness, past shops and businesses with names like Miller's Feed and Seed and Rosenberg's Dry Goods and Ashbyville Curb Market, where men unloaded huge baskets and crates of fruits and vegetables and piled them in bins: red and yellow tomatoes, big green sweet peppers, corn sporting fuzzy brown tassels, yellow crookneck squash, long striped watermelons.

In the market, she searched every young man's face, hoping she'd see Byron's deep-set eyes. Her heart told her he'd do what he had vowed: come to Ashbyville to seek his fortune.

Would anyone come to Ashbyville looking for her? They had chased her in the car, and she had managed to slip away, but they might come to town looking.

She glanced around nervously and saw nothing but a stand where a woman in a canvas apron was setting out baskets of plump red plums. The woman looked friendly, the kind Tenny could ask the way to the mill. The woman pointed down an alley. "Take that way—it's a shortcut. Head toward the sun."

Tenny thanked her and turned to leave. "Wait, honey," the woman said. "You could use a little smile in your soul." She held out a rosy peach smelling of summer. Tenny bit into it at once, licking every drop of juice off her lips, and felt a little better.

The alley opened into a hilly street of shops and she turned left, still heading toward the rising sun. The peach had just made her hungrier. It had been a long time since the syrup biscuits of the night before, and the food she'd packed was long gone. She unwrapped the last square of Hershey's, melting fast, and savored it on her tongue.

In the next block, bacon and coffee hung in the air, and she spotted a man wearing overalls going through a screen door. The sign above it read Mabel's. She still had the dollars she'd stolen—no, earned—and she pushed the screen door open.

She recognized nobody. Men forking up hotcakes and eggs crowded elbow to elbow on stools at a counter, while a hefty colored man behind the counter worked the sizzling, smoking grill. Tenny stared at the prices posted on the signboard back of the counter and bit her lip. She noticed a pot of sorghum syrup on the table, counted her money in her head, and approached the dough-faced woman taking orders. "Coffee and two biscuits."

"Fifteen cents," said the woman.

Tenny reached into her patch pocket, came up with a dollar bill, and thrust it at the woman. Two of the men looked at her and muttered something under their breaths. Tenny dropped the change the woman gave her down into her boot.

When the woman set the coffee and biscuits in front of her, she took her plate over to a rickety trestle table in the corner where four others sat, choosing it over an empty stool at the counter between two men. She sipped the coffee, trying to make it last, poured sorghum over her biscuit, and watched the men at the far end of the table. Dull-eyed, they shoveled in ham and grits, paying her no mind.

When her coffee and the last biscuit crumb were gone, she left the cup on the table, gathered up her croker sack, and walked past the counter toward the door. One of the men spun his stool in her direction. "Hey, blondie."

Startled, she turned and met the eyes of a heavyset graying man with a fleshy nose. The stable boy had looked at her like that: sizing her up, figuring what it would take to get what he wanted. She looked away and edged toward the door.

"Look at miss high-and-mighty," he said to no one in particular. "Ain't got much to be high-and-mighty about."

She walked out, letting the screen door bang behind her, scattering flies. She hurried down the street, down the hill, distancing herself from the café. The shops became fewer and the road widened, and then it came to an end.

She found herself facing the gates of a cemetery, where stone monuments rose among rolling acres of grass, gravel, and good red clay. The grounds looked deserted except for a colored gravedigger who was kicking clay off his shovel. She crossed a street, walked through the gates, and hesitantly approached the man.

"Uncle, can you tell me how to get to the mill?"

He looked up from his shovel and raised an eyebrow. "Now why you want to go yonder?"

"I'm looking for a job."

"That place chew you up and spit you out," he grumbled.

"I don't have a lot of choice," she blurted. "I ran away from home and I've got to live somehow."

He gave her a searching look, leaned on his shovel, and then pointed northeast toward a stand of pines across the street, where a broad smokestack rose beyond them. She turned to go.

"Wait," he said. "They ain't gone let you take that croker sack in the mill. You mought smuggle out some of the goods."

"But what can I do with it?"

"They hold it for you. So they say. But some peoples tell me they lose it, or lose what you got in it."

Tenny bit her lip. The old man looked honest. "Would you keep it for me? You wouldn't steal my dead mama's Bible, would you? There's not much else in it."

He drew himself up and stared at her. "I preaches the word of the Lord."

"So you preach and dig graves too?"

He nodded. "It gets they attention in church, child."

She looked at the sack in her hand. She looked at the man, leaning on his shovel. He was not quite old and not quite young, and he wore a shapeless old hat over nappy gray hair.

"I have to trust you," she said, and handed him the bag.

"I'll keep good care of it," he said. "By the way, they call me Digger John."

"Thank you, Digger John. If they don't hire me today, I'll be back pretty soon."

She took one last look at her bag, then ran across the street and toward the pines.

Through the trees, down the hill, she saw the bridge, and on the other side of the river, the enormous red brick building and its smokestacks. The high windows at the top caught the morning sun, shimmering silver. It looked like the Promised Land.

Workers were milling and talking outside the gate. The whistle blew, the gate opened, and the crowd—mostly women and girls—filed in.

Taking a look behind her to make sure nobody was following, she walked down the hill. So this was the place that took the cotton she and her family had sweated over and turned it into yarn. Drops trickled down her forehead. She didn't go in at once, but skittered down a path to the river's edge and dipped a handful of the water. Might as well clean up a little.

When she raised her hands to her face, she smelled a peculiar odor, not like the sweet, muddy smell of the river where she had bathed the day before. She dried her face with the hem of her dress and walked across the bridge.

Tenny Oakes was the name she gave the man. When he asked where she lived, she told him she hadn't found a place yet, she was new in town. "You have to have an address before we can hire you," he said, looking her over carefully.

She hadn't thought about that. She thought she would get a job and then look for a place to stay nearby. Somebody whispered something to the man, and then he said, "Well. One of my sweepers didn't show for work. I don't usually use a girl for sweeping, but you can fill in today. I ain't promising anything for tomorrow."

The man led her to the floor boss. Her heart sank when she saw the big-nosed man from the grill. "Burton will show you the ropes," the hiring man said, and left.

Burton grinned. "Well, well, well. Time to start your education, linthead. Get to work." He found her a push broom and a bucket of oiled sawdust and a cart. The sawdust was to be sprinkled on the floor to gather the lint before she swept. The sweepings would go into a cart to be dumped into a pit out back.

She did everything he asked of her, even though the oil smelled bad and her sweeping stirred up the linters even more, making it hard to breathe. She felt his eyes on her constantly, just like the eyes of her family's landlord from his high horse. The sun poured through the upper windows, heating up the place. At the spindles, the workers' faces shone, the color of raw meat.

She wasn't sure which job was worse. In the fields there were bugs and the sun right on your head if you didn't wear a hat, and the heavy weight of the cotton bag on your shoulders, and fingers bleeding from the bolls, and hands sore from the chopping.

In the mill the heat was suffocating, and the lint got in your nose and mouth and everywhere, and, Lord, the clatter of those machines was like to deafen you. She knew now why some of the girls wore handkerchiefs around their faces, but nothing covered their poor ears. But she wasn't going to give up now.

Finally, all the sweeping was done, and she collected the day's pay of seventy-five cents. She was told to come back with an address and they'd see if they had a place for her, but not to count on it. Lots of girls showed up every day.

Tired and hungry, she trudged out, and almost didn't hear the woman with blonde frizzy hair nudging her. "Hey, kid," she said. "I heard all that. We got a spare room 'cause my nephew quit and went back home. We got to rent it or move out. My name's Myrtle Mincus. Come on with me."

Tenny's shoulders ached and her nose felt all stuffed. "They won't promise me a job."

"That's okay. Just pay me for tonight."

Myrtle Mincus led the way to the mill village, a collection of small frame houses with dirt yards built close together, each with a front and back porch, painted mostly in greens and blues.

"Here we go, kid." She led the way up the steps of a blue one with peeling paint. Clete Mincus met them in the kitchen. He wasn't very tall, but he slouched in an arrogant way, maybe because he was good-looking, with dark straight hair that flopped over his forehead.

Myrtle lit a cigarette, leaving red lip-prints as she smoked, picking strings of tobacco out of the lipstick and flicking them at her husband while she explained that Tenny needed the room and they would like a nice quiet girl.

Clete checked Tenny out through heavy-lidded eyes, and his lips curled in a funny smile. "Glad to have you, toots," he said. "Call me Clete."

Mrs. Mincus chirped, "And call me Myrtle, dearie."

Myrtle showed her to a tiny room, almost a closet, but Tenny was ecstatic. It was a room just for herself, more than she'd ever had at home. Room and board would be a dollar and a half a week. She stretched out on the lumpy bed gratefully and fell fast asleep. She awoke when Myrtle yelled that supper was ready.

Supper wasn't much—dry cornbread and thin vegetable soup—and Tenny hurried through it so that she could get back to the graveyard and find Digger John.

Digger John had gone and the gate to the cemetery was locked. Tenny felt a tight chill in her belly. There went her mama's Bible, and him saying he was a man of God. She would go back again. She would go back until he gave her that Bible.

The next day they told her she could sweep again because the sweeper was sick, and so she swept, and the sweeper boy never came back, and somebody murmured that he was dead of the typhoid from swimming in a farm pond, and they were going to hire a strong boy and this puny girl would be out. But rain fell for a week. Huge storms slashed the sky and raked the air with lightning; thunder boomed in the lowlands, and she was still on the job. She huddled inside her small room after work.

Saturday night, the Mincuses went next door to visit. Tenny's window was slap-up close to the neighbors, and she could see into their front room. The four of them sat laughing, holding glasses and cigarettes; they danced the foxtrot in the tiny room to a record on an old Victrola, Myrtle's earbobs swinging.

Tenny had never seen such fun in her life. Nothing like that had ever happened in Weedy Grove. She promised herself that someday she was going to dance, with a feathered band for her head.

# Chapter 4

G ussie Pemberton, in a gown of green beaded silk and feathered headband, stood by the open French window of the Burketts' vast colonnaded ballroom, watching party guests below jockey their cars into place on the smooth lawn. The sweet August night chirred with cicadas, and a bullfrog thrumped from the goldfish pond.

"Looking for somebody?" Pete thrust a crystal cup of something orange-pink and fizzy at her, while the jazz quintet struck up "Five Foot Two, Eyes of Blue," the bass bumping out the rhythm.

"I haven't seen your gal." She took a sip. "Methodist punch."

"There she is with the Vincent guy." Pete's gaze followed Swanee Burkett, her jet-black bob swinging, knotted pearls dancing over her raspberry silk gown, as she shimmied across the floor with Russell Vincent, the senator's son who'd just earned a law degree from the University of Georgia.

"I thought you were supposed to be back at school." Gussie patted her curls and adjusted her headband.

Pete flushed. "I couldn't miss her big party. I'll get there before classes start. Barely."

Gussie gave him a scathing look. "Be an idiot, then." She grabbed a canapé from a passing waiter and bit into it. "Mmmm. I love rich peoples' parties."

"Green-eyed monster, hmm?"

"Not a bit. I like being me."

Pete set the Methodist punch on a table. "I'm going to slip out for a nip. Want to come?"

Gussie glanced at her parents sitting at the far end of the room with Russell Vincent's father, Senator Albion Vincent, and the agriculture commissioner, Eugene Talmadge. "I'm surprised at you, Pete. You're always telling me to behave myself."

"Come on. I've got something to tell you."

"Copacetic. Let's go!"

He grabbed her hand and they left through the French door, crossing the raised stone patio glowing with Japanese lanterns. They clattered down stone steps and onto the lawn. Stumbling a bit in her flimsy T-straps, Gussie held Pete's hand as they scampered out to the tall pecan tree where Pete had parked his borrowed roadster.

From a compartment under the rumble seat, Pete pulled out a silver flask. Gussie noticed a couple necking in a Ford a couple of cars away, and she smelled cigarette smoke from the shadows.

They sat on the running board, passing the flask back and forth in the still night, smelling fresh-cut grass, honeysuckle, and cigarettes, surrounded by the chirr of cicadas.

Gussie patted Pete's arm. "Come on, what's the big news?"

He pulled a ring box from his pocket and opened it. Amethysts and opals set in chased gold gleamed in the moonlight. "I'm going to ask Swanee to accept this tonight."

Gussie almost choked on her sip of bourbon. "Tonight? Pete, I'm going to be Dorothy Dix. Don't do this."

"Well, I didn't write to your column. She doesn't want to marry Vincent."

"It's arranged. Like dukes and heiresses."

His smile broadened. "She told me Russell Vincent was a jug-eared bore."

"Bores quite often have lots of money, Pete dearest. Our Swanee loves money more than . . . well, love."

Pete stared at the ground, so quiet that Gussie thought she might be getting through to him. But then he took her by the arms and looked directly at her. "Gussie, you just don't understand. I love *her*. I've loved her for years. Sometimes I think I love her more than life itself."

Gussie, astonished at the passion in his voice, raised her arm to shield her eyes from the headlights of a car backing into a space nearby. The lights went out, and the moonlight revealed a man in a white dinner jacket closing the door to a yellow Pierce-Arrow. He strode toward the high white columns.

"Well," Gussie said. "If it isn't Mr. Mill Manager."

Pete's eyes glittered. "What did he want with Uncle Mac the other day, if I may ask?"

Gussie snorted. "The vulture! He wants to buy Arcadia. What would your mother say?"

"Indubitably," Pete said, "Mom would send him packing. Frankly, Grandpa was nuts to leave the farm to them both. When have they ever agreed on anything?" He took one more gulp from the flask, capped it, and slid it under the seat. "Come on. I've got the waltz with the girl I love."

Gussie got up and flung her stole around her shoulders. She wouldn't tell Pete about the guy she'd seen Swanee with just last week, one of the band musicians. Could be they were just talking about music for the party, but . . .

Before Pete could step away from the car, Gussie put out a hand to stay him. "Chaperones." She pointed to the patio, where Professor Rolfe Moon and Miss Ola Stratton peered out toward the grove. Professor Moon, with his widow's peak and little goatee, looked like the very devil, and Miss Ola, a faded belle of fifty, wore a tight befringed orange gown and a little too much rouge.

Miss Ola said something to her cohort, and they began to make their way down the stone steps.

"Spit! Looking for somebody who's been gone too long. They won't see us." Pete put his arm around Gussie and held her close. The night sounds seemed to quiet down all at once, and she was scared to even breathe. That's all she needed right now, to get caught drinking by Miss Ola Stratton, who would go straight to Papa, and there she would be, confined to the house for a month.

Shoes rustled on pine straw and twigs snapped as the chaperones passed between the cars.

"Follow me. Now!" Pete murmured, grabbing her hand. They tiptoed turtle-backed between the cars, rushing to the front of the house. They almost collided with a man standing in deep shadow. "Oh!" Gussie stopped suddenly, teetering a little.

In gaslight the three stared at each other. "Miss Pemberton, of course," the man said. He extended his hand. "Good to see you again." He turned to Pete. "Hello, Godwin."

Pete reluctantly thrust out his hand. "Fletcher."

Gussie blurted, "We saw you drive up. Why are you still out here?"

He smiled. "Admiring the house. I'll have one just as fine someday."

Gussie set her jaw. "Not Arcadia, I think."

"We need to be getting in." Pete tugged her arm, and the three walked up the front steps. The ebony-skinned butler opened the door before they rang. "Hello, Marcus," said Pete. "We've just been out taking the air."

The butler nodded and took Ned's hat. "How are you this evenin', Mr. Fletcher?"

So Marcus knew him well. Gussie, scrambling after Pete down the wide hall, digested this information. They burst into the ballroom just as the chaperones Ola Stratton and Rolfe Moon emerged from the patio door with two young flappers in tow. The smokers, Gussie guessed.

Swanee Burkett glanced up from the knot of admirers surrounding her, and with eyes shining and lips parted, hurried over and clasped Ned Fletcher's hands.

Gussie glanced over at Pete, who'd gone rigid as a cigar store Indian. The band struck up the waltz, and Pete walked over and placed himself firmly in front of the twosome. "I believe this is my dance, Miss Burkett."

Swanee barely disguised a pout as she disengaged herself from Mr. Fletcher and went to dance with Pete to the strains of "Bye, Bye, Blackbird." Gussie turned to leave and a hand touched her arm. "Miss Pemberton? Would you like to dance?"

Her pulse quickened in surprise. "Mr. Fletcher." She consulted her dance card. "I'd be delighted."

Ned glided through the dance as smoothly as Vernon Castle, and Gussie reluctantly admired his skill. She asked him where he'd learned.

"Virginia. That's where I grew up. Cotillion, all that."

Gussie raised an eyebrow. "I heard you were from the north. Or Florida."

"Spent some time in both places, learning business, learning about mills." He led her effortlessly across the floor.

She leaned back enough to look him in the eye. "Why did you come to Ashbyville, Mr. Fletcher?"

He swooped her in a dip. "Mr. Burkett had contacted a friend of mine in Savannah about an experienced mill manager. Somebody with modern ideas." He lifted her up and took a gentle turn. "So sorry about the tragedy here with young Toby."

She didn't want to talk about Toby and glanced away. Then she turned back with an innocent smile. "I've been wanting to ask you. Why are you interested in Arcadia?"

"I miss the old family place in Virginia. Arcadia's beautiful, though not as large."

Gussie wrinkled her nose. "Papa says it's too far from the courthouse and there's no electricity."

"I hate to think of that lovely old house standing empty."

Gussie shrugged. "Papa's thinking about tenants. He already rents out fields, because my aunt wants to keep the place. She's sentimental, and my cousin Pete might want it someday. He says one day they'll bring electricity to the country. And we do go there for picnics and things."

A shadow crossed Ned's face. "Tenants would ruin the place. Sentiment doesn't pay the bills. And picnics? Ashbyville has a wonderful river."

Gussie shook her curls. "Arcadia's been in our family for a hundred years."

"Maybe I ought to join your family." Ned gave her a lazy, sensuous smile, one that made her catch her breath.

Gussie tamped down the flutters and pretended nonchalance. "You can try to marry my sister Jessie."

"Oh?"

"She's a schoolteacher. My other sister, Anna, is married already."

They glided and swooped until Gussie felt dizzy, her gardenia perfume rising from her bodice. "You're a good dancer, Miss Pemberton," Ned said, "and you smell good."

She pursed her lips. "You're a shameless flatterer. They almost threw me out of cotillion for being too energetic. They said it wasn't ladylike."

Ned grinned. "You're refreshing, you know that?"

"That's not the word some people use," she said.

"What do they say?"

"Troublemaker."

The music slid to an end on a mournful clarinet note, but Ned kept a hand on her waist. "Just my type. Would you like a cup of punch?"

"I need to find my cousin," she said with a melting smile. "It's a matter of utmost importance. Thank you for the dance." She'd better keep her distance from Ned Fletcher. Maybe until he lost interest in Arcadia.

She took off across the dance floor. Maybe she could catch Pete and head off the proposal. She bit her lip. He loved Swanee more than life itself? What if she rejected him? Would he follow poor Toby into the river?

She didn't see him anywhere. Maybe it was already too late.

"Gussie!" a gaggle of girls who were also Essie Swift-bound cornered her, eager to talk about school.

It was impossible to break away without being rude. Glancing around frantically, she spotted Swanee easing one long leg through the door from the patio. Pete followed her, white-faced and stiff with dignity, like a soldier about to face a firing squad.

"Excuse me," she whispered to her classmates, patting each one on the shoulder, "I'm on a mission of life or death." She headed toward Pete, but he ducked to the outer hall and descended the staircase towards the men's smoking room. Gussie stood at the door to the hall, hands on hips.

"Miss Pemberton? Did you save me a dance?"

Startled, she looked up into the eyes of Henry Benedict. Tall and lanky, Henry obviously didn't spend time at the barber shop. His hair wouldn't stay slicked back. Some girls might have thought he was good-looking in his dinner jacket, but her father's students were always too smart and too serious. Not jazzy. And she liked jazz.

"I don't recall your asking me." Gussie arched her brows.

Henry bowed low. "My mother volunteered me at the last minute to fill in. Can't have a dance without enough guys, can you? Taking the trolley was embarrassing in this monkey suit." He lifted her hand and kissed it. "May I have a dance now?

Gussie, surprised, lifted her chin. "Too bad. My card's filled." She patted her hair and looked up at the ceiling.

"I don't see anybody coming. Anyhow, you look thirsty. I'll get you a cup of punch." Henry walked off, leaving her to fume.

She watched Henry stop to say hello to Papa and Mama. Okay, he was Papa's student, but why did Papa like him so much? They were grinning and joking together.

Gussie figured that meant that Henry was always going to be around, and Papa would probably hire him as clerk. That disqualified him right there as a suitor. There sure was more to life than staying in Ashbyville with her parents breathing down her neck.

Henry arrived promptly with two cups of punch. She thanked him, took a sip or two, and then put the cup down. Maybe Pete had come out of the men's room now. "I think I'll go for some fresh air," she said. "I really need to find my cousin. I think he might be very unhappy right now."

"Pete? He's a big boy. Better leave him alone."

"Henry, you just don't understand." She shook her head and circled the floor, eyes out for a head of rusty hair. Swanee was dancing away, this time in the arms of her future husband.

Pete was nowhere to be seen. Henry, drat it, was right behind Gussie, following her all the way out to the patio. Beyond the warm orange glow of the Japanese lanterns lurked deep shadows where lovers could kiss. Palm leaves were rustling. A few couples were taking advantage.

Barging ahead, she leaned over the stone balcony. She saw Pete's rented roadster in the light of the moon, and then she spotted a figure lying face down on the grass beside it.

Suddenly she was glad for Henry's presence. She grabbed his hand. "Come on!"

# Chapter 5

G ussie strode up to the rack of penny dreadfuls in the station, intending to buy one for Pete to read on the train. She and Henry had picked him up off the ground completely ossified and taken him home in the borrowed roadster.

Men with briefcases hustled by, dark-skinned redcaps rolled baggage carts, trains chuffed and brakes squealed, while oily smoke and coffee smells clashed in the air. Dusty sunlight filtered from the high windows onto the rack where Gussie extended thumb and forefinger to one of the more lurid-looking books, its orange cover featuring a gun-toting bad guy in a fedora.

She marched up to the counter and presented the book to the smirking clerk, a young man in steel-rimmed glasses, and realized Pete was breathing down her neck.

"Are you really going to read that?" Pete, wearing argyle vest, knitted tie, and corduroy coat, stood with his ticket to Atlanta in one hand and soft valise in the other. His eyes were bloodshot and his face pasty, and he'd used too much hair tonic.

She wrinkled her nose and laughed. "It's for you." She paid for the book, took it from the clerk, and handed it to Pete.

Pete shifted uncomfortably and shook his head. "I have things to study."

He'd probably sleep the whole way. They walked away from the kiosk, and Gussie fingered the book. "Maybe I'll read it for the juicy parts."

Pete set down his valise and checked his watch. "I'll take it after all. Almost time to board." He knuckled her cheek and took the book, stuffing it into his pocket. "Watch out for yourself."

Gussie crushed him in a bear hug. She'd sworn she was going to keep her mouth shut, but she burst out, "The way Swanee treats you! Forget about her, Pete."

The train whistle blasted, throaty and shrill. Pete drew away and kissed her on the cheek. "I'll write. Thanks for giving me a ride. And the book."

"Sure. You've done a lot for me."

He hesitated, then, as if there were something more he wanted to say. He glanced up at the high windows, at the dust motes shimmering overhead and then looked directly into Gussie's eyes. "Would you write to me? About her, I mean."

Gussie frowned. "Why don't you write her yourself?"

He shook his head. "Come on, Gus. Just a little news every now and then."

The look in his eyes made her take back the *No* on her lips. "All right. It's your funeral."

Pete smiled bitterly, hefted his valise, and strode off to the waiting train.

She steered her father's Hupmobile back through town with a nagging foreboding. What Pete had confessed still bothered her. Loved Swanee more than life itself? Would he sacrifice everything for a girl like that? When had it begun, this obsession? When had he become so silly over the girl who had guys dangling from all ten fingers?

A policeman stopped Gussie at an intersection. Speak of the Devil! Swanee herself crossed in front of her in that cream-colored DeSoto roadster, a present from her father, and pulled into a parking place in front of the drugstore, where a yellow Pierce-Arrow just happened to be parked.

At the policeman's signal, Gussie turned the corner rather than go straight, as she'd planned. She found a parking spot a little way down from the drugstore, but didn't kill the engine.

The pleats of Swanee's silky peach dress swirled as she slinked across the sidewalk. At the drugstore window, she peered at her reflection. She adjusted her cloche and pouted in the glass before she pushed open the door.

Gussie considered the looks that had passed between Swanee and Ned Fletcher at the dance. She'd wanted to find out what made the man tick, why he wanted Arcadia, and now Swanee had him in her sights. Damn what that girl was going to do to Pete! Gussie backed out, stepped on the gas pedal, and drove home so carelessly she almost ran into the back of a tall, thin man driving a mule and wagon. "Bless you," he called to her as she screeched to a stop. "Be safe."

Swanee jerked the roadster into reverse and pulled out of the parking place a little too fast, narrowly missing an oncoming taxicab. The driver honked and yelled about how women had no business driving, crazy, ought to stay home. Swanee gritted her teeth as she raced away. How dare Ned Fletcher snub her!

Well, not a snub exactly, but he'd acted as though he hardly knew her. Some secret business he and the druggist had been transacting—whiskey, most likely. When he'd finally noticed her, he'd just tipped his hat, spoken politely, and walked on out. Any *other* fellow she knew would have been Johnny on the spot, offering to buy her a sundae, a milkshake, or a cherry dope. Any other fellow would be sitting in a booth with her right now.

She felt a perfect fool. People had been looking at her in that drugstore, because people always looked at her. She'd held her head high, bought a couple of things, and walked out. He hadn't acted like that at her party. She'd show him a thing or two!

She wheeled the roadster into the garage and turned off the engine, wondering if her mother had heard her come in. Hoping to avoid a confrontation, she slipped in through the sun porch.

To her consternation, Clara Burkett, forehead wrinkled and her mouth pursed, popped out of the parlor to meet her. "Thank goodness you're back. My head is splitting."

Swanee, still annoyed, said, "Well, Mother, you did drink a lot of punch last night."

"What! How dare you speak to me like that?"

Swanee recovered and flushed. "I forgot to get your headache compound."

Clara snorted. "What have you been doing all this time?"

Swanee forced herself to speak in her most endearing manner. "I got all the way to town and couldn't remember what you sent me for." She hoped her mother wouldn't notice the bulge in her handbag where she'd hidden the packet from the drugstore.

Clara narrowed her eyes. "You're not the forgetful type."

Swanee honeyed her voice still more. "Do you really need that headache remedy, Mother? I can rub your neck."

"Of course I need it!" The older woman grimaced. "There's a bridge tea today. How can I win with a headache? I'm not letting Coralee take home the prize again."

"Yes, Mother. I'll go back." Swanee gritted her teeth.

Her mother shook her finger. "You do that. I'll expect you back in twenty minutes, or I'll speak to your daddy. There's not much point in your having a car if you can't help me out from time to time."

"Maybe you ought to learn to drive, Mama." Poison crept into Swanee's honey-voice. "You could drive yourself to bridge."

"There is no need," her mother said with icy calm. "Your father will drive me. He has an appointment in town." She sniffed. "You can come after me when we're through."

"Of course, Mother." Swanee turned on her heel and left. Daddy wouldn't take her car away! She loved it too much, and he loved her having it. Still, she needed to stay on Mother's good side.

It was almost an hour later before she could unwrap the packet she'd bought at the drugstore the first time she went.

She set the bottle of scarlet nail polish and the blood-red lipstick on her dressing table. Wait till Mother got a look at those! She'd squawk at first, but in the end, she'd be proud that her golden girl had so many beaux.

Humming, Swanee washed her hands, oiled and pushed back her cuticles, washed again, then she brushed a coat of scarlet on the nails of her left hand. She held it up for inspection. Perfect! Bye-bye to the baby pink stuff Mother insisted that the manicurist at the beauty salon use.

She attacked the right hand—a little trickier, but she stroked slowly. The shade was just the shade of the roses Pete Godwin had sent her as a good-bye gift with that silly card "Remember me." She was tired of his hang-dog looks.

It had just been a silly whim. She'd had too much to drink at that party two years ago and he'd offered to take her to get some coffee in his father's car, and he meant it. But a little devil got into her. He was too good to be real, so Boy Scout, and she wanted to see how far she could get him to go.

It was pretty far.

What a good thing he'd been off at Emory College most of the time, or it could have gotten messy. Ever since then, he'd been after her, but she'd held him off, liking the feeling of power it gave her. She realized that if she ever let herself fall for anyone like Pete had fallen for her, the tables would be turned and she'd be lost.

Ned Fletcher would be her conquest, for sure. She liked his rugged looks, his broad shoulders, even the scar that creased his chin. It made him look like . . . oh, a pirate. Swashbuckling.

A warm breeze blew in, billowing the sheer curtains. Her nails done, Swanee took her Chinese fan from the table, unfolded it carefully, and thoughtfully fanned her nails dry.

And her father wanted her to marry Russell Vincent! All the fellow ever talked about was politics. Still, it might be fun to be a governor's lady someday and sit up there in Atlanta and have swell parties and balls.

On the other hand, Russell hardly ever tried to kiss her and frowned on her smoking. He might expect her to do good works, like Mrs. Belinda Pemberton. He was worse than Pete. At least Pete didn't judge people.

She folded the fan and laid it back on the dressing table. Why should she be a pawn in her father's political schemes? It might suit her to marry Russell Vincent—and then again, it might not.

She edged onto her vanity bench and picked up the new lipstick, blood-red. She dabbed on a very little bit—just a hint of red, perhaps. She fluffed her face with powder.

She tilted her head and inspected her rouge. Why had Mr. Fletcher been so indifferent today? Well, of course. He had to be respectful. She was the boss's daughter, and Daddy would have a fit if they were seen together. Ned was being careful. The first move would have to come from her, but not appear so. She changed her mind about the lipstick and dabbed on enough to make a perfect, bee-stung pout.

She reached across her dressing table for the signed photograph of Russell Vincent, smiling blandly in its silver frame. She unfastened the back panel and slid the picture out. Then she walked over to the beautiful little white-painted carved desk that Daddy had ordered her specially from France, and opened a brown envelope that had been delivered the day before.

Swanee picked up the silver frame and exchanged the picture in it for the photograph that had arrived in the brown envelope. She wrapped it in brown paper, secured it with string, and inscribed her father's name on the outside.

It took a week before the time was right, late afternoon. Swanee tossed a new leather bag over her shoulder, pulled her straw cloche over her bob, and spritzed with Chanel No. 5. One more glance in the mirror. Her fresh peach dress clung to her body, wilting in the early September heat. Peach was her favorite color, because it suggested both warmth and sweetness, and because it became her.

She hurried downstairs clutching the parcel and, finding the house empty, strode through the kitchen and out the back door. Even Lessie, the cook, had gone for the day.

She drove with the top down, the fragrant air rushing past her cheeks giving way to the dustier air in town and the smells of gasoline and horse dung. She didn't slow as she passed the mill village, swerving to avoid a child who'd run out into the street.

Little lintheads! She wondered why Belinda Pemberton wasted so much time on them. Not much you could do with ignorance and dirt. Daddy did his part, what with providing places for them to live, and getting that nurse for them, and even paying the preacher at the Baptist church.

Still, she hated the way they looked at her, with those blank eyes you couldn't see behind.

When she got to the mill, breathing the odd river smell, she sailed through the gate and parked in the spot reserved for her father. The guard, Alvin, came out from the back door, and his frown relaxed when he saw who was smiling his way.

They exchanged greetings. "You looking for your daddy?"

"I see his car is gone." She gave Alvin a pout and fluttered her eyelashes. "Where is he?"

The guard shrugged. "He don't tell where he goes."

"Well," she said, "I wanted to surprise him with a little present." She brandished the parcel wrapped in brown paper. "Maybe I'll just go in and lay it on his desk, so he can find it in the morning. We'll just let that be our little secret, won't we, Alvin?"

The burly guard grinned. "Sure thing, Miss Swanee."

The offices at Burkett Mills were all on an upper level; from there they could reach the catwalk that looked out over the floor. Swanee glanced down as she walked the distance to her father's office at the far corner, the office with a view of the river.

She approached the office of Mrs. Mahala Benedict, the secretary and assistant bookkeeper. She peered in, smiling, holding up the parcel. "I'm just going to put this on Daddy's desk."

Mrs. Benedict raised her eyebrows but gave a faint smile. "The door's not locked. Go ahead. How are you, dear?"

"Fine, thanks. Bye now."

Mrs. Benedict nodded and turned back to her work. Gosh, what a life, typing letters all day and helping with the accounts. She shuddered. She would hate to be a widow and have to work. What had Daddy said about the secretary's husband? Died in a car wreck? There had been something else about the wreck, something about it that wasn't supposed to be discussed in front of her, among other things, like her brother's death.

Golly, she missed Toby. They had been such pals, and he was always telling her what dress looked best on her, what hat. Her older brother had occupied the softest place in her heart, and she keenly felt the lack of his lazy smile.

Her steps hesitated as she approached Ned Fletcher's door; she bit her lip and tried to calm her pulse. What if her plan didn't work? Still, if she didn't try, nothing would ever happen.

She glanced in. He was reared back in his chair, feet propped on his desk, telephone in his hand. He looked up, saw her, and brightened, his smile eerily like Toby's. "I've got to go," he said into the phone. "I'll be in touch."

He hung up the phone and rose. "Well, Miss Swanee. To what do we owe this pleasure?"

She stood demurely, trying to quiet the wild throb in her throat. "Hello, Ned Fletcher," she said. "I came by to see my father, but it seems I missed him. I have a li'l ol' present for him." She held up the package.

"It looks like a picture," Ned said.

"That's what it is, sure enough." She dimpled. "Would you like to see it?"

"Very much. Please come in," he said.

She sauntered through the door, alert for evidence of a sweetheart. On the wall behind his desk hung a pastoral scene, with rolling fields and placid cows. He displayed no family photographs, no plaques, awards, trophies: nothing which might have told her anything about his life. A man of mystery? More and more interesting.

She laid the parcel on his desk and untied the string, then held up the picture to the light. "It was just delivered today."

Ned gazed at the picture. "You and your father at that swell party you had. It's a beaut. Wish I had one."

Swanee gave a musical laugh. "What? A picture of the boss on your desk? That might be seen as currying favor, don't you think?"

Ned locked eyes with her. "And what of the boss's daughter? What would they say about that?"

She lowered her eyelids and rewrapped the picture, pouting in concentration, her movements deliberate, delicious. He'd given her what she needed. She looked up and gazed deep into his eyes. "They'd be scandalized," she murmured, touching her upper lip with her small pink tongue.

He drew closer, put one arm around her waist, and pulled her to him. "Are you afraid of scandal, Swanee?"

"I've never been afraid of anything." She leaned into him, and he lowered his lips to her throat where it pulsed. He pressed her body to his, and then his lips crushed hers. She thrilled to the mushroomy scent of his breath, the hint of musky cologne, of sweat. The kiss became deeper, and she felt him against her yielding belly. Her face flushed and her breath deepened, and her head swam with confetti and stars.

She laid her head against his chest, willing herself to keep back, keep back, but her body opened at the steady, quickening rhythm of his heart.

"I've wanted you, mademoiselle." Ned pulled back just enough to stroke her cheek.

"We've wasted time, then," Swanee murmured.

Ned gave her a quick, delicious squeeze and then let her go. "I've heard the talk. They're already laying bets on how soon I'm going to move in on the boss's daughter. You can bet your dear daddy has heard the talk too, and let me know it's over his dead body."

Swanee bit her lip. Her voice came soft, breathless. "He wouldn't have to know."

Ned smiled at her without mirth. "My dear, how long do you think we could get away with that?"

"As long as we wanted to!" The words were stronger than she intended, and she sank to a whisper, thinking of the secretary just down the hall. Through the closed door she heard the muffled roar of the factory and hoped the words had been drowned out. "We just need to be careful."

"For how long, eh?" An ironic smile played across his mouth, but his flushed complexion betrayed how much he wanted her.

As they gazed at each other, the very motes in the air ceased their motion and the two were alone in an expanding universe.

A footstep, a ring of shoes on metal outside broke the spell.

Swanee touched Ned's cheek and whispered, "We'll find a way."

His smile was wry. "No, we won't."

"Ned. We've got to. And now I've got to go. Mrs. Benedict will be wondering what's taking me so long."

"My God, Swanee," he said through his teeth, "I could ravish you right here on this desk."

Swanee lowered her eyelashes demurely. "Hush," she whispered, but her tone was an invitation.

"Sunday," he said. "Go driving with me on Sunday. Can you get away then?"

"I'll see," said Swanee. She blew him a kiss and ducked out of his office, tingling to her core.

She left the wrapped picture on her father's desk and hurried back the way she came, barely glancing into Ned's office, hearing him on the telephone. She bade a cheery good-bye to Mrs. Benedict and to Alvin.

She drove by the mill village without a glance. When she got home she saw her father's electric-blue Cadillac. No sense in being cautious; her blood raced with the delicious challenge of how she was going to get around him. This might be the adventure of her life.

# Chapter 6

Tenny awoke late Sunday morning to a soft pattering rain and found both Mincuses had already left the house for church, although Clete usually stayed in bed. She dressed, went to the kitchen, and ate the oatmeal that Myrtle had left her for breakfast and washed the pan and bowl and spoon. By that time, the rain had turned to mist, and she figured it was time to set off for the cemetery to see about retrieving her Bible and her sack.

By the time she had hustled uphill a mile to the gates, the sun had come out in a blaze of high, pale yellow. People were just beginning to arrive to visit loved ones, as most were still at church. If Digger John was a preacher, he wouldn't dig on the Lord's Day, would he?

Did they have funerals on Sundays? She didn't know. She'd never been to one, except her mother's, and she remembered only confusion and sadness and the kindness of Mrs. Brown, the wife of Brother Jethro, who sat her down and told her that Jesus loved her, and no, he had not taken Ma no matter what some people said.

Underneath a huge spreading oak, Tenny sat and waited, thinking hard about her Bible, hoping Digger John would appear. That Bible held the names of all Ma's brothers and sisters and aunts and uncles, and her grandma and grandpa who died before Tenny ever knew them.

Pretty as a movie star, Ma had been once, and sometimes you could see flashes of that prettiness when she was reading the Bible under the light of the oil lamp, and her face got smooth, and she read the old words to herself, moving her lips silently.

When Tenny's eyes spilled over, she scrambled in her pocket for the handkerchief Ma had told her to always carry.

She'd just touched it to her face when a voice seemed to speak from on high. "It will get better, my child. Her spirit lives on in you."

Startled, Tenny looked up, expecting to see God, or at least a pillar of cloud. Instead, she saw a tall man dressed in a long, dark coat and string tie. Though his voice had been deep and soothing, his words alarmed her. She jumped to her feet. "Who are you?" she quavered. "How did you know about my mother?"

"Isn't that your mother?" the man asked. Tenny followed the man's gaze and found she'd been sitting near a gravesite adorned with fresh daisies, the resting place of a woman who'd died at just the age of her mother, according to the dates carved into the stone.

"No," Tenny said. "My mother's grave is . . . is not here. I miss her."

The man bowed. "I understand. Allow me to introduce myself. Some call me The Reverend Peregrine Falkner, but I prefer Brother Perry. I'm a preacher of the Gospel, and I came to Ashbyville with a mission."

"You're a preacher?" she said hopefully. "Please, do you know Digger John?"

"Indeed I do," said the man at once, raising his bushy eyebrows. "What might you want with that good man?"

Tenny took a deep breath. "I gave him my Bible to keep for me, and now I can't find him."

The man nodded slowly. "He's gone away to help some of his people. He preaches here and there, wherever they need him. I preached with him once."

"Oh!" said Tenny, astonished that a white preacher would preach with a colored one.

"And you are?" He smiled gravely.

"Tenny Oakes. I work at Burkett Mills." She said this a little proudly. She had a job, however temporary.

The preacher nodded. "I am here, mainly, to help the mill workers. This industry is not a spiritual environment, and this particular mill is not kind to its people." He frowned. "You are too young for that place."

"But I don't want to leave," Tenny said, her heart pounding. "I need to earn money."

"There are better ways of earning money," Brother Perry said gently.

Tenny's face warmed, and she glanced over at a man and three half-grown children who were placing lilies on a grave. "Better at the mill than on the street, begging your pardon."

The man paused and considered her carefully, and his long face set itself in deep lines. "Digger John will return with your Bible, but you need to leave that mill."

Tenny shook her head. "Thank you for the advice, sir. It's been nice meeting you."

"Not sir. Just Brother Perry," the preacher said. "I hope we meet again." He held out his hand.

Tenny smiled weakly, shook hands, and made her way down the sandy path back toward the cemetery gates. What did that preacher know? Maybe he was not what he pretended to be. Brother Perry's shadow seemed to follow her as she strode away from the monuments as if she had somewhere to go.

Back at the gate, she watched the face of every visitor whose car rolled in, who walked in, just in case one of those faces was Byron. She didn't want to go back to the Mincuses' house, so she kept on walking, down tree-lined streets with white houses, down store-lined streets with sidewalks of red bricks, always away from the mill. Birds scuffled in the grass and chirruped above.

She remembered to look behind her. It wouldn't do to get too used to being hidden. She came to a place called Madison Street Park, filled with leafy oaks and swept-dirt paths, green-painted benches and children in swings, and even an ice cream man pedaling a tricycle cart, ringing a bell. She sank to a bench and watched boys and girls, not much younger than those who worked in the mill, ride velocipedes and play chase. And buy ice cream.

Watching cold mist rise from the cart, she spent a precious nickel for an ice cream sandwich. The treat was so good, so creamy, and so cold, that she licked every crumb of the chocolate wafers off her fingers.

Around suppertime, she made her way back to the Mincuses' house. Nobody asked her where she'd been. Myrtle did say to her, "Honey, you can do better than that old washed-out dress and them boots, can't you? They like the girls to look a little better than that." Tenny lay in bed that night brooding on clothes and spending her hard-earned dollars, but soon fell asleep. That factory whistle blew at six in the morning.

The next Saturday, after the half-workday had ended, she walked up to a second-hand shop Myrtle had told her about, near Mabel's café, where she spent some of her hard-earned money on a blue calico frock, as well as some lace-up shoes. She hated shoes and would rather have worn none at all, but rules were rules. She also bought a blue bandanna to keep the lint and dust out of her hair.

On the way home, hugging the parcel of clothes tightly to her, she noticed a small red brick African Methodist Episcopal Church with a sign out front that told her the Reverend John Woods would be preaching Sunday on "Sermons in Stone." Could that be Digger John? She crept all around the small building, but she didn't see anyone. She heard someone inside playing the piano, singing a hymn in a rich, mellow voice, but the voice was a woman's. Afraid to disturb the practice, she walked away disheartened.

She stopped by the cemetery. A crew was busy down the hill with picks and shovels, but Digger John wasn't among the workers.

She wore her new bandanna to work on Monday, cheered by smiles of approval. A freckled girl, a spinner, motioned her over. "Want to swap kerchiefs? My red would look good on you."

The red kerchief was liberally fuzzed with lint. "No thanks. Mine's clean as a pin."

The other girl sighed. "The blue would look swell with my red hair."

Tenny shook her head. "Red with *my* hair? Folks would stare."

The freckled girl smiled quizzically. "Too late, girl. By the way, I'm Ramona. See you at lunch time."

What had Ramona meant by *too late*? At lunchtime, Tenny found the girl at one of the picnic tables out back. Ramona waved her cigarette and beckoned Tenny over. Minus her lint-dusted kerchief, Ramona sported a bob of bushy auburn hair and a grin as big as a watermelon slice.

Tenny plopped down across from her. "What did you mean, it's too late?"

Ramona shrugged. "Girl, people just naturally look at you. Your hair lights up the room." Ramona's voice carried a nasal twang, harder than the soft voices of home.

Tenny's fist clenched. That hair Shackley had clutched. "Say, are you from around here?"

Ramona drew on her cigarette. "North Georgia, the mountains," she said. "My whole family's here. We left a mill up in Big Rock."

Tenny sat back eating a rat cheese sandwich while the girl ran on like a busted faucet about how the family farm couldn't make enough to live on, so her brothers and sisters had to work at the mill up there, but there weren't enough jobs for all of them, and they heard about this place. She paused for air and pointed a finger at Tenny.

"I hear you live with Myrtle Mincus."

Tenny shrugged. "She was looking for a roomer."

Ramona shook her head. "That Clete Mincus ever try anything with you?"

Tenny looked around, as if he might be lurking nearby, and tightened her jaw. "Myrtle watches him."

"She's got reason to be jealous."

Tenny shrugged. "He's got nothing I want." The whistle blew, and they reluctantly picked up their battered tin lunch pails and filed inside.

That afternoon the big-nosed man, Burton, came by and gave Ramona a pat, stroking the back of her faded polka-dot dress. Tenny edged her broom out of his line of sight, but not before she saw Ramona give him a smile.

"Why'd you let him do that?" she asked Ramona fiercely after he'd gone.

"He can make things easy." Ramona tossed her head. "Don't you know nothin'?"

"I know too much," Tenny said, thinking of the taste of chocolate on her tongue, but she never wanted to use her body out of desperation again. Maybe Burton's crude advances would lead to a promotion for Ramona, maybe to one of the weaving rooms. She saw the drawbacks to this kind of trading. He could give, but he could sure take away.

And she was still sweeping, day by day.

It wasn't long before Burton came her way with a look she knew too well. She pretended not to understand. "Oh, Mr. Burton," she sang out. "Ramona's been showing me how to spin. How about it?"

His face darkened. "We'll see," he said. "Going to get me a new boy for this job if you don't smarten up."

With a sinking feeling she saw the lay of the land. Give in and get a better job, or get fired.

As Burton stalked off, Tenny gazed upward into the hazy light to see if maybe God would help. On the catwalk that surrounded the floor, a man was looking down at her—a dark-haired man in a suit, a man with a mustache.

A man who looked just like Byron.

Except Byron's hair had been light brown, and he'd never worn a mustache. He'd left for the Army seven years ago. She wondered if he still cracked his knuckles.

She stared up at him, willing him to recognize her, and then she took off her kerchief and waved, like they used to do in Weedy Grove when somebody was leaving. He turned abruptly and walked away.

"Are you crazy?" one of the women hissed. "Get back to work before the boss man sees you."

Tenny grabbed her broom and pushed it for dear life.

She elbowed her way over to Ramona in the crowd leaving the mill that evening and towed her out of hearing range of the others. "Who's that good-looking boss man?"

Ramona's eyebrows shot up. "First time you've seen him? You go around with your head down all the time. His name's Mr. Fletcher."

"He favored my brother. If he didn't have a mustache."

Ramona snorted. "Lucky you. Don't know what your brother was like, but this'n's bad news for our kind, honey. Talk is that he's going after the big boss's daughter. Among others." She looked almost wistful. "He could put his shoes under my bed anytime."

"Girls liked my brother too," Tenny said. He'd been big and strong, not like skinny old Pa, and could do twice the work of all of them. But he'd never been stuck-up. He'd been a good son, a good brother. Why had he left them?

That mill manager couldn't be Byron. After all, he looked down on her, just like that landlord Arno Shackley. Of all the faces she'd seen in this town, not one had ever looked so much like her brother. And this wasn't him.

At the Mincuses' dinner of biscuits and gravy and thin fried pork chop, she waited until Clete was digging into his food and then looked sideways at Myrtle.

"Myrtle, how would you go about finding somebody who was lost?"

Myrtle shrugged.

Clete guffawed, leering at her. "You lost a sweetie, kid?"

She flushed from her shoulders to the tip of her head. "I was just curious, that's all."

"If the person don't want to be found, tough luck." Clete took a long swig of sweet tea. "Myrtle, this is a puny damn supper. Slice up some of that watermelon."

Myrtle silently rose from the table. She picked up the knife, long and sharp, and ran it across the stone they kept for sharpening. Tenny saw her looking at it thoughtfully before she split the melon with a resounding crack.

Tenny, not wanting to be alone in the house with Clete, accepted Myrtle's invitation to church. The sermons bored her, because they were all about encouraging the congregation to be good workers in their vineyards. To obey their masters.

Clete refused to go for this reason, he said, but Myrtle said he had a corn liquor hangover. "Look at Bobby Lee Prewitt next door," she said. "A temperance man. He goes out with his pole and bait to the river Sundays, but always comes back in time for the evening service with a string of fish."

Tenny stood the sermons as long as she could. Finally, one Sunday, claiming she didn't feel well, she stayed behind, hoping Clete would sleep long enough for her to escape the house. After Myrtle had been gone a quarter of an hour, she dressed in her secondhand blue gingham frock and straw hat.

So as not to wake up Clete, she inched the sash up on the window, trying not to make the raw wood squeak. The Prewitt's chickens squabbled out back, and then the most ungodly hollering came from their house next door.

Tenny caught her breath. Polly Prewitt hadn't closed the bedroom curtains, and she and her husband were writhing around, squealing like a stuck pig. But that man was not tall Bobby Lee Prewitt. Those were the hairy buttocks of Clete Mincus.

She slammed down the window, whirled away, and ran out the front door, her bag flapping over her shoulder, and tore all the way to the cemetery. She wandered among the peaceful gravestones until her heart slowed, and then she roamed the surrounding streets, in some cases little more than muddy tracks, and she forgot the way to the A. M. E. church. She doubled back to the cemetery, thinking about the church. She understood the African part, but why was it both Methodist and Episcopal? Maybe she'd ask Digger John.

Digger John wasn't at the cemetery..

She made her way to the river and rambled barefoot along a river path. Then she found her way to the park, ate another ice cream, and went back by the cemetery again, with no luck.

She returned to the Mincuses' house that afternoon hungry, her new shoes all muddy, and went straight to her room, leaving the shoes on the back porch so Myrtle wouldn't yell at her.

At supper she gobbled pork and beans, wiping the plate with a scrap of cornbread. "You should'a been there at church, Tenny girl," Myrtle said. "They was passing the plate around and Polly's youngest kid Obie snatched some money out! His brother snatched it back and threw it at the plate, and them eight pennies went all over the place, and then he got down under people's feet after them and some of the women screamed that he was looking up their dress."

"I'm sorry I missed it," Tenny said. She glanced over at Clete's smirk and promised to go next Sunday. For the next three weeks, Tenny appeared scrubbed and shining, ready for church. As the preacher ranted and pointed and boomed them into being good stewards in their vineyards, she learned to wiggle her ears.

She prayed every time that she would find her Bible.

And then came a Monday morning in October, the mild, fresh dawn promising silky air and soft sun. Tenny felt awful anyway. She gazed without appetite at bread fried in bacon grease topped with a brown-edged egg from the Prewitts' chickens. Myrtle poured her a cup of coffee and pushed it over, then she poked her fork in Tenny's direction. "Don't waste food. Costs enough to feed you, girl."

Tenny sipped at her bitter coffee and choked down half the eggy bread. Clete ate the rest with no comment. Walking to work, she nearly stumbled over rocks in the path. And on the floor, after the first few pushes of the broom, nausea shot over her in waves. She sank to her knees, dazed and foggy.

Alarmed, she saw Burton bearing down past rows of spindles in her direction. "I'm sick." She pushed herself to her feet. "Can I get off?"

He grinned like the devil himself. "Can't leave without an excuse from the nurse, but you're a lucky little girl. She's here today."

Tenny knew about the nurse. Word was that a social worker named Mrs. Belinda Pemberton had raised Cain about unsafe working conditions. The lady had found out about Polly Prewitt's missing finger and the cases of TB and the coughing fits they called "mill fever." Finally, Burkett Mills had hired a nurse to come in Tuesdays and Thursdays.

Tenny trudged up the long metal staircase from the floor to the offices. She knocked on a door marked NURSE, sank to the hard wooden bench outside, pulled off her kerchief, and mopped her face. She hoped she wouldn't sick up right here on the nice clean floor.

Down the way, a woman with salt-and-pepper wavy hair came out of an office and glanced at her, and then a man in a pinstriped suit came out of another office and talked with the woman. Lord, was he the same man who'd looked down on her from the walkway, the man who looked like Byron? His eyes. They were the same hazel eyes, but it wasn't the same Byron behind them.

The nurse's door opened and a man lumbered out, his hand wrapped in a bandage. "Next?" A tall, stocky, dishwater-haired woman in a white uniform beckoned her in. "Get up on that table, kid," she said. "Are you hurt?"

Tenny did as she commanded. "I feel sick to my stomach."

"How long have you felt like this? What did you eat this morning? Does your head hurt?" The nurse shook down a thermometer while Tenny answered, and then said, "Under your tongue, and keep your mouth shut until I tell you. I've been an Army nurse, and I don't take any guff."

"You were an Army nurse?" Tenny blurted. The thermometer bobbled on her lips. The nurse popped the thermometer back in and held Tenny's mouth closed.

"I went to France with the Red Cross. Let me tell you, honey, nearly tore my heart out. Them poor boys. I married one of my patients. Gassed and gimpy but he's a good man. Hold still. I need to check your belly." She poked and prodded. "You got a fella?"

The stable boy and Arno Shackley weren't her fellas, that's for sure. She shook her head. The nurse removed the thermometer. "No fever. Have you been with a man, is what I mean."

Her mouth opened but no sound came out.

The nurse nodded. "You could be pregnant. When were your last menses?"

"I don't remember."

The nurse frowned and Tenny shrank back.

"No, ma'am, I mean, I just can't be expecting." She swallowed. "My momma died in childbirth."

"And you're just a kid." The nurse's expression softened. "Could be malnutrition. Could be coming down with flu. You're little and you're pale. Could be anemia. Yes."

She took a bottle from the shelf and poured a spoonful of a thick, dark, evil-smelling liquid and popped it into Tenny's mouth. Tenny gagged, but got it down. The nurse capped the bottle and gave it to her. "Two spoonfuls of this iron tonic every day. Get more at the drugstore when it runs out."

Tenny stared at the bottle. "Can I ask you a question?"

"That's what I'm here for."

"How would you go about finding somebody who was in the Army? I mean, my brother went off and we never heard from him again. Never got any letter saying he was missing."

The nurse looked surprised. "Honey, you just write to the Army. Say what you just told me. Give his full name and home town. They'll send you a letter telling you when he was discharged and his last known address, if it's different."

"But I don't know where to write."

"Come see me when I'm here Thursday. I have that Army stuff at home somewhere. Now I'll write you that work excuse. If you don't get better in three days, you'd better see a doctor. On your way now, and get some rest."

Tenny left clutching the bottle and the note, biting her lip. Doctors cost money.

It was lunchtime, and the workers had emptied out. Just as Tenny headed toward the stairs, a raven-haired girl cocooned in peach silk and trailing perfume emerged from a side door and swept past Tenny without so much as a glance. She was wearing a perfect cloche hat and T-strap heels like the ones Tenny had seen Miss Rose Shackley wear when she went around giving folks Christmas baskets. The girl slipped into Mr. Fletcher's office.

Could that be the boss's daughter they'd talked about? She was just as stuck-up as that Mr. Fletcher. Tenny edged her way down the iron stairs to the floor and began to look for the red-nosed man.

It was only after the whistle blew to return to work when she finally saw him slipping in, grinning like a fool, probably from drinking. She walked up to him and handed him the note. "Here's my excuse, Mr. Burton."

He tore it into little pieces. "We don't need you any more, girlie."

She blinked. "You got no reason to fire me!"

"Sorry, missy," he said. "My sweeper boy's coming tomorrow, and I don't need no more spinners."

Tenny fought to control her rage and kept her voice low. "Mister Burton. This place is worse'n a pigsty, full of lint. I worked hard. Harder than most of these folks."

"Well . . ." Burton stroked his chin and looked her up and down. "You know, missy . . . if you *behave*, I might be able to try you out as an apprentice spinner."

She clenched her fists. Ramona had told her about that little dodge. They didn't pay you till you learned the job, and then they fired you and took on another apprentice. And she wasn't about to *behave* for him.

Tenny could barely drag herself back to the Mincuses' house. If she could rest a spell, maybe she could move on, find something else. Waiting tables, maybe. She pushed open the door to cigarette smoke in the air.

She stiffened and crept in, but she had to pass the kitchen, where Clete sat at the table, a cigarette between his fingers, a crumpled pack resting beside his coffee cup. They must have switched his shift.

He looked up. "What're you doing here?"

"I'm sick." She held out the bottle of tonic like a shield. "I'm going to lie down."

"Relax," he said, smiling lazily. "Myrtle would say you need a cuppa tea. How 'bout some?"

Her mouth was bitter from the tonic and tea sounded good. She hesitated. Clete gazed at her like a snake eyeing a rabbit. She shook her head.

"Suit yourself." He lifted a tin of tea out of the cupboard and sat it on the counter. "It's there if you want it."

Her mother had given her hot tea when she was sick. Hot tea and milk toast. Shuddering with the pain of missing her mother, she stumbled back to her room, collapsed on the bed, and closed her eyes. She woke, maybe an hour later, her mouth dry as wadded paper. She slid out of bed, padded to the door, and peered out.

Clete wasn't in the kitchen. She slipped in, took down Myrtle's rose-patterned teapot, and spooned in tea. She filled the kettle with water, but the matchbox was missing from its usual spot on the shelf above the stove.

Clete walked in the back door, cigarette in hand, holding the matches. He slid over and lit the gas for her. He set the kettle on the stove.

Then, pivoting quick as a frog's tongue, he caged her against the counter. "Now ain't I nice to you? I been out and about and heard a few things. Poor kid. Got no job no more. Reckon you can't pay the rent." His voice came silky as clabber and he stroked her arm. She felt too weak to fight. The water fizzed, beginning to boil.

"I know folks," he said. "I could get you back on." He laid the cigarette on a cracked dish and kneaded the back of her neck. It felt good. She wanted to believe he had some good in him. She wished he would go away and finish his smoke. She was so tired.

The teakettle sang, and he filled Myrtle's teapot. She watched him shut off the gas. He smiled and took her hand and pulled her to him. He leaned forward and trapped her, breathing tobacco.

He and Myrtle were much of a height, but Tenny only reached his chin. "Pretty little girl." He kissed the top of her head.

She felt him hard against her. She had to keep calm. "Please don't, Clete."

"You know you don't mean that," he whispered, stroking her hair. "You ever been pleasured by a man?"

She shook her head violently. It had been anything but pleasure.

"You don't know what you're missin'," he said. "I've got them slow hands." His voice stayed low, cajoling. "Let me in, sweet baby." Quick as a tadpole, he slipped his fingers under her skirt, under the elastic of her bloomers.

His face buried in her neck, her hair falling over his ears, his fingers insistent, Clete didn't hear the footsteps on the porch. Tenny, seeing her chance, gathered her last bit of strength and shoved back at him.

A voice screeched, "Clete!"

He jerked back. Tenny blinked back tears. Myrtle stood in the doorway, her face contorted and her red-painted lips making cuss words Tenny had never ever heard, not even when Pa was at his drunkest.

When Myrtle lunged for the kettle on the stove, Tenny bolted, ducking around Clete. She slammed the door to her room and stuffed her few clothes and her toothbrush into one of Myrtle's tatty pillowcases. In the kitchen they were still yelling. Clutching the case and her bottle of tonic, she climbed out the window and dropped to the ground.

She made it to the bridge before she threw up, thick and sour, the mess barely missing her new calico dress. She broke into tears. Now she'd never see that nurse again. How could she find Byron?

# Chapter 7

The rolling land stretched in front of Tenny, grave markers white in the bright October sun. Somewhere, a deep bass voice belted out "Swing Low, Sweet Chariot."

She followed the notes down dirt paths past obelisks and angels, past clumps of sweet shrub and tea olive. At the top of a rise, she saw Digger John and another man, a little way down the hill, shoveling earth into a red-dirt hole beside a folded canvas awning.

When she'd left the mill, she had found him, like Brother Perry had prophesied. Maybe that Brother Perry was a real prophet.

She stood and watched, sweat running down her brow, until Digger John looked up and saw her. He put his shovel aside and spoke to the other man, who nodded and took out a cigarette. Then Digger John walked up the carriage path to meet her.

"Well, little lady. You's come back for your sack."

"I came before but you weren't here. I thought you had gone off with my Bible."

He took a pipe and a poke of tobacco from his back pocket and stuffed the pipe. He looked at her hard. "Where'd you come by that Bible, child?"

Tenny caught her breath, then hung her head. There was no point in lying. "I stole it from Pa. I wanted something of my poor dead mama's, and Pa never read it."

"You sure about that?" Digger John rattled a matchbox, struck a match, and lit the tobacco. He gave a pull on the pipe before he spoke. "That the only reason? Somethin' more, maybe?"

Tenny thought of Pa in the car, the day after she'd left home, when they'd found her, him and Mr. Shackley, hollering and screaming about the Bible. "Well, Pa was awfully upset. He chased me, him and Mr. Shackley, in Mr. Shackley's car. But I got away from them in the swamp."

"Mmmm. You lucky you didn't meet no cottonmouth. Sometimes thieves suffer for they sins."

"I don't feel like a thief. Maybe I shouldn't have taken it, but Pa never even went to church."

Digger John puffed on his pipe, and then his hard look softened. Then he said, "Child, he weren't missing the word of God. He were missing his money."

"Money?" Tenny choked on the word.

Digger John beckoned for her to follow, and she trailed after him, heart pounding, to a gray stone mausoleum. He unlatched its iron gate, and taking a deep breath, she stepped into the cool, gloomy interior. He removed the cover from an empty crypt and extracted the croker sack. He took out the Bible and fanned the pages to reveal five five-dollar bills.

Tenny's face grew hot. She had never seen that much money in all her life. "I swear that money wasn't there the last time I looked."

The old man chuckled softly. "There was a buryin' here and the preacher forgot his Bible. I reckoned you wouldn't mind if I let him use your'n. Lord, what a surprise."

Tenny shook her head. "I don't know how my Pa came by that kind of money."

Digger John cut his eyes at her. "Mebbe that boss man give him money for somethin'."

What could it be? "I can't give it back," Tenny moaned. "I can't go home. And I just got fired from the mill from no reason." She swallowed. "Do you suppose the Lord would mind if I borrowed this money?"

Digger John murmured, "Maybe the Lord providin' for his lamb. You take it and do good."

She gingerly slipped out one of the bills and pressed it into his hand. "You too."

He looked down at it as if trying to decide whether to keep it. Then he folded it and slid it into his pocket. "I thankee kindly," he said, tipping his battered hat. "Me and the Lord can use it."

She bade Digger John good-bye and left the cemetery, making her way toward town. How had Pa gotten the money? It hadn't been there long, because she'd just been looking through the Bible a few days before she left.

What did Shackley pay Pa for? The corn liquor went to pay off his debt at the store. Twenty-five dollars, when she'd made seventy-five cents a day at the mill! She didn't want to use the money, but she'd need food and a decent place to stay.

What if—what if Pa had sold her off to Shackley! What had the landlord said to her that horrible night? "You're mine now, girl."

The Bible trembled in her hands, and she gripped it tightly. Were Pa and Shackley still looking, wanting her and that money? She walked back past the shops and the livery stable, not even glancing up at the loft. She couldn't, wouldn't do *that* again.

She blindly kept walking, not sure where she was going—just away from the river, away from the mill. She found herself in a neighborhood of houses bigger than the mill houses, tidy white and yellow and pale green cottages, colorful with pansies in the flower beds.

She loved one yellow house with blue shutters, the color of the sky on a June afternoon, and stopped to admire it. The door swung open, and the lady of the house glared at Tenny before she swept up a cloud of porch dust with a fierce-looking broom. Tenny sneezed and edged out of her sight.

Her steps grew slower and heavier, and she longed for a place to rest. She felt she must be near that Madison Street Park, the park she'd found earlier, and headed toward the town center. Silly with joy to find the park entrance, she followed its well-swept paths past azaleas and tall magnolias until she came to a white octagonal bandstand.

Dropping her sack to the ground, she collapsed onto a nearby bench. She stretched out and drifted off into a hazy, sunlit sleep.

She woke at a tap on her shoulder. Heart pounding, the western sun in her face, she squinted up. Had they found her? She struggled to her feet, ready to run. But on the next bench, big hands on his knees, sat the tall preacher Brother Perry.

"And here you are, Miss Tenny," he said. "You have left the mill, and I see you have your sack."

Tenny blinked, the fright still with her. "It's all I have."

She leaned to pick up her sack, and that awful feeling came over her, and she sicked up right in front of the preacher man, missing his old coat but splattering her own best calico.

"Be still, child, and wait right here," he rumbled. Tenny bent double, trying to clear her head. Maybe he meant to get someone, maybe a church lady, maybe the law, to take her home. No, never! She took a couple of steps, but the sickness swelled again.

She breathed in and out, in and out, trying to overcome the nausea. Brother Perry brought a towel and a stoppered jug of water and, dabbing gently, cleansed Tenny's face and most of the soiled dress.

"I thought of influenza," he said. "But you're not fevered. Is it possible that you are in the family way?"

"No, no!" The mill nurse's words came back to her, and miserably, Tenny covered her face with her hands.

"I know someone who may help you," Brother Perry said gently. "Will you allow me to take you there?"

She opened one eye. "Promise you're not taking me to the sheriff?"

He smiled. "Here in Ashbyville, there are city police, but I think the law is not needed." He extended his arm to help her up. "I'll bring your sack."

"No." Tenny clutched the burlap for dear life.

Tenny rode tucked under a quilt in the back of Brother Perry's mule wagon, and as the mule clip-clopped through the streets of Ashbyville, she half-dreamed of Arno Shackley's face, his breath on her neck, his fingers raking her plait. She woke drenched with sweat when the rocking of the wagon came to a halt.

A gentle hand touched her shoulder, and she opened her eyes. A plump lady stood over her, a lady who reminded her of Mrs. Brown, Brother Jethro's wife, a lady with a brown frizzy halo of hair above rosy cheeks. "Hello? Would you want some help, dear?"

Tenny, shivering, inhaled sharply.

"Don't be afraid," said the lady. "My name is Verity Hapsworth, and I'm here to help you and your child."

"My *child?*"

"Well, not yet," the lady said soothingly.

The lady and Brother Perry helped Tenny out of the wagon, propping her as they walked toward a big, blue two-story house with fancy cut-out railings and a tall round room like a tower.

At the front door, Tenny noticed a small nameplate under the brass knocker: *Inez Callahan Home for Wayward Girls.*

The door flew open, and girls flurried out and flocked around Tenny. They were Dulcy, Mary Beth, Marjorie, Hephzibah. Most of them looked older than she was, and each one of them was pregnant and wearing a blue smock.

*Dear God, no,* she prayed silently. *Not me, too.* Tears stung her eyes. The girl called Dulcy stepped forward and took her arm. "Come on. It's not so bad here," she chimed. "Nobody looks down on us."

After Brother Perry bade Tenny farewell, Dulcy and the girls led her upstairs to a clean, tiny room furnished with a white iron bed, a plain pine nightstand, a lamp, a painted dresser, an old school desk, and a rag rug. "This used to be a storeroom," Marjorie said.

"Too bad you don't have a roommate," said another.

"Let me put this away," said another of the girls, reaching for Tenny's croker sack, but Tenny shook her head and held it tight.

"You'll need to get cleaned up. You stink." Hephzibah, the tallest, shook her long brown braids and wrinkled her nose. "Where's her suitcase, Miss Verity?"

"That sack's all I have," Tenny said.

"We'll get clothes for you." Verity turned to one of the girls. "Dulcy, bring up a few dresses, small ones, from the donation closet. A smock and nightdress and robe too."

She turned to another girl. "Mary Beth, start filling the bath. Bring a fresh cake of Lifebuoy."

"Bathroom's down the hall," Mary Beth told Tenny.

"Right now?" Tenny didn't want to undress, didn't want a bath. Hadn't she got washed clean in the river not too long ago? She was used to a hip bath once a week by the woodstove in the kitchen.

"Right now," said Hephzibah, nodding, swinging her plaits. The girls marched Tenny down the hall, shimmied her out of her clothes, and tossed her into the tub. They soaped her hair and streamed warm pitcherfuls of water over the pale strands. Then they handed her a washrag, hung a fresh white towel on a hook, laid a robe and a clean nightgown on a bench, and left.

Tenny soaped herself all over, rinsed, and then pulled the plug. The dingy grey water gurgled away, and with it, maybe, some of her fear.

When she finally emerged into the bedroom, tingling with cleanliness, Hephzibah and Dulcy attacked her with towels. "We'll dry your hair. It's unhealthy to sleep with it wet." They propelled her out to the back yard, where they sat her in a scrap of sunlight, combing and rubbing the strands.

"So did you love him?" Dulcy asked.

"Love who?"

Hephzibah shrugged. "The one who got you here."

Tenny shook her head, grimacing.

"Too bad," Dulcy said. "I really loved Whit, but his daddy sent him away to military school. Whit promised he'd come back for me, but he stopped writing. They're going to make me put the baby up for adoption."

She kept talking, and Tenny let the words drift away. She had questions—lots of questions—but first, she wanted to sink into that nice bed.

"It's dry as it's going to get," said Hephzibah. Dulcy, plaiting the warm, damp hair into one long braid, said, "I'll bet Miss Verity is going to want you to bob this."

"No!" Tenny's hair was the thing people said was pretty.

"Short hair is fashionable," said Hephzibah. "Modern."

"And easy to wash," said Dulcy. "Especially if you get lice." She made a face. "Nasty things."

"I *don't* have lice." Tenny white-knuckled her braid. Long hair made her feel safe, covering her ears and neck.

Dulcy shrugged. "We're supposed to give you a drink of water and take you up to nap. Miss Verity says you're exhausted."

Tenny didn't argue.

Drowsing in bed, she heard the faraway, lonesome hoot of the train. She remembered crossing the tracks when she'd come to town. On the very edge of sleep, she saw the face of the boy at the gas tank beside the livery stable, the boy in the black automobile, the boy who wore round eyeglasses. The boy who'd looked on her with wonder.

Where was he now?

# Chapter 8

Making his way back from afternoon lab, Pete wasn't holding his breath for a letter. Like an idiot, he'd written Swanee faithfully, once a week, since he'd returned to campus, and all he'd gotten in return so far was a scribbled "Thinking of you, darling Pete" on the back of a postcard of Rich's Department Store.

He knew she was stringing him along, as surely as he knew that human beings were made up of water, bones, and dreams. He'd write one more letter, and that was it.

Sometimes he thought about the river girl, as poor as Swanee was privileged, and just as unreachable.

He fought his way up the boardinghouse steps, lab notebook against his coat, through stinging winds. He pushed the door open into the musty smell of the old house. The day's mail lay on the mahogany hall chest, and he reached for the bundle without hope.

There would be no letter, of course. What did he expect, after that awful night at Swanee's party? He'd taken her out to the terrace, where the moon hung in the sky like an exotic Chinese melon. She'd gazed at him with that wonderful mischievous tilt of her head, and then kissed him full on the mouth. "Where's that present you promised?"

God help him, he'd dropped to one knee like somebody in a Victorian novel and held out the opal and garnet ring that had belonged to his great-aunt Obedience. She'd smiled vaguely while he slipped it on her finger and asked her to be his wife.

"It's too big, I know," Pete said. "Aunt Beedie was a woman who loved life in a big way. I'll have it sized for you."

Swanee raised it and admired it, dimpling. "It's pretty."

Pete closed his eyes. *Say yes. Please say yes.*

She twirled it once more, sighed a little, and slid it off. She placed the ring back in his hand, curling his fingers around it. "How sweet of you, Pete. I can't accept it."

He pushed himself to his feet stiffly, not willing to give up. He clasped her hand. "Take it. For friendship."

Still smiling, she slipped her hand away. "That wouldn't be fair. It isn't the time for me, Pete. Now, why don't you kiss me again? For friendship."

And he did kiss her. He ended the kiss at the proper time for a friend, too soon. "When will be the right time?"

She touched her scarlet-tipped finger to his lips. "Pete, favorite jelly bean, you'll know." She winked, and blew a kiss, and glided away, her body caressing the air.

He'd stumbled off and annihilated his stash of hooch. He'd have missed his train to school if Gussie and Henry Benedict hadn't dragged him away and sobered him up with three cups of coffee, then driven his car back to his house, found his suitcase, and plunked him at the station in time to catch the 3:30 a.m. Dixie Flyer to Atlanta.

And good old Henry even returned the car to Abner Jones the next day.

That was one reason Pete wasn't going home for Thanksgiving. He felt too guilty, too crappy. He didn't want any questions from anybody, and certainly no pity.

Settling his lab notebook on a chair, Pete sorted through the magazines and letters. One from crazy Gussie. Now what had she gotten into? He ripped open the blue envelope and unfolded the sheets and smoothed them out.

*October 14, 1924*

*Dearest Pete,*

*Sorry I haven't written in so long, but that's life at the Essie Swift Female Institute. It sounds like a hospital for crazy women (no comments from you). I get some photography study as part of art class. The prof, Aloysius Bontley, is a crusty old thing, but he says I have talent.*

*Big news! I finally developed the film we took by the river, and your nekkid girl showed up, a perfect fluke! The print, enlarged and cropped, looks great. Mr. Bontley wants me to send it to a contest. What would Papa say if I won! Think he would change his tune about New York?*

*I'm on the staff of the school paper, and I run around shooting pictures of the dean opening convocation and things like that. And get a load of this! Because of the women's fencing competition in the Olympics, Miss Lindstrom decided to start a fencing class. I'm in. You'll have to watch me.*

*Swanee News. She didn't come back to school this semester. She decided she wanted to learn Daddy's business while she's having her debutante season! That's a joke. I hear she goes*

*down to the mill for a couple of hours a day doing a little
typing and filing, but the rest of the time she plays canasta and
goes to deb parties and helps her mother with the Red Cross.
Not to mention taking the train to Atlanta to shop.*

*She's still not engaged to Russell Vincent or anybody
else, but don't get your hopes up. I think she's stuck on this
Ned Fletcher and that's the real reason she goes to the mill. If
Daddy gets wise, Katie bar the door.*

*Your studies sound fascinating, but methinks me would
faint at the sight of a cadaver, much less take a knife to one.*

*Are you coming home for Thanksgiving? Are you coming
to the big debutante ball at Christmas?*

*Love always,*

*Gussie*

Ned Fletcher! Pete stalked up to his room, carrying the letter and his
notebook, and flung both on his bed. He stuck his hands in his pockets
and paced. Outside his bedroom, dead oak leaves rattled in the cold
wind, the rattle of dry bones against grimy clouds that scudded across
the sky.

Swanee didn't want him, she didn't want Russ Vincent. She couldn't
be serious about that Fletcher! He was such a fake. How could she be
taken in by him? She'd looked at him at that party like—like a shark looks
at dinner swimming by.

Still, Elias Burkett would never let his daughter marry anybody who
couldn't bring something to the table. But, yeah. She would pull a stunt
like working at the factory to get near to her crush, right under Daddy's
nose. It wouldn't last. Swanee would get tired of him, the way she got
tired of everybody else, or Daddy would get wise. Fletcher would be
out, no girl, no job.

Pete viciously crumpled the letter and shot it at the wastebasket across the room. It hung on the rim for a moment, and then dropped in.

Ned Fletcher leaned back in his chair at Burkett Mills and read the note slipped into his hand just a few minutes before. Lord, she loved to take chances.

Why did Swanee have to come here, to the mill? He didn't want any trouble. He needed time. Time to become indispensable at the mill, time to acquire some acres of land and a suitable house. Maybe then the old man might come around to seeing him as a prospective son-in-law.

Someone who could give her material comforts, a place in society, and a secure future was the kind of son-in-law Elias had in mind. Ned could achieve that. He had the talent, he had the brains. All he'd ever lacked was a family name, and by damn, this was the South, where it mattered. And he'd been cheated out of his.

Swanee would be his jewel, and she deserved the setting: Arcadia, as well as an impressive house on Vasco da Gama Boulevard, and Burkett Mills. He had to make himself indispensable. He'd do the job better than young Toby, that poor schlump who drowned in the river. Suicide, people said. Didn't make sense to Ned. Why would a guy with everything throw it away?

He felt his face warming. There had been another guy who'd had everything, his buddy, Eben Shackley. Eben hadn't thrown anything away. He'd had it taken from him by an enemy bullet over in France. Ned had dragged him to safety, had gotten him to the casualty tent, but gangrene got him. That last day, when Ned had gone to check, Eben knew he wasn't going to make it.

Ned decided that Eben, since he was dying, might as well know they were brothers. That they had the same father. He hated to tell Eben the truth about why.

Eben said that he had always suspected it. He'd gone to war just to spite the old man, and now Ned might as well know about a stash of gold coins that bastard had hidden in the camp house at his farm, the coins that his mother, Miss Rose, had inherited from her dead Yankee uncle. Said his father had stolen them and hidden them because he thought women ought not to have money. Made them uppity, his father said.

Eben told Ned to go and get the coins, if they were still there. Maybe the old man was dead. Enough people hated him.

Ned remembered those missing gold coins. He remembered that s.o.b. sheriff searching all the croppers' cabins for those coins. He remembered the deputies digging and ruining their vegetable garden. The family had little enough to eat.

Mrs. Benedict, the secretary, appeared at the door. "Mr. Burkett wants to see you in his office," she said. Cursing beneath his breath, he grabbed his coat and went to see his boss.

When he came back with a stack of letters from more customers to placate and more figures to work with, he read the note from Swanee again. She'd meet him Sunday at their favorite tree by the river. The pile of work now seemed lighter. He put the note aside and got down to business.

Mr. Burkett needed something Ned felt he could deliver. An infusion of Yankee capital would tide them over this slack period, and the boss wanted good figures to take to the investors. The mill needed to increase production.

Ned leaned back in his chair. Maybe he should try the stretch-out. Maybe he could shave the hour-long lunch break. More lunches in pails, forty minutes out back. He could get the carpenters to knock together more picnic tables.

He took out a sheet of fresh green paper, whittled a point on his pencil with his pocket knife, and began to figure.

# Chapter 9

"What are you going to do when you get out?" Mary Beth washed a spoon and handed it to Tenny, drying cloth in her hand. It was the second month of her stay at the Home.

"I don't know." Tenny polished the spoon and looked at her upside-down reflection. "I wish I could stay here."

"You're nuts, Tenny," Mary Beth said, flicking her light brown bob. "I can't wait to leave. The bad part is I'm not going back home. My parents are moving to Atlanta and they've arranged for me to go to Agnes Scott College. Don't you want to go home?"

"Nothing to go back to." Mama was dead. Pa had sold her to Shackley. He'd fought Byron and made him leave home. Some father *he* was.

Mary Beth burst into tears. "I'll never see Robert again, never see my old friends. My folks say they have to move so I can find a good husband, one who didn't know about my . . . my . . ."

"Hey, gal," Tenny said. "If that Robert wouldn't marry you, you're better off without him."

"He was engaged to somebody else—he was my best friend's brother—" Mary Beth sobbed. "I loved him."

"And now you lost a friend too," Tenny said. "What a creep." The Byron she remembered would never have done such a thing.

They finished the dishes in silence. Tenny still marveled at the water piped directly into the kitchen and bathrooms, tubs of hot water appearing without having to boil kettles on a wood stove and carry buckets, and she had bathwater all to herself. No nasty, gray, used water!

She snatched a leftover biscuit from under its napkin. In this kitchen, there was always something to eat, and the work at the Home was a sight better than chopping cotton. She hung up her apron and patted Mary Beth on the shoulder. "Come on, or we'll be late." She looked forward to English class. She was reading and writing better every day.

"We're not having classes this morning." Mary Beth sniffled a little. "Remember, the doctor's coming. We're supposed to keep on with our chores until we're called."

Tenny clenched her fists. Ma had done their doctoring with turpentine, a drop of whisky, and warm salt water. Ma said you didn't give in to sickness. You had to pretend it wasn't there to survive.

Ma had all the babies at home, all healthy but the last one, who never drew a breath. Ma's fever afterward made the preacher's wife summon a doctor, but that doctor couldn't save her. Ma died after four days.

On the back porch, rolling wet sheets through the wringer, she heard the doctor's car arrive. Stomach roiling, she cranked away faster, hoping she'd be overlooked. No such luck. Just as she'd handed the last sheet to Hephzibah to hang on the line, she heard, "Tenny Oakes!"

She dried her hands and, as instructed, changed into her bathrobe with nothing underneath. She waited with hunched shoulders in a straight-backed chair outside the infirmary, listening to the murmur of soft, familiar voices.

If she was pregnant, in a few months she'd have to leave. What then? Marjorie, close to delivery, had rich parents down in Savannah waiting for her to come home from her "fancy boarding school up North." She

giggled and told them she wrote letters to her friends, and her parents
then had them sent from a school in Connecticut where they knew the
headmistress.

Marjorie's baby would be adopted by a couple who needed a baby
and could give it a good home. Tenny's own baby would be adopted
too. How else could she work? How else could she find Byron and help
the others get away from Shackley's farm?

The door opened and Marjorie waddled out, her pretty face merry.
"It's almost over." She gave Tenny's shoulder a squeeze. "Say, kid, you
look awful. It's not that bad."

It would be bad. She felt cold all over, nailed to the chair.

"Come on in, young lady," the doctor beckoned.

She edged into the alcohol-smelling room. The doctor stood behind
the examining table, the sleeves of his white shirt rolled up, his natty
bow tie a little askew, his gray, curly hair springing in all directions. He
adjusted his round eyeglasses and held out his hand.

Miss Verity prodded Tenny forward to take the doctor's hand. "Dr.
Godwin, this is Tenny Oakes, a new friend."

"Tenny? Is your name Hortense?" said the doctor. His voice was
kind, if a little gruff.

"I was named for a poet. A lord." At his gesture, she climbed onto the
table.

His eyes crinkled at the corners. "Aha. Better than Alfred, I guess. I had
an aunt Hortense, called Tenny." His gray bristly mustache twitched, and
she let herself finally break into a smile. He checked her ears and throat,
and listened to her heart and tummy. His touch, as he probed her belly,
was firm but tender. Then he told her to slide down on her back and put
her knees up. Tenny shrank back, wide-eyed.

"Miss Verity? Do I have to?"

"Do as he says, dear." Verity stepped alongside and held her hand.

Tenny shut her eyes and submitted to the cold instrument and the doctor's probing. When he had finished, he washed his hands, then gazed at her for a moment.

"We'll do a lab test, but I don't think there's any need. From what Verity tells me, you've had a hard life, young lady. You're doing all right now. You're small, but with that wide pelvis, you could have a dozen with no problem at all."

So she could stay at the Home! Tenny, sitting up, folded her arms over her chest. "I'm not having any more children."

The doctor patted her shoulder in a fatherly way. "No time soon, young lady, but you'll change your mind when you marry."

"I'm never going to marry!"

Dr. Godwin raised his eyebrows and regarded her over his glasses. A flush warmed Tenny's neck, and she clenched her jaw.

He snapped his bag shut, then turned back to her and stroked his chin. "If you don't intend to marry, my girl, you'll have to make a living. Or do you plan go back home and keep house for your parents? Maybe work on a farm?"

Her throat tightened, and she choked out the words. "I can't go home. Or to a farm. Maybe I'll just get a job at a . . . at a café or something."

The doctor and Miss Verity exchanged glances.

"You're awfully young, dear. You need more education," she said. "At least finish high school."

"Why not become a nurse?" the doctor asked. "We need good, strong young women at our hospital. Verity, the two girls you've sent us have been a great success."

Verity smiled with knitted brows. "Oh, Emmett. I'm so glad. Tenny's really very bright. If she wanted to become a teacher, she could qualify for the Inez Callahan Scholarship."

Dr. Godwin folded his arms. "Verity, we *need* bright girls, girls with gumption. I think this young lady fills the bill." The doctor nodded at Tenny. "Think about it."

"I don't have any money for school," Tenny said in a small voice.

The doctor patted her shoulder. "Don't need any. You'd have room and board and a small allowance. Three years and you'd be ready to earn a living."

"You'd work her to death while she's there." Miss Verity, chin down, spread a fresh sheet on the examining table. "She could go to Essie Swift College."

Tenny felt excitement stirring. Essie Swift! Wasn't that in Atlanta? Or just south of there? She could be far away from Weedy Grove.

The doctor turned to Tenny. "It's a great satisfaction to help people get better."

"A doctor didn't help my sister!" Tenny blurted.

Dr. Emmett Godwin stopped what he was doing and looked at her. "Tell me about it."

"You still have to see Hephzibah." Miss Verity gestured toward the wall clock.

Dr. Godwin leaned forward, elbows on knees, as if he had all the time in the world. "Tell me."

Tenny found herself describing how Shelley had been run down by the horse, how Shelley's head had landed on that rock and how she'd never been right since, getting fits so that people thought she was afflicted with devils and stayed away from her. Tenny went on, "I had to leave her at home. One day I want to go back for her." *And get my family out of that trap*, she didn't say.

"You know what, young lady? My son's in medical school right now, and he's learning new treatments every day. If you train at my hospital, you just might learn ways to help your sister."

She perked up. "How long does it take? Is it a long time before I can earn money?"

"You'll have a little money right away," he said, "and in three years you'll have a profession. It takes longer to become a teacher." The doctor nodded to Verity, picked up his bag, and turned to go. "You've got six and a half months to think about it." He winked at her and slipped out the door. Hephzibah was waiting.

"He's awfully nice," Tenny told her.

"Humph," Miss Verity said.

Later that afternoon Tenny shaved soap into the mop bucket, stirred it into suds, and began to mop the back porch. She hadn't forgotten Byron. Hadn't forgotten how they all needed his help. Maybe Verity or Dr. Godwin would tell her how she could find the nurse at the mill, who knew how to send a letter to the Army.

If only that tall, handsome, stuck-up Mr. Ned Fletcher could be Byron, Byron like he used to be! But then again, Byron was surely dead, or they'd have heard from him. He wouldn't have deserted his favorite sister. She swished the mop back and forth over the boards.

Six and a half months to go. Miss Verity had impressed on them that they had to lead a respectable life if they wanted all the good things that came with it. Based on what she'd learned of the world so far, she wondered if that might not be the most difficult thing of all.

# Chapter 10

Five minutes before nine o'clock on the Friday before Thanksgiving, Tenny stopped dusting the parlor, tucked her feather duster under her arm, and answered the doorbell.

Before her stood an elegant girl wearing a raspberry-colored dress and cloche hat that must have cost a ton of money. Silk, too, she reckoned. Surely this girl wasn't coming for help!

"I've come to see Mrs. Verity Hapsworth." The young lady's voice sounded like falling raindrops. "Please tell her Miss Burkett is here."

Tenny froze with shock. *This* was the girl she had seen going into Ned Fletcher's office. "Will you wait in the parlor?" She swallowed, aware of her own shabby work smock and kerchief, and showed the girl, wafting clouds of French perfume, to the velvet parlor sofa beneath the portrait of Mrs. Inez Callahan. The girl sat, crossed her silk-stockinged legs, and pulled at her gloves. She stared at Tenny's carpet sweeper.

Tenny seized the sweeper, returned it to the hall closet, and hurried back to Verity's office to tell her about the visitor. Upstairs, treadle sewing machines clicked away. Tenny had finished her required maternity smock, and would be allowed to sew another if she liked, to be left behind for the next unfortunate.

Miss Verity strode from her office to meet the girl. Tenny lagged in the hall with her feather duster, curious. The young woman sat gazing out at the last of the drifting leaves. When greeted, she rose smoothly and stepped forward to shake the director's hand.

Miss Verity gave her a welcoming smile. "Miss Burkett! So nice to see you. It's been a while. Your mother's benefit tea was so helpful!" The older woman folded her hands. "Now, Miss Burkett, how can we help you?"

"Please, call me Swanee." The girl glanced out at Tenny. "Can we speak in private?"

Miss Verity nodded. "Of course. Tenny, please bring coffee to my office, and then you can finish the dusting."

Tenny poured two cups from the electric percolator in the kitchen and arranged them on a tray with sugar and cream. When she entered Miss Verity's cramped office, conversation stopped. She placed the tray on a side table, noticing that Miss Burkett, posed in her chair with calm composure, held one hand tightly with the other.

Tenny closed the door on a bucketful of questions. Was this girl really Ned Fletcher's sweetheart? And why was she here? Tenny retrieved her duster but hurried upstairs and slipped into Hephzibah's room. She wiggled behind the bed and put her ear to the heating vent above the office, stifling a sneeze.

Verity was saying, "Are you engaged to be married? Shouldn't you consult your own physician?"

There was a long pause. "Dr. Paxton, our family doctor, knows my father socially. I thought I could rely on you to be discreet."

Again, a pause. Tenny's ear was heating up, and she wanted to pull away, but she couldn't. "We do give the young ladies advice when they leave here." Miss Verity was probably leaning forward and clasping her hands. "And we tell them to have a commitment before they become intimate with a young man again."

Tenny's heart beat faster. Oh, she knew that speech. That was Miss Verity's *birth control* speech. Could it be that Swanee Burkett was asking for . . . ? The furnace burped, roared, and blotted out the sound, and Tenny wriggled away. When the noise died down, Tenny lowered her other ear and heard "We try to instill good judgment in our girls. We treasure them, but we don't want them to return."

Swanee's voice rang clearly through the metal pipe, firm with an edge of desperation. "We are secretly engaged. To tell you the truth, Mrs. Hapsworth, my father is being difficult. He has my future husband picked out and won't accept anyone else."

"Ah," said Verity. "Fathers sometimes have our best interests at heart." Tenny imagined that the director paused, closed her eyes, and steepled her fingers, the way she did when she suspected you were fudging the story.

"Not this time," Swanee said heatedly. "Papa thinks he's some medieval king who can hand me over to the highest bidder! I want to be with the man I love."

"I see," Verity said. "If it's true love, it will wait, won't it? You're still young."

The silence grew long. The furnace roared. ". . . pregnant out of wedlock, he'll disinherit me. I'd be damaged goods in the marriage market." Another long silence.

This time Swanee spoke smoothly, handing each word over. "You know, I'd like to make a donation to the Home now."

The machine treadles clicked and the girls in the room down the hall chattered. Her ear was too hot, and she couldn't make out the murmurs. But Miss Verity always needed money.

A sharp question: "Does your young man use a prophylactic?"

"Sometimes." The words were choked. Miss Verity had ways of making you feel embarrassed.

"Birth control only works when you use it." Miss Verity proceeded to explain about condoms, pessaries, douching, and the relative effectiveness of each.

"A pessary, you say? He doesn't have to be involved?" Miss Burkett's voice rose in hope.

"You must obtain it from a doctor. The doctor who attends our girls is Dr. Emmett Godwin. He is very kind."

"Oh, no!" Swanee blurted, and then she said quietly, "His son is . . . is a friend."

The sewing machines clattered to a stop. Tenny scrambled up from the floor, barely making it out of Hephzibah's room before the girls spilled into the hall and streamed downstairs for a break before the next class.

Tenny followed them down, swished the duster across the rest of the parlor tables, and then knocked at the office door to ask if more coffee was needed.

"No, thank you, my dear," Verity said. "Please tell the others I'll be there shortly for the cooking lesson." As if on cue, the back doorbell rang. The cooking teacher had arrived, and they'd all prepare lunch and dinner.

Tenny delivered Miss Verity's message and waited until the girls had trooped to the kitchen before she slipped back into Hephzibah's room. Okay, she'd be late for the cooking lesson, but being pregnant was a

great excuse for getting out of things. You could always say you felt
nauseated and had to lie down.

"... douche bags are found at the pharmacy and you must make the
solution yourself. But I really would recommend you see your doctor for
a pessary, if you are determined."

Blood roared in Tenny's ears.

"I'd better go now." A chair scraped.

"This pamphlet might help you," Miss Verity said.

"Margaret Sanger? *Woman Rebel*?" The voice was soft, but the tone
was sharp. Another chair scraped. And then, from Swanee: "I appreciate
your advice, Mrs. Hapsworth, and I appreciate the work you're doing."

A pause. A drawer opened and closed. "The girls and I appreciate
it, Miss Burkett," said Verity. "I hope you never need us." Tenny could
almost see Verity's one raised eyebrow.

"Thank you." Miss Burkett's voice had cooled. Tenny vaulted herself
off the floor and raced to the stairwell. From above, she saw Miss Verity
accompany the girl to the heavy front door with its blue stained glass
pane. She opened it. "Good-bye," she said. "Good luck."

The girl murmured something. The door closed. Tenny ran to an
upstairs window and looked out just in time to see a beautiful cream-
colored roadster roar away.

Tenny had no envy of this Swanee, of her clothes and her car and
her airs and graces. She was no better than the rest of them. Tenny was
envious of just one thing, and she would speak to Miss Verity about it
right away. She wanted to talk with a voice like that girl's, a voice like
falling raindrops.

On the way downstairs, she met Miss Verity, and the good lady's
conspiratorial smile told her Miss Verity knew she'd been eavesdrop-
ping. The lady put her finger to her lips. "Not a word to anyone," Miss
Verity said. "She's not the first debutante to come here."

"No?"

"Certainly not. But she's the least likely to listen I've ever seen."

# Chapter 11

O ver the Christmas holidays, Swanee made her debut with a spectacular private ball in the Burketts' own splendid ballroom, decorated all in white for the occasion. White roses and lilies from the florist, white satin covers for the chairs, white damask and ribbons for the table. Her escort was Russell Vincent.

Gussie watched them dance, hearing people murmur about what a handsome couple they made, and that they expected an engagement any day now. Swanee certainly danced as radiantly as a girl in love.

Pete had stayed away. She didn't feel guilty about telling him about Swanee's flirtation with Ned Fletcher. She watched the two at the dance, but the minx didn't vamp, didn't tease, and kept her distance from the mill manager. Had Swanee's father caught on? The girl was coming back to school in January.

Deep in thought, she started when Ned appeared at her side and asked her to dance.

"Did I frighten you?"

"Of course not." Gussie smiled with real pleasure. Swanee would hate it.

Gliding with her across the floor, Ned gazed at her with that offhand, sleepy way he had. "I heard you had a dove shoot out at Arcadia over Thanksgiving. I wish you'd invited me."

"It was really more of a family picnic plus a few of Papa's friends. You like to hunt?"

"I'm very good at it. What are you good at, Miss Pemberton?"

Gussie smiled sweetly. "When I shoot, it's with a camera."

"A nice hobby."

Gussie gave him a cold smile. "It's my career."

He raised his eyebrows and spouted, "Don't you want to be a normal girl and get married?"

If it hadn't been for her headband slipping, she would have stung him. "Of course not," she managed, sliding the band back into place.

"Why do you say that?"

"Why should men have all the fun?"

Ned executed a twirling dance move, swooping her down so that she was looking up at him. "Fun?" He grinned. "I thought most women liked to lie in the lap of luxury."

"Have you ever scraped for a living, Mr. Fletcher?"

He hesitated just long enough for Gussie to know she'd made a direct hit. "More than you know." He cleared his throat. "It wasn't easy after my family lost that farm in Virginia."

She widened her eyes sympathetically. "Oh, that's right, you did. Where was this farm, exactly?"

Once again the hesitation. He was saved when the music ended and Swanee headed their way like a locomotive under full steam. Gussie thanked him for the dance. He looked relieved.

Watching the two take the floor, Gussie felt Swanee's involvement with Russell Vincent was a sham to fool her father. Anyhow, at that moment Russell was dancing with a girl Gussie knew from Essie Swift, a toffee-haired girl named Jean Claire who liked to play golf, Russell's game. And she was laughing at his jokes. Not only that, she was a niece of the Governor.

Gussie was glad Pete hadn't come, but it was strange that she hadn't heard a peep from him since October.

Back at school in January, she mulled over that remark of Ned's that her photography was just a hobby. Was that what they all thought? She'd show them! She spent every spare moment behind the camera and blackened her fingers with developing solution. She talked with Mr. Bontly about letting her have a show on campus. She could write the show up and send the article and photos to the *Ashbyville Clarion*, where the editor, a fellow her father liked, was her sister Anna's brother-in-law.

In the meantime, while she was waiting to become famous, she'd have fun. She acted in student plays, wore baggy trousers, smoked cigarettes, and sneaked off with boys on Saturday nights to dance in speakeasies and drink bathtub gin.

The required chapel service the next morning was hell, and sometimes she slept upright in the pew. Sunday afternoons she napped and wrote letters and then went off to take more pictures.

One particular Sunday in February she tapped her pen against her teeth. She ought to write Pete, find out if he was all right. She had news about Swanee, but would he want it?

She dipped the nib into the ink and wrote:

> *I know you said you were through with Swanee, but I just*
> *thought you might be curious. Stop reading here if you don't*
> *want to know.*

*Now she's back at school. Far as I can see, she's studying hard, being nicey-nice to all the professors, and giving the housemother little presents. She's got her lackeys that scuttle along behind her hoping some of her glitter drops off and lands on their heads.*

*They had the Honor Court nominations last week and of course she's on it. The bookies here (joke) are saying the odds are 2-1 that she'll be May Queen. And to think she stayed out a quarter? Yours truly has too many demerits to ever be considered, so no need asking if I'm on it. Who cares!*

She paused, pen in air, and glanced at the clock. From her second-story room the front walk was in plain view, and she'd noticed from her letter-writing perch that Swanee left the dormitory dressed in hat and fur-trimmed coat every Sunday at 2:00 exactly: on foot, in heels. Girls were not allowed personal automobiles on campus.

And here she was, clipping down the walk in hat and coat.

Where was she going? Maybe Pete would like to know. Gussie had always liked the idea of being a spy. Wasn't photography a kind of spying, trying to find the inner life of people and objects?

She shrugged a duffel coat over her sweater and corduroy knickers. Braving the misty chill, she hurried to spot the figure in cocoon coat and caramel cloche, intending to shadow her like a private eye in a penny dreadful. Where was she going, heading away from town, cafés, and movie houses?

And here she was passing into Oakwood Cemetery? The students hardly ever went there. The Dean of Women told them it was dangerous because of the gully right behind it. Vagrants might be hiding there. Ghosts would be more likely.

Ducking behind an ancient oak, Gussie watched Swanee crest a gentle grassy rise and disappear. She followed, keeping out of sight, scooting from obelisk to tombstone like a soldier dodging enemy fire. When she reached the hilltop, she saw only a yellow Pierce-Arrow driving away from a bare dirt parking area.

So that was how it was. Gussie shoved her hands into her pockets and ambled back to the dormitory, mulling things over. This flirtation had lasted longer than Swanee's other wild flings. If the girl wasn't careful, she'd lose Russell Vincent and Fletcher both and wind up ruined. Pete would be glad then—or would he?

She went back to her letter and wrote one more paragraph to Pete about the horrible stew and cornbread they were forced to eat in the Dining Hall, surely made of horsemeat or sawdust. She asked if he'd met any girls that were alive. She signed the letter with *tons of love*.

And then she added her P.S.:

> *Mr. Bontly sent some of my nature photos to a magazine and they bought them! No, I didn't let him see the naked girl. Not yet. I'm saving it for you, anyway. I now have a check for fifteen dollars to wave at Papa.*

# Chapter 12

Tenny, slipping into her dress, gazed at the envelope on the small desk in her cozy room and felt a thrill of anticipation. Her future? No more winters in a drafty shack with just one kitchen woodstove for the whole house? She glanced out at a tracery of frosted black limbs against a dull gray sky and shivered.

She didn't ever want to be that cold again.

She pulled up the white chenille spread and tucked it around the pillows, her rounded belly making her clumsy. Satisfied that her room would pass inspection, she picked up the envelope, walked to Miss Verity's office, and tapped on the half-open door.

"Come in, Tenny. Sit down." Miss Verity smiled kindly and gestured to a steaming teapot on the desk. "It's a good cup on a cold day." She poured tea for each of them.

Tenny nodded, her throat dry. She reached for a sugar cube and cream, stirred her tea with a silver spoon, and waited.

"Now," Miss Verity said, "I've found just the school for you. The Berry School's mission is to educate rural mountain children, but they might take you. Mrs. Callahan knows Mrs. Berry and could arrange it. You are from a rural background, are you not?"

She couldn't deny it. Her country speech gave her away. "Yes, ma'am."

"Well, then." Miss Verity smiled like a cat in the cream. "You'll spend a year or two in this school, working for your tuition, and at the end you'll get a high school diploma. Then you'll be prepared for college."

Tenny, heart racing, gripped her envelope so tightly she creased it. "Miss Verity, I'm really grateful, but I can't spend that long. I need to earn money as soon as possible." Should she tell about her sister?

Miss Verity pressed her lips together. "Young lady, listen to reason. With education, you can become a teacher, quite respectable, and can make a good marriage. Or, perhaps become a stenographer, if you're bent on a career."

"Yes, ma'am, but . . ."

"But?" Miss Verity clasped her hands together.

*Oh Lord, don't let her steeple her fingers.* Tenny thrust the envelope on the desk. "Dr. Godwin sent me an application to nursing school." She took a deep breath and sat up straight, unable to hold back a smile. "I've filled it out, I'm ready to mail it, and the director, Miss Wells, wants a recommendation from one of my teachers."

She sank back in her chair, biting her lip.

"Slow down, my dear." Miss Verity took the application and quickly scanned it. Tenny didn't like her expression, the one she used when faced with a stubborn girl.

"Let's give a thought for what will happen if you become a trained nurse. You'll find yourself looking for private positions, with no guarantee of work."

"Miss Verity, why are you trying to discourage me?" Tenny leaned forward. "Maybe I could get a job like the nurse at the mill. I'm good at looking after people and I like it. I looked after my . . ." She blinked and swallowed. She mustn't mention her sister.

"What is it, Tenny?"

She sidestepped to cover her mistake. "The mill nurse was going to tell me how to write to the Army and find my brother."

"You have a brother?"

Tenny had covered one slip with another. She nodded. "He went away and we never saw him again."

"And your brother's name? Is it Oakes too?" Miss Verity allowed herself a small smile.

Tenny looked at her shoes, her face warming.

Miss Verity's brow furrowed. "It isn't, and you don't want to say why."

Tenny slid back and clasped her hands, silent.

"You don't want anyone finding *you*, is that it?" Verity leaned forward, her voice soft. "You've run away from home and changed your name."

This lady saw right through her. "Tenny is my real name. As for Oakes, I borrowed it off a sign. My Pa, he's alive and he's a drunk. I can't go back there."

Verity's face turned severe. "The truth, now. Was it your father that got you here? Or your brother?"

She shook her head violently. "It wasn't. I swear it." *But he sold me. He sold me for twenty-five dollars.* She wanted to confide in Verity, but she was so ashamed.

"You were compromised, weren't you? You should report it to the sheriff."

She opened her mouth to protest that the sheriff was in the pocket of Arno Shackley. That's what Mrs. Brown, the preacher's wife, always said. But the words wouldn't come.

"I'm quite serious," Miss Verity replied.

"They wouldn't believe me." Tenny shook her head, wishing she could disappear. "Please, I want to forget all about it. If I could just find Byron. My brother. I know he's out there somewhere. I'd know if he was dead. I'd feel it."

"Your brother? You don't want him to exact revenge, do you?" Miss Verity gave her a sharp-eyed stare.

"No," Tenny said. "But the brother I knew would do that. No, I want him to help Pa. Help Pa stop drowning in 'shine and find the courage to leave that place. Help him find work somewhere else. Maybe Byron has a good job by now."

"I'll see what I can do about your brother," Verity said. "Now will you let me write to the Berry School for you? Nursing can wait until you have a high school education."

Tenny clenched her fists. "Miss Verity, what if that school turns me down? Can I go ahead and send in my application to Mercy Hospital? And a letter from you? Please? And may I have an envelope and stamp? And may I go to the Post Office?"

"My, my," said Verity, sipping the last of her tea. "So many questions. You seem determined, so against my better judgment, I'll write the recommendation. And I'll hold you to your word."

"Yes, ma'am!"

Tenny felt like saying "Yee-Haw!" like Pa used to do in the old days. Now she was really on her way. She gave the envelope to Miss Verity, who promised to have everything ready to mail after classes that afternoon.

When sewing class finished, Tenny put away her new smock and clattered down the steps to the donation closet. She needed a warm winter coat for this weather. In the understair space she rummaged around until she found a gray and red wool plaid with a tatty fur collar. She didn't much care for it, but it was the only one that fit her childlike frame. In a cardboard box of knits she unearthed a faded red woolen tam topped by a pompom. Hair tucked under the tam and coat buttoned tightly, envelope in her pocket, she fought a sharp wind seven blocks to the tall marble steps of the Post Office. She raced up, tugged open the heavy door and, once inside, shoved the application through the shiny brass mail slot.

She stood a few moments by a front window, rubbing her chilled hands and basking in her accomplishment. She was on her way! Across the street, in front of the courthouse, two men stood talking. A slim dapper type in a gray fedora and overcoat seemed to be arguing with a heavyset man in a cowboy hat and moleskin coat.

Tenny caught her breath, her heart plummeting. That man in the cowboy hat stood like Shackley, gestured like Shackley. And when he turned and looked directly across the street, she *knew*. What business did he have at the courthouse? Was he still after her for stealing a Bible with money in it? For being a runaway? For stealing herself away from him?

Gnawing her cold knuckles, she watched as Shackley turned away from the dapper man, got into the black Ford parked in an angled space, and drove away. She couldn't stop trembling. A postal clerk called out, "Say, girl, you all right?"

She swallowed and nodded to the clerk. "I'm okay. Sorry." She pushed open the heavy door and burst out into the sharp wind. She scurried down the steps and marched head down towards home, glancing up from time to time at passing cars. Black Fords were everywhere.

Had Shackley seen her? He wouldn't have known her, with her pale hair stuffed under her hat. Her jitters subsided and she clenched her jaw at the memory of what she had endured. Angry warmth flushed her face.

She didn't need Byron to take revenge. She could easily kill Shackley herself.

The wind whipped up and caught her tam, and she tugged it tightly to her head. Motorcars roared in the street, honking at pedestrians. The occasional mule and wagon clopped and creaked, leaving road apples. The chill, the steaming dung, and the fumes of gasoline made her nose water.

Just as she dug in her pocket for her handkerchief, a hearty gust whipped off her red tam and carried it. She ran after the hat, wind whistling through her braid, whipping it loose. A car in the street screeched to a stop.

"Hey, girl," the man in the car yelled over the traffic din. "Hey, girl, I know you."

Blood pounded in her ears. She darted into an alley, dodging a delivery truck. A horn blared. She kept running, her feet smacking the cobblestones. She stumbled, unused to her extra pounds and growing belly. At the end of the alley, she reckoned that Shackley would come around the block to chase her, so she crossed the street and ran in the opposite direction.

Her breath came hard and her chest was beginning to hurt. She darted through a crowd of people waiting for the trolley, jostling a man with a bulging briefcase, barely missing an old woman. Cries followed her. She kept going. Her right ankle turned, and she winced, but slowed only a little. She ducked into another alley, rounded a corner, and emerged onto a side street.

Panting, she paused to rest in a shop doorway. A black Ford slowed. She ducked into the shop, and a bell clamored as she shut the door behind her.

She peered back out at the street, quaking in all her limbs. Her ankle was beginning to throb.

"May I help you?"

Startled, she turned to see a slim man with a narrow fox face and hair almost as pale as her own, as finely dressed as a mannequin in the shop windows downtown.

His polite manner, his mild expression calmed her. Why, he even wore a fine silk handkerchief in the breast pocket of his blue blazer. Miss Verity would say he was a *gentleman*.

"I'm sorry to come bustin' in like this," she said, forgetting her careful speech. "A man was after me."

"H'm," said the fox-faced gentleman. "Your hair is very untidy." He lifted her pale tresses and examined them as if they were a skein of silk. "Yet it's glorious." He shook his head and sighed. "I can see why you haven't bobbed it."

She pulled the locks away from him and closed them in her fist. "Sir. I'm running for my *life*."

The man put his finger to his chin. "Should I believe you? You look like a ragamuffin. Why was this man chasing you? Did you steal something?"

"I never stole anything in my life!" She immediately blushed, thinking of the Bible. That *wasn't* stealing. She'd *borrowed* it.

"Really?"

She gave him a furious look. "I was on my way home from the Post Office, minding my own business, and this man started chasing me in his car! He wanted to kidnap me!"

"How very odd," the man said. "Most kidnappers want ransom, and you don't look as if you came from money."

Tenny stomped her foot in protest. "That has nothing to do with it!"

The man smiled at her outburst. "You are just a child, aren't you? No need to get upset." He gave her a slight bow. "Allow me to introduce myself. My name's Lyman Stratton. These"—he swept his arm in a semicircle—"are my antiques."

Tenny gazed all around, bemused. The place smelled of dust and furniture polish and some kind of perfume and was full of tables and chairs and bric-a-brac and lamps and rugs, more than she'd ever seen. Somebody's sour-faced grandma and grandpa with long straggly beard gazed down on her from the high walls. "I can't figure it," she said. "They're all so fancy, but kind of shabby. Why don't you sell new stuff?"

Lyman laughed. "People pay me good money for this shabby stuff. Who *are* you, mystery girl?"

She looked at him skeptically and decided to trust him. "I've come from the Callahan Home. My name's Tenny Oakes."

Lyman picked up a pencil and tapped it on the counter. "Callahan Home—for Wayward Girls. Verity Hapsworth's establishment. That wouldn't have anything to do with this kidnapper, would it?"

Tenny flushed warm from head to foot. She'd make something up, close to the truth. "Yes. He's a white slaver. He wants to catch me and sell me to the Sultan of Borneo, and I escaped from him."

Lyman pointed a finger at her. "That's a good story, but I don't *think* the Sultan wants an expectant mother."

Tenny's heart sank; a deep-chiming clock bonged five. Tenny laid a hand on Lyman's arm. "Okay, I'll be serious. Please help me," she said. "Is there a way I can get back to the Home through the alleys?"

Lyman nodded slowly. "It's closing time. I'd take you back in my automobile, a delightful Pierce-Arrow, but I'm expecting a crate of goods from England, and my delivery boy should be back from the station with it any time now. That Home is on Magnolia Street, right?"

She nodded and Lyman gazed at her for a moment. "You really could be a beautiful girl," he said. *"There is no beauty that hath not some strangeness in the proportion."*

Tenny furrowed her brow. "What does that mean?"

"Perfect girls are rarely beautiful," he said. "Sir Francis Bacon said that. Tell you what. I'll give you a good-luck charm that's strange and beautiful."

He went behind the counter, reached into a case, and took out a silver pendant which held an oval stone, milky white with an iridescent blue sheen. Glancing again at her, he also took out a silver chain.

"Tenny," he said, "lift up your hair."

Too surprised to protest, she did as he asked and he fastened the charm around her neck. "This is a moonstone, and it's said to protect women," he said.

She touched it. "Miss Verity says never to accept jewelry from a man unless you're engaged."

"I know the good Miss Verity," he said. "I promise you, this will be all right with her. All I ask in return is that you come back someday and buy something from my shop."

"Me?" She glanced at the price tags on the jewelry in the case. "That's funny! I'm never going to be rich enough."

Lyman gave her a mysterious smile. "You will surprise everyone, including yourself," he said softly. "You have spirit, and you have imagination. Now, come on. I'll tell you the quickest way home."

He locked and bolted the front door, flipped the sign to *Closed*, and then he escorted her past rolled oriental carpets, fancy standing lamps, and cases of figurines: porcelain horses rearing and demure ladies in ball gowns, fans in hand.

He led her into the musty-smelling storeroom, piled high with crates and boxes, then out to the loading dock, which looked out onto a hard-packed dirt driveway, trash barrels, and an alley. The late-afternoon sun glowed in the west, and the wind gusts had died down.

Lyman pointed to the right. "Go down the alley, and it will bring you out onto Vasco da Gama," he said. "Left for half a block then a right down another alley, which will take you to Magnolia Street. You can get home from there, can't you?"

Tenny nodded.

"A word of advice." Lyman reached out and touched her head. "That hair. That's why that man noticed you. I'll bet he never paid attention to your face. Not really."

Tenny shook her head. "No. He didn't."

"If you want to avoid being recognized, then put some hair dye—light brown, not red, not black—on that fabulous hair. You get it at the drugstore. It might be called henna, but it isn't. True henna is only red, and you don't want that."

Tenny clutched at her hair once again. Hair was a woman's crowning glory, Ma always said. She couldn't put dye on her crowning glory, the hair that matched Shelley's! She thanked Lyman again and gave him a quick hug. He smiled at her in return.

She hurried down the alley and turned left on Vasco da Gama Boulevard, as he'd told her. She passed in front of Walgreen's, paused for a moment, and then hurried on down half a block and turned right down the alley. And there was Magnolia Street! She tingled with relief, but then she bit her lip. Lyman Stratton was right. With her hair, Shackley would notice her wherever she was. Even if she went to Atlanta. He could go anywhere.

She backtracked to Walgreen's. She was already late. A few more minutes wouldn't matter.


"Tenny! I was just about to send out a search and rescue mission!" The director's lips tightened and her eyes narrowed. "You've lost your tam, and your hair's all tangled!"

"I'm sorry, Miss Verity," Tenny said, closing the door behind her. "The wind blew it off, and it went out into the street, and then I stopped . . . in a shop because I had . . . um . . . twisted my ankle . . ."

"A shop!"

"It was an antique shop," she said with dignity. "Mr. Lyman Stratton gave me this pendant to . . . to cheer me up." She lifted it up for inspection.

Verity regarded the moonstone. "Mmmm. I have a feeling there's much more to your story," she said, "but I don't have time to winkle it out of you right now. Those girls are making a frightful muddle in the kitchen. I never should have allowed them to bake a cake. Come see me after dinner. I have some news."

"Yes, ma'am." Tenny scooted upstairs to her room, happy that Miss Verity wasn't angry. But what news? Good or bad?

On the high shelf of her closet, she pulled out a cigar box one of the other girls had given her. She opened the box and deposited a packet of light brown hair dye. She fingered the Bible lying there, but didn't open it. It still made her think too much of her mother, and of the baby to come. Please, dear God, she prayed, let this baby have a good home. And thank you, God, if you answered my prayer before and it isn't that son-of-a-bitch's.

She touched the stub of her first movie ticket, the wrapper of her first bar of store-bought soap, the list of house rules Miss Verity had given her. She thought of her keepsakes back home that she hadn't brought—dried pods and buckeyes, pebbles and broken shards of pottery and arrowheads. She'd left them for Shelley. The thought of her sister wrenched her.

She yearned to see her, to know she was all right, and that Shackley had not taken a fancy to her. She was a child, and she would always be one, and would have nothing inside to protect her from someone like him. The child could not rely on her father Jubal Chance, wrapped up as he was in his own misery.

Maybe Tenny could write to Mrs. Brown, the pastor's wife. After Ma had died, Mrs. Brown often dropped by with the pastor, bringing a jar of honey from her bees or beans from their garden, and asking the children if they needed anything. Pa wouldn't talk to them. He retreated out back and sat on the porch until they left. Merry said he was mad at God for taking Ma away from him.

"Tenny! Come on, girl! You've got table duty!"

That was Dulcy. Tenny closed the box, shoved it back on the high shelf, and hurried downstairs. Fish and chips, Miss Verity had promised them. Tenny smiled. It would be catfish and fries.

After dinner, Tenny sat at the kitchen table along with Dulcy and the other girls who were doing lessons. She opened her notebook to a fresh sheet of Blue Horse paper and picked up her pencil.

> *Dear Mrs. Brown,* she wrote in her best penmanship,
> *I pray you will forgive me for running away but I had to. I need to ask if the other kids are all right, esp. Shelley. I am inclosing two dollars for them, and please don't tell Pa. Maybe you could just buy what they need and say it came from the church.*
> *Please reply soon. I will be looking forword to your letter. Please use the name below, she is a friend of mine.*
> *Your friend,*
> *Tenny*
>
> *Send to Miss Oakes, Box 125, Ashbyville, Ga.*

She was fortunate that Miss Verity had taken a Post Office box for her girls. She wrote one more line:

> *P.S. Please tell me is anything happening in Weedy Grove.*

It was an off chance that Mrs. Brown might know why Arno Shackley was at the courthouse. She generally knew everything that went on, since Pastor Brown went calling on folks and they liked to talk. She didn't want to ask directly about Shackley. She didn't even want to think about him, and would've shut Weedy Grove out of her mind forever if it wasn't for her brothers and sisters.

The Tenny that people could hurt was gone forever, stuffed in that old croker sack she brought from home. She would keep that old sack to remind herself where she'd come from, and one day, she'd toss it in the fire.

She was hurrying upstairs, notebook in hand, when Miss Verity called out to her from the parlor. "Come to the office, dear."

Gosh. Was Miss Verity still mad about her being late?

Biting her lip, she followed the director. But when they reached the office, Miss Verity opened her desk drawer and pulled out a slip of paper. "You said you wanted to find your brother, didn't you?"

Tenny blinked, her mind racing. "Yes! But what . . ."

A Mona Lisa smile crept across Miss Verity's face. "I telephoned the nurse who works at the mill. The one you told me about."

"You *found* her?"

"One does need a telephone in her profession."

Miss Verity handed Tenny the slip of paper. "For Army records, you write to the National Records office in St. Louis, Missouri," she said. "You tell them you're a relative, with some details that prove it. And you'll need a return address. The P.O. Box, of course."

Tenny's knees went weak, and she swiped away tears. So much had happened today! "Yes, ma'am. Oh thank you, ma'am!" Still, she hesitated, searching for the right words.

"Yes, Tenny? Is there something else?"

Tenny hung her head and toed the ground. "Yes, ma'am. I've been thinking. Maybe I was too quick. Is that Berry School far away from here?"

Miss Verity gave a crisp nod, smiling. "Yes, and it's on a farm in the country. You've done farm work, I take it?"

"Yes, *ma'am*." Far away, that's where she ought to go. The farther the better.

"And?" Miss Verity prompted.

"I've changed my mind," Tenny said. She wanted to be far, far away from Arno Shackley.

# Chapter 13

Tenny read the letter again, then folded it and slid it into her desk drawer. She'd been accepted into Miss Berry's school, to start in the fall. She sighed and wished she hadn't had to tell Dr. Godwin that she'd withdrawn her application to join the fall nursing class at Mercy Hospital. He'd just cocked his head and raised one eyebrow. "Very well. If you change your mind let me know."

She bit her lip. Maybe she could find some way to make money after a year at Miss Berry's. Maybe it would be possible because of her new speech lessons. She was learning how to talk like a lady!

Miss Verity had used a special contribution to hire Professor Moon, the speech teacher, to give them all lessons. Before that, during the winter, they'd studied George Bernard Shaw's play *Pygmalion* to see how speech changed one girl's life, and she'd loved the drama. Still, it had been spring before Professor Moon could arrange the time. The wonderful thing was that he liked her!

"Ah, if only we had time for a few more lessons, Miss Oakes, I'd have you speaking like a stage actress. It's marvelous what you've accomplished in these few weeks."

"Thank you, Professor Moon." Tenny smiled at the dapper little man in the brown suit. She glanced down at her belly. She'd been worried that she wasn't going to be able to finish the lessons, but this was the last session.

She was going to speak so well when she got to Berry College, they'd never believe she'd come from the country! Verity had been tickled when Tenny got her acceptance letter to finish high school there, and she'd encouraged her to apply for the Callahan scholarship when she was close to graduation.

"Come now," the professor was saying. "Turn in your books to the third chapter and repeat from the Bard:

"How sweet the moonlight sleeps upon this bank!
Here we will sit, and let the sounds of music
Creep in our ears: soft stillness and the night
Become the touches of sweet harmony."

Tenny had just gotten to "Creep in our ears" when the backache that had been nagging her for two days attacked like a wild boar. She gasped, nearly choking with the effort to ride out the pain.

"What's wrong, Miss Oakes?" Professor Moon was frowning, his expressive lips pursed.

"Dr. Moon! Oh, oh! Somebody run and get Miss Verity!" She clutched her back. "A mule is kicking me!"

Tenny lay on a trolley in a curtained-off labor room, twisting as the pains hit her. Miss Verity squeezed her hand from time to time and smiled encouragingly. "Dr. Emmett should be here soon," she told her. "He's been delayed by an emergency. They've called Dr. Golightly."

"Isn't this an emergency?" Tenny groaned.

"It's natural," Verity said. "Don't worry. Count your contractions."

"I'm cold."

"You're frightened." Verity patted her hand and went to ask the nurse for another blanket.

Tenny's teeth chattered and she tried to keep track of the pains, coming now at regular intervals. The clattering murmurs and air that reeked of chlorine fought with the sensations wracking her body.

The curtains parted. A curly-haired young man wearing a short white jacket and round glasses stepped in. He gave her a nervous smile. "How are you doing?"

Was this boy really a doctor? "You're not going to deliver the baby, are you?" Tenny's eyes frantically searched the room for Miss Verity.

"No need to look so horrified," the young man said. "I'm Pete Godwin. Pop asked me to look in, and Dr. Golightly's scrubbing. He'll deliver you."

Verity and the nurse arrived with the extra blanket. "Hello, young Emmett," the nurse said, tucking the blanket around Tenny. "Home for the summer? Have you been studying OB?"

Pete hated it when people called him by his real name, but he only repeated what he'd told Tenny. "Think I could attend?"

"Don't I have any say in this?" Tenny broke in.

Pete stepped forward. "Well, if you object, then of course I'll leave, but . . ." A strange look crept over his face.

"What's wrong? Why are you staring at me?" Tenny scooted back and propped herself up on her elbows.

"Now, now, dear." The nurse gently urged her back down.

The boy doctor's eyes softened and he smiled, a silly smile. "I think I've seen you before."

"No, you haven't!" Then she knew. He was the young man at the gas pump. He was the young man who had looked at her with wonderment. And he was looking at her like that again, and here she was, all sweaty and greasy and, from what she remembered of her mother's childbirth at home, would soon be bloody and screaming.

She sucked in air, afraid, exhilarated, heart racing. The curtains parted again, and Dr. Golightly, bearded and bespectacled, strode in. "Let's get the show on the road. You staying, young Pete?"

A contraction seized her, and Tenny squealed, "No, please!" as much from protest as pain. Pete gave her one last look before he slipped back through the curtain.

"Let's take a look at you," the doctor said, and the nurse raised the drape. Tenny bore the examination breathing deeply, not complaining, and when he'd finished, he smiled. "You're coming along. Eight centimeters. How do you feel?"

"Plowed under." The contractions were coming about three minutes apart, and were getting stronger. A shiver wracked her body. "I'm not going to die, am I?"

The doctor lifted her cold hand and patted it. "Of course not. I'll see you soon."

She saw him next in the delivery room, standing behind a nurse lowering an ether cone.

Tenny blinked awake to sun streaming in through the high windows, with a sick sour feeling in her stomach. Between her legs she throbbed and burned. Stitches, someone had warned her. And they had to put disinfectant on them. She found herself in a white iron bed, in a ward with two other women.

Through half-closed eyes she saw Pete Godwin at the bedside of the woman farthest from her, and she pretended to be asleep. He talked and joked with the patient, then he chatted with one of the nurses. He paused before Tenny's bed, watched her thoughtfully for a moment, and then moved on.

A nurse, her hair cut in the latest shingled style and wearing a blue-and-white striped uniform, came up to Pete and asked him a question. They walked over to the door and Tenny slowly turned her head so she could see them.

Flirting! That nurse was flirting with him—dimpling and simpering, briefly touching his arm. He nodded but didn't return the flirtation. Before he walked out he gazed back toward Tenny's bed. She kept her eyes almost closed until he was gone. She didn't want to talk to him and ruin her memory of that boy in the car by the gas station.

The shingled nurse came over to refill Tenny's water jug, and Tenny glanced at her name tag. It read *E. Barlow.* She might have been pretty without that expression on her face, as if she'd just smelled doo-doo. "Good morning," the nurse said. "How are you feeling?"

"Like I just fell off a barn," Tenny said.

"That's normal," the nurse replied airily.

Nurses ought to have more compassion that that. "Can I ask you something?" Tenny used her best Professor Moon voice.

"Oh?" The girl raised an eyebrow and smiled, but the smile was only with her lips, a professional smile.

"Is this your first year?"

Now the nurse frowned. "Yes. We're the ones with stripes. Why?"

"Do you like it?"

The young nurse shrugged. "It's hard work, but it's an opportunity."

"To help people? To be on your own?" That's what mattered to Tenny.

The girl tittered. "What ideals you have! No, the opportunity to meet a doctor. Or a prosperous patient, for that matter."

But most of the doctors were married, weren't they? Tenny thought of Pete. Interns, of course. "Do all the nursing students feel that way?"

"More than you might think," said the girl, with a grin. "Now get some rest, dear. Don't worry if you leak. Your milk will soon dry up, since you won't need it."

She sashayed off. So this nurse knew Tenny's baby was going for adoption. Well, of course, if Miss Verity had brought her here. This nurse was maybe a little—snooty? The girl acted perfectly friendly, and yet it wasn't the right kind of friendly.

Tenny ached all over and her breasts were tender. Another nurse came in to bind them. Tenny was a little bit sorry, because she'd never had such large breasts before. Miss Barlow came back with aspirin and an ice pack for her head, with a comment that Tenny ought to appreciate not being wakened to feed a baby. Finally, around one in the morning, the night nurse gave her a hypodermic to make her sleep.

The next morning, she was still woozy from the sleeping medicine when Dr. Emmett Godwin appeared at her side. He patted her shoulder. "You're looking very well, my dear. Came though like a champ. How old did you say you were?" He picked up her chart. "Turning sixteen next week?"

She nodded. Then his face turned serious. "I'm sure you must be wondering about your baby. The little fellow is doing very well, and there's already a couple who want to adopt him."

A boy, then. And parents who want him. "What . . . what color hair does he have?" Oh, please let it be stable-boy red, she prayed.

The doctor chuckled. "Ah, he's a towhair, like you."

"Towhair," Tenny murmured.

Dr. Godwin frowned. "It will change, for certain. You haven't changed your mind about adoption, have you? Miss Verity will be here with the papers this afternoon, but she'll give you another day to think about it."

Tenny shook her head. "I haven't changed my mind. I can't give him a home. I don't even have a home myself."

The doctor took a seat beside the bed and leaned forward.

"If you change your mind about that Berry school, let me encourage you once again to apply for our fall nursing class. I know you're a bit young, but you seem more mature than most."

Tenny decided to tell him the truth. Almost. "Miss Verity convinced me. She says with farm work I can pay my tuition and learn a trade there, and maybe later try for the college scholarship."

The doctor looked at her shrewdly. "That's Verity for you. You'd be better off here, I say. Do you really want to go back to a farm?"

"How . . . how did you know?"

"I've seen plenty of farm girls. Tan, calluses, sturdy feet. Hard to hide, even with that fancy talk you learned."

Tenny couldn't meet his eyes. She really would rather be at this hospital, but she couldn't take the chance on meeting Arno Shackley in Ashbyville. "No, Doctor, I think I'd better go on to Berry."

The doctor rose and patted her on the back. "My offer still stands. I'll be happy to have a word with Miss Wells for you, if you change your mind."

She watched the door close behind the doctor. She would not change her mind. She was sure. She would never forget that night. She would never forget what brought her to this place.

# Chapter 14

She'd been born in a tenant shack on the outskirts of Arno Shackley's farm to a cropper named Jubal Chance and his wife Emily. They spent their days planting and chopping cotton and picking, dragging the heavy bags as they worked the rows in the broiling sun, just like the black folk there.

Sometimes people asked her if her name, Tenny, was short for anything. Her long name came out of Ma's poem book, but she didn't like to tell people that.

When she was nine, her mama had died a few days after childbirth along with the baby, and raising Tenny fell to her eldest sister, Meredith. People used to say that Tenny and Shelley, her twin sister, were smack-dab pretty, that is, until Shelley got run down by Eben Shackley's horse, and she had fits after that and was not right in the head.

Tenny begged Pastor Jethro Brown to tell her why God let this happen, but the good man never had an answer that satisfied her. We can't question God, he said. Tenny thought sometimes that God wasn't really looking.

And then Byron had left them, hopped a freight train out of Weedy Grove. He'd left home right after Ma died, telling people he was going to join the Army to fight in France. He'd never come back. And they never got any letter to say he was dead. Tenny was sure he was out there somewhere.

Tenny had watched the dirt road by their shack, hoping it would bring Byron in one of those automobiles, but the road brought only peddlers and traveling salesmen, who'd barter goods with Pa for moonshine. Sometimes the traveling men stayed the night.

One night, one of these men crept in bed between herself and her sister Emmy Dee, fouling the air with his badtooth whiskey breath. She lay there, stiff and hardly breathing, until a hand reached over her back and snaked down her stomach. She jumped up, screaming.

"Aah, wha'd you do that for?" the man grunted. "I ain't gone hurt you."

She heard Emmy Dee stifle a giggle. "I'm over here."

Tenny knew what was about to happen, because it had happened before. She scrambled out of bed, ran over to the open window, and jumped out, landing with a bump on her backside. The old hound began to bark. Oh, Lord, he'd wake up Pa from his corn liquor dream and there would be hell to pay.

Then she remembered Shelley, lying in her corner pallet by herself, and hoped the man wouldn't take an interest in her. She went back to the window and peered in.

The man was lying on his back, smoking a cigarette, the smoke feathering up to the water-stained ceiling. He paid no mind to Shelley on her pallet. She'd lost most of her looks since the accident, becoming slack-jawed and lank-haired. Maybe, if God had to let that happen, this was His way of protecting her.

Tenny crawled under the house into the soft dirt, hunkering down with the warm smelly hound and the doodlebugs until she dropped off to an uneasy sleep.

The next day the man was gone, and Emmy Dee showed Tenny the dollar she'd earned. And what did Emmy do but run off after Pa had found out and whipped her, heading for town and more easy money, that's what Merry had said. Pa spent a day and a night looking for her but didn't find her. Good riddance, he said, and made Tenny drop out of school to help with the cooking and the cotton.

Tenny missed school. She snuck Ma's family Bible off the table by his bed and read what she could. She puzzled out the parable of the talents. She read of escapes. She read of wandering in the wilderness. She told the stories to Shelley, who listened open-mouthed.

And she gazed at the fine photograph of Byron in his Army uniform that Pa had stuck in the Bible, the only picture they had of him. He had sent it to them after he joined up. No return address, just a scrawl that said he was fine and he missed them.

She just knew she had to look for him and make him come back. She kept a croker sack under her bed and filled it with the things she thought she might need if she left—a folding knife and some string, a pair of step-ins, an old work shirt of Ma's, a pair of her brother Milton's outgrown boots.

Tenny felt a twinge of regret that Shelley would have to take over all the sweeping and washing and doing what Pa and the others told her to do. But she felt sure if Byron knew what a mess they were in, with Pa being drunk all the time and owing Shackley, he would come back to help them. Maybe he'd get all of them out of Weedy Grove and away from that boss man.

Tenny had always tried to keep clear of Mr. Shackley, out riding the fields next to theirs on that big roan horse of his, wearing a belt with a big silver buckle that shone in the sun.

Of late he'd been staring at her, at her pale hair.

He sometimes dropped by in the evening for some of Pa's corn whiskey. They'd stay up until all hours drinking and talking hunting, for Miss Rose Shackley didn't allow liquor in the house. Pa would get so liquored up he'd tell anything Shackley wanted to know, such as who among the other croppers was keeping back more than their share. He had been weak like that ever since Ma had died. It was like all the gumption had leaked out of him, leaving him like an empty gourd.

The night it happened, the night she finally left, Tenny lay in the bed she now shared with Shelley and listened to the voices from the kitchen, hoping Shackley would go home soon. The moon had risen high above the pines, high and white and pale, like the round crackers in barrels.

By and by she heard the burr of snores coming from the kitchen. She slipped out of bed, tiptoed to the door, and pushed it open a crack. At the kitchen table, Arno Shackley stared at a near-empty glass, while Pa's head lay on his folded arms.

She pulled the door to and walked over to the window, waiting for Shackley to leave. Shivering a little in her thin, grayish nightdress, she looked out at the big cracker moon and hugged herself, wishing it was her ma's arms around her. From the kitchen came the scrape of a chair, heavy footsteps.

Shelley slept on, a lump under the sheet. The footsteps became louder, then the door creaked open. Tenny's breath fluttered. She felt his eyes on her, outlined against the moonlight from the window, her long, pale hair in a braid down her back.

The steps grew closer, and still she did not turn. She felt her braid being lifted, and then the hot vapor of breath on her neck.

"I had my eye on you, girl. I always had my eye on you. I reckon you're ripe." Tenny shivered, remembering the first time she had seen him riding in the fields, looking down at her with his pig-bright eyes.

Shackley's thick fingers raked the strands of her plait apart, paining her scalp, but she didn't cry out. He mouthed her neck and she shuddered. She froze when he unfastened the belt with the big silver buckle. She swallowed and looked at the window. If she fought him, if she tried to get away, they might all suffer. She stole a glance at the sleeping Shelley.

"No," she whispered, cold to her toes.

He grasped her arm. "I got a right to you, girl."

What did he mean by that? And then he was pushing her numb body down on the bed, pushing back the sheets which should have been washed a long time before.

Shackley heaved his weight onto her, reached down, and roughed her legs apart. She turned her head, and his mouth landed wetly in her neck. He grunted and shoved his way into her, and then came the pain—dull, aching, burning, searing. Stifling a cry, Tenny bit her lip and tried not to take in his reek. She didn't know how he could keep on, drunk as he was.

Finally, he sighed, rolled off her, and fell asleep. Tenny lay still until the hateful, drooly, sticky feeling ebbed away. She willed herself to stop trembling. It was no time to give in to faints.

She slipped out of bed and washed herself with the old rag that hung beside the cracked pitcher on the washstand. She looked at the pinkness on it, spat on it, and shoved the rag under a crack in the floor. She put on her dress and silently searched Shackley's pockets. She figured she was due five dollars, by Emmy Dee's reckoning. From under the bed she retrieved her croker sack and put the five dollars into it.

Shelley rose from the bed and stared at her with big eyes. Tenny laid her finger to her lips and tiptoed over to her. "Go out on the porch and sleep there," she whispered. "I'm leaving. I'll find Byron and he'll help us." She hugged Shelley. "Sister mine, I hate to go off and leave you. I'm really sorry, but it's the only way we'll ever get out of this mess."

"Tenny . . ."

"Sssh. Remember now, I love you lots and lots. Look up at the moon in the sky and know it's shining down on me, too, and I'll come back for you someday." She fought back a tear, and then she took another look at Shackley. She hoped to God she never had to lay eyes on his ugly face again. Unless it was to shoot him.

Shelley, thank God, sniffed a little, then, casting a frightened look at Shackley, did as she was told.

Pa was still passed out on the kitchen table. Tenny padded into his room and lifted the Bible from the bedside. He never read it, anyhow, and it had Byron's picture in it. Before she could pick up Mama's book of poems, too, she heard him stir and snort.

She thrust the Bible into her croker sack, darted out the front door, and took off running along the moonlit dirt road. She was aiming for the highway, for she knew she could follow it to Ashbyville. They'd gone to the state fair there one good crop year, and it seemed to be the place where everything in the world could be found. She felt in her bones that Byron had to be there. He'd said so, that day at the fair. *I'm coming here one day, Tenny,* he'd said, looking all around while the Ferris wheel turned and barkers shouted from the sideshows. *I'm going to make my fortune, and then I'm going to come back home and take you away from all this.*

Before long, Tenny was hungry and thirsty. She stopped and dipped water from a stream with her two hands, saving the water in the canteen, and she ate sweet, plump blackberries from tangled canes and sour yellow plums from overhanging bushes on the side of the road.

She walked on barefoot while the sun rose, her soles thickened and callused from the sand in the tobacco rows. She ducked into the bushes when she saw or heard the clop of a horse, the rattle of a wagon, or the clatter of a motorcar.

At a crossroads, she found a country store called Oakes Grocery, and she fingered her dollar bills. It was too early for the men who liked to stop in and while away the time playing checkers, too early for the farm wives who came in for a sack of meal, too early for boys to stop in for a snack of Vienna sausage and soda crackers. She went in.

The storekeeper leaned on the counter, sleepy, drinking coffee from a white mug, not taking too much notice of her. Just another one of the cropper kids, plentiful as weeds.

With one of her dollars she bought a hunk of rat cheese and some crackers from a barrel and an apple. She wanted a Hershey bar, but it would melt in her sack. She bought a box of Cracker Jacks instead. She ate the first three outside sitting on a tree stump; the Cracker Jacks she packed away for later. She drank a dipperful of water from Mr. Oakes's well.

She liked the name. It made her think of sturdy trees and acorns and red leaves in the fall. As she slid off the stump and hoisted her sack, she figured she'd call herself Tenny Oakes and be done with Jubal Chance, who had turned out to be not much of a father.

A few miles further, she came to the main road. She turned left toward the church steeple in the distance, as the storekeeper had told her, and that road would lead her to Ashbyville.

She walked all day, her strong feet becoming sore. She couldn't hide from traffic here, so she tied an old calico kerchief over her hair. Cars puttered by; farm wagons creaked along with loads of melons, and from time to time she was offered a ride. She shook her head and kept walking. The fewer people knew her business, the better. It wouldn't be long before she got somewhere.

By late afternoon, when the sun hovered low in the sky, she stopped and hunkered down on her haunches by the roadside, shifting the load off her back. Her body was beginning to flag in the heat. She uncapped the canteen and took a long drink.

A car's horn blatted behind her. She jerked her head around and froze. Arno Shackley's Ford automobile was bearing down on her with Pa in it, shaking his fist, yelling and screaming about a Bible.

Clutching the croker sack, canteen dangling, she leapt off the highway and scrambled down the bank. She staggered, then took off running along the sandy bottom of the ditch, sandspurs bobbing and tearing at her legs. She glanced behind her. The two men were edging sideways down the embankment. She ran through a culvert and found herself looking into a swamp.

Alligators and water moccasins might live there, but the swamp was her only hope. She shoved her feet into the boots and waded into the sucking muck, breathing hard. Deeper and deeper into the marsh she waded, through blackish-green water with floating debris that smelled of rotted plants and spreading fungus.

She pushed on, not looking behind her. Any minute she might step into a hole, might sink, might run into a cottonmouth or rattler.

Finally, she came to a string of rusty barbed wire meant to keep cattle from wandering into the swamp. Breathing hard, she ducked through it and crawled out onto the edge of a muddy field corrugated with hoofprints. She looked behind her, and saw only the twisted trees and draping moss of the swamp.

Night was falling, a soft, gray pall in the east, and a screech owl hooted behind her. Animals, possums and raccoons, scuffled and snuffled. She skirted the swamp water, silver-tinged from the last light, and finally came to a branch of the river.

A live oak, limbs reaching toward the water, clung to the bank with massive roots. Between the roots the ground was dry, and there she curled, the croker sack spread over her, and drifted off to sleep.

She awoke to a brilliant yellow sunrise, mist rising over the fields. She stretched her aching limbs. The air was already warm and oppressive, promising a scorching day. She ate the rest of the cheese and crackers and some of the Cracker Jacks, and drank from the tin canteen. She oriented herself by the sun. She could follow the river into Ashbyville.

She would have to find a job and earn some money while she looked for Byron.

She made her way beside the limpid water, out of reach of her pursuers for now. Why these men should bother so much with a worthless girl—Pa had told her she was worthless many times—she didn't know.

Well, she had washed their words and her past away in the river.

And now she was going to school.

# Chapter 15

M iss Verity brought Tenny home from the hospital after two weeks.

She was greeted at the front door by an excited bevy of her housemates, who'd baked her a plate of sugar cookies and gathered her a bouquet of daisies from Miss Verity's garden.

"You've got a letter!" they chorused, waving it around. "From the Army!"

Tenny snatched the envelope and hurried to the kitchen. She grabbed a table knife from the drying rack, plunked herself into a chair, and slit it open.

She read it slowly. The letter told her that Corporal Byron Chance had served in the Allied Expeditionary Force in France, had won a medal for bravery, and was honorably discharged in 1919. The address on file was Route 5, Weedy Grove, Georgia. Yes. A brave Byron was the brother she loved, but she was no closer to finding him than she'd been when she came to Ashbyville. The nearest she'd come was that plant manager, Ned Fletcher, who looked like his evil twin.

It struck her that once she went away to Martha Berry's school, she'd be buried deep in the country with no way to find her brother, even if the remote school protected her from running into Arno Shackley.

She slid the letter back into the envelope. Her recuperation time was up, and it was time to leave the Home. Miss Verity had agreed to let her stay until fall term began at the Berry school, working for her room and board. She'd move into a converted storeroom next to the kitchen and sleep on a cot so the new girl, Etta, could have her room and bed.

When Sunday Chapel came, she figured she could stand taking her mama's Bible out. She wanted to give thanks that she'd come through safely. She took it out and laid it on her desk, and just for a moment, she slid out the blurry picture of Byron in his uniform and slipped it back. Maybe she could show it to people.

She gazed at the clothes hanging on wall hooks. She didn't fit into her old dresses, and she was so tired of the shapeless sacks she'd worn for six months. And then she saw it on the farthest hook—a new dress! Miss Verity or one of the girls must have found it for her in the latest batch of donations: a pale green artificial silk, not too worn.

The dress fit well enough. She gazed at herself in the mirror and pleasure brought a spot of color to her cheeks. She brushed her pale hair until it shone, pulled it to the crown of her head, tied a wide satin ribbon around it, and let it cascade down her back like a schoolgirl's. She picked up her Bible.

The doorbell rang as she was going into the parlor, and she stopped to open it. How strange! Here stood a young man holding a golf cap, wearing a striped shirt and plus fours. His wiry auburn hair was backlit by the morning sun, and he was grinning like a monkey. "And here you are," he said.

What on earth did he mean? He knew her?

"Remember me?" the young man was saying. "Pete Godwin? I'm sorry to drop by unannounced."

She gasped. This was the boy doctor she'd dismissed from the delivery room. And he was also the boy at the gas pump.

She found her voice. "It's about time for chapel, but if you need to see Miss Verity—"

Still that grin. "No, no, it's *you* I've come to see. I'm on my way to a golf match, and my father asked me to drop this by. He said this is his last offer."

He held out an envelope. She glanced at it, then back at him. Their eyes met. She held out her hand for the envelope, and he gave it to her, touching her fingers.

Behind Tenny the girls filing into the parlor, the curious glances, the hymn from the parlor piano, disappeared. Her world tilted a little, letting in fresh breezes blowing in with scents of geraniums and phlox and heavy, lemony magnolia.

Dulcy waddled up, shattering the moment. "Wondered who'd be here on a Sunday morning." She fluttered her eyelashes at Pete. "Hi. Want to join us for chapel?"

Pete gave a stiff bow. "Appreciate the invitation, ladies. I'd better be off." He touched Tenny's arm lightly. "I really do hope to see you again," he said, and then strode back to a Packard waiting at the curb.

Tenny's legs felt numb, rooted to the spot. Her fingers tingled.

"He's cute!" Dulcy said. "Who is he?"

Shoes clicked in the hall behind them. "Who do you mean? A man was here?" Miss Verity peered out just as the Packard sped off.

"Dr. Emmett's son." Tenny glared at Dulcy and turned the envelope over in her hands, chewing her lip. "He said it was a message from the doctor."

"May I?" Verity reached for the envelope, and Tenny nodded. The envelope wasn't sealed. Verity pulled the contents out and scanned them before placing them back in the envelope.

She handed the envelope back to Tenny. "Emmett Godwin, that old scoundrel," she said.

# BOOK II

~~~~

## Chapter 16

The summer of 1925 was the Summer of Weddings, a female summer of afternoon trousseau teas and canasta parties and showers, with the men joining them for surreptitious cocktail parties. Still, Gussie found time to spend in her darkroom, for she'd found a postcard company that wanted her river and town pictures—even the mill and the cotton gin and the bales waiting by the river to be shipped.

She had no idea that summer would change her life forever.

With grudging fascination, she watched how Swanee Burkett and Ned Fletcher carried on their secret romance during this party summer. They thought they were so clever. Swanee always left the parties early. She had to be meeting Ned, for he wasn't a member of their crowd.

Gussie forgot about parties when a postcard company bought some of her pictures, the mill and the cotton gin and the strapped bales waiting by the river to be shipped. She roamed the town in her khaki knickers and canvas shoes, much to the despair of her mother. She stuffed all her earnings in her New York fund.

And then a woman drowned in the river, some said pushed by a jealous husband. The judge grumbled that river drownings were becoming too common for his liking. It was dangerous, he said, a young woman alone roving the city. Pete was home, but working all hours at the hospital. No more driving alone.

Gussie wailed that her idol, Margaret Bourke-White, climbed skyscrapers to get her famous pictures. She reminded her mother that postcards with her pictures circulated all over the state and maybe even to farthest Alabama. Her father remarked that it was too bad she had to sell them as A. J. Pemberton.

Her exasperated mother hired a twelve-year-old boy from a mill family to accompany Gussie and carry her equipment, and she was once again allowed to take Papa's Hupmobile. Her mother's ulterior motive was the hope that young Jack Latrelle's outdoor job would postpone his entry into the mill and encourage him to stay in school.

In return for her mother's help, Gussie went to a few parties, even managing to cadge a new dress. Now she saw that Swanee stayed to the end and often left with one of her former beaux. Was the romance with Ned cooling?

She usually saw Ned at the First Methodist Church most Sundays, always alone, sitting in an aisle seat. He would wink at her, and she would ignore him.

Then came that fateful Sunday in late August.

Gussie didn't particularly want to go to the outdoor garden party to celebrate the engagement of their second cousin Calista Pemberton and the son of the best mortician in town, but her sisters persuaded her.

Anna's husband, Wyatt, drove them in his new Hanson Touring car, and they trooped through the rose trellis entrance.

Gussie scanned the crowd. So Ned Fletcher was here, slicked-back hair and striped jacket, smoothing his suave mustache. Jessie turned to her. "Why are you staring at that lounge lizard, Gus?"

"He's a strange mixture of charm and loathsomeness."

Jessie's face twisted with scorn. "He's about as charming as toilet paper."

"You just hate men." Gussie reached for her Japanese folding fan.

"I don't like *that* one," Jessie said. "He's like a student whose homework got eaten by the goat."

Cousin Frances, Calista's mother, rushed over and greeted them, and dragged them over to a group of young men in conversation.

"You know they killed Benedict," someone was saying.

Gussie's heart gave a lurch. *Benedict?*

"Frances has brought us some chicky-boos, Alf," a second voice warned. The group grew quiet.

After the introductions, Alf commented on the ghastly heat. Gussie was dying to ask *Benedict? What Benedict?* She asked instead if anybody had read that new novel, *The Great Gatsby.* Nobody had.

The talk turned to the Scopes monkey trial. Jessie, who taught high school biology, jumped in, arguing with those jelly beans that it was perfectly obvious they were descended from apes.

Gussie, half-listening, watched as three men clustered around Swanee under an arbor. Her sheer white lawn dress and white picture hat, its one red rose like a splash of blood, caused heads to swivel in her direction.

Ned stood nearby. Swanee accepted a crystal bowl of ice cream from a passing waiter. She poised her silver spoon, red lips parted, and then she turned and gazed at Ned. He caught her eye with a flick of his lashes. She dipped, then slowly closed her lips around the spoon, licking it clean.

Gussie, face flushed, turned back to the conversation, which seemed to have slid into the topic of Governor Hardwick, defeated in the last election by the Klan.

Jessie spoke up. "My father says the present governor is in their pockets, therefore despicable."

Alf shrugged. "He won't get very far in politics, honey."

"They're modern-day knights protecting women and children," a male voice insisted.

"As long as the women stay in their *place*," Jessie said scathingly, and Gussie knew the battle had begun. She slipped away in search of refreshments and gossip.

Armed with a dish of peach ice cream and a spoon, Gussie spotted Miss Ola Stratton's nephew Lyman, the antique shop owner, next to a row of tall marble statues of Greek gods and goddesses. Sun dappled his light fawn sport coat, and with his taffy hair carefully pomaded, he looked so very cool.

She walked over to him. "Hello, Mr. Stratton."

"Well, Miss Augusta! Do you like these beauties? Please! Let's sit down." Grinning, he indicated a green bench.

She sat, straightened her dress, and dimpled. "Actually, I do like them very much. We're studying mythology this year. Isn't that one Hebe, cupbearer to the gods?"

"Right. I have a small replica in the shop if you're interested."

"I'd love one," Gussie said, "but I keep spending all my allowance on photography equipment."

"One day, I'll get your money. When you have a house of your own."

"Not me," Gussie said. "I'm going to New York and become famous."

"More power to you, dear," Lyman said. "I love your picture postcards, by the way. I'd be glad to carry your work in the shop if you'll frame them. They're uncommonly good for a woman."

"For a woman, indeed!" huffed Gussie. "You can just wait a long time, Lyman Stratton, to furnish a house for me. For one thing, I'm not planning to marry. I think I'll just live in sin."

"Oh, honey," said Lyman, "you can't shock me. I know you. You'll get married. Even silly old Aunt Ola wants to get married."

"She *what*?"

"The old dear thinks she's in love," he said. "She met some impossible old yahoo named Arno Shackley at the hospital when she was taking flowers around for the church. Unfortunately, he recovered from his apoplexy. She's invited him to dinner next week!"

"Arno *Shackley*? You're kidding!"

"Darling! You know him?"

Gussie spooned the last of her ice cream. "Papa does. His place is down past Arcadia, Grandpapa's cotton farm between here and Weedy Grove. He tried to buy Arcadia from Grandpapa once."

Lyman shifted on the bench. "He's got his eye on Aunt Ola's money, that's for sure. Why she'd have any truck with a redneck planter I'll never understand."

"Maybe she just wants to be married," said Gussie. "Tired of being the eternal chaperone. Weddings seem to be in the air this summer. Be sure and tell me how the dinner goes."

"Oh, dreadfully, I hope," said Lyman. "That man is the last person I want in the family. He'll just make Aunt Ola miserable and God knows he'll hate *me*. I might wind up like poor Toby, in the river."

Gussie turned sharply. "You'd jump in and drown?"

Lyman was quiet for a minute, and then he looked Gussie straight in the eye. "Toby Burkett didn't kill himself, my dear."

Gussie caught her breath. "But, Lyman! You're saying . . . ?" Who would want to kill Toby?

A deep voice broke in at Gussie's left. "Mind if I join you, or is this a private conversation?"

Gussie looked up to see Ned Fletcher settling a wrought-iron chair next to her bench. She stiffened. "My, isn't it warm," she murmured, flapping her fan.

Lyman shifted on the bench. "Oh, Mr. Fletcher. I know you really want to talk to Miss Augusta. I'd better go speak to Keenan and Calista about my new shipment of English country pieces. And some lovely Bokharas—if you'll excuse me . . .?"

He stretched, rose, took the silver-topped walking stick he didn't need, and sauntered off.

"Queer bird," said Ned, sinking onto the bench.

"I'm very fond of Mr. Stratton." Gussie looked away from Ned and dusted some imaginary lint off her sleeve.

Ned leaned toward her. "I'd like to ask you something."

"Do I look like an agony aunt?" Gussie raised her eyebrows.

Ned smiled wickedly. "I have no romantic problems. No, I just wondered what Stratton was saying about a man named Arno Shackley."

"Oh, you eavesdropper." Gussie flipped her fan at him. "Why do you want to know, if I may be so curious?"

"You may not be so curious. Private business."

"Then I will say Mr. Stratton and I had a private conversation."

"You were out here in the open." He gave her that dratted mysterious smile.

Lyman wouldn't keep it a secret. He loved gossip. In fact, Gussie had never met a man who didn't like gossip. Why did they say it was a woman's vice?

She sighed. "Lyman's Aunt Ola seems to have taken a fancy to the man," she said. "I can't imagine why she wants to marry him."

Ned's face darkened like thunderclouds piling in the west. "The old goat. Looking for a respectable wife while he—" He stopped himself. "I beg your pardon, Miss Gussie."

"You *know* him?"

Ned straightened. "Let's just say I've found out a few things while looking for property to buy."

Ned Fletcher was judging Shackley and carrying on in secret with Swanee? A passing waiter took Gussie's bowl and spoon, and she folded her hands, fan dangling from her wrist. "I don't know if he's an old goat, but Papa says that he's a hard man to his tenants. Gets them in debt to him and acts like he owns them. And I hear he's doing just as badly with his cotton as the rest of the farmers. And Papa says there are other things, terrible things . . ."

"Murder?" asked Ned. "Lynching?"

"I've said enough," Gussie replied, looking around. "I need to find my sister Anna. I came with her, and she doesn't want to stay long. She's got a new baby at home."

"But you just got here," Ned said.

Gussie gave him a hard look. "Have you been spying on me?"

He smiled and shrugged. "I notice all the pretty girls."

Gussie rose from her seat and smoothed her dress. "Nice to talk to you, Mr. Fletcher."

Ned jumped to his feet. "Miss Pemberton, may I walk with you?"

"Suit yourself." She walked down the path toward an arbor, not slackening her pace.

Out of the corner of her eye she noticed Swanee at the center of a group of parlor sheiks with pomaded hair. Ned couldn't have missed it. He leaned over and murmured, "I'll take you home. I think you'll like riding in my Pierce-Arrow."

"I think not." Gussie walked on. After a few more paces, she had the uncanny sensation of Swanee looking daggers at her.

"Better go see to your girlfriend," Gussie said.

"*What* girlfriend?"

Gussie angled her head in Swanee's direction. "I saw her sneaking off to meet you at school. She left parties this summer for you."

"It's all over," Ned said.

"I saw the ice cream!" Gussie shot at him.

She continued along the path, and this time he didn't follow her. She found Wyatt and was informed that Anna and Jess had gone in search of the powder room.

She walked back to the house and entered under an arch to the back patio. There, under the wisteria arbor, Miss Ola and Miss Edith sat with Calista's grandmother, funeral home fans flapping back and forth.

Miss Ola pointed her fan at Gussie. "Augusta, were you talking with that Fletcher man?"

Gussie shrugged. "What of it?"

Miss Ola whipped her fan into action, her spectacles glittering. "You know he boards right near me, at Sweet Mangam's house."

"Yes?" Gussie gazed toward the back door, hoping she hadn't missed Anna.

"Women go into that house when Sweet's not there."

"Miss Ola," said Gussie, her face pinkening again, "Mr. Fletcher's private life does not concern me." She slipped quickly past them and through the back door into the house.

Finding neither of her sisters, she left the house by the front door in case they were on the veranda, but they were not.

She was heading back through the side garden when she felt a hand grasp her arm. She turned and faced a white garden-party hat and the ice-blue eyes beneath it. Swanee's breath rose and fell. "What were you talking about with Ned?" she hissed.

Gussie gazed calmly at her. "Ice cream."

Swanee let go of Gussie's arm and raised one eyebrow. "He's not your flavor, dear."

Gussie was truly tired of Swanee's swanning. "I won't know without tasting, will I?" She turned her back and walked away. She made another circuit of the party without finding her sisters, and stopped to ask Lyman if he'd seen them.

Before Lyman could reply, Ned Fletcher appeared from behind a hedge. "Ah, the lovely Miss Augusta. I told your sisters I'd take you home. They've left."

"You *what*?"

"I had a feeling you'd change your mind. I've said goodbye to our hostess for both of us."

Gussie opened her mouth to protest, but she had that feeling of daggers in her back again. She glanced over her shoulder. Swanee was sipping another glass of champagne and pretending not to glare at them.

Gussie shrugged, took Ned's arm, and walked out through the rose bower. She didn't look back. And when Ned suggested a drive by the river and a nip of good bourbon, she thought *why not*?

# Chapter 17

Tenny, acceptance papers in one hand and a cardboard case with all her earthly belongings in the other, mounted the five stone steps to the huge pile of ancient red brick that served as the Nursing School of Mercy Hospital. She'd hardly slept the night before. Could she do the work? Would she fit in, being so young? The girls at the Home had been welcoming, but they needed each other.

At least people didn't stare at her anymore. Her poor hair looked awful with that Browntone color she'd bought from Walgreen's. Though Dulcy and Mary Beth had protested, she'd applied the smelly mixture as soon as she'd been invited for an interview with Miss Iphigenia Wells, Director of Nursing.

Tenny dreaded meeting Miss Wells again. The interview a month before had almost sunk her chances for school.

The spare-looking Miss Wells, her shiny brown hair marcelled into waves that marched in military precision across her scalp, had peered at

Tenny's application through rimless spectacles. A frown creased her pale square face. "You're really sixteen?"

"Of course," Tenny lied. After all, she'd be that age before the year was out.

Miss Wells tapped her fingers on the desk. "You're sure of that?"

"Yes, ma'am." Tenny's heart pounded but she held her gaze steady.

The director cocked her head. "I have a feeling you're not telling me the whole truth, young lady. I ought to send you packing."

"I'm just small for my age." Tenny waited, hands in her lap, frozen.

"Dr. Godwin thinks very highly of you," Miss Wells had said finally. "I've decided to give you six months' probation, instead of three. You'll have to be especially good to prove someone so young can handle this important calling. And you must keep your hair pinned under your cap. It must be scrupulously clean at all times."

"Yes, ma'am." The cap would disguise her hair roots when they began to grow out.

Uneasy at the recollection of the interview, Tenny tucked a stray hair under her cloche and reached for the door handle. At that moment the door flew open, and Tenny leaped back to avoid the young woman charging out. The girl paused. She didn't apologize for almost knocking Tenny down, but looked her up and down, with an expression Tenny remembered, as though she smelled a dead rat.

"You're a new girl," she said. "I'm Enid Smith Barlow."

This was the nurse who'd been so offhanded to her when she'd delivered her baby. The nurse who'd been flirting with Pete Godwin.

Tenny swallowed what she really wanted to say and smiled. "Yes, it's my first day. I'm Tenny Oakes. Pleased to make your acquaintance."

"Pleased to meet you. Must run." Enid Smith Barlow frowned and hurried down the steps. Tenny watched her stride away, noting her crisp uniform and neat appearance, shiny as one of Miss Verity's polished tables, perfect as one of her china figurines. Though the student's skin was creamy-smooth and her glossy hair bobbed in the latest style, her green eyes had been cunning and shifty.

Tenny glanced down at the cheap suitcase she carried. The door ahead of her looked more like a barrier than an entrance. Miss Verity had always reminded them to be proud of having the courage to get on with their lives, to not let one misfortune limit them. Tenny picked up her bag and walked in.

Points of light from a tarnished, dusty brass-and-crystal chandelier fluttered around the soaring hall, illuminating the gilt flaking off the ornately carved woodwork. Her steps echoed on the marble floor.

It must have been a grand residence once in the prosperity days Ma used to talk about, the time when cotton was king, when money seemed to grow on trees and houses like castles rose up along wide, tree-lined avenues.

She'd been too nervous to notice anything before, not even where the office was located. She gazed into a parlor on her right, dim with heavy fringed curtains and a faded red plush sofa.

A voice called out, "Over here!" On Tenny's left, a sign tacked beside an open door read *Miss Iphigenia Wells, Director of Nursing*. A student in a blue-and-white striped dress beckoned from behind a desk. "Come on in. I'm dying of boredom! We're expecting five girls today. You're the very first. What's your name?"

She gestured at the folders on the desk. Tenny pointed out the one labeled "T. Oakes."

"Call me Tenny, please."

"Sure. I'm Alice Hepple." Alice looked young, too, with tendrils of dishwater hair poking out from a white cap low on her forehead. She riffled through Tenny's folder and set it to one side.

"I came in six months ago, and I've got this job temporarily because I'm pretty useless on the floors." She pointed down to her ankle, encased in a thick wrapping. "The Assistant Director left to get married and they let me help out here until they hire a replacement. I've got to catch up on classes and all."

Tenny asked what had happened.

Alice shrugged and looked away. "I slipped and fell in the hall. Tore the ligaments. Some really awful slick things wind up on the floor sometimes. Needless to say, I can't tend patients like *this*." She swiveled in her chair and retrieved a bundle of clothing from a nearby table. "These are your uniforms. Two furnished, any more you'll have to buy yourself. They'll be deducted from your stipend."

"Where do I sleep?"

Alice looked over the folders on her desk, thought a minute, then opened a drawer and took out a key. "Third floor. You'll room with me."

Taking the key and slipping it into her pocket, Tenny was glad. She liked Alice already and hoped the others would be like her, rather than like Enid. She opened her mouth to ask a question, but Alice kept up her patter.

"Bathroom and showers down the hall. All meals will be in the dining hall next door. Lunch is at 11:30; you'll meet Miss Wells at 12:30 sharp for orientation and a tour. Please come in uniform. And do NOT be late."

She opened a folder and took out a sheaf of papers. "Here's your schedule of classes and a handbook. You'll need a notebook, pencils, pens, the usual school supplies. There's a Woolworth's in the next block." She paused. "Oh, I almost forgot."

She unlocked a drawer, took out a plain, serviceable watch like the one she had pinned to her uniform, and placed it on the pile. "Take good care of this."

Tenny picked up the bundle. Now was the time to ask her question. "Alice, on the way in I met a girl in a blue uniform. She said her name was Enid Smith something. What year is she?"

Alice pursed her lips and looked away. "Oh, yes. Enid Smith Barlow. Second year." She sighed. "We don't usually get the debutante type."

"I'm surprised she's here, then." Tenny had heard about debutantes at the Callahan Home. Marjorie would be one, a year late. It made sense, with Enid's poise, her look of things smelling bad.

Alice lowered her voice. "The family came on hard times. Her father was a doctor, and he died suddenly, not sure why. She and her mother ran through the money pretty fast, and then they had to sell their house and move into a rented apartment. Enid signed up here, I guess, looking for another daddy. The sugar kind."

Tenny thought of what Enid had told her in the hospital, about looking for a man. At least she was honest about it. "You don't seem to like her."

"I ought to be sorry for her, right? But I'm not. She just thinks the world revolves around her, forget the patients. Oh, she puts on a big show when anyone's looking, and . . ."

The front door rasped open.

"Here comes somebody. I'd better shut up. Probably said too much already."

"Why the different color uniforms?" Tenny asked. Three blue-clad students walked by and Alice relaxed when they had gone.

"Stripes are for probationers and first-year students. Second and third year students wear blue, and graduates wear all white."

Alice reached for the ringing telephone. "Go on. It's busy today. We'll talk more later."

Tenny walked up the polished staircase to the third floor, then stepped along the cool, musty hall until she came to a dark wooden door with brass numbers that matched the numbers on her keytag, 307. She turned the key in the lock and went in.

The tiny room held two white iron beds, one made up neatly with a plain cotton bedspread, and one with sheets and green blankets folded on top, set against pale green walls. Twin bedside tables, two desks with small bookshelves, plus two small dressers with mirrors made up the rest of the furnishings. Tenny lingered over a picture of Florence Nightingale with her lamp, tending to a wounded soldier.

At the window, she touched the cold radiator beneath it and pushed back white muslin curtains, looking down into a courtyard where girls strolled, talked, or sat on benches studying.

The watch Alice had given her told her she had an hour and a half until lunch.

She unfolded blue-and-white striped shirtwaists with turn-back cuffs and long, white bibbed aprons with broad straps that criss-crossed in back. The cap was of the same material with a broad, turned-back brim. She placed the caps on a shelf and hung the uniforms on a rod, then set her cardboard case on the bed and clicked open the latches. She drew out the worn croker sack that had once held all her earthly possessions, unrolled it, and took out the Bible.

She closed her eyes and opened it at random like Ma used to do, wondering what it would say. She placed a finger on the page.

It was the verse of Matthew: *And five of them were wise, and five of them were foolish.*

Virgins. Well, she wasn't one of those!

She placed the Bible on her bedside table and stowed the sack on the high shelf of the closet. She hung up her few dresses and put away her underthings in the dresser, along with cotton lisle stockings and an extra pair of garters. She arranged her comb and brush, face powder and lipstick in front of the mirror, and then set the bottle of Chantilly eau-de-cologne, a going-away present from the other girls, among them.

She set her handbook and schedule on the desk, flipped on a small gooseneck lamp, and sat down to read.

*Rules: No smoking, no gum chewing, hair must be clean and contained under the cap, uniforms must be clean and pressed. No rouge or lip color should be worn.*

*Students must not leave the dormitory after seven o'clock on weeknights. Older*
*students must be obeyed; they are your superiors. Doctors' and head nurses' words*
*are law. Demerits will be given out for infractions . . .*

Tenny's eyelids began to feel heavy. Maybe she should just rest her
head on her arms and close her eyes a few minutes; she wanted to be
alert when she met Miss Wells again.

"Tenny! Get up! You'll be late and miss lunch!"

Tenny, jolted awake, found Alice standing over her. "Good thing I
decided to come back and check on you," Alice said.

Tenny bounded out of the bed, stripping off her clothes. "Go ahead,
Alice. I'll change and catch up with you. Gosh, thanks."

Alice waved it off. "You're new. Lower level. Follow the smell of
food."

The door closed behind her, and a few moments later Tenny heard
the ominous creak of the descending elevator.

Tenny dressed, fumbling with the crossing of her apron straps. Gazing
in the mirror, she pulled her hair to the top of her head and twisted it into
a knot, secured it with hairpins, then pulled on the white cap. She looked
very different. Good! She pinned on her cap and her watch, wincing
when she jabbed her pointing finger. Sucking on the wound, she hurried
out the door and pattered down three flights of stairs.

After a couple of wrong turns, she skidded into a high-ceilinged
room full of girls in uniform at rows of tables. The din of conversation
nearly overwhelmed her. In the cafeteria line, she received a plateful of
cornbread and turnip greens with a thin slice of ham, along with a raisin
cookie and a glass of iced tea. Plain food, but her mouth watered.

She paused. The dining room seemed full, and she didn't see Alice.
She took a deep breath and approached the one table she saw with an
empty seat. Enid Smith Barlow looked up with the I-smell-something
expression. "I'm sorry, but this seat is taken."

Tenny, hot with embarrassment, swerved past table after table. Far in the back sat a group of colored women in gray, with room to spare. Well, she'd worked alongside those folks in the fields often enough, why not sit with them? Before she reached the corner, she felt a tug at her skirt. She looked down and saw Alice.

"Where are you going?"

"There's room over there." Tenny nodded toward the gray-clad girls.

"You can't sit with the assistants. It's not allowed." Alice pointed to half a space beside her on a bench. "Come on. Squeeze in here." She leaned over and whispered, "They train them just enough to help with the colored patients."

Tenny sat down, glad for once to be slight of body, and dug her fork into the turnip greens. Between bites, she found that the others had been here six months and knew one another already.

Peg O'Dell, a big-boned, jolly girl with chestnut curls, smiled. "Where are you from, Tenny?"

"My folks moved around a lot," Tenny improvised. "I can't say I'm from anywhere."

Peg gave her a nod. "One step ahead of the rent collector, eh? I know what that's like."

Tenny shrugged.

Alice nudged her. "Eat. You'll need your strength."

Tenny dug in. Back home, no scrap went to waste. Her cornbread had the crunchy edges she liked, and the salty ham was a taste of country. She ate it all.

Alice, glancing at her watch, rose from the table. "I've got to get back to work. Don't be late for Miss Wells, Tenny." Other girls scraped chairs and fluttered out. Tenny slipped the cookie in her apron pocket, left her tray on a kitchen cart, and followed.

A window at the end of the hall looked out onto a strip of green and a parking lot. Going by, she happened to see Pete Godwin and his father crossing to the parking lot. Hand over her heart, she watched them get into a black car and drive away.

Pulse racing, she hurried on to the classroom. At the door of Room 3B, she remembered the rule book she'd left on her desk.

The four other girls watched her sink into a chair-desk near the door. The director, head down reading a paper, didn't glance up. "Miss Wells" was written on the blackboard.

The director finally stood up and told them to take out their manuals. Her cool, severe gaze rested on one, then another, of the girls as she called roll. "Oakes."

Tenny sat up straight. "Here."

Miss Wells raised an eyebrow. "Where is your handbook?"

"I'm sorry, ma'am. I left it in my room. But I did read—"

"You were told to bring it. One demerit." Miss Wells made a mark in her book. "Quarles?"

After roll call, Miss Wells went over the rules once again, and then the schedule of classes: anatomy, medications, basic patient care. She sniffed. "Your book studies are important, but the real learning will be on the wards. Any questions before we take the tour?"

Tenny glanced over at the other students. They sat straight and silent. Tenny, with a demerit already, decided to keep her mouth shut, follow orders, and not ask even one of the hundred questions she had.

# Chapter 18

September melded into October, and on an Indian summer Sunday afternoon ripe with the fragrance of Russian olive, Swanee lay in a four-poster mahogany bed among rumpled sheets in a gentleman lodger's room hung with tan muslin curtains against green walls bedecked with hunting prints.

Golden light sifted through Venetian blinds, striping Swanee's bare flanks. Ned, sitting on the bed's edge, reached out and outlined each bar, finally dipping into the curve between her legs. She stirred restlessly. "Mmm, Ned, I'm sleepy. Let me sleep."

He continued his exploration, caressing her again and again, and beneath his hands she responded and her breathing became heavy. Finally she rolled over and with a catlike purr, took him in her hand. "Ready Neddy, that's you."

"It's you, sweetheart. You do this to me." He let her pleasure him, and then he leaned over and placed kisses on her belly, working his way downward. When he had her almost where he wanted her he topped her, taking his weight on his knees. He arched himself into her, slowly, slowly, and then came the thrusting, and he smiled at her cries of pleasure.

When he had spent himself and she lay panting, happy, he kissed one pink nipple, drew back, and began to dress himself. She rolled and propped herself on one elbow. "Ned, where are you going?"

Now he was in shirt and drawers, flexing his muscular calves. He looped his tie, fingering the silk. "It's late, darling. You need to be getting along. God knows what would happen if the old ladies came home early from their trip to the country."

Swanee dragged herself from the rumpled sheets, lifted her bob, and let the silky strands fall. "Maybe next time we can go to the river. I love these Sundays. It's so funny to go to church and listen to the preacher and think about what we'll be doing later."

Ned, by this time, had pulled on his trousers. Studying himself in the mirror, he combed his hair back from his forehead and smoothed his mustache. "Swanee. I don't know how to say this, sweetheart, but we can't meet like this again."

"You mean here at your place?" She smiled and dimpled. "Is it Miss Ola? I know she followed me once, but she hasn't done it again, and this time I know she's out visiting, taking those flowers to the hospital."

Ned laid down his hairbrush. "It's your father. He's read me the riot act. If we were discovered, I'd lose my job, and I'd have to leave Ashbyville. Can't you see, Swanee? It's hopeless."

"No!" She pushed up on her hands, alarm in her eyes, and slid off the bed. "I'll find a way to bring him around. Give me some time, Ned."

He took out a cigarillo from the humidor on the dresser, then he trimmed it and lit it with a small gunmetal lighter. He liked the cool feel of the lighter in his hand, the sudden flare of the flame. "There's something else. I'm getting married."

Swanee's eyes narrowed. "Ned, you fool. Don't try to tease me that way."

"I assure you, my sweet, I'm deadly serious."

First came a little choked cry, and then a thick glass ashtray whizzed by his head so close he could feel its wake. It smacked into the wall beside the mirror, digging a gouge in the plaster. Chalky chips scattered on the carpet.

"My God, Swanee, you might have killed me!" He wheeled to face her, her perfect features twisted into a murderous sneer.

"I didn't throw it very hard," she said. "If I had wanted to kill you, I would have, Ned Fletcher. How dare you . . . *discard* me like this!"

He walked over to the bed and tried to embrace her, but she backed away, slapping at his hands. "Don't you dare touch me."

"Hey, hey, kid," he said, gazing at her with real sadness. "I wanted one last time, and I thought you'd want it too. You know your old man would have never let me marry you. I'm the new guy in town, blew in from nowhere. He's told me in so many words. I thought you were engaged to that senator's son, anyhow."

"It's not official. I can get unengaged. I want you, Ned."

Ned leaned over, picked the ashtray up from the floor, and rested his cigarillo in it. He took a deep breath and looked at her in the mirror, his heavy eyebrows drawn together. "There's another reason I can't marry you, Swanee. There's a . . . there's a kid on the way."

Swanee scrambled forward, pressed her breasts against his back, then circled his neck with her hands. Her voice went down a register and she squeezed a little, with hot and trembling hands. "You bastard. Who is it?"

Ned twisted around and grabbed her wrists, pulling them away. She glowered at him through her thick lashes. "Some street tramp you got careless with? Just pay her off. You need money? I can find it."

Ned dropped his hands, but he met her eyes. There was no point in hiding anything now. "I don't need money, Swanee. It's Augusta Pemberton."

Swanee's eyes widened. "My God! You've been rolling with that silly flapper in khaki who runs around taking *pictures*?"

"She didn't bring her camera," said Ned dryly.

Swanee gave a disgusted huff, took a comb from her bag, and sat on the bed, flipping the comb through her hair. "Did you knock her up on purpose, Ned? Are you that obsessed with having Arcadia?"

He shook his head. "Of course not. She'll make a decent wife." He got up, walked to the dresser, and picked up the gold cuff links Swanee had given him. He rather liked the curved Art Deco style. They caught a spark of afternoon light as he slid them through his cuffs.

Swanee's lip curled. "A little housewife, Ned? But it's me you *love*."

Ned looked around on the dresser, but he was clothed and groomed and there was nothing else to do but make it a day. Except he didn't want to. He said slowly, "It doesn't have to mean the end."

"What do you mean by that?" Swanee's pout remained, but she raised one eyebrow.

Ned turned to face her. Outside, in the distance, a siren wailed. "Well, after a respectable period of time, of course, maybe we can continue to see each other."

Swanee balled her fists. "Are you *insane*? Oh, you're much worse than I *ever* thought. You just wait and see. I'm going to get even with you, Ned Fletcher. One day I just might shoot you." She slid off the bed and grabbed another ashtray.

Ned sprang forward and wrested the ashtray out of her grasp, trying to pin her arms. "Try it, baby."

"Let me go!" She twisted away from him and rolled across the bed to get to the other side, scrabbling for her peach silk teddy. "Shooting's too quick. I'll find a way to make you suffer."

"You're not going to do that," he said. "You love me too much." He flopped on the bed, reached for her, and pulled her to him. She tried to resist, tried to push him away, but then he was unknotting his tie, loosening his suspenders, and the silk teddy slithered to the ground.

"Damn, Swanee," said Ned, when it was over, his lips against her flushed and fevered neck, her scent all musk and seashore. "How can I ever let you go?" He gazed at her, hungry to see those passion-chewed lips, that look of satisfied desire. But she turned her face away.

"You've found a way," she said.

They barely got out of the house in time. Ned was rounding the corner when he spied Sweet Mangam's automobile bringing her and Miss Bessie home. "Get down," he whispered, but Swanee only shot him a hateful glance.

Now he realized he hadn't considered how difficult the hour and a half drive back to the college was going to be. It had been careless of him not to consider it. Swanee came up with a solution before he did.

"Drop me at the station," she told him.

"You don't have to do that."

"Yes, I do."

"I'll buy your ticket."

"No, you won't. Drop me a block from the station."

When he didn't immediately reply, she said, "I mean it, Ned. I'll jump out of this car if you don't."

Reluctantly, he turned the corner leading to the railroad terminal. They said good-bye in front of the Federal Building, or rather, she told him she hoped he burned in hell. She got out, slammed the door, and strode rapidly down the sidewalk.

My God, thought Ned, she was magnificent.

He headed back toward the boarding house, hating that he would have to wash off her scent. When he passed the hospital, he noticed a slip of a girl walking toward the red brick building next door. There was something familiar about the way she walked, about her slim figure. He slowed the car, and then he caught his breath. That girl at the factory— was this the same girl? He couldn't see her hair for her cloche.

The guilt hit him then, the guilt for what he had done—not acknowledging the girl at the factory. Looking right through her. *It must have hurt her*. He banished the thought. He hadn't seen Tenny since she was a child. How could he be sure the girl was his little sister? And how could she have recognized him?

He told himself firmly that Tenny didn't belong in the factory, or in Ashbyville. She belonged back home, and it was better that way. It would have been death to all his plans to have had her identify him as Byron Chance. Survival was the reason he'd had to deny her.

He watched as the girl mounted the steps of the once-grand house, and then he drove on. *That* girl couldn't be Tenny. What would his Tenny be doing at the hospital?

He rounded the corner and pulled into Miss Sweet Mangam's driveway. In just about an hour he'd be on his way to the judge's to eat a civilized supper with his fiancée in the dining room of that Georgian house, with candlelight on the table and the harvest moon rising in the sky. He saw his future spread out before him like vast white fields of cotton.

# Chapter 19

G ussie wasn't scared a bit. Papa had insisted that Havana was full of Chicago mobsters, but Ned insisted it was the best place to honeymoon, the place where all the New York swells went to escape Prohibition and jazz it up. Gussie begged to go, she just had to. Papa relented, but with reservations.

At the cavernous Ashbyville station, Mama and Papa and Anna and Jessie had smothered them with kisses, and Papa had swiped at his eye with a handkerchief, declaring it must be soot in the air. When Ned's back was turned, he slipped her a new Kodak Autographic for her train case. Ned had forbidden her to pack her Graflex and tripod.

Mr. Wyckham, Ned's Savannah friend and best man at the wedding, was traveling with them to Savannah. She didn't like Wyckham, a skinny man with strange ears, thinning hair, and a slow, cultured drawl. His good-old-boy act hid a devious mind. She worried that none of Ned's family had attended the wedding. He claimed his parents were dead, and he'd lost touch with his sister, Sarah, after she'd married a traveling salesman. Papa said it sounded fishy, but that was just Papa.

Gussie fanned the stuffy air of the train car and wiggled out of the jacket of her Glen plaid traveling suit, stuck to her cotton blouse. She fitfully ran her hand over the seat's plush fabric and glanced over at Ned, deep in conversation with Wyckham.

"Sell it now," Wyckham was saying. "I've heard rumors."

"It's just talk." Ned waved his hand dismissively. "That land's going up, and it'll make my fortune." Gussie winced. Ned had been at Papa again about Arcadia, saying he'd sell his Florida land to buy it. Of course, Papa refused. Still, it bothered her that Ned was so determined. Was that why he had married her?

She turned and gazed out the window, where vast fields of picked cotton rushed by, ragtags on black, shriveled stems waving in the breeze. Flattened lint lay by the side of the tracks in wavy patterns, and at the occasional tenant houses, dark children played in the dirt yards or sat morosely on their porches watching the rattling cars go past, on their way to somewhere else.

Glancing once again at Ned, she wished he'd stop talking with Wyckham and talk to her about Cuba instead of having endless debates about the price of Florida land. Something about a bubble. Something about swamps.

Bubbles, swamps, alligators—enough to make anybody queasy. She called a porter for iced tea to settle her stomach. How could she have been such a dunce?

She'd been so smug, going off with Ned after the garden party. That ride to the river had been such fun! The warm afternoon light on the water, and sips of hooch from Ned's flask, and *poems*. She'd never felt so warm all over, bubbles coursing through her like champagne in her veins, too breathless to do anything but kiss and kiss. She'd met him in secret three more times, and she wondered if there was any reason to hold back. Swanee had been mean, and Papa wouldn't let her go to New York, and she had always wanted a lover.

The exhilarating, scary stolen hours turned to panic one morning when she realized she'd missed her monthly. Nerves, she told herself.

After she'd missed a second, she knew it wasn't nerves. She ran down to the breakfast room and confessed. Her mother's fingers rose from the Remington and she looked over her spectacles. "Gussie, maybe you should have taken an interest in my lectures on birth control."

Her father, after a long draw from his pipe, said, "Tell him to come see me."

There had been a horrible, embarrassing visit to Uncle Emmett, then a family conference, and then she and Ned had been married without delay in the chapel of the First Methodist Church. She'd worn her sister Anna's dress, so as to disguise the reason for the hasty marriage, and the guest list had been small. Gussie was only seventeen. Ned was twenty-eight.

The train whistle blew, the rhythmical clacking slowed, the depot of Savannah came into view. A sigh escaped her lips. Ned gave her a tender look and patted her hand. "Tired?"

Gussie smiled and put away her unread Elinor Glyn romance. Under flickering gaslights, she cheerfully waved good-bye to Wyckham when they boarded the taxi to the hotel. They'd left Ashbyville at seven that morning; it was now after eight in the evening. They'd spend the night and catch an early train to Tampa.

At the door to their suite she paused in anticipation, but Ned walked ahead of her into the room, showed the bellboy where he wanted the bags, and tipped him. The bellboy left, wishing them a good evening.

Ned stared at her, amused. "Are you scared to come in?"

Gussie tried to make her voice light. "Aren't you going to carry me over the threshold?"

A look of momentary panic crossed his face before he smiled mischievously. "Am I supposed to?"

"Oh, Ned, quit teasing," she said.

Grinning broadly, he scooped her up, carried her in, waltzed her around twice, and laid her on the bed. Then he leaned over and kissed her. "Alone at last." His voice was tender, as on those long afternoons by the river, and his eyes glowed. Yet Gussie couldn't shake off a feeling of unreality, that this had really happened, that he really loved her. And she wanted that love, hungered for it. It had to make up for her lost dreams.

The steamship from Tampa left at 9:30 in the evening and would arrive at the port of Havana in the early morning. The other passengers were delighted to see newlyweds and gave them a lot of ribbing. The good-natured banter embarrassed Gussie, but Ned enjoyed it, shaking hands with everyone he could, just like all those politicians on the courthouse steps when Papa was running for judge.

At least she wasn't seasick, and she was too excited to sleep much. As the dawn rose, she and Ned stood at the rail, smelling salt spray and rocking with the swell of the sea, while the haze on the blue horizon faded into the contours of the island. Gussie wanted a map.

"Wait a minute," Ned said. He left her at the rail and in a few minutes thrust a guidebook into her hands.

Gussie glanced at the title. *Havana, Mexico, and the West Indies: Kepple's Tours.*

"You can look at the map inside. You know about the Spanish-American War, don't you?"

"Yes," said Gussie. "We had to fight the Spanish because they sank our ship, and I was never quite clear about why they did it."

Ned had pulled out his binoculars and was staring at the shoreline. "They wanted the Spanish out of Cuba, basically, and the Spanish wanted to stay in control. That didn't stop the political fighting. I hear they throw old regimes over the seawall to the sharks. Hey, I think I see one now."

"A shark? Oh!" She stepped back from the rail and began to thumb through the guidebook.

Ned liked to tease the kid; she was funny that way. He lit a cigarette at the rail. So he was hitched again, to the daughter of a judge! A step up from the daughter of a widowed bicycle-shop owner. All he could hope was that Sarah wouldn't show up from out of nowhere wanting her money. He'd covered his tracks pretty well: she didn't know where he was; she didn't know he even had money. Ah, what if he'd never met Curtis Wyckham in that bar, never read that brochure about Florida land!

He'd seen a way then, a way out of his postwar fortune-seeking, a wandering that had fetched him up in Savannah. He saw a path to all that he wanted to accomplish. All he needed was money. A lot of money.

He'd had to make Sarah a lot of promises, but in the end she'd agreed to risk the money they were saving for a house. Ned had filled her with dreams of a mansion on Reynolds or Monterey Square if it all worked out, with plenty of room for dear old Daddy.

Well, the Florida land had gone up; he'd made money. He'd sold, banked some, and bought more land from a wealthy widow and specula- tor intent on becoming a tycooness. The future tycooness saw in Ned the man she needed at her back, and he could see a good thing in this arrangement.

He kept postponing the time to go back to Sarah until he saw no reason to go back at all. He moved in with the widow and left no for- warding address. Sarah probably assumed he was dead by now. Maybe she'd even remarried.

"Ned? Look!" Ned unclenched his fingers and wrapped his arm around Gussie. A little green at the gills, she was gazing down at a circling dorsal fin.

"Baby, sharks don't eat honeymooners."

"Are you sure?"

"Only political prisoners."

She squealed and pretended to slap him, and they both laughed.

When the ship steamed into Santiago bay, the outline of Havana in the rosy dawn shimmered against the tropical sky. Gussie hung over the rail as the ship glided near the imposing bulk of Morro Castle, its sides pockmarked from shelling. Breathing in the windy salt tang of the sea, her soul seemed to expand in excitement, and she gripped Ned's hand.

The taxi racketed to the hotel, too fast. The magical old city seemed a world away from the dusty, plain, cotton-lined streets of Ashbyville. And the Sevilla Hotel? A palace, with its cream stucco exterior and iron balconies trailing lush scarlet blooms.

A doorman welcomed them, summoned porters, and ushered them through the massive hotel door. "Baby, the sky's the limit," Ned said. "We're going to enjoy ourselves in style."

They swept into the lobby past friendly, smiling faces in shades from black coffee to milky tea. Gussie stood tall, holding Ned's arm. He was her husband now, her protector. She forgot Wyckham, the train, the frowns, the roily stomach, and Papa.

The bellhop opened the door into a tall-ceilinged room with pale mango walls. Its main feature was a massive carved bed, flanked by French doors opening onto a balcony. A ceiling fan turned slowly, drawing in the silky evening air.

Gussie exclaimed over the basket of tropical fruit and went to sniff the fragrant white lilies on the dresser. She longed to bounce on the imposing bed's white coverlet.

The bellboy uncovered champagne in an ice bucket and two stemmed glasses. Ned tipped him lavishly and, after the boy left, popped the cork and filled the shallow glasses to the brim.

He handed one to his bride and lifted his own glass high. "To our future."

Gussie raised her glass carefully, smiling through her tears. So this was what it meant to be happy.

Abuzz with champagne, she lay on the bed and kicked off her shoes, and she heard, faintly, Ned murmuring something about shopping, but she was so tired.

She blinked awake to the sound of Ned stacking parcels on a chair. "Ice-cream suit, a Panama hat, and a box of cigars," he said. "Now, let's go to the beach. The hotel can make us a picnic lunch."

The adventure had started! She scrambled out of the tall bed, splashed water on her face, and gathered bathing suits and towels into a canvas bag.

Her buoyant mood flagged when, on the taxi ride to the beach, the sweaty, cigarette-smoking driver took a route that veered away from majestic, pastel buildings and lush plant life and passed through quarters where houses were little more than hovels, and half-naked, dirt-streaked children roamed the streets. She felt a glimmering of the difference between herself and others, a difference she'd been blind to at home.

An hour later, she was trying to forget those hovels as she lay back in a striped sling chair under a sun hat, sipping a rum punch Ned had ordered from the attendant.

"I'll go find us a boat for hire."

"But Ned, can't we just . . ."

He had already left. She closed her eyes and once again drifted off to sleep. She dreamed she was running down a road, and the farther she ran, the darker it got. She couldn't see where she was going, and the road suddenly was gone, and she was falling, falling . . . She screamed and struggled awake, heart racing.

A voice cut through her sleep-fog. "Whats'a matter, honey?"

Tobacco smoke tickled Gussie's nose, and she sneezed. Reaching for a handkerchief, she peered from under the hat brim. In the sun's glare, she made out a woman's knobby knees and orange bathing suit. "It was just a nightmare," she told the woman.

"You better watch that rum if you're not used to it. Pleasedtameetcha. I'm Sylvia Herbert, from Chicago."

Chicago? Gussie, now alert, pushed herself up and dabbed her nose. The knobby knees belonged to a lean, big-boned woman with a wide mouth and hennaed hair, who waved a cigarette with a hand sporting a huge diamond.

"I'm Gussie. Gussie Fletcher. We just got here."

"Yeah, I noticed. Where's that handsome sheik? I'd steal him from you, only Max might object."

"Max?"

"My old man. Hey, here he comes now." Sylvia gestured in the direction of a man, his dark hair glistening on a sweaty pate, carrying two fresh drinks festooned with lime slices. His loose lips fondled a cigarette. He handed a drink to Sylvia and nodded at Gussie. "Hiya."

"Hi." Gussie noted the tanned complexion, the five-o-clock shadow, the suspicious leer. She wished Ned would hurry.

Sylvia turned to her husband. "Max, these kids just got here. Gussie and her sweetie."

"I don't see no guy. Where you from?" He lowered himself with a grunt into the beach chair next to her.

"Ashbyville, Georgia." She tried to edge her chair away, but the sand gripped it. "We're newlyweds."

Max took a last drag of his cigarette and stubbed it into the sand. "I figured something like that. Been to the casino yet?"

"Why, no," said Gussie.

His smile was friendly, but his eyes glinted maliciously. "Looka here. You and Bub join Sylvie and me after dinner and we'll show you all the best joints. Whaddaya say, little lady?"

"It's Ned, not Bub," said Gussie, looking around anxiously. "There he is."

Max Herbert glanced at Ned walking across the sand. "Ned? He don't look like a Ned."

Ned gave no sign that he'd heard, barely glancing at the Herberts when he handed Gussie her drink. He stepped behind Gussie's chair and kneaded her shoulders while she made introductions. "They're from Chicago."

Max Herbert regarded Ned with interest. "Haven't I met you somewhere before, Bub?"

"I don't think so. It's Ned, and I've never been to Chicago."

"New York?"

"Nope."

"Miami?"

A flicker of a shadow crossed Ned's face. "I must look like somebody else. An evil twin named Bub."

Max shrugged the joke off and smoothed his hair. "I want to invite you kids to join us at the casino this evening. Sylvie and me like the company of young people."

Gussie took a deep breath and risked a lie. "Ned promised to take me dancing tonight, and I was so looking forward to it. I want to learn the rumba."

"The casinos are open late," interrupted Max. "Some have dancing too."

"Tell you what, Max." Ned glanced at Gussie. "How about another night? We're here for a week."

"Fine," grinned Max. "You at the Sevilla?"

Ned nodded and touched Gussie on her arm. "Come on, honey. I've got a boat lined up for the afternoon."

"Going back to the hotel first?" Max gave Ned a broad wink.

Gussie pretended not to notice, but she was blushing as she followed Ned across the sand. When they were out of earshot of the Herberts, Gussie said, "Ned, I don't like that man. Sylvia's all right, I suppose, but . . ."

"I'd just as soon not see them again," said Ned. "Maybe we can figure out a way to duck them."

"I didn't come here to gamble, anyhow," said Gussie. "I came to be with you."

"No point in skipping the attractions of Havana," said Ned. "We'll fish, take trips to the countryside, go to the dog tracks . . . and the casinos. We have the rest of our lives to be together."

Gussie supposed he had a point, but . . . "All right."

They cruised in the boat, they went dancing that night, and Gussie tried to learn the rumba. It was one o'clock when they got back and after two when they finally sank into an exhausted and blissful sleep. At noon they woke and made love again.

Gussie, basking in the afterglow, said, "Life is going to be perfect, now, isn't it?"

Ned stared up at the ceiling, at the slowly turning fan. "Sure, baby. Let's go to the casino tonight, not wait till tomorrow." A shadow crept slowly across Gussie's sun for an instant, and then it was gone.

# Chapter 20

In the soft gaslight of the casino, Gussie's kitten heels clicked over honey-colored terrazzo tile. Under the dappled starlight from prismed chandeliers, she slipped through the crush of people and clatter of voices and clicking of roulette balls.

Cards riffled, people murmured, and a winner slapped the table and did a jig. Closer to the lounge, a jazz band thumped a tango while couples slinked hotly around the floor. Smoke wafted from fragrant cigarettes, curling up into the shimmering crystals.

Gussie even forgot that she was queasy. She'd only eaten half of the swell dinner. If only she had her camera! She'd snap the postures of the players, their expressions as they sat at the tables. And the dancers! Women, faces painted, wore jewels and silk shoes and beaded dresses in red, yellow, magenta, teal. The men sported white dinner jackets, and Ned was dressed exactly like them. Oh, gee. Why had she let Mama talk her into bringing Anna's white debutante dress? It was *all wrong*.

Gussie bit her lip when they spotted Max and Sylvia at roulette, Max chewing on a cigar, Sylvia in turquoise, a peacock feather in her headband. Sylvia, seeing them, waved and smiled enough to crack her rouge.

Ned took Gussie's hand and half-dragged Gussie to the table near Max and Sylvia. "Don't let us interrupt you," he said.

Max turned and patted his breast pocket. "I quit while I'm ahead." He looked Gussie up and down and grinned. "You look like one of them sacrificial maidens."

Sylvia tapped him on the arm. "Shut up, Max. You're embarrassing her." She extended a packet of Fatimas to Gussie. Glancing at Ned, Gussie took one and let Max light it. Ned cocked an eyebrow but said nothing.

Gussie, trying to look sophisticated, took a long draw, intending to let the smoke curl out slowly and sensuously like she'd seen Swanee do. Instead, she had a coughing fit and her nose began to run. She dug out a handkerchief and almost burned her dress until she figured out how to hold the thing. She should have stubbed out the nasty butt, but she continued to puff at it without inhaling, not willing to admit defeat.

Someone handed her a rum punch, and at least that washed down the awful taste of the tobacco. She set her glass on top of the cigarette, quashing it. The delicious punch, and more punch, made the evening pass like a dream, a dream of chips and clicks and murmurs and smoke, at least until the room itself began to slowly revolve. A kaleidoscope turned before her eyes, faces going by, people she didn't know. She woozily made her way over to Ned, standing at the roulette table. She clutched his arm. "Can we go home?"

"What?" Ned glowered at her the way Daddy did when she wore knickers. "Not while I'm winning."

"But will you go if you start losing?" She gave him her best pout. "Pretty please?"

He shrugged. "Another half hour, honey."

"It's after twelve, or one, or two, Ned." She was finding it hard to stand up straight. "Whoooo." She grabbed the back of a nearby chair and held on for dear life.

Ned patted her on the shoulder. "Hey, chickie, they go on island time here. My number's coming up. Just you wait and see."

Humph. Ned was brushing her away like a horsefly. She found herself a velvet chair in a cocktail nook and sank into it, leaning back. Ned looked back at her, beckoned a waiter, and a few minutes later she was served a glass of ginger ale.

She took tiny sips, because she was thirsty. She felt like crying. Surely he would keep his word. Finally Ned motioned her over and she pushed herself up with a smile. Was he finally ready to leave?

When she'd toddled close, he put his arm around her waist and whispered in her ear, "Didn't your old man give you some spending money, sweetheart?"

She closed her eyes, nausea growing. She held up her tiny fringed evening bag and opened it to reveal lipstick, compact, handkerchief, and coins Ned had given her for the restroom attendant. She would never mention the "mad money" she'd hidden in her corset.

Ned peered in, then shrugged. "Max'll gimme a loan."

She glanced at Max, leaning on the bar beside a rough-looking man in a pinstripe suit with wide lapels and a gardenia in the buttonhole. "Please, Ned. Can't we go?"

He abruptly turned back to the table. "Just leave me alone. Go back to the hotel if that's what you want."

Go back alone? It hit her. The nausea. Oh, oh.

She ran for the ladies' room and got sick right there, barely making it to a commode. Fortunately, the attendant was there with damp towels to help her clean up, and didn't seem surprised at all. Gussie gave her all the coins.

The white silk dress was ruined.

Now sobered, Gussie extracted money from her corset. She found her stole and wrapped it around her to hide the stains. She walked to the entrance and asked the doorman to call her a taxi. The whole thing had been crazy. She was going back home tomorrow and let Papa get the marriage annulled.

By the time she arrived at the hotel, her head was clear but aching. Their steamship passage was booked for the following Monday and she had no idea whether the tickets could be exchanged.

She wobbled to the front desk, wrote out a telegram to her father. NEED COME HOME NOW STOP HELP STOP LOVE GUSSIE, and shoved it at the night clerk. "Please send that as soon as possible."

The clerk raised his eyebrows. "Please," she added, wondering if a tip was necessary—but she couldn't very well get it out of her corset right here. "Add it to our bill."

The clerk nodded, and she saw concern in his dark eyes, and maybe a little pity, which made her flush.

She stepped into the creaky elevator and was carried to the third floor. In their honeymoon room, she peeled off the white dress, damp with perspiration, stained, and reeking of cigarette smoke. She stuffed it in the wastebasket. She never wanted to see it again.

After a bath, wearing the white silk nightgown from her trousseau, she inspected herself in the mirror. A child, she looked—a child of seventeen, with bobbed strawberry blonde curls and freckles on her nose. A sacrificial maiden.

Worst of all, she still loved him.

She cried until she was all cried out and slipped into a restless sleep beneath the thrum of bass and maracas from the jazz club across the way.

The next morning she awoke with a hammering head and a looming, dark feeling that something bad had happened. When she peeked over at Ned snoring beside her, the night before rushed back at her. She had no idea when he'd come in.

She touched his shoulder. His skin was slippery with sweat, and in his deep stupor, he didn't even twitch. She'd rather not be around when he woke.

She splashed cold water on her face, helping the headache a little, and then she tugged on a blue linen frock and slid into canvas espadrilles. She dabbed lipstick into a bee-stung pout and plopped a straw hat over her damp curls.

In the dresser drawer, she reached under a stack of handkerchiefs and drew out the rest of the money Papa had given her. She tucked it into her shoulder bag.

Ned's wallet was lying on top of the dresser. Her hand hovered over it, her mama's teachings about privacy clashing with her instinct for survival. Survival won. A few pesos lurked between the leather folds, along with a sheaf of one-dollar bills.

She laid the wallet back on the dresser, slung her bag over her shoulder, and hurried down three flights of carpeted stairs. She stopped at the desk. Was there a telegram for the Fletchers?

A clerk she hadn't seen before glanced in their box and shook his head sadly. "No, señora."

Gussie swallowed. Perhaps Papa had not received her message. Perhaps the clerk had never sent it. "I'll check later," she said.

She plunged out into the sun and made her way down the boulevard, and from a cart-vendor she bought a roomy straw basket, paying too much, she was sure, but she didn't know how to haggle. Ned would have insisted on a better deal.

The scent of pastries from an open-air café drew her in. The nausea had gone and she was famished. She ordered coffee and a guava *pastelito*, eating it slowly while hawkers passed by. Women balancing banana baskets on their heads implored her to buy; smiling men dangled cages of brightly colored birds.

Revived by the pastry and coffee, she pressed on through the crowded streets. Off the main boulevard, the sidewalks narrowed to single file. Above her head, baskets hung in profusion; alongside, taxis rolled right onto the sidewalk to go around mule wagons or carriages or pedestrians.

She stopped at a fruit stall. She'd never seen so many different kinds of bananas, from tiny finger-sized ones to big green plantains to short red ones. She bought a bunch of the red bananas, ate one, and found it delicious. She tucked them into her basket.

She walked past open-air shops and added to the basket a sword letter opener for her father, a lace mantilla for her mother, a *Don Quixote* book for Jessie, old Spanish coins for Pete and Wyatt, and a fancy inlaid comb for Anna.

She wanted to find something for her baby, and perhaps Anna's little boy. The dark-haired woman at the shop where she bought the comb told her, in halting English, where to buy hand-embroidered baby clothes. "*Muy* cheap," she said.

Gussie hesitated. Should she return before Ned got up? No. Let him stew if he didn't like it. She turned one corner and then another, fascinated by the sounds and smells and colors, until she realized she had turned into a street of ramshackle shops, with trays of wilting produce and fly-ridden, dusty merchandise. A rat scuttled across the street.

Gasping, she hurtled around another corner, only to find ragged and dirty children playing in the dirt and washing flapping in the breeze. Smells of frying and decay filled the air.

She mustn't panic. She mustn't! She just needed to retrace her steps. After resolutely marching back three blocks, she found herself back where she'd started, recognizing nothing. Panic seized her, and she struck out in a new direction.

Conscious of her new American clothes among the shabby dwellings, she broke into a trot. Heart pounding, she rounded a corner and collided with a child, tossing them both to the ground. "Oh!" A boy of about ten, with tousled black hair and a smear of dirt on his brown cheek, picked himself up, trying to look dignified. *"Perdóneme, por favor, señora."*

He helped her to her feet. She scrabbled in her bag for a coin. "I'm very sorry. Here's something for you."

He bowed and took the peso. *"Gracias."* He peered into her basket and looked up hopefully. *"Bananas?"*

Gussie broke two from the bunch. He peeled and ate both, then tossed the peels over a crumbling stucco wall. *"Adiós, señora."* He saluted, darted away, and disappeared.

Gussie pressed on, picking up her pace. But the shops became fewer in number and further apart. Rumpled residents squatted in doorways of rundown buildings and regarded her with suspicious eyes.

In her halting Spanish, she tried to ask an elderly toothless man directions to the Hotel Sevilla, but he just pointed to the sky and laughed incoherently. Breathing hard, she dashed to the end of the street.

Looking up and down the narrow street, praying hard, she picked the direction that seemed to lead to taller buildings. She'd walked only a little way when two young men dressed in red-spattered, whitish shirts and pants advanced toward her, talking and laughing, casting sly glances her way.

She ducked her head and hurried by, but not before she had heard the muttered words *yanqui chiquita.* She rounded the next corner and stared at a dead end.

Ned! If she didn't come back, would he come looking? Her breath came in short gasps, she felt paralyzed. She wanted him, wanted him here with her. She *needed* him.

Perspiration trickled from under her straw hat, and her throat ached from thirst. She darted down an alley in the opposite direction and found that it opened out onto a track beside an open field of cane and grass, and beyond that, she supposed, the bay. She skirted the field and followed the track until it curved back into a street of shuttered shops, virtually deserted. In the distance she saw a mule and wagon and a few pedestrians.

She raced down the street of shuttered shops, trying to keep the tall buildings in sight, her heels clattering on the cobblestones. Just then the two young men in red-spattered white rounded the corner at the end of the street and walked straight toward her.

She broke and ran back the way she had come, hearing their shouts and running footsteps behind her. Panic seized her. Suddenly, the small boy she'd knocked down emerged from a low wooden doorway and motioned for her to follow him. She ducked back through the low wooden door and found herself in a courtyard. He motioned Gussie to a half-open door and she entered it, finding herself in a long, low room, completely bare, with bars on the windows. The boy pushed the door shut, and she wondered if she had escaped from the bloody men only to find herself in a prison. The boy lowered a bar to the door and they flattened themselves against the wall.

For agonizing minutes they stayed there, hardly breathing, hearing the two men outside the door, walking around, muttering in rapid Spanish Gussie couldn't understand. Finally the voices receded.

She peered through a crack in the wooden door, and saw nothing but rubble and a tumbledown building with barred windows.

"What is this place?" she asked the boy.

He shrugged. "La Casa de Recogidas. *Prisión de mujeres.*"

Gussie understood "prison for women." She took a deep breath, and could only manage a little squeak. "Prison?"

The boy shrugged. "It is empty. *Abandonado.* How you say, *la fantasma* live here."

Gussie thought that meant ghost, but she didn't believe in ghosts. "What's your name? You've saved me!"

*"Me llamo Rafael."*

"Well, Rafael, ghost or no ghost, I need to get back to my hotel. The Sevilla."

He shrugged. "I take you to a *fotingo*."

She'd learned that was a taxi, and the hard knot of fear began to loosen. "Oh, yes, please!"

Rafael slid the splintery wooden bar back and crept out of the courtyard. He looked up and down the street and motioned for Gussie to follow. He ran like a wild animal, a fox, ducking down one street after another, and Gussie panted after him, dizzy. They burst out into a bustling street of prosperous-looking shops and honking taxis.

"Here," he said. He stepped out into the street and waved and a taxi stopped. Gussie dug into her bag, and, since she was out of pesos, pressed a dollar bill into his hand. She stepped into the taxi.

Ned was just waking up when she burst into the room. She crashed onto the bed, sobbing.

He rubbed his eyes and then stared. "Hey, you're hot as a firecracker! What's wrong?"

"Hold me, Ned, just hold me," she said. She lay back, and he held her, and the fan turned, and the breeze cooled her trembling body. She closed her eyes and soon was conscious only of the rhythm of her breath and his presence beside her.

"Don't worry. You can tell me later." He stroked her hair, and the sun glowed through the slats of the shutters while the air blew in from the sea, and the fan lazily turned. He made love to her, slowly, slowly, and the currents of her body ebbed and flowed like the tide, sparkling like sun on the water, alive as salt marshes and phosphorescent eels.

She wondered how she could have ever doubted him.

When she came out of her doze, Ned had ordered coffee and sat on the balcony engrossed in a Miami newspaper. The telegram to Papa! She slipped into her shoes and her dress, edged out of the room, and hurried downstairs to the lobby. She sent another telegram to Papa, instructing him to disregard the previous telegram.

She joined Ned on the balcony, sipped coffee, and told him about getting lost in the city. She told him only that she'd found her way back to him alone. And that she'd rushed out because she was expecting to hear from Papa.

But there had been no telegram from Papa.

After lunch, they fished in a rented boat and had a grand time, turning brown as islanders. That evening, Gussie dressed in pale green linen, a gardenia behind her left ear, and they ate grouper and fried plantains and black beans at a restaurant overlooking the harbor. The gulls mewled just beyond the railings, and from a nearby club the rhythms of a band sparked the moonlit night. She felt once again a bride.

"Do you think we might go to a show tonight, Ned?" She'd seen the placards in town.

"Max says those things aren't worth the money." He leaned back and lit a cigar. "We'll go to jai alai, and then hit the tables." He smiled knowingly. "Don't worry your sweet head. I've just had a little run of bad luck. Tonight I'll win it all back plus diamond-necklace dough."

Gussie licked her lips. He'd given her roses and was now offering thorns. "I don't want a diamond necklace, Ned."

He reached over and tweaked her cheek. "Sure you do. Max knows where I can get one wholesale."

Gussie grasped his wrist, searching his face. "Don't have anything more to do with Max and Sylvia, please. If you've spent all your money, maybe we'd better go home."

"Don't be silly." He laid her hand on the table and patted it like an unruly puppy. "I can wire my bank." He paused. "Max is teaching me things."

Chicago things. Cold settled in Gussie's stomach and she shivered. Ned blew smoke and watched it drift out toward the gulls. "Trust me," he said.

Gussie wrapped herself in her fringed silk shawl. "That breeze is cold, Ned, and I'm not feeling too well. Maybe you should go without me."

He gazed at her for a long moment. "Suit yourself."

# Chapter 21

The sun was climbing past the balcony when Gussie woke. The barred light through the shutters played over Ned's sweat-sheened form. He lay so still that she checked to make sure he was breathing. She hadn't heard him come in.

She stretched her limbs to work the kinks out, then slid out of bed. Ned's wallet, resting on the dresser beside an empty bottle of rum, looked suspiciously thin. She ignored the temptation to riffle through it. She didn't want to know.

She dressed in a white middy blouse and navy linen skirt. She wasn't a sacrificial maiden this morning, but a schoolgirl. Mama hadn't let her buy new clothes for a trousseau. "You'll just grow out of them in a couple of months," she'd said practically.

Gussie craved coffee, orange juice, fresh air, sunlight, and freedom. The light-barred room seemed like a prison this morning.

She slipped the Kodak her father had given her into her straw basket. At least she'd get some pictures out of the trip. At the hotel café, she took a table in the tiled courtyard around a fountain. The happy, animated faces around her made her feel guilty for being miserable, and her nausea was returning. She ate some cubed pineapple and papaya and mango, and felt better.

Out into the steaming morning, she struck off in the direction of the cathedral spire. She'd barely gone two blocks when the boy, Rafael, darted through a group of tourists and appeared at her side. *"Señora!"*

The guidebook slipped out of her hand. "Rafael! You frightened me!"

His small face solemn, he picked up the book and handed it to her. "I saw you, señora, and followed you. It is not good for a foreign lady to wander alone." *Especially one as naive as you,* his eyes seemed to say.

"You speak good English," she accused him

He shrugged. "The padre teaches me. He say listen before speaking. He say I am quick. You need a guide?"

"No. I want to be alone." She looked away.

His voice grew softer. "I take you to a church."

She shook her head. "I'm on my way to the cathedral."

"Not San Cristobal." Rafael tugged at her hand. "Come. Not a church for tourist. A church to pray. "

She turned then, and smiled. "I'm not a Catholic."

*"Es posible* to pray, *señora,* even a Protestant."

The humor caught her unawares. She gave a little laugh, then tears sprang to her eyes. He silently held out a grubby square of cloth, but she shook her head, touched. "I have a handkerchief, thank you." She drew out a square of embroidered linen and wiped her eyes.

Watching her, he angled his head, his dark eyes meeting her sea-colored ones. This street urchin was stealing her heart, but could she trust him? He'd already saved her once. And if he was fishing for a tip—all right, she'd give him one. "Lead on, guide."

He took her past the square: past the park and the palace, past the cathedral. On the broad tree-lined boulevards street hawkers jostled; laughing women sold fried pies, while carriage horses clip-clopped in flop-eared resignation. Colorful flower sellers' buckets gave off a drifting fragrance. Gussie, entranced, snapped them all, offering coins in return.

They approached a stately stucco house fenced with wrought-iron railing. Gussie drew back, startled, to see two painters in whitish suits spattered with rusty red. They dipped their brushes in rusty red paint and slapped it on the fence.

The boy frowned. "We go this way." He gently steered her toward a side street.

She wished she could have photographed the painters against the railing, even as they frightened her. For hadn't Papa always said to confront your fears? He said fears are like bad dreams: in the brightness of day, they fade into oblivion.

Four blocks they walked, Gussie peering in gates at grand houses behind high walls, at palmy courtyards where fountains cooled the air. When they passed an iron-barred gate, Gussie caught a glimpse of white-habited nuns crossing the courtyard with brisk purposefulness. She stopped and peered in to see patients in shapeless cotton pajamas slumped on benches.

"What is this place?"

"*Es hospital. Leprosos,*" he said, wiggling his fingers and then folding them down. Gussie shrank back.

Rafael laughed. "You cannot catch it through the bars."

"But it seems so terrible to be shut up like that, away from the world, away from everyone you love . . ."

"I think, *señora,* you have not seen much of the world."

She didn't reply. That was what Pete had been trying to tell her, that she'd been too sheltered for her ambition. She'd make a poor photojournalist if she shrank back from realities.

What did it matter? She wasn't going to be anything but a wife. And mother. Her spirit rose in protest. There must be a way out.

She lifted the small Kodak to capture the image of the lepers, but Rafael was moving on. She snapped a shot through the bars, then ran to catch up. In the next block they stopped before another wrought-iron gate, and Rafael pushed it open with a squeal into a spacious cobbled courtyard fronting a chapel.

An elderly padre in a white homespun robe, inspecting a handful of small green bananas on one of the trees that grew there, turned at the squeal of the hinges. "Ay, Rafael," he said, *"Buenas tardes, señorita."*

*"Señora, por favor, padre,"* said Rafael, and chattered in such rapid Spanish Gussie couldn't follow, but she realized she was being introduced. "Augusta Pemberton," she said, and did not correct herself. The old priest held out his hands to bid them enter the arched wooden doors. *"Señora."*

Inside the tiny chapel, a dark Virgin brooded over the altar, a crowd of votives flickering in the dimness. Two old people hunched in a pew. Gussie stopped, mesmerized by the melancholy light. "Why are all these candles burning?

"These candles burn for *los muertos*. In the war," the padre explained. A woman in black walked up the aisle, took a candle, placed it in the bed of sand, and lit it, and then dropped a small coin into the waiting box. At last she walked out, head bowed beneath a *mantilla*.

Gussie gave Rafael a coin and nodded. He gave her a quick, brief smile of thanks and lit two candles.

She glanced up at the carved wooden Virgin above the altar. It looked very ancient; maybe it had even come over with the Spanish in the 17th century. Such sad and sorrowing eyes, as if this dark lady knew something of her pain.

Gussie allowed the sadness to wash over her. Shadows loomed and receded. Calmness and peace descended into that still place, and she realized peace had eluded her ever since the day her yearning for Ned had ended her dreaming childhood forever. How far away now were the innocent days by the river!

The boy knelt in prayer, and Gussie awkwardly, hesitantly, sank to her knees. A great warm wind, full of sweetness, washed over her.

Her face and body glowed, and her surroundings receded into the flame of pure radiance from the altar candle. She prayed with all her heart, for the lepers and for Ned and for her unborn child, for her sisters and her cousin Pete, for Rafael and the splattered men, for all of the poor people in the streets. Finally her mind was quiet.

Rafael, at length, whispered, "*Señora*, are you well?"

She opened her eyes. The radiance had faded. There was the quiet church and its flickering candles, its dampness and cool decline.

She struggled to her feet with rubbery knees. She brushed her skirt, and then walked with Rafael out into the blazing morning sunlight. The elderly padre in the garden smiled.

"Father, will my prayers be answered?" she asked, hoping he understood.

The old padre replied, "*Sí*. Our prayers, they are always answered."

She waited for him to say something more, as the minister at home always did, about how we may not recognize the answer when it comes, but he did not.

"Thank you. *Gracias*."

She took a picture of the old priest and Rafael. He nodded and smiled and bade them a good journey.

"What was this church called?" she asked Rafael as they passed through the gate to the street .

"La Iglesia de la Nuestra Dama de Soledad," he replied.

Our lady of loneliness, Gussie whispered to herself . She glanced at her watch. It seemed she had been in the church for hours, but only twenty minutes had passed since she first entered. Her heart was at peace, and she wanted to give the boy something.

"Where is your family?" she asked, thinking he might have hungry brothers and sisters.

"*La iglesia,*" he said.

"At the church?"

"I help the padre; he gives me food and a place to sleep," Rafael said. "He teaches me English. He is *mi familia.*"

"Are you an orphan?"

Rafael nodded sadly. "My father was killed in the war. My mother died of typhoid. I ran away from the orphan's home."

Now she knew why the two candles. They passed the park and backtracked along the *avenida*, now hot and growing noisy and lively with the noon traffic. Rivulets of sweat poured down Gussie's face. She kept her head down and followed Rafael through the narrow side streets, so narrow that they had to walk in the road, moving to the sidewalk when a car or carriage came along.

A stout, threadbare woman with snaggle teeth and a basket of religious medallions approached them. Any other time Gussie would have ignored the woman, but now she stopped. The boy peered into the basket and held up a St. Christopher medal. "*El padrone de Cuba.*"

"Would you like one?"

The boy brightened for a moment, then shook his head. "You must have."

"I'll buy two."

The medals were bought. When one was resting in her basket and the other hanging by a cord around Rafael's thin neck, he said, "Now I leave you. The hotel is one block." He pointed, and she saw the hotel's marquee in the distance.

"Wait," she said, opening her purse. She counted out half of her last twenty dollars and gave it to him. "Give some to the padre," she said. "Some to the lepers. The rest for you."

Rafael nodded. "*Gracias, señora. Vaya con Dios.*"

Like the click of a shutter, he disappeared.

Gussie lagged in her steps toward the hotel, wondering what to tell Ned this time.

She stopped in front of a shop to think, not seeing at first the Panama hats, each with a string to secure it under the chin. The shopkeeper hurried out to greet her in English. "This hat is of the finest straw, *señorita.*" Did she look so obviously American? "*Confortable,*" he said. "*Muy bueno* for the fair of face." He took one off its peg and held it out to her. "Try, *por favor!*"

The sun was climbing high in the sky, and sweat trickled down her neck. She handed her cloche to the shopkeeper and tried the Panama on. Wonderfully light, it fit well and provided more shade than the cloche.

The shopkeeper produced a mirror, and she turned this way and that scrutinizing her reflection, and finally smiled. She could tell Ned she'd been shopping.

"I'll wear it," she said, and paid a sum she thought was too much, even when he said it was a special price. He tucked her cloche in a hatbox and bowed as she left.

Ned was still asleep when she returned. She placed the box on the dresser and opened her bag. Seven dollars, more or less, to last them until they could return home.

She went back down to the lobby and checked at the desk. A message was waiting for her. With trembling fingers, she opened the envelope. What was Papa sending her? She tore it open and found a money order, enough to cover their hotel bill.

All at once she began to laugh.

But what would Ned say? She slipped it in her pocket. This would be her secret. To be used if disaster fell.

# Chapter 22

E nid Smith Barlow was now Tenny's supervisor.

Tenny had survived six weeks on the job, barely. She slammed open the door to her empty room at nearly nine p.m., bone-weary and close to tears. Alice was probably down the hall having a bath. Alice would understand about her day.

Enid had kept her long after her shift had ended at seven.

On the TB ward, the patients were too sick for Enid's flirtation and the coughing was awful. While Tenny cleaned, mopped, served meals, fetched supplies for doctors, and emptied sputum cups and bedpans, Enid somehow found errands to run elsewhere. Tenny, counting the hours until her shift was over, rejoiced when she saw a fellow probationer coming their way. She stepped over to Enid just in time to see her slide a magazine under a patient chart. "Miss Barlow, Miss Jones is coming to relieve me."

Enid stared at her watch and raised an eyebrow. "You can't go yet. Miss Powers wants the supply room straightened. She complained about the floor. It's got to be scrubbed. And those bedpans need carbolic."

Tenny, wishing she could throw the bedpans at Enid, gritted her teeth while Enid walked off with her magazine. No use complaining. She headed to the supply room.

Probationers got the jobs nobody else wanted, and Enid was known for running them ragged, while she slithered between beds with coos and smiles, especially if the men were good-looking or appeared to be rich. She patted their cheeks and fluffed their pillows, and then came back to the nurses' station and dropped the mask, wishing them all to the devil.

Tenny tossed an old copy of the *Ashbyville Clarion* on her study desk, hoping the sun in the sunroom had disinfected it sufficiently. She sank down on the bed, kicked off her sturdy shoes, and rubbed rosewater and glycerin cream on her raw, red hands. There were never enough rubber gloves to go around, and she suspected Enid had walked off with the last pair.

Then she massaged her aching feet, scooped up the newspaper, and stretched out to relieve her back. She flipped past pages telling of starving peasants in China, a surrealist art exhibition in Paris, and the speech on tax cuts by President Coolidge. She stopped and read an editorial about better sanitation at the mill village.

Then she turned to the society section, where she liked to read Aunt Polly's advice to the lovelorn and the helpful household hints. She lingered over the photographs of brides, who wore ankle-length confections of lace, satin T-strap pumps, and long, swooping trains. Veils floated from jeweled caps, tiaras, and headbands.

One picture caught her eye. The bride looked so wistful, such a sad smile. She read the caption: *Pemberton-Fletcher*. Could that be Mr.

Fletcher at the plant? She read the tiny print more closely. *Miss Augusta Pemberton, daughter of Judge and Mrs. McIntosh Pemberton, and Mr. Edmund Fletcher, son of the late Mr. and Mrs. E.T. Fletcher of Roanoke, Virginia . . .* she skimmed until she read *Mr. Fletcher is the well-regarded manager at Burkett Mills.* She felt stunned. Yes, it was *that* Mr. Fletcher, the one who looked like Byron.

She wished there was a picture of him so that she could study it. *Her* Byron was clean-shaven, thin, and lanky, and this mustached man was filled out and muscular.

And they were going to Cuba on their honeymoon? Where was Cuba, anyhow?

On the second society page, another item caught her eye. Miss Swanee Burkett and her mother had departed on the Dixie Flyer for New York, where they would take the *Mauretania* for London, and from there take the Grand Tour of Europe.

Miss Burkett was the one who'd been so rude to her. The idea, so la-de-da and wanting birth control! Tenny had seen them kissing, her and Mr. Fletcher, and now he'd married someone else? Was she going away because he'd left her, or had she refused him for someone richer?

Tenny studied the picture of Miss Burkett and her mother beside the enormous ship. The younger woman wore a glamorous traveling ensemble, dress and coat set off by a corsage and pearls, a stylish cloche pulled low over her brow. Her stout mother smiled, showing lots of straight teeth, in a cocoon coat trimmed with lush fur.

Tenny closed the newspaper. She wanted to tell Mrs. Brown about the mill manager, because Mrs. Brown had known Byron.

She took out a sheet of the pretty stationery Miss Verity had given her as a going-away present, and wrote:

*Dear Mrs. Brown,*

*Thank you for your nice letter. I'm happy to hear everbody is well. I miss them so much and you and Brother Jethro. I do hope Pa stops getting lickered up. I hope Brother Jethro will talk to him and pray for him and hope he can get out of debt so he can move on and work for somebody else. Thank God for Milton. He is a good brother.*

*Speaking of brothers, I saw somebody who looked like Byron here but he dident know me. Or pretended that.*

*Please don't let anybody know I'm in Ashbyville, especially Pa and Mr. Shackley. Let them think I have just disappeared like Byron.*

*Your friend,*
*Tenny*

Tenny scrawled a signature that looked as unschooled as it had been when she left home. Her penmanship was perfect now, but she'd just as soon nobody knew how much she was learning. She added a P.S. to send it to the same P.O. Box as before, and hoped Miss Verity would forward it to her, or let her drop by and pick it up.

She wished she could tell Mrs. Brown about school, about the long hours and the hard work and the terror she felt when she was in charge and wasn't sure she knew what to do, as when she was changing the linens and the patient suddenly started projectile vomiting, and all she could do was drop the sheets and run for help. On that occasion, she was blessed out by Miss Powers, who informed her that *nurses never run.*

Licking the envelope, she thought of the exam at the end of the week. Her eyes felt tired and grainy, but she'd better have that bath before she fell asleep. Tomorrow night, if she could get off in time, she'd study.

She got up and opened the window, hoping a deep breath of the chilly air would cut the fog in her brain. She caught the drift of cigarette smoke and gazed down at the gaslit courtyard, but saw no one with a cigarette. A curl of smoke dissolved before her eyes, and she realized it was coming from the open window just below hers, the window that belonged to Enid Smith Barnes, who had a whole room to herself.

Tenny closed the window just as Alice clumped in, wearing robe and slippers. "Guess what? Ellen down the hall has one of those electric hair dryers! She said I could use it. You want me to ask her if you can too?"

Tenny, used to plaiting her long hair and sleeping in it, shook her head. "Is the bathtub free?"

"Better go quick."

She gathered her towel and washcloth. "How does Enid get away with smoking?"

"Same reason she gets away with everything else, with wearing lipstick and all that. Her uncle's on the board. Her father was a genius, according to Miss Wells."

"What did he die of?" asked Tenny.

"Ooh, that's a mystery. Nobody wants to talk about it."

Tenny was intrigued, but Alice didn't know any more.

"As for Enid," Alice said, "they'll keep bending the rules as long as nobody complains. Nobody important, that is."

Tenny wasn't about to be the one to complain. There was something she wanted to ask, anyhow. "Say, Alice. Where is Cuba?"

# Chapter 23

The sea rippled in steely corrugations, and the sailboat whizzed over the water. Clouds tumbled across the sky, and Ned, the sun and salt spray raking his face, clearly enjoyed the excitement.

Gussie's headscarf fluttered and loosened, whipping in the wind, and she unwrapped it and tied it around her wrist. Her hair slapped and stung her face. The fabulous champagne lunch Ned had ordered rose sourly in her throat, and she swallowed. She didn't want to be sick in the boat. She wished she'd never come.

He hadn't asked where she'd been when she got back from her walk to the church. He'd believed, or pretended to believe, her story about shopping for a hat. He'd embraced her and told her he loved her, and she'd softened a little, still sore about his gambling, and kept Papa's money order to herself.

Ned handled the boat well. Still, he didn't seem to notice the clouds banking to the east, or the choppy waves now slapping the boat, or the pervasive smell of rain. Gussie felt sick. "Ned—"

Ned, laughing, yelled at her to grab the boom and swing it around. She obeyed, and was almost knocked overboard.

"Ned! Please!" She leaned over the side of the boat and a rogue wave slapped her full in the face. She lost her lunch right there.

"We might as well go in." He grumpily handed her a wet towel. "I want to have a drink with Max, anyhow."

She glanced over at him, his hair blowing in the breeze, furious that he could be so casual at her distress. But she had to hang on and get back home.

"Ned, look at those black clouds. A storm's coming."

He snorted. "A rain squall, most likely. It's too late in the year for a tropical storm."

She clutched the side of the boat until her fingers paled and didn't stop until they reached the dock.

After a soak in the claw-footed tub, wrapped in her new baby blue silk cocoon robe and her feet luxuriating in satin slippers, she should have felt better, but her shoulders were way too warm. She touched them gingerly. Not a sunburn on top of everything else!

Ned handed her a rum punch he'd ordered and invited her to sip it on the balcony. She frowned. It was a little windy, but the wind would feel good on her shoulders.

She'd barely lifted her glass to the breeze when he told her that Max had lent him some "capital." Tonight he was going to win everything back.

Gussie's heart sank. Just when she was beginning to think things were better. "Ned," she cried, "you don't have to win it back. Papa sent us some money for the hotel."

He stared at her and then shook his head. "You keep it, honey. I'm not taking your father's money."

"But—"

"That's it, Augusta. You just have to trust me."

She sighed, leaned back in her chair, and studied the orange and lime slices in her punch. The palms rattling in the wind sounded to her like skeletons dancing. She closed her eyes. Could you pray for success at gambling? Was that what Papa had meant when he said gambling would destroy your faith in God? Maybe not, but she prayed anyway, and wondered if the dark Virgin in Rafael's church would listen and make Ned lucky for the sake of their baby.

In his dapper white suit, with his slicked-back hair, Ned gazed at her earnestly. "You look lovely."

She stirred in her chair and sipped her drink, the wind teasing her curls. She smoothed it down. "It's going to storm, Ned."

He smiled. "An island squall, dearie. It'll be over by dinnertime. I've reserved a table at the Beach Club."

"Don't you have to be a member?"

"Max got me in."

Gussie turned aside. "I wish Max would go play with the real sharks."

"He's all right, Gussie."

"I think he's—" She never got to finish her sentence, because the rain came up quickly, pelting them with drops like BB shot. "Oh!" She grabbed the drinks and hurried inside. Ned followed, closing the French doors behind them.

"My hair—" She set the glasses on the dresser and gazed in the mirror at the limp mess.

"It looks beautiful." Ned shucked his coat and tie, crept up behind her, and encircled her with his arms, placing a slow kiss on the back of her neck. Lightning flashed outside, magnesium bulbs illuminating their charged bodies.

At first she resisted, but then her nerve ends came alive beneath her silken underthings. The fan clicked overhead, slicing the sultriness, the flush on her neck, while the rain raked the tiles in thundering ripples, sluicing in great sheets. Somehow their clothes slithered to the floor.

Ned vaulted onto the massive bed and pulled her to him. The rain-cooled air feathered their hot bodies, while Gussie's soul stirred somewhere else, back in the church with the sundust, back where the roseate windows grew and expanded until the sky filled with stained-glass kaleidoscope shards.

Afterwards they clung together, sweating in the chill, almost not hearing the pounding, BAM BAM BAM, on the door, and a hoarse voice: "Come on madam, sir, everyone down to the ballroom, there is a *tormenta . . . huracán . . .* take the stairs please, not the elevator . . . down the hall please step lively *señoras, señores . . .*"

Gussie grabbed lounging pajamas, topped them with a raincoat, and slipped her feet into the espadrilles. She gathered cigarettes, magazine, hair comb, and slipped her money into her pocket.

"*Venga, señora, señor . . .* BAM BAM BAM . . ."

They joined other guests straggling down the corridors, talking and complaining and carrying books and papers and one small, forbidden dog. Bellmen and clerks stood at the foot of the stairs, guiding guests toward the ballroom. "This way, please, everyone hurry . . . *venga, venga . . .*"

Max Herbert saw them first. "Hiya, Ned, little lady." He walked over to them, jabbing his cigar into the air to make the point. "I told Sylvie there was gonna be a storm and she didn't believe me."

Sylvia, wearing cerise from head to foot and sporting a long cigarette holder and a jeweled skullcap, paid no attention, being engaged in a game of contract bridge with three other women. A bartender arranged bottles on a portable bar in the corner, and a piano player pounded out a rumba in the light of the flickering candles. Smoke floated toward the high ceiling, wafting through a smell of mustiness and faded flowers.

"Want a drink?" asked Ned. Gussie shook her head, hugging herself.

"I'll join you, bub," said Max Herbert, and the two walked over toward the bar.

Gussie wandered over to the French windows that gave out onto the courtyard. The wind screamed and bellowed, and the slanting silver wall of rain rushed past them, tumbling patio chairs and pitching palm fronds, bits of roof, a flurry of papers, and an unfortunate chicken.

She took a seat near the cardplayers and watched Ned and Max across the room drinking, absorbed in conversation.

Was Rafael all right? Surely he was in his church with the padre. Surely. A child of the streets like that, he must have a million hiding places. *Prisión de mujeres . . .*

By eight the storm had passed; people filtered back to their rooms and left the hotel staff to the cleaning: the overturned chairs, the inside-out umbrellas, the uprooted trees, the pool full of storm water and silt.

Word spread quickly. The Beach Club and the casino had suffered storm damage and were closed. There was no point in going anywhere now. Gussie and Ned took a candlelight dinner at the hotel; its ancient charcoal stove worked well. The Herberts wandered off to continue their card games.

The party at the hotel went on for hours, and Gussie finally left to go upstairs and sleep alone.

The next morning she woke early, closed the door softly behind her, and ventured outside with the Kodak.

She waded through the debris resolutely, clicking the shutter again and again, recording the storm's destruction. She felt light, expansive, as if she'd come home after being away for a long time. That camera in her hand felt *right*, and her fog lifted as she snapped the shattered sign of the hotel, fallen awnings on the street, splintered donkey carts, rivulets of deep brown mud.

She hurried down several blocks, dodging debris, and a policeman frowned at her but didn't try to stop her. She arrived at the padre's church. The banana trees in the courtyard had bent clear over and their leaves were tattered, but they hadn't broken. The church was unharmed. She didn't see a soul. The place looked deserted.

Walking back to the hotel, she framed images with her photographer's eye and wished she'd brought the Graflex. How had her obsession with Ned blinded her into giving up her dream? She stared at the little camera in her hand, meant for capturing honeymoon memories.

She wheeled around to capture a donkey and cart, its driver picking through the trash. Happily, the outdoor café had escaped the storm. She bought a cup of fragrant dark coffee, doused it with cream, and sipped it on a damp chair, her invisible shackles falling away.

At the hotel, she demanded that the harried concierge get their steamship tickets exchanged for billets on the next ship out, never mind the port, Tampa or Miami. She slipped him a chunk of Papa's money and asked to have their luggage delivered to their door.

When she returned to the room, she found that Ned, still in his pajamas, had ordered up coffee and rolls and fruit. He was drinking rum and orange juice. "Just for you, pet," he mumbled.

"We're leaving, Ned."

Ned paced silently, sipping his drink, while the fan clicked overhead. Gussie folded shirts, sorted underwear, and answered the door when their luggage arrived. She tipped the harried porter. Finally he blurted, "You go on home. I'll stay and win back our money!"

Gussie didn't look up as she opened the trunk and lowered Ned's undershirts into it. "Ned, the casino suffered roof damage and no one knows when it will reopen. Anyhow, you told me not to worry, that you could afford the loss."

"I hate to lose," he mumbled.

She tucked the precious gifts she'd bought into the corners of the trunk. "Suppose you lose again?"

"Where's your faith in me, Gussie?" He sounded hollow. Trying to make her feel sorry for him.

She edged away from him and lifted another pile of clothing. "I've seen things here that can't be explained. That storm was a sign to leave. Why don't you sell that property in Florida and pay Max what you borrowed?"

Ned said nothing.

An icy calm stole over her. "You have to come. I can't travel back alone. Papa would have a fit."

At the mention of her father Ned flushed. "I'd rather your father didn't hear about any of this."

"How could he not hear, if I came alone? What excuse could I possibly give?"

Ned remained silent for a moment, then he came to her and touched her shoulders. "Your muscles are tight," he said, and kneaded them. Gussie relaxed her muscles but tightened her resolve. Ned gazed outside, into the sunshine and mist, and dropped his hands. "I'll talk to Max. He said he'd be in the hotel café this morning."

"Then go, and make whatever arrangements you can." Gussie turned away from him and stuffed handkerchiefs, coconut candy, magazines, her Kodak into her straw basket. She didn't look up when the door clicked shut.

Standing beside the taxi outside the hotel, Gussie thought she'd never seen air so bright, and the colors had never seemed so green nor the sky so blue nor the buildings such melting shades of pink and coral and green and yellow.

The driver was loading their bags when Max and Sylvia showed up, Sylvia this time wearing poison green. "Just wanted to tell you kids good-bye." Sylvia shook Gussie's hand. Max, chewing on his cigar, clapped Ned on the back. "I'll be in touch."

"I'll bet he will," muttered Gussie as they pulled away from the hotel. Their driver, the same gold-toothed man who had driven them from the casino, said, "So you friends with Señor Jerbert?"

He was clearly impressed. Gussie looked behind her, but Max and Sylvia were no longer at the curb. She thought of Rafael, and the church, and lovemaking in the *tormenta*. Cuba, their *honeymoon*, had been a long dream and nightmare all rolled into one.

"He took an IOU," Ned finally said.

Gussie said nothing.

Her eyes would not stop leaking. She searched in the roomy straw bag for a handkerchief among the sweets and magazines. She found one in the bottom of the bag, along with a dried red banana peel.

By and by she cast the peel out into the harbor.

# Chapter 24

G ussie paced the room at the Fernando hotel. They'd arrived in Savannah late in the afternoon and exchanged their train tickets. "Ned, I'm going down to send a telegram to Papa."

Ned leaned back in his chair, trimming a cigar. "What's your worry? You sent one from Havana."

"I couldn't explain. Too many people jostling and shoving in the telegraph office. Just said we were on our way home."

Her shoulders tingled from the sunburn, and now she wanted nothing so much as to feel Mama's arms around her, to wake up and be back in her own room again, to soft morning light and honeysuckle, to coffee and bacon and Papa behind the paper.

A loud rap at the door jolted her out of her reverie.

"It's our drinks." Ned laid the cigar aside, walked to the door, and admitted a bellboy trundling a cart rattling with glasses, ice, tonic, and limes. Gussie pivoted toward the window and glared at the river, where a tall sailing ship was anchored. She didn't turn back until she heard the click of the door.

Ned was pouring gin into a frosty glass.

"Where did you find gin?" She felt her shoulders tighten, and the itch from sunburn begged her for a rub.

"Just knew who to ask, is all." He held his glass up for a toast and winked at her. "Cheers, darlin'. I've got to go meet with Wyckham. Won't be an hour. Then we'll have a good dinner."

Wyckham. Of course he'd know the bootleggers. Savannah was probably wide open. She sipped the drink she didn't really want, the fizz of quinine tickling her nose. "Can't I come?"

Ned smiled indulgently. "You'd be bored." Gussie ran her finger down her glass, drawing patterns in the condensation." How much money did you lose, Ned?"

Ned's smile froze. "I'll deal with it."

A lump rising in her throat, Gussie turned and walked over to the window. She pushed aside the curtain and looked down on the street, and her hand flew to her mouth. Henry Benedict was standing on the sidewalk! What on earth was he doing here?

Ned didn't seem to notice her unease. "See you later, kid," he said.

"I might take a walk." Gussie's eyes were still on the figure below.

"Suit yourself." He drained his glass, set it on the dresser, and walked out, the heavy door closing with a dull thud.

Gussie slipped into a blue-and-white striped cotton dress and set the Panama hat from Cuba on her head. She peered in the mirror and dusted a little powder over her reddened nose, and then caught the elevator down.

By the time she walked through the big revolving door of the hotel, Henry had disappeared. Had he followed Ned? Perplexed, she gazed at the street and sidewalk. Was that him heading down Liberty Street to the square? Papa had something to do with this, she was sure, and she was going to find out.

She strode across the street, then crunched her way down a pebbled path under low-hanging Spanish moss, searching for a glimpse of Henry's tan coat. Streaks of orange sliced across the sky, and the breeze blew in from the river, carrying the salt-marsh smell. No Henry.

A friendly black mongrel with floppy ears came to trot alongside her, tongue lolling, and she was glad for the company. In the darkening sky, the stars were beginning to come out, and the gibbous moon hung low. She wasn't going to find Henry before it became too dim to see. She turned to go back to the hotel, but a low-hanging live oak branch snatched her hat off. It fell to the ground before she could catch it.

The black dog seized the hat and loped off down the path. "Hey!" Gussie chased him, her shoes slipping on the pebbles.

Henry appeared from out of the dusk and whistled to the beast. "Come on, boy."

The mutt, wagging its tail, approached him and dropped the hat in front of him. Henry scooped it up.

Gussie, panting, hurried to his side. "Henry, I didn't know you had a dog!"

"I don't. Never saw this guy before."

She sighed. "I never know when you're putting me on. What on earth are you doing in Savannah?"

Henry held out the hat to her, grinning like an idiot.

She took it and held it loosely. "Thank you. You haven't answered my question." The dog pranced around, wanting to continue the game.

Henry met her gaze frankly. "Your father asked me to come meet you and . . . well, escort you home if you needed that particular service."

Gussie's face warmed. "I'm all right." Oh, that telegram to Papa—

"He's just concerned for your safety. You're coming home suddenly."

"I don't suppose he heard about the hurricane, the storm?"

"No word of it."

"The hotel staff was up to their ears. I had to go to the telegraph office—" Her hand on the hat met a damp spot and she finally lifted it to see. Teeth marks and drool decorated her poor Panama, her souvenir of Cuba. "I'd better go back and send a wire now." She strode a few steps back toward the hotel, the dog following, Henry alongside.

"Let me escort you, Gussie. It's getting dark. Where's Fletcher?"

"A business meeting," she said, her mouth tight. "Honest, I'm perfectly fine."

"Miss Augusta, I want to be your knight in shining armor."

"I'm not locked in the castle, Mr. Benedict." She looked down at the tatty chewed hat and suddenly burst into laughter. She turned the hat while she walked, Henry beside her with his hands shoved in his pockets. Finally she tossed the hat into a waste barrel. The dog trotted off.

"Are you staying at the Fernando too?"

Henry laughed. "Not likely. I'm staying at a boardinghouse. I was on my way to call on you when I saw you leave the hotel. I was curious where you were going so I played spy." This time it was his turn to blush.

"Actually, I saw you and came looking for you."

They both laughed, and Gussie got the giggles so hard she choked. She sobered when they approached the hotel. On the dining terrace a figure in a white suit paced up and down, smoking a cigar. Gussie stopped. "There's Ned, looking for me."

Henry laid a hand on her shoulder. "Shall I come up with you?"

Gussie hesitated. She felt secure with Henry's hand on her shoulder, but it wouldn't do for Ned to find out Papa had sent someone down. Not when he'd acted so funny about the money. "No," she said. "Please."

"Then I'll say good-bye, Miss Gussie. I'll see you in Ashbyville. Don't worry about the telegram. I'll send one to the judge, or perhaps try the telephone and tell him you're safe and sound." His touch lifted, and

Gussie felt a lifting away of comfort, home, Papa. Then she pulled herself up, remembering she was about to start a new life.

She held out her hand. "Good-bye, Mr. Benedict."

He took her hand in both of his. "Good-bye, Mrs. Fletcher. Good luck."

She turned and ran up the steps to the terrace. Ned turned and saw her then, smiled, and she was struck at how handsome he was, what a fine figure he cut. Anyone would think she was a lucky girl.

Her husband stepped forward to meet her and scooped her up in a hug. "Did you have a good walk?"

"Yes. Did you worry about me?"

"It was getting dark, little one." He guided her to a table where he'd already ordered ginger ale and nuts in silver dishes. From his pocket he took a small silver flask and poured them both a generous shot of bourbon. "What am I going to do with this wanderlust of yours?"

She smiled. "Perhaps you can come with me next time." She told him about her adventure with the dog and the hat, except she substituted a gallant stranger for Henry.

Ned thought a moment. "Don't worry about the hat. I'll buy you another one. Finish your drink and we'll order dinner."

A new hat wouldn't carry the memory of the Iglesia de Nuestra Dama de Soledad. "Ned, that's sweet of you," she said. He'd forget about it. She took a sip of her drink to help the lump in her throat.

In the high, palmy hotel dining room, Ned ordered for them both, while Gussie traced patterns on the white damask tablecloth with her table knife. "How was your meeting?"

The waiter placed icy bowls of shrimp cocktail before them. Ned blinked and shrugged. "Fine, nothing to worry about. How long before we can move into that house?"

Gussie dipped a shrimp in the red sauce. "Papa's given the tenants two months."

"He's the landlord. Why can't he just chuck them out right now?"

"He's not that kind of landlord." Gussie squeezed lemon on her last shrimp.

"But we're family," Ned gobbled the rest of his shrimp and shoved the dish away. "Maybe he'd let us buy it at a good price, or maybe even give it to us."

Gussie didn't see the difference between her father giving them the house and letting them live in it rent-free, but she didn't argue. Instead, she turned to the practical. "We'll have to get it painted, and then we'll have to buy furniture, rugs . . . a crib . . ."

"You'll need some help," Ned interrupted. "A baby nurse for a month, and a cook."

That hadn't occurred to Gussie. "Can we afford it, Ned? I'm not afraid of work."

"Have you ever done any housework, my little flapper? You know, Negroes are cheap."

Gussie opened her mouth to protest that Mama didn't like that kind of talk, and that she had always tidied her room and made her own bed, but she was interrupted by the arrival of quail and grits and greens. She resolutely attacked the bird with knife and fork while Ned tore off a quail leg and sucked the meat.

Mama wouldn't like those manners. Strange—sometimes Ned had good manners and sometimes he didn't. She wanted to ask more about his life but was afraid he'd brush her off, the way he had when she'd asked about his sister.

At last the waiter brought a quivering white blancmange and set it in front of her. She picked up her silver spoon and prodded it. She felt like that.

They went up to the room after coffee, and Ned kept his distant preoccupation and didn't complain when she said she felt too tired to make love. She closed the window curtain on the moonlight, wondering what Henry was going to tell her father.

Maybe she could have gotten over her doubts about Ned, the botched honeymoon, if the next day had not happened.

They were standing outside the hotel waiting for a taxi when a trolley rumbled by. A tanned woman with gray hair in an untidy bun leaned out the window and pointed at Ned. She screamed a word that sounded like . . . *France?*

Gussie faced Ned in surprise. "Do you know that woman? Did she meet you in France?"

Ned shook his head. "Of course not. Off her rocker. Thought I was somebody she knew." Gussie noticed a sheen of sweat on his forehead, but the morning was cool, with a light breeze off the river.

The taxi rolled up, and while the driver took their bags, Gussie gazed at the trolley lumbering down the street. When it stopped at the next corner, the old woman hopped off and, surprisingly agile, headed their way. Ned threw the last bag in the trunk, yanked open the taxi door, and hustled Gussie in.

"Station, and fast," he said to the cabby. "I'll make it worth your while."

The cabby took off with a screech and Gussie leaned out the window of the taxi, but the taxi rounded a corner, putting the old woman out of view.

Ned pulled Gussie to him and kissed her the way she'd always loved. "I'm sorry the honeymoon's over," he said. "I wish it was just beginning."

"Why, Ned," she said, mollified but not melting, because of the *France*. Why France?

He held her hand until the taxi pulled up in front of the station. He paid the driver and summoned a redcap for the bags. Gussie spotted Henry Benedict outside the terminal and steered Ned away toward a newsstand, sweet-talking him into buying her two fashion magazines, a *Delineator* and a *Vogue*.

When they alighted at the Ashbyville terminal, Papa and Mama and Jessie and Anna were waiting with kisses and hugs and happy tears, and Henry had drifted away.

This wasn't a dream. This was her life.

# Chapter 25

A siren screamed outside, almost drowning out the hoots of the seven o'clock morning train from Florida. Tenny shrugged it off. TB patients rarely arrived in ambulances.

Today was a split shift, and the first leg meant hustling. Until eleven o'clock she bathed patients, helped them into fresh bedclothes, changed sheets, and collected sputum cups. Leaving the lab, she had just a few minutes to get to her anatomy lecture.

Outside the classroom, Alice, face gaunt with exhaustion, struggled on her gimpy leg. Tenny stood aside to let her enter first.

"Oh! What a morning!" Alice shook her head as they settled into their seats. "Where's Dr. Hooper?"

"Did you hear that siren? Hope he's not called to an emergency." Three other students filed in and took their places.

Alice shook her head. "They brought one in last night. I had to help out. It was awful."

"Lucky you. What happened?" Tenny took out her notebook and pencil.

Alice shook her head again. "A girl came in all beat up. From the mill village. She made the mistake of getting between her boyfriend and some troublemakers. Sounded like the fight had to do with strike plans."

Tenny shivered. "Is she going to be okay?"

Alice sighed. "Battered head, lots of bruising. Cranial hematoma. The surgeon operated, but nobody knows how much it'll affect her brain when she recovers."

Tenny's stomach clenched. The pictures would never go away: her sister's head with that gigantic bruise, the grim look on the doctor's face. "Alice—what was her name?"

Before Alice could answer, Dr. Hooper strode into the room, impassive behind his neat beard, a pointer in his hand. He walked over to the flip chart at the side of the room and heaved it open. Pink and glistening illustrations of intestines in both front view and cross-section greeted the students.

"Today we will study the digestive system," he said crisply. "Open your books to Chapter 5." Tenny hardly heard the first part of the lecture. The night Shelley had been run down had been a freaky cold one for September, wind whistling around the eaves and slicing through the chinks in the little house. Poor Shelley lay on a narrow pallet, and it seemed an eternity until the doctor came around in his tin lizzie.

The smoky kerosene lanterns guttered in the little room. Deathly pale, Shelley lay motionless as the doctor drew back the clean blanket that covered her. He gazed down, frowning, at her injuries. He touched and gently prodded her limbs and ribcage, but the main bruise was to her head, now purple and swelling.

"What happened?" the doctor asked flatly.

Tenny's mother, belly out to *there*, choked out a wail, chewing on the edge of a knotted handkerchief. Her father took another swig from a Mason jar.

Meredith stood up from her chair by Mama's bed. "The little 'uns was out picking muscadines by the side of the road, so we could have us some muscadine jelly, they did love that jelly . . ." She stopped for a moment to compose herself, gulped. "The boys come along, three of them, racing along the road. I think they was having a horse race, you know." She swallowed. "They run her down, they did."

"Are you saying they did it deliberately?"

"Nossir. I swear I don't know how it happened." Merry hung her head. "Tenny seen it."

Now all eyes turned to Tenny. She looked over at the doctor, and he was gazing at her, encouraging. "Yes, Tenny?" She licked her lips and darted a look at the dark-haired nurse, and wondered if she was the doctor's wife.

"I didn't see much," Tenny said. "It happened so quick." She closed her eyes and tried hard to make sense of her jumbled thoughts.

"Take your time," the doctor said. "What were you doing before?"

That was easier. "Shelley said there was some vines on the other side of the road hanging low, and she headed over there. I still had some ripe ones to hand, so I didn't follow her. Just then I heard all this whooping and hollering and they come over the rise, these boys, and Shelley stood in the road like she didn't know which way to go and she jumped the wrong way and two of them missed her but the other one didn't. Knocked her slap down and the horse stumbled and the boy almost fell off.

"He slid off the horse and came over. It was Eben Shackley. He picked Shelley up and carried her back to the house, about a mile."

The doctor nodded. "It was Eben who telephoned me," he said. "She needs to go to the hospital. We'll take her there."

Her mother looked up with swollen eyes. "We can't pay."

The doctor set his mouth. "Arno Shackley will get the bill, I believe."

"No," Ma said, white-faced, gripping the chair. "We can look after her here."

"She must go," the doctor said, "or she will surely die."

It was Meredith who finally spoke. "We're in debt to him, already, you know, at the store."

"I'll have a word with Shackley," said the doctor.

They took Shelley away in the car, and when a nice lady from the county finally brought her back, Tenny knew she had lost her twin sister. In her place was this vacant-eyed stranger. She felt as though half of herself was gone forever.

Nothing had ever been said about paying the doctor or the hospital, but Arno Shackley took more of the crop and Pa started making moonshine for him.

"Miss Oakes?"

Tenny's eyes snapped into focus. "Yes, Doctor?"

"I would suggest you pay attention. When you do your colonic irriga-tions, you need to know what's happening inside."

"I'm sorry, Doctor." She felt a deep flush creeping up her cheeks.

"Please see me after class."

"Yes, Doctor." She bent to her book, heart thudding, for she knew Dr. Hooper's reputation for strictness.

After the lecture was finished, the doctor closed the chart and stood by while the girls filtered out of class. Tenny approached the desk and swallowed while he drummed his fingers on the desk, waiting until the last girl had left before he spoke.

"Miss Oakes," he said, "you're one of my best students. You're a girl who knows what she's about. But I will not tolerate inattention in my class. The thing you miss will be the thing you need to know at a critical moment."

"Yes, sir."

His voice was hard. "May I ask what you were doing? Dreaming of some *boy*?" The last word had a knife edge. Did he know of her background?

"No, sir." She cleared her throat and straightened her shoulders. "Somebody told me before class about a patient that got knocked down in a fight, cranial hematoma, and it started me thinking of my sister. She's not right in the head."

Doctor Hooper frowned. "What?"

Tenny flushed. "I mean she had a brain injury. Run down by a horse."

His eyebrows raised and his tone softened. "I see. Where is she now?"

Tenny grew still. She knew she had to answer. "She's helping to keep house for my daddy. My mother's dead."

The doctor's expression relaxed. "All right, Miss Oakes. I'll give you some extra reading on the brain. I'll bring the book next class. For today's lapse, please outline Chapter 5, answer the questions at the end, and bring the pages back to me."

"Yes, sir. Thank you!"

It could have been much worse. On her way out, Tenny glanced down at the watch pinned to her uniform. She barely had enough time to get to the next class, eat lunch, and make it back to the ward for the afternoon shift.

Her mind was still on Shelley as she made her rounds of the men, taking temperatures, updating the chart, assisting with toileting. She was becoming hardened to it by now. She was entering the bathroom with a bedpan when Enid appeared with the medicine tray.

"Carry it more securely, Oakes," Enid said. "You'll slosh urine all over the floor."

"I've never lost a drop." She tightened her grip on the pan. She'd like to overturn it on Enid's head.

"You can distribute the medications. Be sure to wash your hands."

*Wash her hands,* indeed. As if she needed to be told. "Isn't medication your job?"

Enid narrowed her eyes. "I'm giving you more responsibility, Oakes. I'll leave the tray just inside the door."

When Tenny came back from dumping the bedpan, hands scrubbed raw, Enid was nowhere in sight. Where had that wretched girl gone? Tenny, tired of covering for the older student every time she disappeared, walked the rows of beds, handing out pills in small metal cups and filling water jugs. Then she emptied their sputum cups.

She'd heard tales of careless nurses catching TB, so she scrubbed again when she finished.

She was wheeling one of the older men out to the solarium when Enid strode back down the hall, a mysterious smirk on her face. Tenny, nodding briefly, passed her.

"Wait. Where are you going, Oakes?"

Tenny stopped and took a slow breath. "Mr. Dodson needs to walk now."

"I can take him back. I want you to scrub the floor of the medication room."

Tenny tightened the grip on the chair handles. "Mr. Dodson needs to get up, or he'll get bedsores."

Mr. Dodson, thin, with a long shock of white hair and an angular, knowing face, looked up at the mention of his name.

"I can take him," Enid said, reaching for the handles of the rolling chair.

Mr. Dodson's wrinkled face hardened and he glared at Enid. "My name's Dodson," he said, "and I don't want *you.*"

"Now, Mr. Dodson," Enid said.

"Don't you *Now, Mr. Dodson* me," he growled.

The tense silence mounted. Someone laughed, far down the hall. A door closed. Tenny waited. And then Enid took a step back, face unreadable. "Go ahead, Oakes. But that floor had better be clean before you go off duty."

The old man winked at Tenny as they rolled away.

In the solarium, Tenny helped Mr. Dodson shuffle around while he talked about his youngest son. "He promised to come see me after he got off work," he said. "Good boy, but I wish I had a daughter. Just like you,"

"Oh, Mr. Dodson." She tapped him playfully. "How do you know I wouldn't be trouble?"

"Nope," he said. "Not you. I wouldn't want one like that Nurse Barlow. Always sneaking off to see her fella."

"Her fellow?" Tenny stopped in front of a tall window and gazed out at sunshine dappling the lawn and the tall oak trees.

Mr. Dodson grabbed a paper handkerchief from his pajama pocket and had a fit of coughing into it. Then he said, "One of them interns. Us sick-uns see plenty when they think we don't."

"Mr. Dodson, don't spread gossip."

"I'm just telling you. You think about that when you're down there with that scrub brush." He coughed again. "You go ahead and leave me here for a spell. I'll be fine."

Tenny replenished Mr. Dodson with handkerchiefs, left him in the solarium, and went for the bucket and scrub brush. She scrubbed the medicine room thoroughly—and thoughtfully.

When she went back for the old man, he was tired, and she wheeled him back to his bed, settling him in for a nap. Right before he closed his eyes, he said, "Watch out for that Nurse Barlow, now."

The old man knew more than he was telling her.

When Tenny got back to her room that night, she found her roommate at her desk, pen in hand. "I was just writing to Dan," Alice said.

"Finished your studying for the Materia Medica test?"

"I need to study." Alice sighed and laid down the pen. "But I haven't written Dan in days and days, and I miss him so." She picked up her book on medicines from the bedside desk and flipped its pages. "I'm already behind a quarter. Do I really want to be a trained nurse? I ought to just go back home and marry Dan."

"Why did you come, then?" Tenny spoke a little sharply, but Alice had always had people to look after her. Her father, a Methodist preacher, always had something nice to say to them, and her mother, who played the piano at church, brought the girls cookies shaped like harps and lyres.

"It was my raising," Alice said. "Service to humanity. Mother wanted me to study music like her, but I can't even carry a tune. I thought I might be a missionary to Africa. Doesn't that sound thrilling? The church will send you more quickly if you know nursing, so I came here. I didn't know it would be so *hard*."

Tenny sank to her own bed. "Alice, don't take the easy way out. What if something happens to Dan? Or your folks? You don't want to marry somebody just to have a roof over your head."

"Of course not." Alice smiled sheepishly. "I like nursing, really. Just not tests. Let's study together."

"Copacetic. One question first. That mill girl that was in the fight. Did you get her name?"

"The main thing I remember," said Alice, "is that huge amount of curly brown hair I had to shave off."

Tenny's stomach gripped. Could it be her one friend from those days? "I might know her," she said slowly. "Is her name Ramona Finch?"

"Finch? That might be it. Why?" Alice scooted up higher in bed and leaned forward. "Tell me about her."

"A long time ago," Tenny said, "I worked in the mill."

"Oh," breathed Alice. "The mill! Was it terrible?"

"It wasn't too bad," Tenny said, edging the truth. Half the TB cases were mill workers. Sheltered Alice probably wouldn't believe her if she told her what the conditions were really like for the girls. "I'd like to go see Ramona, if it's Ramona."

"If she pulls through." Alice looked away.

Tenny clenched her fist. "She's tough. She'll fight."

"Come to her room around lunchtime," said Alice. "We'll be clearing trays for the patients."

Tenny nodded. "I'll be there." She reached over and picked up her Materia Medica book. She opened it to the study questions page. "If a patient's temperature is 102.6 on a clinical Fahrenheit thermometer, what would it be on the Centigrade scale?"

"I'm doomed." Alice laid her head on her desk and covered it with her arms. "And why do we need to *know* that?"

Alice was still struggling with their materia medica test when Tenny turned in her paper and left the room. She stopped by the dining hall and folded a large square of cornbread in her handkerchief. She slid the bundle in her pocket; that would do for lunch.

She hurried down one corridor, up two flights of stairs, and down another corridor to the women's surgical ward. She wanted to check on the mill girl that had gotten injured.

Scanning the rows of beds, at first she didn't see anyone she knew. Then she saw a head turbaned with bandages, cheek bruised, lips swollen, eyes closed. She quietly stepped over to her side. When she saw the freckles, she knew the patient was her friend Ramona. She touched the sleeping girl gently on the arm; the girl's eyelids fluttered open and then blinked.

"I don't believe what I'm seeing," the patient croaked.

Tenny crouched beside the bed. "It's me, Tenny. I'm a nurse in training here."

"Holy cow. Look at you in that striped dress and white apron and that cap. That's a damn cute outfit." She looked harder. "What the heck happened to your hair?"

Tenny laughed with relief that Ramona was still the Ramona she remembered. "Sssh. Tell you later." She laid a hand on Ramona's shoulder. "How is the pain?"

"Worse'n yesterday," Ramona said with a grimace that told more than words.

"It'll be better tomorrow," Tenny soothed. She held Ramona's wrist and felt for the pulse. Strong, steady. Tenny's fear and dread eased.

"I'll make it out of here." Ramona's voice was weak, but determined. "It's my job I'm worried about. That Mr. Fletcher'd soon fire you as look at you."

Tenny took a deep breath. "I saw in the paper where he got married. Went on a honeymoon to Cuba."

"Marriage won't change him none," Ramona said, struggling to lift herself up. "Just make him meaner, is all."

"Easy, now." Tenny plumped the pillows and caught Ramona under the arms, helping her to sit, then she straightened her blanket. "Have you seen his wife?"

"Not hardly. Hurry-up wedding. They say it was shotgun."

"Holy cow!" Tenny said. "I wonder if she'll come here to have the baby."

Ramona giggled. "What if you met him!"

"Oh, I doubt I'll be doing OB then, anyhow," Tenny said. Maybe there was some way she could finagle the assignment, but students spent three months on each duty before rotating. "Enough about me," she finally said. "Tell me what happened."

Ramona gave a deep sigh. "Do you remember Joe Kinley? He's my sweetie now. He's in with the union crowd, wants one so we can stop getting stomped on. He and some of the other guys have been meeting in secret. We were all leaving the meeting late one night and a gang jumped us."

"A gang? Who was it, do you know?"

"Hired gang, I think, supposed to scare us," Ramona said slowly. "Joe took it bad, did some damage. He was in France, you know, and knows how to fight. I was trying to pull him off before he finished off a goon and I got clobbered with a two-by-four. One of our guys got away and called the cops, or we might all be dead."

"Oh, Lord." Hair prickled the back of Tenny's neck.

"What galls me, is how they knew where we were."

"Somebody had a big mouth," Tenny said.

"I suspect that Clete Mincus." Ramona's voice hardened. "Too many women, too much talk." She paused. "Or he's a spy, paid by the boss to be a turncoat. There's bound to be more fighting."

Alice, returning to the ward, caught Tenny's eye. Tenny glanced down at her watch. "Oh gosh, I've got to go on duty," she said. "I'll try to get back to see you."

"I don't suppose you have any pull with the kitchen? They're trying to starve me," Ramona said.

Tenny laughed. "Alice here had kitchen duty last quarter. Ask her to see what she can do."

She hurried down the long corridors and up three flights of steps and still came into the men's TB ward panting. Enid stood by the door, face stony.

"Five minutes late, Nurse," she said. "For that you can stay an extra half hour."

"Enid," Tenny stopped, her hand on the door frame. "Why do you have it in for me?"

Enid narrowed her eyes. "People like you need extra discipline."

"People like *what?*" Tenny's spine stiffened.

Enid raised her well-plucked eyebrows. "You had a baby in this very hospital and gave it up for adoption. You have three months extra probation."

Tenny dug her nails into her palm to stop herself from lashing out, conscious of ears beyond the nurses' station. A motion from the ward caught her eye. "Excuse me," she said in clipped tones. "I think Mr. Dodson needs me."

She walked over to his bed. "Lean closer," the old man whispered. She put her ear near his mouth, but not too near, conscious of tubercle bacilli.

"They're still at it."

"Be quiet, Mr. Dodson," she said, calmly smiling.

"Catch 'em," he urged.

Catch them? The problem was that Enid was threatening her, intimidating her so that she'd never complain about the cigarettes or the extra duty or picking up Enid's work so she could sneak off with an intern.

Did Enid think Tenny was afraid of people knowing she'd been an unwed mother?

She was, actually.

Miss Wells had told them the nursing profession was bent on wiping out the last remnants of bad nursing, the slovenly duty that Florence Nightingale fought against. Nurses should be seen as professionals, as healing angels.

A fallen angel would never do. Especially not one with three months' probation still to serve. Miss Wells knew where Tenny had come from, of course, and had admitted her anyway. But few others knew. How long could Dr. Godwin's protection hold out?

She'd fight to keep this chance.

She gazed over at the patients, mostly napping, and picked up a chart to review. She knew that this hospital was where she belonged. It felt right, being here. After Shelley had been hurt, Tenny had cared for her, and the caring had made her feel needed. She missed Shelley now.

She made a notation and set the chart aside, deep in thought. A long time ago, Ma had showed Tenny the special pages in the back of the Bible where she'd written down healing receipts she'd copied from her grandmother, who had learned them many years before from an old granny woman who was part black and part Creek Indian.

Tenny hadn't yet learned her letters then, but she helped Ma make the potions and poultices.

She'd begged Pa to let her go to school. She wanted to read. Why, he grumbled, did a girl need to learn to read while there was plenty of work at the farm? He finally agreed to send her to school after Mrs. Brown, the pastor's wife, came to call one Sunday afternoon bringing blackberry jam.

Mrs. Brown oohed and aahed over Tenny, saying how smart she was, that if she knew her letters she could read the Bible and the Farmer's Almanac to them all. Then Pa thought that might be useful, because Milton couldn't read worth a durn, Ma needed new specs they couldn't afford, and Byron was usually out hunting or fishing.

When the midwife came to assist at her mother's birthing, Tenny stood by, carrying water and clean rags, and then the birthing had turned terribly wrong, and her brother Byron had taken off as fast as he could on the mule to fetch the doctor. The doctor couldn't help much. The baby was gone, and Ma lived only a few days after that. Childbed fever, they called it.

And they buried Mama next to the baby Meredith named Charles Lamb out of Mama's poem book, because he was an innocent lamb.

Pastor Jethro Brown came to pray with them, and Mrs. Brown came to visit every week for a while. Tenny took wildflowers to the baby's small grave—long stems of blue-flowering flaxweed in springtime and Cherokee roses in summer and wild asters in the fall. She would sit there and pray and wish she could have saved them.

That evening, one of the patients died.

Tenny found him already gone while she was making her rounds. Enid had left on one of her "errands." Choking back tears, Tenny sent another probationer, Bessie White, for the doctor. She would get used to deaths. She had to.

When the doctor arrived at the ward, Enid slipped in the door just behind him and joined the other two nurses.

"Were you here when it happened?" the doctor asked Enid, the senior nurse.

"I'd gone to the sterilizer," she said. "These two were here," she said, indicating Tenny and Bessie White.

The doctor raised an eyebrow, and Tenny told him what had happened. He said nothing but frowned at Enid. Enid at once sent Bessie and Tenny to pull a sheet over the patient and screen the bed while she found the patient's chart.

"She didn't go to the sterilizer," Bessie whispered to Tenny as they pulled the wood and canvas screen in place.

But what could they do?

# Chapter 26

NOVEMBER–DECEMBER 1925

P apa wasn't through with Gussie. She waited for days after they'd arrived home while the judge, busy with court cases and lectures, went about his business as if nothing had happened.

Then one morning at breakfast, after Ned had left for the mill grumbling about a rumor of union organizers, the judge finished his coffee, put down his *Atlanta Constitution*, and rose from the table. "Augusta, I want to talk to you."

"Now?" Gussie crumpled her napkin and laid it carefully beside her plate. The morning queasiness she'd thought was gone was returning, and her heart raced.

"I have a class to meet, young lady," he said. "I'll see you on the porch after supper, without the King of Siam."

"Oh, Papa. Why do you call him that?"

"Because he acts like he's got a fancy pointed crown on his head and expects people to bow down. Especially you."

"Oh, Papa. I do wish you'd like him." Gussie kissed his cheek, saw him off to work, and went upstairs to lie down until the queasiness went away. As soon as she felt better, she got up, made the bed, and tidied the room, hanging Ned's bathrobe in the closet. She noticed two valises he'd brought over from his rented room. Not only were they taking up closet space, the unpacked cases made her feel uneasy. What was in them?

She'd just dragged the first one out of the closet when Velma called to tell her that a package had been delivered. She shoved the case back and went downstairs.

The department store box was addressed to Mrs. Ned Fletcher, c/o Judge Pemberton. "Late wedding present," Velma remarked.

Gussie cut the string, lifted the top off the large square box, and parted white tissue paper. "Oh!" Gussie lifted out a floppy Panama just like the one the dog had chewed.

Velma frowned. "Who be sending you a *hat*?"

"Oh, Velma. I think Ned has surprised me." Who else could it be?

Velma chuckled in approval, and Gussie hustled the box up to her room before she pulled out the card stuck under the band. A man's visiting card. *Mr. Henry Franklin Benedict.* On the back, *Sorry I couldn't save it.*

Gussie couldn't breathe for a moment. She shook her head and stuffed the card in her pocket. She'd never told Ned about meeting Henry. If she told him now, he'd think she had something to hide. Of course she didn't, but Ned had never even missed the hat, had he? Why stir up trouble?

Henry probably spent the money he'd earned from her father to buy the hat. She ought to return it, but she had loved that hat and its reminder of the church, of the old padre, of the boy, Rafael.

She bit her lip and stuffed the hatbox under the bed. Then she placed the hat on the shelf and tore up the visiting card. She hoped Velma would be discreet.

That evening, after a good supper of pot roast, carrots, and Irish potatoes, after Ned had settled by the fire in the library with the *Ashbyville Clarion* and the *Wall Street Journal*, the judge nodded to Gussie and headed to the front porch with his pipe.

Gussie, taking her shawl, joined him. Papa rocked in a slat-bottomed chair, fragrant smoke floating into the twilight. A gas streetlamp flickered into flame, and the moon climbed above the trees. Her throat felt dry. "Papa?"

"Sit down, my dear."

Gussie settled in a rocker, wrapped her shawl, and creaked in the gray evening dimness. "Don't you want the porch lamp?"

"Draws bugs," the judge said, "and this way I get a show." With the stem of his pipe, he pointed across the street, where the lace curtains framed pretty Mrs. Evelyn Marbury practicing her piano, the scales tinkling up and down.

"Papa, you're incorrigible," Gussie laughed.

"I think you know what I want to talk about."

"Now, Papa . . ." She felt her voice rising an octave.

"You're in a snit because I sent young Henry to check up on you. You've been afraid to ask me about it."

She leaned forward. "Papa, why'd you do it?"

The judge drew on his pipe. "I was alarmed to get that telegram, Augusta. In my line of work I see plenty of meanness. I see women beat up and the man thinking it's his right. Sometimes he even gets *them* to thinking it's his right."

Gussie burst in, "Papa, I swear to you Ned's never laid a hand on me. It was just a . . . just a lover's quarrel, and I was . . . I was just being silly."

The judge took a few more puffs, rocking. "If it's two wills clashing, then it's one thing. More serious if he hasn't been honest with you."

Gussie took short, shallow breaths. "I don't know about that, Papa."

Her father stopped rocking. "Then you need to find out. My girl, you're so blinded by moonbeams you can't see his character. I hope Ned's a good man under all this Barnum and Bailey show, because he's hiding something."

Gussie closed her eyes. "I'm not blind, Papa."

Her father gazed outward, smoke drifting off to join clouds scudding across the moon. "Pity things happened the way they did."

"Papa," Gussie said. "Ned loves me. He tells me all the time."

The judge paused for a long moment. "He's told us plenty—about losing the family farm in Virginia and seeking his fortune in Florida and Massachusetts. We haven't met any of his people."

"But, Papa," she said. "They're all dead except one sister, and he doesn't get along with her."

"So he says. But aunts, uncles, cousins? All wiped out in the influenza epidemic of '18? Seems farfetched."

Gussie looked at the floor. She agreed with Papa but didn't want to say so. Of her twelve aunts and uncles, she'd lost only one to the epidemic. She raised her chin. "Oh, Papa. Don't be such a judge."

The judge shook his head. "I don't have enough evidence to convict Ned of intent to break your heart. I won't keep you any longer, daughter. But you need to find out more about him."

"Maybe he'll tell me in good time, Papa," she said. "I'll leave you to your pipe." She rose and went to the door before she realized there was something Papa hadn't told her. She turned and faced him. "Can I ask you a question?"

"Shoot."

"Why do you like this Henry Benedict so much?" There. Was Papa throwing him at her?

Papa gazed at her, smiling mysteriously. "I give him jobs because he can use the money. His widowed mother supports the two of them doing office work at the mill."

"How do you know them?"

"His father was the district attorney," the judge said. "As good a friend as a man could have, and I still miss him. I still believe he was murdered."

"Murdered?"

"Automobile crashed into a tree out in the country," the judge said. "No witnesses."

"I didn't remember," Gussie said in a small voice.

"You were a little miss of twelve then," the judge said. "Ruled an accident. Henry thinks not. Talks about poking around like Sherlock Holmes. I told him to stick to his education. I don't want him killed too."

Gussie stood in the shadows and watched moths bat against the door. "You know who did it, don't you?"

"No proof," the judge said. "They made sure of that. Go on, that's all I have to say now."

"All right, Papa." Gussie could hear Papa drawing on his pipe as she opened the screen door and slipped back into the house. The way he said "they" meant it was the Klan.

"By the way, Augusta," her father called. "I'd like to see the pictures you took with that gadget I gave you."

The pictures! They were downstairs in the darkroom drying. She'd nearly forgotten them. She smiled uncertainly. "I'll have them tomorrow. I think I hear Mama calling me about those dishes."

She was glad to be at the sink. She plunged her hands into soapsuds, scrubbing, scrubbing, scrubbing. She ought to tell Papa that Ned had borrowed from that Max person who looked like a gangster, but she just couldn't.

"Damn!" Ned, tie draped halfway around his neck, was dressing for work the next day. "Where are those cuff links you gave me?"

Gussie smoothed the bed covers and plumped the pillows. She'd last seen them in Cuba. "Have you unpacked everything from the trip, Ned?"

"Sure. How about looking around today for me?"

"All right." Gussie dug a toe into the rug and bit her lip. What if Ned had sold them for Max's gambling debt and was trying to make her think he'd misplaced them? Was Papa was making her doubt Ned? Still, the cuff links had been 14-karat-gold ones that had belonged to Mama's father, Grandpapa Poe, a distant cousin of the writer.

Ned thrust his jaw and tied his tie, then dove into his cuff link box and brought out another gold pair, very modern. Art Deco.

Ned and Papa and Jessie departed, Mama attacked her typewriter, and Velma shooed Gussie out of the kitchen, saying she had to wax the floor. The sky outside hung gloomy and overcast, a November chill settling in and the smell of rain tickling the air. No day for taking pictures.

Gussie hurried down to the darkroom for the Kodak shots of Cuba, mostly scenes of the hurricane's destruction. Papa would like the lepers and Rafael and the padre. She unclipped the prints from the line and laid them on the worktable. The little camera had done its best, but the quality of her Graflex wasn't there.

There were only two photos of her and Ned. She'd asked the *fotingo* driver to snap them as they were leaving the hotel: standing by a downed palm tree on the curb, stalwart hotel in the background, Gussie in linen dress and long jacket, Ned in his ice-cream suit. He'd pulled his hat brim low, his white teeth gleaming, an Ipana toothpaste ad. On the first shot he looked toward the camera; on the second he appeared to be looking past it. The smile appeared forced.

That was just before Max and Sylvia had come to say good-bye, and she'd snapped them too, because they posed, grinning, Max's arm around Sylvia's shoulder. She placed the print apart from the stack of prints for Papa. Something caught her eye, and she picked up her magnifying glass to examine the Max and Sylvia picture. What she saw made her stomach knot.

She tugged the first case out of the closet and unbuckled its strap. A beautiful array of haberdashery lay before her. She lifted out colorful silk ties, soft suede gloves, silver cuff links, a supple leather wallet, two crisp folded shirts of finest cotton, a black velvet bag of collars, a set of silver brushes, and a bottle of French cologne. Gifts, by the look of them. Someone had given these things to Ned. Who?

She shoved the case aside, not bothering to repack it, and tackled the second valise, a heavy one. She found it full of books, fragrant with the scent of leather and old paper.

She lifted out a Webster's dictionary, a history of the United States, a biography of Teddy Roosevelt, a couple of Tarzan novels, and a book called *Poise: How to Attain It*, one of the Mental Efficiency Series. Here was another, *Opportunities: How to Make the Most of Them*, as well as *1000 Things Worth Knowing* by Nathaniel Fowler. She gazed at a manual of bicycle repair. Perhaps he'd owned one when he was younger. She was about to lay the manual aside when she noticed the edge of a photograph stuck between the pages.

With thumb and forefinger she pulled it out.

A pretty young woman in a shirtwaist and long skirt, her wavy hair piled atop her head Gibson Girl style, stood gripping a pair of bicycle handlebars. Her mischievous smile revealed that she was fond of the photographer. The sign behind her read *Grady's Bicycles*, and behind the bicycle grew three Spanish bayonet plants and two azalea bushes. Gussie flipped the photo over. *Sarah Grady, 1917* was scrawled in blocky handwriting.

Was this the sister Sarah Ned had mentioned, the sister who married the man she loved instead of rescuing the family plantation? Or some other Sarah? She tucked the picture into the pocket of her dress and lifted the last book out of the box. A popular novel, *The Lyttons of Carrington Hall*. But she'd never seen Ned read a novel. Maybe it had belonged to this Sarah.

A stack of papers lay on the bottom of the box. Just as Gussie reached for them, door hinges squealed behind her. She sat back on her heels, heart thumping, and looked over her shoulder. Her mother filled the doorway, hands on hips.

"Augusta! Didn't you hear me calling you? And whatever are you doing?"

She shrugged. "Unpacking Ned's cases."

Her mother raised an eyebrow. "You'd best let them be. If he thinks you're snooping, he might be angry."

"Let him be rabid," Gussie said stubbornly. "He lost the cuff links I gave him. I was looking for them."

Belinda gave Gussie that *mother* look. "I understand. But everyone is entitled to some privacy, married or not."

Gussie clenched her jaw and stared at her toes. "Papa wanted me to find out more about Ned."

Belinda stopped for a moment. "Let's discuss this later. You need something to do. I'm going to the Inez Callahan Home today to take them a few things: books, a bundle of clothes from the church, soap, shampoo. I'd like you to help."

"But I was going to take pictures," Gussie said crossly, knowing a command when she heard one. "Why do I have to go?"

"You ought to see how good you have it with a loving family," her mother said. "Your Uncle Emmett told me of a girl he got into nursing school because she couldn't go back home. Those girls need support after their babies come, and I can help them. Now put all that away and get your coat."

Gussie reluctantly stacked the books back in the valise, covering the papers she'd wanted so badly to examine. Her mother wouldn't stop talking.

"We can have lunch in town afterward and do some shopping. I've made an appointment with Mrs. Dalrymple this afternoon at three, and I want you to pick out some fabrics. Those slim little dresses won't fit you much longer."

Gussie laid the dictionary on top and closed the case. "Mama! Why didn't you ask me if I wanted any dresses made? Ned will complain that he can buy them."

Her mother's smile turned rueful. "He'd better be grateful. You've never turned down any gifts before. What's gotten into you?"

Gussie laid the beautiful shirts in the first case and placed the other gifts as best she remembered. "Mama, Ned has his pride." She closed the top and tried to rise to her feet, but it wasn't easy.

Her mother held out a hand to help. "Please explain, then, why Ned is pressing your father to give you two that rental house outright?"

Gussie, on her feet, reeled. "He keeps saying he doesn't want Papa's money. I don't understand it."

"Methinks he doth protest too much," her mother said.

"Oh, Shakespeare—*ouch*!" Something was jabbing her stomach. She yanked at her knickers and found that the safety pin holding them together had burst open. Her favorite frock had ripped at the seam yesterday. She *did* need some clothes.

Grumpily, she set the valises back in the closet, changed into her roomiest dress, got her coat and hat, and followed her mother out. She would never tell her mother that Max the gambler was wearing Ned's cuff links.

On the way back from the dressmaker, Gussie asked her mother, "Mama, did you ever read a book called *The Lyttons of Carrington Hall?*"

"I don't think so. Why?"

"Oh, somebody on the boat was reading it. I was just curious. I could use a new book."

"Then get yourself to the library, my dear."

She hoped Mama wouldn't mention the book at supper. Luckily, Jessie, the bookworm, was helping with a school event and wasn't there. If only Gussie hadn't dropped the darn fork.

When she bent down to retrieve it, she felt a hand at her pocket. "What's this? Cuba?" she heard. The hand plucked the photo she'd found and she bolted up straight, only to find Ned staring at the image.

He was smiling. "You found this picture of my sister! I thought I'd lost it."

He passed it around the table, saying, "my sister Sarah." He patted Gussie's hand. "Where'd you say you found it?"

Gussie let his hand rest on hers and composed herself. "Marking a place in a bicycle repair manual. You hadn't unpacked two bags in the closet, and I thought I might as well do it while I was looking for your missing cuff links."

Ned withdrew his hand. "There was no need to unpack, Gussie. We'll be moving shortly." His voice was low, almost threatening.

"Well, I put everything back. Mama was ready to go help the wayward girls." Gussie forced a nonchalant tone, and he seemed to relax, but Mama shot her a displeased glance.

Papa and Mama complimented Ned on his fine-looking sister.

He explained smoothly that the bicycle shop belonged to the man her sister had married for love in Roanoke, the town near their ruined plantation. He was angry that she'd chosen this man of commerce over a man from their own circle: if she'd married a man of property, he could have bought their land and kept it in the family.

Sarah had become the ungrateful sister who didn't know her duty! The bicycle shop had a lot to do with why they didn't speak. When the picture came back to Ned, he slipped it into his billfold.

Gussie's jaw clenched. Hadn't he told her that his sister had run away with a traveling salesman? Maybe that was just his name for Mr. Grady. Or not. She kept her composure while the toasted pound cake and ice cream was served, and then she said she was feeling puky and fled to her room without looking at her mother.

She heard Ned's footsteps on the stairs behind her. He followed her into the room before she could close the door. "Why did you go looking through my things?" he said mildly, almost as if it didn't matter.

Gussie sank to the bed. "I told you. You said you had lost my grandpapa's cuff links. For all I knew, they might be in there."

"I see." He snapped his fingers. "Well, I'll take care of those cases. Right now."

Gussie had learned that a brisk, artificial manner meant Ned was rattled and trying not to show it.

He unpacked all the haberdashery and put away the beautiful shirts and silver cuff links in the dresser, and then he picked up the case of books and papers. "I'll take these books to the office. There's room in the bookcase there. I'll take them to the car so I won't forget."

He didn't come back upstairs. Gussie heard her father's new radio, and figured Ned had stayed listening with Papa, although not much was broadcast tonight except sermons and music.

Maybe he would benefit by the sermons.

He didn't return until bedtime, and when she tried to ask him more about Sarah, he shrugged and said he didn't like to talk about her. Maybe one day. Then he bent and kissed Gussie and ran his hands up and down her body, giving her long soulful kisses that tasted of honey and licorice lozenges. He whispered that she was his own, his lovely, his beautiful Augusta . . .

Despite herself, despite her misgivings, despite his evasions about Sarah, she melted. The little devil of outrage about the cuff links climbed down from her shoulder, but the devil's pitchfork left a prickly stab.

Gray shoals of sleep were overtaking her, Ned gently snoring by her side, when she suddenly blinked awake. Something had not been right about that picture of Sarah. The question teased her and vexed her in the pale sliver of moonlight until she finally fell asleep.

# Chapter 27

C hristmas Eve. Tenny walked the halls after their supper of corn
chowder and ham biscuits with pickled peaches and didn't see
Pete Godwin anywhere. She'd put too much hope that he'd spend his
holidays here.

She didn't mind being at the hospital. What she missed were the old
days when Ma was alive with songs and love and presents, conjured
from scraps and spools and home-dyed yarn, when Pa's punched tin
lantern transformed their bare wood walls into a star-speckled sky.

Tenny's only present this year was a box of chocolates from Mr.
Dodson, which made her smile, and her tree was the one in the hospital
lobby, with real store-bought baubles and tinsel.

She was on her way to the children's ward with some books she'd
collected to read to them while they were waiting for Santa. Shelley, her
child-like sister, had always been so excited about Christmas. She wished
she could read to her too.

Enid Smith Barlow passed her in the hall, walking at a rapid clip, and barely nodded. So she was on duty? How had that happened? Couldn't her uncle get her excused? The night couldn't get any worse.

Pete Godwin admired the Christmas tree in the big waiting room at the hospital, enjoying its fragrant woodsy smell, its colored lights and silver tinsel. He'd rather spend Christmas Eve at the hospital than go with his parents and brother to Uncle Mac's get-together, with all those lawyers.

He hurried up the stairs, hoping to see Miss Oakes, his father's recruit, who'd refused to let him watch the birth of her baby. A quick talk with the floor nurse revealed that the young probationer was reading to the children in the pediatric ward.

Miss Oakes intrigued him. Her hair had so much resembled that of the girl he'd seen on the riverbank, the girl he'd seen in front of Jones's livery stable. Miss Oakes herself was a bit of a mystery. He wondered how she'd come to be at the Callahan Home. She didn't seem like any type of wild or loose girl. He wondered if she'd loved anyone. Or had she been forced?

He made his rounds and focused on the patients, trying to bring comfort to those who were lonely, wishing they could be elsewhere. He took a stroll by the pediatric ward and glanced in; sure enough, he spotted Miss Oakes at the far end, book in hand, making funny faces at the children as she read.

He became aware that a tall man was standing by his side, watching over his head. "She's come a good ways, hasn't she?"

Pete recognized Brother Peregrine Falkner. "You know Miss Oakes?" he said in astonishment.

"Took her to the Callahan home after I found her in the park. They'd fired her from the mill. I might speak to her after she finishes reading."

Pete, embarrassed at being caught watching Tenny, said he had patients to see and left Brother Perry standing there. He mulled over what Brother Perry had told him. So she'd worked at the mill. Where Fletcher worked. His mood grew dark.

After checking on two patients, he stopped by the staff lounge for a cup of coffee.

"Hello, Pete. Merry Christmas." Enid Smith Barlow's face shone like tinsel when she saw him, and she gave him a quick hug.

"Enid, nice to see you. Merry Christmas. Why aren't you out celebrating?" He poured a cup from the electric percolator and sank to the sofa. She used to be a regular at Swanee Burkett's parties. In school they'd been thick as thieves. But Swanee was spending the holidays in Europe this year.

She shrugged. "Why, I wanted to help out. Uncle George told me how much it meant to some of the girls to get this night off, and since Father died, well, Christmas just isn't the same."

Pete sipped his coffee. He had no illusions about Enid. She was no Florence Nightingale. After all, Enid had not been able to make a debut, as it would have been unthinkable for her to go to parties in the year after her father's death. Not to mention the question of money. Enid and her mother had run through the inheritance pretty quickly.

"Won't your mother miss you?"

Enid lifted her shoulders. "Mama's gone over to Granny's, and I might as well be here, where people are glad to see me."

"Isn't your Granny glad to see you?"

"Well, you know how she is." Enid pouted. "Living there with Aunt Ola and Aunt Ethel and Cousin Lyman. What a nutty bunch. I'd just as soon be here." She looked up at him from under her eyelashes. "And I'm glad you're here tonight."

Enid took out a cigarette. "How about a light?"

"Put that coffin nail away or I'll have to turn you in," Pete said.

"Hey, jelly bean, it's Christmas."

"Then I guess I'd better leave. But heaven help you if Miss Wells should happen to drop in. I don't think even Uncle George could help." He drained his coffee cup, rose, grasped her arm, and kissed her on the cheek. "Merry Christmas, Enid." And then he walked the quiet hall down to the children's ward and peered in. The ward was dark, save for the glow of a night light. He walked on, vaguely disappointed, and contemplated searching for Tenny. Before he got very far with that idea he was paged. A patient with a heart attack and other injuries caused by electric shock from a string of Christmas lights was brought in, and he saw Tenny no more that night.

Christmas morning, when Pete opened the back door of his house, aromas enveloped him of fir and pine, of cinnamon and nutmeg and roasting turkey. His mother, in a red cocoon robe and a ruffled white apron tied around her waist, took off an oven mitt and kissed him on the cheek. "Everything okay down at the hospital?"

He smiled. "Fine. I'm going to hit the sack."

"Dinner at two o'clock," she reminded him. "And we're having two more guests, strays your father invited. Oh, and Gussie gave me a present for you last night."

He grimaced. "I didn't get her anything."

Pete's mother laughed. "I don't think she expects anything. She looked mischievous when she handed it to me. Go ahead and open it. I'm dying to see. Red paper, white ribbon."

Pete found the flat rectangular package on an end table in the living room. He slid off the wrappings, too tired to be more than mildly curious.

He held an eight-by-ten frame of weathered wood. A photograph. A girl, naked, stood on the river bank with one foot in the water, her long pale hair piled atop her head, hands outstretched, at the moment of hesitation before she plunged in. A remarkable picture.

He felt his mother behind him. "Gussie took that? I wonder what Belinda said?"

"Gussie probably didn't show it to Aunt Belinda," Pete said. "But she shouldn't object. It looks like a naiad."

"A naiad, a water nymph? Yes, I suppose it does, but still—"

At that moment his father and brother thumped down the stairs. He plunged the photograph under a cushion, unwilling to share. Charlie would make snide remarks, and Pop would tease. His mother, understanding, kissed him on the cheek and went to attend to breakfast.

He hadn't slept in twenty-four hours. He wished the family Merry Christmas, retrieved the photograph, and then climbed the stairs to bed.

He gazed at the picture once again before he tucked it in his leather book satchel. The girl on the riverbank was surely the girl by the livery stable, the girl having the baby, the girl Pop recruited for nursing school. But Miss Oakes' hair was a strange shade of brown.

Maybe he'd ask her about it the next day.

But he woke with a scratchy throat and a temperature. "Goes with the territory," his father said, and ordered him to stay home and rest until it was time to go back to Atlanta. No matter. He'd be back in the summer. He hoped Miss Oakes wasn't going anywhere.

# Chapter 28

G ussie's father had surprised her on Christmas. He'd promised to
sell the little house to her and Ned for the price of one dollar.

Gussie, unsettled, stared out the parlor window at the rare dusting
of snow, feeling as crazy as the children running, trying to catch flying
flakes on small tongues, clapping patchy white smatters on the grass into
ragged snowballs that fell apart in the air.

She dropped the curtain and turned away. Ned was not pleased at the
gift. Only Gussie's name appeared on the deed. Oh, yes, on the outside
he was grateful, but Gussie could tell he was smoldering underneath. "In
case anything happens to you," the judge had explained to him. "It'll be
easier for Augusta."

"Nothing will happen to me," Ned growled under his breath.

The renters would move out at the end of February, and the cleaners
and the painters would come, and then Gussie would gather together
all the furniture she could summon from attics and spare rooms. Aunt

Amelia had volunteered a fine pair of velvet curtains of her late mother's, along with a coffee table she'd bought from the widow next door who'd decided to move in with her daughter.

Ned growled like a bear a lot these days on the phone to Wyckham in Savannah. The properties in Florida. Gussie begged him to sell some of them so that they could at least buy a rug or two for the house, and maybe a brand new bed, but he'd told her he had something else in mind. Papa wouldn't change his mind about Arcadia, so what could it be?

Ned paced the floors, talked on the phone, and ducked out in the evening "to meet people for dinner." Who could have known that the rocketing land boom in Florida seemed to be fizzling like a wet firecracker? And why did he hold on? He was secure in his job, wasn't he? Maybe if he worked hard he'd get a raise and they could buy a rug.

An Oriental rug would look so nice, and be so much better for a child than a cold floor. A child! She was really going to have a child. She wasn't ready to be a mother. She thought with longing of the Hospital Ball, of doing the Charleston and having a swell time.

She missed Pete and the good times they used to have, those long lazy days by the river. She'd driven him to the train station when he'd gone back to school, a little pale from the chill he'd suffered.

She'd seen the other Godwins at the Burketts' party, and she'd asked Uncle Emmett where Pete was, and he'd told her Pete was at the hospital. She was glad Pete wasn't at the party. Swanee and Russell Vincent had made their engagement official that night.

The rumor was going around that Swanee had decided she'd better accept Russell, because the next man her father had in mind was a politician who'd already buried two wives. Gussie shivered a little at the thought.

After the long, cold winter, she and Ned would move into their own house, and it would be so lovely, and the time of waiting for the baby would nearly be over.

Maybe Ned would be happier then.

Tenny spent the winter quarter in the diet kitchen, learning about nutrition and how to prepare meals for invalids. She was surprised to learn that the country diet they ate at home, with the vegetables they grew and fresh milk and eggs and lean game, the berries and the wild plums they gathered, was actually good for people, except maybe for the salt and fatback they cooked the vegetables with.

Kitchen duty was all right, but she was looking forward to spring, when she expected to be assigned to obstetrics. It was likely that Mrs. Fletcher would have her baby then.

Easter week, Tenny was thrilled to find a postcard in her mailbox. She gazed at the photograph of the Emory university chapel and tuned it over slowly, heart hammering. There were just two words: *Happy Easter!* It was signed *E.G., Jr.*

She pasted it in her scrapbook that night beside the other postcard she'd received in January, the one with Emory University Hospital on the front. It read: *Dear Miss Oakes, Sorry I missed you at Christmas. Best wishes for a happy new year.*

It was also signed. *E.G. Jr.* Emmett Godwin, Junior. Pete.

# Chapter 29

D r. Emmett, senior, made a notation on the chart and raised one eyebrow. "You getting exercise?"

Gussie sat up on the table in the white examining room that smelled of alcohol and cotton. "Well, we've moved into our own house, and for a month I've been unpacking and hanging curtains."

"You need fresh air, my girl."

"Ned bought me a new bicycle. I'm just waiting for this rain to stop and I'll be off again. I ride from my house to Mama's all the time . . ."

"Bicycle?" Gussie's uncle tapped her tummy and shook his head. "Your balance is off, and you might take a spill."

"Pooh. I'm a good rider, Uncle Emmett."

The doctor frowned. "I've known you since you had frog legs, Gussie Pemberton. Something catches your attention, flower, bird, that's when it happens. I don't want to see you in the hospital before your time. You stay off that bicycle."

"Oh, Uncle Emmett." She wanted to change the subject. "What do you hear from Pete?"

Her uncle grinned. "The boy wants to intern here. I told him somewhere else'd be better, but he's got his heart set on coming back. I'm glad it's not because of that girl. She's getting married, right?"

"So they say." Gussie wrinkled her nose. Swanee and Russell Vincent hadn't yet set the date.

He nodded and patted her arm. "Good. Come back in two weeks—in one piece. No bicycle."

Gussie crossed her fingers behind her back. "If you say so, Uncle Emmett." She was sick of staying inside while the endless April rain lashed against her windows.

Walking out of the waiting room with her mother, Gussie told her what her uncle had said about Pete coming home.

"I thought Emmett wanted him to intern at Emory."

Gussie shrugged. "Pete's got his own agenda."

"Surely it's not Swanee," Belinda said. "She's going to be married."

"I'm not holding my breath." Gussie held the door for her mother, and they emerged into an overcast sky, the sun silver-edging the clouds. They stepped down a rain-washed walkway thick with dogwood blossoms and passed a flower bed lively with two plants like round green porcupines.

"Mama, wait!" Gussie tugged on her mother's arm. "Look at that Spanish bayonet. Does it grow in Virginia?"

Belinda gazed at the spiky shrub. "Probably not. It's a warm-weather plant. Cold winters kill it back. Why do you ask?"

Gussie swallowed and thought quickly. "Ned said something about planting some at our house."

Belinda gave Gussie a curious look. "Ned's interested in plants? That's news to me. Tell him that with a small child, it's not the best choice."

Gussie agreed. They rode home in silence, Gussie thinking about the photograph, of Sarah. Of Spanish bayonets in Virginia.

Gussie's mother stopped at the newly painted house. "Are you happy with the house?" she asked. "You seem a little moody."

"Of course, Mama!" Gussie protested. "It's just the baby."

She got out of the car and kissed her mother good-bye. Happy with the house? What was happiness anyway? It was as elusive as a perfect photograph: if everything lined up, she could get it right, but light, objects, shadows, were shifting, moving out of focus, appearing out of nowhere.

Gussie wished she could dispel her doubts. She should have been full of joy that Uncle Emmett said she was coming along so well.

She sank to the red velvet sofa that had come from Grandmama's and surveyed the empty room in the empty house. It wasn't that she missed living at her parents' house. Here, she and Ned had privacy—maybe too much privacy. With others present, she and Ned were a couple. Teammates.

Here in the tiny house, they'd sit and face each other night after night, and tell each other pretty lies. Now she knew the truth of a secret. Whatever you keep from someone is another brick in the wall between you.

And her truth, the truth she hid, was that she had never wanted to be tied down in Ashbyville with a house and a baby and a husband. Play the cards you're dealt, that was what Papa always said. Oh, Ned had seemed a King, hadn't he? Now he was a wild card. A Joker.

His truth was—what? The woman in the picture? Sarah? The family he said was dead? Too many things didn't add up.

In Savannah, she'd seen the angry look the woman in the trolley gave Ned, calling "France!" She'd seen his fear. And then there was Wyckham. She'd never liked weasly Wyckham.

She glanced around at the trunks of clothes, at crates that held wedding presents, at hand-me-downs from generous relatives. They still didn't have a rug for the parlor. Ned joked that she should try braiding one from scraps. As if she knew how to do that!

She'd hold out for an oriental rug like those Lyman Stratton wanted to sell her cousin at the garden party.

Ned was in no mood to discuss floor coverings with the morning paper full of gangland killings. In Chicago, someone named Hymie Weiss had been gunned down in front of a flower shop.

Nothing to do with Max, he'd said.

The Burkett ladies had arrived home from Europe and planned a tea to show off their souvenirs of the Grand Tour—their Bavarian cuckoo clocks and Spanish mantillas, their English porcelains and Paris frocks. Gussie was invited along with Mama and Jessie and Anna, but she'd stay home, of course. They'd be shocked if she arrived in her condition. She penned her regrets in a charming note.

She was just sealing the envelope when Ned flung open the front door and stalked into the parlor. "The boss is going nuts about those labor organizers," he said. "What does he expect me to do?"

Gussie had no idea what he was talking about. "I'm sure you'll think of something," she said, and held out the envelope. "Would you put this in the mailbox on your way to work tomorrow?"

Ned took the envelope and stared at it. "Why are you writing to old lady Burkett?"

Gussie sighed. "Regrets to their party. Mama says it's the rule."

"What party?"

"Swanee and Miss Clara, of course, giving a tea and talking about their time abroad. I wish I could go. I'd like to go abroad someday."

"You've been to Cuba. That's abroad." Ned stalked out of the room, but not before Gussie saw a flush rise to his cheeks. All she'd done was mention Swanee and Miss Clara. She shivered.

He stalked back into the dining room when she called him for dinner. When he took a few forkfuls of a chicken pot pie, crust broke off in large, stiff chunks. The gravy ran thinly off his spoon, and the carrots crunched between his teeth. "I think it's time to get a cook," he said.

Gussie twirled her hair around her finger so tight it hurt. Couldn't she do anything to please him, except in bed? She looked down at her blue-green cotton calico dress, curving above her swelling belly. *I have his child.*

During the next weeks she read cookbooks and plunged herself into cleaning and painting. She tried to knit tiny garments like her aunts did, but all she got for her efforts were a few rows of white and yellow stitches, unraveled many times.

She stared out at the bare and weedy back yard, with its one chinaberry tree and a fledgling bamboo grove. Mama had suggested daffodils and crocus and azaleas, roses growing up the porch railings, and sweet shrubs for the scent.

She didn't want to dig or plant, to put in roots. She missed the river: the play of light on the water, the sandy roads, and the plum bushes heavy with fruit. No one had time to take her, and Ned forbade her to go by herself.

Where could she put her studio in this house? Her darkroom? The house had no basement, only a ramshackle garage that needed work. She'd make a room of her own there, but right now there was too much to do in the house.

She gave up and called her mother.

The very next day her mother came over with a basket of sliced ham and fried chicken, potato salad, and jars of pole beans and vegetable soup. "Here's some dinner for you," she said. "Why didn't you ask me for help sooner?"

Gussie burst into tears. "I didn't want to admit that I'm no good at cooking," she sobbed. "Ned hates my food."

"Now, now." Her mother embraced her. "Right now you're over-wrought, and the baby will soon be here."

Gussie sniffled and reached for a handkerchief.

"You need something to do, to take your mind off this. How about helping me to stuff and address envelopes tomorrow? We'll have lunch, and Velma can give you a cooking lesson."

Gussie smiled. Mama was up to her old tricks again. The world was all right.

The next day dawned sweet and clear. Gussie, her bag slung over her shoulder, locked the back door, excited to be out. Nobody could tell her she was too far along to walk! She'd take her time, savoring the sweet smells of early roses and the sight of wisteria blossoms trailing over fences.

Her bicycle beckoned to her from the garage.

Uncle Emmett had said no to riding, but—*pooh*. It was only a mile. She climbed on the bike, made sure she could balance well, and headed toward the college campus shortcut, where the paved roads had less traffic.

She pedaled along near the Law building, enjoying the wind in her hair and the scent of flowering cherries, their snowy petals drifting onto clusters of students.

A boy stepped away from the crowd, his nose in a book, right into her path. She screamed and jammed on the brakes, he jumped out of the way, the book hit the road. Her front tire bumped against it, sending the bicycle—and Gussie—sprawling.

On the ground, stunned, she heard shouts, and then she saw a circle of students' faces above her. Her back hurt, and her knee hurt. A pair of arms reached for her, and then the whole world turned gray.

Ned sat at his desk jotting figures on a pad, the picture of Sarah tucked away deep in the second file drawer. The day was steamy, the office was steamier, and sweat broke out in his forehead. He'd been sending Max half his salary for five months now; they hardly had enough to live on, especially now that they'd moved out of Gussie's old man's house. And now Max was demanding the rest of the money all at once.

Wyckham was no help. He hadn't come up with a buyer for Ned's land at any kind of price. Everyone was selling, he said, and the big operators had sent their runners, their land scouts, back up North. "Should have sold when I told you to," Wyckham had groused.

The market would turn around. There had been a rally in March, and there was no place to go but up. He'd counted on that land sale to buy Arcadia from the judge and his sister, that is, if the geezers could be persuaded to sell. And he'd heard that Arno Shackley was after Arcadia too, and was courting that rich old maid. He crunched the paper in his fist and hurled it against the wall.

Damn! At this rate he'd have nothing left. He started to figure again. How much would it take to pay back what he'd borrowed from the company? He'd meant to square it when the land sold, and before anyone cottoned onto his bank accounts in Atlanta and the nonexistent suppliers he'd set up. One or two fairly big checks went a good ways toward keeping Max happy. The cuff links had only been a drop in the bucket.

He stared at the letter in front of him. There were certain legal eagles, Max wrote, that wanted money for services rendered, and they were putting pressure on him, Max, and so he regretted that he, Max, would have to put pressure on Ned.

Ned ripped the letter to bits and shoved them into the wastebasket. Underneath, a dark stain relentlessly crept across the floor. The office roof had sprung a leak during the heavy April rains, and roofers kept finding excuses why they couldn't come. Thank God they were now on their way.

On his desk, a newspaper lay folded to a picture of Miss Swanee Burkett and her mother preparing to give a tour of their gardens. He folded the paper carefully back to its original state and slid it into the wastebasket.

Damn foolish to think of her. He was in enough trouble.

As he began a letter to Wyckham, a sharp rap sounded on his half-open door.

"Come in," he said, pen poised. It was none other than old Burkett himself, followed by Mrs. Mahala Benedict, the secretary. Salt-and-pepper hair in deep waves, she wore a neat collared dress. Lightly plump and still pretty, she settled a shrewd gaze on him through wire-rimmed spectacles. He shifted in his seat.

"Well, young man," said Elias Burkett, "the roofers have arrived. I'll have Mrs. Benedict's office repaired and repainted—she got the worst of the leaks, you know. She'll share your office for a few days."

Ned rose at once. Why hadn't Burkett warned him? He held out his hand to Mrs. Benedict and smiled. "Welcome." He intended to be as affable as possible. He'd learned his lessons well.

"I'm off to my luncheon meeting," Burkett said. Chewing on a cigar, he walked out.

An electrician in coveralls appeared with a telephone, and commenced to knock a hole in Ned's office wall just as another two men hefted a desk in place beside the door, waiting for instructions.

Ned fidgeted while Mrs. Benedict pondered the best way to place the two desks for maximum work space. He'd just voiced his opinion when Belinda Pemberton, his mother-in-law, for God's sake, appeared in the doorway.

Out of breath, her hair jammed untidily under her hat, she stared at him thin-lipped. "Get to the hospital at once," she said. "It's Gussie."

# Chapter 30

Gussie's baby was delivered by Dr. Emmett Godwin the next morning at one a.m. in Mercy Hospital. Ned, who'd gotten tired of waiting in the hard wooden chairs provided by the hospital and gone out for late-night barbecue at the Pig and Poke, had stayed on sharing a jug of corn liquor with the proprietor. When he finally wandered back to the hospital, he dozed off on the lone horsehair sofa.

The next thing he knew, a firm female hand was shaking him. "Wake up and see your little girl!"

Ned rubbed sticky eyes. Little girl? Where was that boy, the heir that was going to carry on the empire he was going to build, the one that would inherit Arcadia? He blinked, breathing a fug of sweaty clothes, coffee, and disinfectant.

Pink and brown and white blobs above him resolved into his mother-in-law, those two sisters of Gussie's, and a white-coated doctor with a bushy gray mustache. Standing a few steps back was a nurse holding a pink bundle.

He heaved himself off the sofa and staggered over to the baby. The nurse wrinkled her nose, and the doctor raised his eyebrows, but damn, nobody said a thing. He pushed back the blanket to get a better look at the baby's face.

A wrinkled monkey, yes, just like Ned's sisters and brothers as babies. "Well, I'll be damned," he mumbled, thick-tongued. They all looked at him with stony disapproval. Well, what was he expected to say?

"How's my wife?" That seemed to melt them a little.

"She's groggy from the anesthetic." The doctor inspected Ned too carefully for comfort. "She had a hard labor. Maybe you'd better see her later. She needs to rest."

What? They wouldn't let him in to see her? To hell with them. "I'll be back," he grumbled. He could feel their eyes on him as he walked toward the swinging doors. He wasn't spending what was left of the night on that damned itchy sofa.

He turned back, lifted a hand to half-mast. "Give her my undying love." He stumbled a few steps and stopped to glance back. That nurse had looked vaguely familiar.

Tenny, holding the baby, watched him go. She hoped with all her heart that horrid man was not her brother. After she'd returned the baby to the nursery, she took the bath cart to the new mother's room and found Enid Smith Barlow brandishing a metal cup of pills.

"Here's something for pain," Enid told the patient. "Nurse Oakes will give you a sponge bath." Tenny waited with the basin and cart, numbness and a kind of wonder stealing over her. This patient, this Mrs. Fletcher of the strawberry blond hair and kewpie-doll eyes, might be her sister-in-law.

She watched Mrs. Fletcher take the pills and the glass of water, watched Enid take her temperature and pulse, ask more questions, and make notations on her chart.

Her tormentor finally gone, Tenny let out her breath. "Well, let's get started." Tenny drew back the sheet and scooted a folded flannel pad underneath her patient's hips.

She wielded the cloth gently, more confidently than usual, because something about this young woman put her at her ease. Maybe because the other girl was more scared than she was.

"How long have you been here?" Gussie asked, trying to prop herself up, but Tenny urged her to relax.

"It's my first year. Don't worry, they train us well."

"But where's the baby? She's all right, isn't she?"

"Of course. They'll bring her soon, after we get you comfortable." Tenny smiled. "Are you planning to feed her yourself? Most young ladies want to feed formula and get flat chests as soon as possible."

Mrs. Fletcher shrugged. "A flat chest would be nice, but I'll have a fight with Mama if I use formula. She's in the Women's Movement and they're all for natural feeding."

"The Women's Movement?" Verity Hapsworth had told them about the long battle for voting rights and the fight for rights for women. It hadn't been so very long ago that all a woman's possessions belonged to her husband. Not that any woman she'd known had any possessions to worry about.

"Do they really believe in free love?"

Mrs. Fletcher shook her head and smiled. "Mama says that free love isn't free of trouble. They just think women ought to have satisfaction doing it, the same as men."

"Your mother told you *that*?" The washcloth slipped out of Tenny's hands to the floor. At the Callahan Home, trouble was emphasized and nothing said about satisfaction.

The young mother gave Tenny a wry look. "My mother's a social worker. She believes in birth control as a way to relieve poverty, women's deaths, and child labor. She's trying to get better treatment for women workers. Specifically mill workers."

Tenny retrieved the washcloth, placed it in the pan for soiled linen, and took a fresh one from the pile on her cart. "Sorry," she said. "I dare say those workers need some help." But she forgot and said "he'p."

Gussie Fletcher looked at her oddly. "Where are you from, Miss Oakes?"

Tenny took a deep breath. Not only was it hard to get the country out of her speech, Miss Verity's expressions sometimes crept in. But she had prepared her story. "Call me Tenny. My folks moved around a lot. My pa was a carpenter. He went around looking for work and we followed him. Now turn on your stomach."

"But that's fascinating!" Gussie protested. "You must have seen a lot of the country."

"Now, Mis' Fletcher," Tenny said. "You know you don't want to keep my other patients waiting while I tell my life story. No, sirree. Now turn over."

Gussie grumbled, but did as she was told.

After the bath, Tenny was preparing to leave when a blue-and-white striper walked in with the Fletcher baby, wrapped in a pink blanket. Tenny gazed once more at the little girl's downy dark hair and deep blue eyes, like most babies' eyes, before they settled into their real color.

Something twisted inside her. Where was her own child, the one she'd given up? She shoved the memory into the croker sack she carried in her mind, roped it tightly, and hurried to her next patient.

Tenny haunted the hall during the next day's visiting hours, hoping to see Mr. Fletcher, but Enid intercepted her with linen duty. Tenny was trundling the cart back from a newly-supplied room when she heard a male voice behind Mrs. Fletcher's door. She stopped, excuse ready, and raised her hand to knock.

"I'll be back from Savannah tomorrow morning," she heard. "I hope you'll have decided by then." Then, without warning, the door swung wide. She leaped back as Ned Fletcher strode out, brushing by her mumbling "excuse me" or maybe "out of my way."

She stared after him. Tall as Byron, he walked like Byron, with a graceful stride covering lots of ground.

She rolled the cart into the room. When her patient saw her, a flush faded from Mrs. Fletcher's face, her lips relaxed, and she let go of the blanket she was clutching.

Tenny gave her a sympathetic look. "Everything all right, ma'am? I thought you might want fresh towels."

Gussie nodded distractedly. "That would be nice."

Tenny lamented the anger and despair in her patient's tone, but what could she do? She laid out towels, then moved a vase of red roses to the broad windowsill. She poured her patient a cup of water. "Got to keep your fluids up for the baby. The milk flows better when Mama's happy."

Gussie sighed and looked down at her hands. "My husband hates the name I picked out."

"He does?"

Gussie leaned back and looked skyward. "I think Sarah's a lovely name, and it was my grandmother's name, and it's his sister's name! I thought it would be perfect!"

Tenny dipped a washcloth into the room washbasin and squeezed it thoughtfully. Gussie sniffed and reached for a paper tissue. "He says no. They don't get along. And his parents are dead."

Tenny dabbed the young mother's face with the cool, wet cloth. That's just what somebody who wanted to deny his family *would* say. Somebody who was pretending to be somebody else. Suppose, just suppose, Ned really *was* Byron. Then that little baby lying in the basket beside the bed was her *niece*.

"It's been a while since your hair's been washed," Tenny said.

Gussie waved her hands. "Can I have a shower bath? I'll wash it myself then. I hate leaning over a basin. Water gets in my nose."

"I'll have to ask the doctor."

"All these rules!" Gussie burst out. "They wanted this name today for the records. Ned said to name her after me, but more than one Augusta per family? Little Gussie and Big Gussie, makes me sound like some kind of Civil War cannon. Mother doesn't want another Belinda. Ned said his mother's name was Emmeline and he says that could be a middle name. He doesn't want to call her Emmy."

Tenny finished the washing and popped the used towels in the bag hanging from the side of the cart. *Emmeline.* Close to Emily, her own mother's name. "My mama liked poetry and named us all after poets. She hoped one of us would have a poetic streak, but it didn't happen. I was Tennyson."

Gussie laughed. "That's nice, but no poets for me. I hope my daughter's joyous and clever and graceful."

"Then how about Joy? Or Grace?"

Gussie smiled. "Or Sophie for wisdom? You know, I like Grace. But Emmeline? Maybe Emily for short. Emily Grace, then. Give me those papers." They smiled at each other conspiratorially.

Tenny took her leave and pushed her cart through the door to the hall, where Pete Godwin neatly sidestepped it. "Hello, Nurse!"

Tenny's heart gave a lurch and her hand went to her throat.

"Am I that alarming?" Pete's face brimmed with good humor and satisfaction, probably because today he was wearing the short white jacket and stethoscope of an intern.

"You startled me." Tenny's hand went to her heart. And then he gazed at her in a way that made her feel as liquid as water rushing over stones in the river, water falling into limpid pools.

"It's nice to see you," Pete said.

"Yes." Seeing him felt like the sun warming her face after a cold, dreary morning. "Thanks for the postcards. Are you back for good?"

"You bet," Pete said. "Came straight here after my last exam."

"Well, I'm glad."

"Are you?" His expression made her catch her breath. Heaven only knew what might have happened if Enid hadn't appeared from around a corner and given them the fish-eye before she'd gone into a nearby room. Tenny reluctantly edged away from Pete. "Listen, I mustn't keep you," she said. "Are you going to see Mrs. Fletcher?"

"Sure thing," he winked at her.

"She'll be so happy," Tenny said, and before she could take another step Enid came out of the room and stared at them.

Pete stepped into Mrs. Fletcher's room. Tenny rolled her cart down past Enid, and greeted her as though nothing at all had happened.

Enid had nothing to say. But she was smirking.

# Chapter 31

Ned paced outside Wyckham's office. Damn Curtis, telling him to come down here and then making him cool his heels. It was going to be a bloodbath, but he was lucky to find a buyer for the Florida parcels at all. He'd hoped, after that great March rally in Miami, that it was back to business as usual.

And now this pile of shit he'd been offered for the Miami parcel. When was he going to get the money? Why was it so slow coming in? And damn! Slow as white trash getting that office redone. With the Benedict woman underfoot, it was harder for him to cover up his adjustments. He was running out of excuses to stay later after she left for home. He'd always intended to put the money back, but now, with the old biddy dogging his tracks, he had to do it soon.

Maybe Burkett suspected something. Maybe he'd put her there to spy on him. Naahh . . . her office was a mess after the leaks. But why hadn't Burkett put her in with the old accountant?

"Ned?"

Wyckham stood at his office door. Ned walked in, thinking Wyckham did indeed look like a praying mantis. Gussie, bless her, had been right.

Wyckham, unsmiling, closed the door. "What the devil's so funny?"

"Nothing, Curtis." Ned positioned himself across from Wyckham and waited.

Wyckham grunted, clearly in a bad mood. "There's very little to smile about."

Ned forced himself to keep a steady gaze. Never let them see you sweat. "The money?"

"They've sold it again," Wyckham said. "Waiting for their money before they send us ours. We'll get it." He steepled his fingers and pursed his mouth. "Your *wife*, Sarah, came by this very office looking for you. Funny you didn't mention you never got a divorce, Ned, when you asked me to stand up with you."

Ned cracked his knuckles. "Good God." He thought he'd never mentioned Wyckham to Sarah. How did she find him?

Wyckham blathered on. "Sarah told me after you took all her money and left, all her relatives and customers from the bicycle shop wanted to help her. She put out the word to watch for you. It paid off."

Ned slapped his forehead, remembering the woman on the trolley. France? Hell! She'd been saying *Chance*, damn her. "How'd she connect me with you?"

"Who knows? She did."

"What the hell? She has no idea where I live now. Or my name. Did I tell you I'm a father? A little girl."

"Congratulations." Wyckham didn't crack a smile.

Ned cleared his throat. "We'd better get down to business. Tell me again what the offer was for the property in Miami?"

"Ten," said Wyckham. "You want to go ahead?"

"Christ," said Ned, running his hands through his hair, destroying the smooth brilliantine finish. "I could have sold it for a hundred Gs a year ago."

Wyckham doodled on a pad on his desk, his face stern, like a doctor recommending surgery as the only option. "You haven't gotten paid for the Mackenzie parcel yet. I have a hunch the bubble's fixing to bust, and bust big time. I'd recommend selling not only that parcel, but the Victoria one too. Right now, while you've got an interested party."

Ned made a rapid calculation. At that price, he could pay off Max, but he couldn't put back what he'd borrowed from the till.

"No," he said. "It's bound to pick up. You told me so yourself."

Wyckham nodded slowly. "Well, yes, a few people are buying. Some fellow in Jacksonville is buying up the Panhandle. Too bad your parcels are around that cow town of Orlando. Developments are going bust, Ned. The sand blows across empty lots."

"Sell the Mackenzie. I'll hang onto the Victoria until the market improves."

"Ned," said Wyckham gently, "sell it all. *Now*."

Ned drew out his handkerchief and mopped his forehead. "It's not enough. It's not enough."

Wyckham cocked his head quizzically. "Not enough for what?"

Ned sat back, coming to himself. Wyckham didn't need to know about his private business. "Some real estate where I live," he said carelessly. He mopped again. "God, it's hot in here. When you gonna buy a good fan, Curtis?"

Wyckham tapped his pencil on the desk. "I hear you've got a pretty good setup."

"A boss who's God and a wife who owns a bungalow," Ned snarled.

Wyckham shrugged. "What'll I tell Sarah if she comes around again?"

Ned finally shucked off his coat and loosened his tie. "Tell her I got killed in Cuba."

"Spirits walk here, haven't you heard?" said Wyckham, grinning. "My advice is to stay out of Savannah."

"I'll grow a beard," said Ned. "Should have done in the first place. Things are gonna be fine." He withdrew a pocket flask. "Come on, have a drink, and then I've got to hop the train. Can't stay away from the mill too long."

Wyckham slid his chair back, opened a drawer, and brought out two tumblers. Ned poured a couple of fingers into each glass. "By the way, Wyckham, my wife found a picture of Sarah. I told her she was my sister."

Wyckham raised his glass. "Ah, let's drink to the lovely red-haired Sarah. She looks like a nice armful. I have a feeling she'd hate being your sister."

"Shut up," said Ned. He raised his glass. "To success."

Wyckham raised his glass and clinked it with Ned's. "I'll drink to the health of your new daughter."

"And plenty of cotton," Ned said. "Where are those damn papers you want me to sign?"

# Chapter 32

Tenny had hoped for another chance to get a good look at Ned Fletcher during Mrs. Fletcher's two-week stay, but it hadn't happened, and the mother and baby had checked out while she'd been off duty. He hadn't come around much for a new father. With that drinking habit, she might see him in the emergency room.

This term, she was assigned to Surgery. She was run ragged supplying instruments fresh from the sterilizer and bringing in fresh drapes and green soap and gloves from the supply room. There never seemed to be enough gloves, and the scrubbing was endless—floors, tabletops, hands and forearms. She hated the nasty green soap they used.

Patients crying were the worst part. She had to learn not to cry herself.

One day, Dr. Hooper allowed her to fit the ether cone over the face of a young man, an emergency appendectomy patient. Her hand chilled as the ether hissed. The patient coughed and choked and finally fell into deep sleep as the big wall clock ticked off the minutes. She stepped back, but the assisting nurse motioned for her to stay and observe.

The surgeon poised his scalpel. Tenny surprised herself by not flinching as the knife separated the skin, the yellow fat of the belly, the muscle. The surgeon deftly flipped out the appendix, tied it off, and separated it from the patient with a flick of the scalpel. He deposited the bit of flesh into a waiting kidney basin and called for sutures.

Tenny took it all in with her cool grey eyes, noting carefully each procedure the doctor performed. After the procedure, she wheeled the patient back to his room. His name was Henry Benedict, and she was there when he awoke from the anesthesia, nauseated, gagging, and grateful for a different kidney basin.

My lady of the slops, he called her.

Tenny liked Henry. She'd just finished irrigating, cleaning, and dressing his wound one morning when a visitor knocked at the door. "It's not visiting hours," she said to the woman who held a basket that smelled of fresh baking.

"But I'm his mother, and I have to get to work."

"Mother," Henry called.

Tenny, missing her own mother, opened the door. "Just a few minutes, please." She saw Enid pass the door. Of course.

Mrs. Benedict, true to her word, didn't stay long. She told him she'd brought him some of his favorite muffins and that Judge Pemberton had called to see how he was.

Henry grinned. "That's made my day."

She left soon after. "Where does your mother work?" Tenny asked, wondering about opportunities for women.

He told her, and her hand flew to her mouth.

"Why are you looking at me like that?" he asked. "She works in the office."

"Sorry," Tenny said. "I was just thinking of some of our patients."

"I wish she worked somewhere else," Henry said. "One day, I hope she can quit. When I graduate and get a job."

"What are you planning to do?"

"Clerk for Judge Pemberton for a while," he said. "Then we'll see. Join a firm, maybe. What about you? Going in for private duty?"

"Maybe," Tenny hedged. "I met Judge Pemberton one day when he was in here visiting his daughter, who'd just had a baby."

A shadow passed over Henry's face. "The judge became a grandpa twice in two years. His other daughter adopted a little boy."

"Adopted?" Tenny caught her breath and grabbed his pillow, plumping it with great energy.

"Yep."

"How . . . how old is the baby?" Tenny settled the fluffed pillow under his head. Was she always going to be like this, always wondering, whenever an adopted child was mentioned? She had to be made of sterner stuff.

Henry shrugged. "I don't know how to tell. I was an only child."

"Not me," Tenny said. "I'm one of six." She smoothed the sheets and then said she had to go. She ached for her brothers and sisters. When would she see them again?

When Henry recovered enough to go home, Tenny had no time to miss him. Another young man was admitted with a concussion, broken fingers, cracked ribs, fractured tibia and fibula, and soft tissue trauma from a riding accident. His horse had fallen on a jump and landed on top of him. He was lucky to be alive.

Thinking of Shelley, she gave him lots of extra attention. Finally, he felt well enough to give her a box of chocolates another girl had brought him, as well as beg her for a date.

She kept the chocolates, but had no intention of going to see Charlie Chaplin with the fellow. He'd forget her soon enough. Five girls had come to see him on Sunday, each one bringing a present.

She took his lunch tray to the cart and trundled to the next room, passing a few Sunday visitors. It wouldn't be long now until three o'clock when she could go to her room, flop on her bed, and open her Elinor Glyn novel.

Unfortunately, when she turned the corner with her cart, she ran smack dab into Miss Ola Stratton, painted and rouged, in a dress of flowered silk crepe de chine, wheeling her own cart of flowers she'd brought from the First Baptist Church. On Sundays, she delivered them to patients, along with a church leaflet of comforting Bible verses.

Executing a quick dodge, Tenny glanced at Miss Ola's companion. The fleshy-jowled man in a tan seersucker suit, gray-black hair slicked back from a reddened brow, straw hat in his hand, stepped back with a rolling motion, like a man accustomed to a ship. Or a horse. A slow, poisonous feeling paralyzed her limbs. Her breath slowed, and her fingers whitened on the cart handle. Arno Shackley glanced at her with a flash of annoyance. "Look where you're goin', girlie," he growled, dismissing her. The two walked on.

Tenny closed her eyes, tears welling. She couldn't break down. That dreadful night came back to her in a rush, and the world closed on in her. She sank to the floor, jostling the cart, and a tray fell with a crash. Dishes, gelatin, cabbage, carrots scattered on the tan linoleum. A metal tumbler clanked and rattle-rolled away, the sound fading into a gray blanket of silence.

When the fog lifted, a hazy someone was bending over her. She blinked, and a young man in a short white coat came into focus. "Nurse Oakes? Can you hear me?"

Reddish hair, round glasses. Pete Godwin. No, no, no. Blood rushed into her head. She struggled to get up, but he held her back. "Easy," he said.

Panic seized her. "Oh, gosh. I guess I fainted. Really. I'm fine. I forgot to eat lunch, I think. I'm so sorry. I'll clean up all this mess. Miss Wells will have my hide." Once again she tried to scramble to her feet, but the gelatin slipped under her.

"I'm helping you," Pete Godwin said in a voice that let her know it was useless to argue. He took her arm and hauled her up. She stepped back, away from the tray and its muddled contents.

"Please," she said. She smoothed her skirt and apron, dismayed to see stains. More washing, eating away at her reading and resting time. "I'll get right to work on this." She gestured at the floor.

"No," he said. "I'll call for a janitor."

"Oh, no, Doctor, I'm supposed to—"

"You can call me Pete," he said. "I'm not a doctor yet."

"All the interns want to be called Doctor," she said.

Pete shrugged. "I'm still learning."

"But you're famous here."

Tenny was surprised to see a faint flush in his cheeks. "I can't help who my father is. Say, I'm going to take a coffee break. Why don't you join me?"

"Look. This is my job." She gestured to the mess on the floor. He took her by the shoulders and gazed into her face. He touched her jaw. "Turn your head to the right."

She obeyed.

"The left."

She obeyed.

"Something's not right with you. A case of nerves. Take ten. That's an order."

"But . . ."

Pete snagged a passing orderly, explained the situation, and asked him to find the janitor and get the hall cleaned and mopped. Then he took Tenny's arm and escorted her to an alcove where an electric percolator steamed. Pete poured out two cups. "I just made some an hour ago."

"You made it?" she said, taking the mug and holding it in both hands. She would have liked sugar and cream, but didn't want to ask.

"All right. Why'd you faint? *Real* reason." His tone was sympathetic, but professional, and she relaxed.

She shrugged. "I told you. I skipped lunch."

He nodded. "Plunging blood sugar. Don't they teach you girls about that in class?"

"Of course. But I wasn't hungry, and there was so much to do . . ." She didn't like the way he was frowning at her, as if he wanted to pinch her and see how much meat she had on her bones. "When am I supposed to find time to eat? Any influence with Miss Wells or the staff nurses?"

Pete laughed. "I've always thought Miss Wells used to teach God," he said. "I'm afraid anything I say would make things worse." He glanced at his watch. "Crackers! That was a fast ten minutes." He looked at her name tag. "What do they call you at home, Nurse Oakes?"

Her heart skipped a beat. He didn't know, he *couldn't* know—then she realized he was just flirting. "Tenny," she said, and though she never told people this, she said, "it's short for Tennyson."

"Tennyson! Poetic! I like Tennyson. *The Lady of Shalott*. Do you know his poems?"

"Just one or two," she said. "My mother had a book of poetry."

"You need a book of your own," he said. "I'd better be off, Tennyson. Be sure to eat, now."

"All right, Doctor."

"I'm Pete." He touched her cheek briefly. "Oh, just a minute." He fished in the pocket of his white jacket and brought out a Hershey bar with almonds. "This will help."

She looked at it as if it might be a black widow spider.

"Go on, take it," he said. "It'll raise your blood sugar."

She stood very straight and accepted the candy. "Thank you."

"You're welcome." He gave her a comical half-bow and walked on down the hall. She finished her coffee, still a little shaky from the encounter with Arno Shackley, washed both cups, and hung them on a peg to dry. And then she ate the candy, all of it, and threw the wrapper in the wastebin. She felt as though a chapter in her life had been closed.

# Chapter 33

Gussie was a long way from those jazz palaces and cocktail parties in New York.

It was all a conspiracy, this adoration of motherhood. The preachers and poets never mentioned the nasty diapers. She took a deep breath, held it, and lifted the first bucket of diapers soaking in 20 Mule Team Borax. She poured the water into the toilet, then filled the bucket with fresh water, swished the diapers, and poured it out again. She flushed and did the same with the second bucket.

Then she dumped the wet diapers into the copper tub of the washing machine Ned had bought her, sprinkled in soap flakes, heated a huge kettle of hot water on the stove, poured it in, and heated another kettle. After that was poured into the copper tub, she turned the hand crank until the diapers were clean.

She rinsed them with hot then cold water, wrung them out through the two rollers of the wringer, and then piled them in the clothes basket.

Yes, she was a long way from the Empire State Building, from the Great White Way. She huffed, clumped into the living room, and fitted a record on the Victrola. She wound it. "Yes, sir, that's my babee—no, sir, don't mean maybee—"

She pirouetted, dancing with the mop, and finished the kitchen floor. She switched to the broom for the back porch. By the time she'd finished, the record was over. Now she was starving and the baby was whimpering with hunger. She looked longingly toward the icebox, where some chess pie was waiting, but the baby began to wail and her breasts tightened as milk flowed in. Just like a farm cow.

"Mooo—" she murmured. She sat in the kitchen rocker, placed a clean diaper over her shoulder, and unbuttoned her blouse. The baby rooted around and fastened, one tiny hand clutching at the fullness. Gussie sighed. It would be a while before she looked fashionable again.

After she patted a burp out of Gracie, she laid her in the bassinet and flung open the icebox. Ned had eaten the rest of the pie last night. This morning, Ned had eaten all the eggs and grits, and then complained because her biscuits were hard. He didn't eat them, threatening to nail them to the wall. She still hadn't washed the pots.

She had enough coffee for another cup. She drank it staring out the window, but she was still hungry. "Come on, Gracie," she said. "Want to go to Grannie's for lunch?"

Gracie cooed and kicked her legs as if she thought it was a swell idea. But first, there were the laundered diapers in the basket. Gussie lugged them outside and pegged them on the clothesline, wincing as she saw her red and raw hands, her broken nails in the bright sunlight.

She thought stupidly of the bright varnished nails of Swanee Burkett at that long-ago dance. The nails on the hand that held a Camel cigarette—the hand that adjusted a feathered headband—the very picture of a flapper. Gussie was eighteen now, the very age Swanee had been at that birthday party. She winced.

She was hanging baby diapers, and Swanee had been touring Europe, having a grand time. Gussie had thought she was such a vamp, leaving that garden party with Swanee's crush, and look how it had all turned out. Some flapper!

Aware of her mother's eagle eyes inspecting her red hands, Gussie dug into a big lunch of fried chicken, mashed potatoes, and English peas. She almost swooned at the delicious smell of yeast rolls.

Velma, her mother's cook, took her empty plate away and plunked a slice of lemon pie in front of her. "Girl, you need to build up your strength."

"I'm all right," Gussie protested.

Her mother frowned. "You're getting too thin, Gussie. You let Mrs. Blackstone go?"

"Ned says money is tight." This inquisition was the price of her food.

"Drives a fancy car," observed the judge. "Seems to patronize the back of the drugstore. Not that I ever go there myself."

"Hush, Mac." Gussie's mother cast a worried glance at the judge.

"Papa, please, I don't want to start a fuss." Gussie lifted a pale yellow forkful of pie with plenty of meringue.

Gussie's father snorted. He placed his napkin on the table, pushed back his chair, and rose. "I've got to get back to the courthouse, ladies. Please forgive me." He kissed Gussie on the cheek. "Stand up for yourself, m'dear." Then he went through the swinging door into the kitchen.

"Velma," Gussie heard him say, "come into my study for a minute."

How humiliating. Was he going to tell Velma to pack up extra food for her and Ned? Was she such a failure at keeping house? She couldn't eat the rest of her pie. She pushed the plate away as tears welled in her throat.

"Gussie, what's wrong?" Her mother laid a hand on hers.

How could she tell her mother how Ned had been behaving these past couple of months? All Mama would say was *I told you so. You're married now.* She forced a smile. "It's hard to get enough sleep with a little one, Mama. Surely you remember."

"Of course. Let me keep Gracie for you. You go upstairs and take a nap."

Gussie lifted her handkerchief to her nose. "Oh, Mama, would you? A couple of hours? A nap, and then I'll do some shopping. The cupboard is bare."

"All right," said Belinda. "Have them deliver your groceries, and when you come back to collect the baby, I'll have some nice leftovers packaged up for you."

"Mother . . ."

"Shush," said Belinda.

Gussie, swallowing her pride, hoped there'd be a lot of leftovers. Ned had been giving her less and less money for housekeeping.

She tried to nap but couldn't. She went shopping and then came back for Gracie and the leftovers, wondering why her mother looked at her so slyly. At least there would be something on the table tonight.

At home, Gussie set Gracie in the playpen, put away the food from Mama, and began to tackle the kitchen. She was just taking the dirty pots and pans out of the oven where she'd hidden them when someone rapped sharply on the back door.

Gussie opened it. Before her stood a short, sturdy young woman with bronze skin, head wrapped in a print headscarf, hoops in her ears like the Cuban women. Her broad nose was sprinkled with dark brown freckles.

"You Miss Gussie?" Her voice was sharp, direct.

"Yes, I'm Gussie Fletcher." That name still didn't fit right. It sounded like a sneeze.

"Trevania Woods. My aunt Velma sent me. You can call me Tre."

Now she knew why Mama had looked that way. Gussie opened the door wide and Trevania walked inside. Hands on hips, she surveyed the grits pot in the sink, the hard biscuits still stuck to the baking sheet, the grease-caked bacon pan, the crumbs under the kitchen table.

She sniffed the air and looked down at Gracie in her wheeled crib. "This baby need changing," she said. "Where you keep them diapers?"

"I'll do it," Gussie said, hastening toward the crib. Trevania held up a hand like a traffic policeman.

"Whoa. I'm the help here."

Gussie slowly understood. "You mean you want to work here?"

Trevania narrowed her eyes. "It sure beat choppin' cotton."

Gussie almost clapped her hands in glee. But what would Ned say? "Gee, I ought to ask my husband."

Trevania tossed her head. "Aunt Velma told me not to study what you say. Your daddy gone take care of it. Now I'm gone change this sweet chile, and then I got to go. My Uncle John out yonder waitin' now," she said.

Trevania changed Grace expertly, then she was out the door with "I be here tomorrow mornin', thank you, ma'am." She bounded down the back steps and sashayed across the yard toward a pickup truck driven by an elderly dark-skinned man, a pickup truck with shovels in the back.

Gussie bit her lip. Would Ned kick up a fuss about taking charity from Papa? Suddenly she didn't care. Was he here helping to wash and iron and cook? And what about his trips at night to those blind tigers? Poker games?

"Trevania," Gussie called out.

The young woman looked back.

"Nine-thirty?" Gussie called out. Ned would have left for the office by then. Trevania nodded a smile, then hopped in the cab of the truck. Gussie watched the truck back down the driveway. She'd have to tell

Ned eventually. She hoped he'd get used to the neat and tidy house before he found out.

And maybe someday—maybe someday—she could get back to her photographs. She'd make her own money and pay Papa back.

And get a manicure.

Sunday at the hospital began under a bright china-blue sky and a light breeze, and patients were in good spirits, which lasted well into the afternoon. Lunch over, Tenny hummed as she rolled the linen cart into a newly vacated private room. The dull green room, stale with lingering odors, needed airing. She walked over to the window, pushed it open, and took a deep breath of the sweet morning breeze.

She nearly choked.

Down below, Arno Shackley and Miss Ola Stratton, arm-in-arm, strolled from the hospital toward the parking lot. She watched, appalled, as he opened the door for her, the door of the same Ford motorcar that had chased a runaway girl down the highway.

Did Mr. Shackley come every Sunday with Miss Ola to the hospital to deliver her flowers from the First Baptist Church? Was he courting the old maid, now that Miss Rose was dead?

There he was, getting in his car, all dressed up, looking like he had been to Sunday dinner at her house eating fried chicken and three kinds of pickles and four kinds of vegetables and biscuits and cornbread and peach pie and pound cake and God knew what-all.

Tenny turned away from the window and savagely stripped the bed. She snapped a fresh sheet into the air and let it float into place, then smoothed it down. Just as she began to tuck it in, the floor nurse appeared at the door.

"Oakes! Thank God you're here! Get down to the basement and bring up a cylinder of oxygen."

Tenny turned. "But I'm—"

"We're short-handed," the floor nurse snapped. "We need that tank now, Nurse. Bring it to the pneumonia ward."

"Right away," Tenny said. She hurried to the nurses' station where the keys were kept and opened the cabinet where they hung. The hook marked *storage* was empty. She turned to the desk. "Who's got the storage key, Tillie?"

Miss Tillman lifted her pen, looked up from an index card, and shrugged. "Don't know. Nobody signed it out."

Someone was already down there.

She clattered down the three flights of steps to the ground floor, hurried past the emergency room and the X-Ray room.

The storage room, where all cylinders of gases were kept, was near the loading bay, at the end of a long hall. Why didn't they keep some on each floor? Did she dare make a suggestion?

She tried the doorknob, but it wouldn't budge. Was that a shuffle she heard inside? She banged the door with her fist. "Anybody in there? I need to get in! Emergency!"

Silence. Maybe the noise had come from across the hall.

She tried the doorknob across the hall. It opened easily, and she found herself staring into a broom closet.

She closed the door with an exasperated moan and hurried to the stairwell, grabbing the door handle. The unmistakable click of a lock echoed in the hall. She ducked into the stairwell, closed the door partially behind her, and peered out.

Enid and one of the new interns, the naive-looking one who looked as if he might be good at baseball, emerged from the storage area. Enid's lipstick was smeared and her cheeks were flushed. With deft strokes, she smoothed her apron.

Tenny burst from the stairwell and dashed down the hall. "Enid! I need the storage room key!"

The key and its tag were dangling from Enid's hand. The intern gave Tenny an uneasy glance and hurried off without a word. Enid stared after him.

Tenny held out her hand. "Quick! Oxygen cylinder for 4B. Pneumonia."

Enid, flushing dark red now, slapped the key into Tenny's palm. "I can make life miserable for you."

"Dry up, Enid." Tenny plunged into the room.

She boarded the elevator and pushed the button for the third floor. At eleven pounds, the tank was no heavier than a three-month-old baby, but it was dead weight, and she felt a little winded when she emerged from the elevator.

Pete Godwin approached just as she got off. "Miss Oakes!" he said cheerfully. "Can I give you a hand?"

"Oh," she said, taking a deep breath, trying to still the pulse in her throat. "I'm fine." She couldn't appear to be weak. Not here. Not now.

"Then carry on." He winked at her. With a second wind, she propelled the cylinder into the room. They should get wheels for these things.

The doctor and the charge nurse were waiting for her. The patient, a young man, skin blue with cyanosis, was wheezing and rasping, each breath labored.

"It's his last chance," the nurse murmured. "What took you so long?"

"I'm so sorry," Tenny said. "The key—"

"Never mind." The rest of the apparatus, with its rubber tubing and wash bottle, was ready. "You students stay and watch," the nurse said to Tenny and a second girl as she took charge of the tank.

Tenny expected the doctor to connect the cylinder to a pharyngeal insufflation apparatus, but the doctor inserted the pharyngeal tube directly into the patient's mouth.

"This is a new treatment," the nurse explained. "See that valve? It controls the oxygen flow under tank pressure. The doctor will turn it on and off, 12 times a minute."

The nurse opened the valve of the cylinder, and the doctor worked the respiratory valve. Tenny watched in amazement as the cyanosis faded. As the young man's skin took on a normal color, his face became familiar. Someone at the mill she remembered as a good man.

"Will this treatment cure him?" She clasped her hands.

The charge nurse shook her head. "At this stage, when the oxygen is stopped, he becomes cyanotic again. We have to keep going. It may take hours. We may need more oxygen."

"May I stay and watch?"

"Bring us another cylinder," the charge nurse said. "Just in case."

But she wanted to learn! At least she still had the key. Disappointed, she headed to the stairs. To her astonishment, Ramona emerged from the stairwell, limping only a little.

She gave her friend a hug. "Gosh, it's good to see you! You're not sick again, are you?"

"It's Joe." She shook her head miserably. "Joe Kinley. He's got pneumonia."

"Joe—your boyfriend?"

Ramona nodded, her eyes brimming. "My husband, really. We got married after the accident."

That's why the patient had looked so familiar! "Oh, Ramona. They're giving him oxygen. A new treatment. It just might work."

Ramona brushed away a tear. "They fired me. And now they'll fire him. It will kill him."

"We'll get him well." Tenny put a hand on her friend's shoulder. "I'll come back and check on him."

She hated to leave her friend, but she couldn't risk any more demerits. She prayed for Joe like she'd never prayed in church. Not even with Brother Jethro.

She delivered another cylinder and was dismissed.

When she finally came off a long, dull shift, she made straight for Joe's room, but Ramona had left and Joe was sleeping. The charge nurse told her he'd get another oxygen treatment the following day.

Finally, Tenny sank to the iron bed in her room and stripped off her lisle stockings. She suppressed a knot of envy that Alice was having supper with her boyfriend, Dan, and wouldn't be back until curfew.

What a day! Ramona, poor Joe Kinley, the storage room—and seeing Shackley again. She would never forget that devil face over her in the moonlight, that foul tobacco breath.

Anger rose to the surface, bubbled, and exploded. Walking arm-in-arm with Miss Ola! Did that old maid know what kind of man he was? She clenched her fist to stop her hand from trembling. Oh, if she just had Pa's rifle! Byron had taught her to shoot, and she'd brought down squirrels and rabbits that went into their meager dinners.

She'd never liked shooting critters, and she was here to heal, not to kill. If only Miss Verity were here to talk to, or her sisters, Merry, or Shelley, or even Emmy Dee. They'd clung together, a life raft in the sea of her father's hopelessness. Her brother Byron had run away, and her brother Milton had become silent, plodding through each day.

With a rush of tenderness she realized how much she missed them all. She shook off the feeling. She had no time to be tender.

She opened her desk and took out the box of letter paper. She took a long look at her small stash of bills and coins tucked underneath the envelopes. The Bible money was disappearing little by little, used for things she needed for school. She hoped, in the end, she'd be able to repay Pa, even if it was evil money.

She began to write.

*Dear Mrs. Brown,*

    *Thank you for your letter letting me know Merry was sick. How I wish I could be there to tend her but I have a job I cannot leave. Flu is a bad thing. I hope the worst has past and I am so grateful you have been over there with soup and good words. Lord knows Milton is no cook and I am not surprise to learn they have been living on pork and beans. I am surprise that Pa was so worried about her dying that he listened to your words about Jesus. Maybe he wont blame him for Mama anymore.*

    *Now I must tell you I have seen Mr. Shackley here in town. It seems he is squiring around a widow with loads of money. That must go along with what you told me about him wanting to buy that farm off Judge Pemberton.*

    *All I can say is, I hope the judge can hang on until times get better.*

    *Now for another one of my newspaper clippings. Here is a picture of Miss Swanee Burkett, whose father owns the cotton mill, and her mother. They returned from Europe where they have been traveling. It also said that Miss Burkett studied painting in Paris. She is very glamorous.*

    *Here is some money to buy medicine for poor Merry. Please write soon and tell me how everyone is doing.*

She signed the letter, sighed, and went to brush her teeth. She had to be up at five-thirty, and the hospital was crowded. Too much rain and then a drought, crops were failing this summer, and sickness seemed to follow in the wake of bad news.

Pete Godwin, at least, was here until September. Being near him gave her a feeling like lying in the shade of a tree by the river, while the sun danced in the leaves and the breeze played a tune in her hair.

She turned off her electric lamp. She ought to forget about him. He might never come back after school was over, and of one thing she was certain: Arno Shackley would be back. She had only her thin disguise of hat and brown hair. If he recognized her, he might threaten them all. She had to think of something else.

# Chapter 34

H enry Benedict brooded as he walked home from classes, his coat over his arm. He should be elated, but, instead, gloom dogged his steps. Mother would be so happy at the judge's praise for his work, for the hint of a clerkship after he graduated. That job might mean he'd see more of Gussie. That was the hellish thing.

Mother knew something was up, from the way he brooded. She'd even wondered if he had a crush on the little hospital nurse who'd looked after him when he'd had that appendix operation. Miss Oakes, who came from everywhere and nowhere, had intrigued him, but curiosity wasn't love.

For him, there was only one woman. Too bad.

As he crossed the river bridge, he stopped to watch an empty barge float by. Later in the year the barges would be loaded with cotton, fewer than the year before. In Lafayette County alone the yield had dropped steadily from 2 million bales in 1911 to 500,000 last year. The boll weevil had marched through the South, and after 1920, cotton mills had geared down when the army didn't need so many uniforms, rucksacks, and bandages.

At the sound of a factory quitting whistle, Henry walked on toward the lowering sun past warehouses crowded with dollies and trams; past docks where barges rocked, tied to piers, while herons flapped lazily across the river. He turned down Azalea Street, a narrow row of neat wooden houses.

Henry's neighbor Emory Latrelle, head mechanic at the plant, was going home, lunch pail in hand. He hailed Henry, grinning, and Henry hailed him back, glad to see him. Emory was the closest thing he had to a father now.

After Henry's father had died, and he and his mother had sold their rambling Victorian house and moved into the cottage on Azalea Street, Emory had often taken young Henry fishing, along with his own boys, Jack and Milford. The youngest Latrelle, Sam, had been just a toddler then.

Henry watched as Sam, now about seven, leaped off the front porch with an athlete's grace and ran to his father. That kid looked like a natural, and he just might play his way out of the mill village. Sam idolized Ty Cobb and wanted to grow up to be just like him.

The paint job Henry had just completed on his mother's house— yellow with white trim—looked good, as did the front flower beds. Mahala Benedict had planted geraniums and marigolds, tomatoes staked among them. It wasn't the gracious old house where he'd spent his early years, but Mother had made the cottage into a cozy home.

She'd been waiting for him. She opened the door and leaned forward to kiss him on the cheek, eyes crinkling at the corners. "How was your day?" she began, but a volley of coughing swallowed her words.

"I'm fine," Henry said, scowling. "But you're not. That damned lint gets everywhere in that plant." He took off his flat cap and hung it on a peg by the door.

She shook her head, hand to mouth. "Not in the offices, Henry."

"Lint travels," Henry said. "Why on earth didn't you apply for that job at the college I told you about?"

She gave him a sideways glance. "Have you forgotten the paltry salary they were offering? Mr. Burkett does pay me well."

Henry snorted. "He couldn't get along without you. All those extra hours he makes you work sometimes . . ."

"Hush, Henry. You know why I do it." And he did. Mother was determined that he fulfill his father's wish, to follow him into the law. Henry vowed that one day he'd be able to look after her, and she could quit that job.

She laid a hand on his shoulder. "Come along to the kitchen. I'll fry some eggs for you."

"No, you won't. I'm taking you to a restaurant." Henry wanted tonight to be special.

She frowned, but her eyes sparkled. "Henry, I won't have you spending your money on me."

He walked over and kissed her on the cheek. "We have to eat, and Mulligan's serves a pretty good blue plate special. We're celebrating because Judge Pemberton gave me the top mark in the class on a jurisprudence paper and hinted he'd offer me a clerkship when I graduate."

"Oh, Henry. That's wonderful. He's the fairest man I know. He'd give you that grade only if you deserved it."

"I hope so. Let's go." He grabbed his cap.


Mulligan's mouthwatering aromas of cornbread and fried chicken and spiced apple pies tempted Henry, but hungry after the long day and longer walk, he gave the waitress their order for the special. The fried pork chops and potatoes, butterbeans and pickled peaches, and buttermilk pie for dessert were just what he needed.

The meal was good, and Henry enjoyed seeing his mother's eyes glow. He'd settled into contentment when the waitress brought their slices of pie and steaming coffee. He'd just lifted his fork when the front door swung open. A young woman glided in, her peach-colored straw cloche pulled down so far Henry couldn't see anything but bee-stung, painted red lips.

The man with her, sporting a well-cut linen jacket and a silk tie, murmured something to the hostess, who then led them to a table in the farthest corner. The man pulled out the girl's chair and made sure she was settled.

Henry's fork stopped in mid-air.

"Henry? What are you looking at?"

"Those people. Uptown types. Slumming, you know?"

His mother sneaked a look and turned back quickly, an odd expression on her face. "What are they doing?"

"Leaning forward. Their hands are touching."

"Henry." Her voice sank to a whisper. "I have to tell you something."

"What?"

"Sssh. I'll tell you on the way home."

They finished the pie and coffee. Henry paid the bill at the front, gnawing on a free toothpick. Mahala let herself outside and waited in the muggy air, and when Henry joined her, they walked in silence, the only sounds their footsteps and the lonely hoot of a train. When they were halfway home from the café, he said, "Okay, Mother. Out with it."

"Henry, promise me you won't breathe this to a living soul." Mahala strode steadily, her hands jammed into her pockets, bag swinging from her shoulder. "It could be completely innocent." Her voice sounded dubious, nevertheless.

"Of course, Mother." Henry waited, the faint wail of a distant ambulance tracking the silent evening, the smell of the river in the air.

"It was the manager from the plant," she murmured. "And the girl with him was Elias Burkett's daughter."

"Ned Fletcher, you mean?" Henry clenched his fists, feeling heat creep up his neck.

"That bothers you," Mahala said quietly.

"He's the man who married Judge Pemberton's daughter." *And now he's two-timing her.*

They reached the corner and turned to cross the street. A Cadillac sped by, too close. Mahala said, "Miss Burkett's been on a Grand Tour of Europe with her mother and cousin, and then she stayed on in Paris to study art for a few months. I'm surprised her mother let her stay."

"I hear she's engaged, too," Henry said. "Funny way to spend your engagement."

Mahala nodded. "I'd like to imagine an innocent reason for those two to be meeting, but it's difficult. I've seen her at the plant going into Mr. Fletcher's office. Does she think I don't notice?" She smiled ruefully.

Henry didn't know what to say. They walked on in the glimmering dusk, greeting an elderly neighbor out for a stroll.

Across from their house Sam Latrelle and his brother were playing catch out in the yard with their father, tossing the baseball around. One throw went wide and the ball rolled into the street. Sam chased after it, scooped it up, and tossed it with an easy side-arm.

"Impressive for a little kid," Henry said, giving the boys a wave. "A natural."

At the house, he unlocked the door for his mother. For Gussie's sake, he hoped there was some explanation for what he'd seen at the restaurant.

"What will you do, Mother? I mean tomorrow at the office?"

She shrugged, gave him a long look, and walked inside. "It isn't my business what goes on outside of working hours, and I don't carry tales about my employer."

Henry hung his cap on its peg. "I don't want Gussie to know of this."

"Gussie? Is that her name, Judge Pemberton's daughter?" Mahala looked searchingly at her son.

Henry realized he'd made a slip, but decided to plunge ahead. "Augusta. The judge once hired me to keep an eye on her."

"Oh," said Mahala, her eyes widening. "I hadn't made the connection. I really should have, shouldn't I?" Henry watched her face, settled and calm, as though she'd found the answer to something that had been puzzling her.

Half an hour later, after his mother had gone to her room to rest, Henry leaned back in his father's cracked brown leather Morris chair, a textbook on torts on his knees. Outside the open window, lightning bugs rose from the dry grass and a sweet wind blustered in. A motorcar was approaching, fast, by the sound of it. He slammed the book shut. He'd get the tag number of the speed demon and let the police deal with it.

Just as he reached the door, brakes screeched and a boy screamed, high and terrifying, and then a man shouted, and the man shouted again, and then he howled, a long and agonizing howl.

Henry slammed open the door and ran out into the street where, in the twilight, a man was kneeling on the roadway.

Neighbors were gathering, some with hands to mouths. Young Sam Latrelle lay unconscious in the road, an ugly red bruise on his head.

Someone handed Henry a flashlight. He played the light across the boy and gritted his teeth when he saw one leg bent like a marionette's. Doors opened, light spilling out. One voice shouted that he'd called the police. "Where's the car?" Henry looked around for the driver.

"Drove right on," said Emory, voice choked, tears running down his face.

"Don't move the boy," Henry said, swallowing and clenching his fists. He needed to be calm for Emory. "Try to make him comfortable. I'll call for an ambulance."

He found Mahala in the living room, robe pulled around her. He told her what had happened, made the call, then hurried back outside to Emory Latrelle's side. "Where's Mildred?"

"Over to her mother's," said Emory Latrelle, his hand over his eyes. "I told the boys to put up that ball and come in. I'd already started up to the porch."

Henry's mother appeared then, fully dressed in coat and hat. "You and I will go and tell Mildred."

When the ambulance came in, Tenny sighed. It was getting along toward eight-thirty, and she'd had a full day of bee stings, heatstroke, sprains, broken bones, concussions. She'd been going hard since three o'clock.

A car accident, a little boy, they said. Tenny's tiredness faded; she straightened her shoulders and entered the room where the duty doctor and the senior nurses crowded around the boy's stretcher truck, trying to stabilize him. Pete Godwin caught Tenny's eye. "Oakes, go tell the boy's parents a bone specialist is on the way."

She found them hovering outside the door in the crowded waiting area and told them about the specialist. "Won't you sit down and have a cup of coffee? Some water?"

Sam's mother shook her head and buried her face in her hands. The father wanted to talk. Tired, a little heavy, he kept running his hands through his graying thatch of hair, words running out in a stream. ". . . the dark was comin' down, and the lightnin' bugs was risin' in the yard, and I told the boys to come on in. I was just goin' up the porch steps, thought they was behind me, when this car come speedin' down the street."

His voice grew hard. "Jack, he threw the baseball at the damn car when it didn't stop. I hope he cracked a window."

Sam's mother started to wail, long, agonizing. One old man in a shabby coat coughed, shifted uneasily, and looked away. A red-haired woman came over and asked if she could do anything. The charge nurse appeared and put her arm around the mother's shoulders and spoke quietly in her ear. The wails tapered into quiet sobs.

Dr. Emmett Godwin strode in with Dr. Huff, the orthopedist. "Ah, Nurse Oakes," he said. "You might as well come on back and scrub up. We'll need extra help."

Tenny gulped. This was part of her education, but she'd never seen them operate on a child. She walked through the big double doors into the surgery area and went to the lockers to find a smock and mask. Then she walked over to the sink and scrubbed well with green soap, eyeing the charge nurse, who was too busy to criticize her scrubbing.

Then she helped Dr. Huff into his surgical gown.

The little boy looked so pale, white face, shock of dark hair, contusion on his forehead covered with gauze padding. The drape was pulled back and she gasped to see his leg, then bit her lip when Dr. Emmett frowned.

Dr. Huff bent over the leg.

She listened to the doctors with a sinking heart. The bone was splintered. Shoulder dislocated. Broken ribs. Broken fingers. She thought of the nurse at the plant, who'd been through a war. There was no war here, but there was horror enough. Had anyone seen that driver? Did anyone know what kind of car it was?

"Ether," the doctor said to the anesthesia nurse, beckoning to Tenny. She stepped forward to help, hearing her own breath behind her mask.

Across the table Pete Godwin watched as Dr. Huff began the operation, exploring the fractured leg with infinite patience to see if he could save it. Finally, with barely concealed anger, he shook his head. "I'm going to try to save this leg if it takes all night. Take that saw away."

Sometime after eleven, Tenny headed to her quarters, looking forward to bath, book, and sleep, preferably until next Thursday.

"Hey, Oakes."

She stopped and caught her breath, and Pete Godwin walked up behind her. "I finally found you," he said, catching her arm.

"What's happened?" Her arm tingled where he'd touched it, and she tensed, waiting for bad news about the boy.

"The kid's doing as well as can be expected," Pete said. "This a social emergency. I need some company. Cup of java?"

So he'd been as affected by that little patient as she had. "Fair warning. If I collapse from fatigue you'll have to throw me on a stretcher truck and push me to quarters."

He shrugged. "Why not? I'm already on Miss Wells's scut list."

Pete emptied black sludge from the newfangled electric percolator, filled it with fresh coffee and water, and plugged it in.

Tenny set out two sturdy white mugs and poured hers half full of milk from the bottle in the icebox. Waiting for the coffee, Pete told her that he'd heard that little Sam wanted to be a baseball player when he grew up.

A tear trickled down Tenny's cheek.

"Sorry," Pete said.

"It's okay. I'm tired."

The coffee was ready. Before they could get up, another intern pushed through the door, not even glancing their way, and filled a mug. They waited until he'd gone before they filled their own and sat down again.

"Let's start over," Pete said. "Where did you come from, girl with a poet's name?"

Tenny shook her head. "Nowhere. Really."

Pete gave her a stop-the-bushwah look. "Smart girl. You're hiding something, but no matter. You know your stuff and you're usually pretty cool. Tonight has shaken you up."

She sank back to the sofa. "This is just cruelty."

"Scum. And I couldn't do anything to help."

"Dr. Huff did all he could."

"Huff's a good man," said Pete. "He'll save that boy's leg if anybody can. I hope I can learn a lot from him this summer."

The conversation faltered, and Tenny looked down into her milky cup. The strain of the day had wrung her dry. She pushed a damp strand of hair off her forehead. "I'd better get to bed before I collapse."

"Tenny," Pete finally said, "one more thing. Why have you dyed your hair?"

She felt the blood drain out of her face. He'd noticed the strand that had escaped her cap. "Dye my hair? What are you talking about? Nice girls like me don't dye their hair."

Pete reached forward and touched the unruly tress.

"You don't want to be found."

She pulled away, rose from the table, picked up her empty mug, and crossed to the sink. She washed it and hung it on a drying peg. "Good night, Doctor," she said.

"I'm pulling a late shift," he said, rising. "And my name is Pete." He grasped her hand warmly. "Goodnight, poet girl."

Spontaneously they embraced, warm bodies comforting each other because of the damnable accident to the child, and Tenny felt her first real peace since her mother died. In some way, she felt she had come home. He kissed her, gently, warmly, a kiss that went all the way to her toes.

She pulled away, breathless at the unfamiliar sensation. He smiled and touched her cheek before they went their separate ways. Tenny stumbled back to her room through the quiet halls, seeing stars and shadows, heart like a raft on a raging river.

# Chapter 35

Ned was two hours late.

Her great-aunt's grandfather clock in the hall ticked louder and louder, tick-tock, tick-tock, *tick-tock*, just like that story by Edgar Allan Poe. The clock chimed the half hour. Gussie adjusted the mosquito netting over Gracie's cradle and gazed down on the sleeping infant. She longed to pick up the baby and hug her, feel the tiny heart beating next to hers.

At the window, she pulled back the light dimity curtain, looking down at the empty garage. Lately he'd been dining out more and more, despite Trevania's excellent cooking. But most restaurants were closed now.

She let the curtain drop. Unable to sleep, she settled into a comfortable chair and picked up the book she'd been reading. She read the same page three times. The hall clock seemed to tick louder. She went downstairs to make herself a glass of warm milk.

Just as she entered the kitchen, Ned's car roared into in the driveway, tires squealing. She stood rooted to the spot, waiting. The kitchen door slammed open and Ned strode in, jaw clenched and eyes vacant. His face looked as pale as one of Poe's corpses.

"Hello, baby." He turned and pushed the door shut. He faced her, breathing heavily, hands hanging by his sides as if they belonged to somebody else. He made no move to kiss her.

She swallowed. "Ned, what is it? What's the matter?"

"Going to Savannah. Tonight."

Gussie's heart hammered. "Ned, what's *happened*?"

"The guy I had dinner with. Needs me to go right away."

"There's no Savannah train until morning. What's wrong? What are you keeping from me?"

"Nothing, babe. I'm taking the car."

Gussie began to tremble, but she forced herself to keep her head. "You'll drive all night. The roads are awful. Not even paved in places. Is it all that important?"

"I have to go." His eyes were bloodshot.

"You've been drinking. You'll end up in a ditch." She leaned forward and grabbed his arms. "Listen to me, Ned!"

"What the hell, Gussie!" He pushed her away. Gussie flinched, thinking quickly. It would be better not to fight him now. "Calm down, Ned. At least let me make you some coffee."

Ned drummed his fingers on the table. "Yeah. And make me a ham sandwich or two. To go."

She opened the breadbox. "I wish you'd wait for the six-thirty train . . ."

She was talking to air. His feet were pounding up the stairs.

"Don't wake the baby," Gussie called. Her hands shook as she cut slices from a fresh loaf.

She spread butter and mustard on bread and ham that Trevania had baked yesterday. She wrapped the sandwiches in waxed paper and put them into a basket. When the coffee had perked, she filled a Thermos bottle, and then a cup.

By the time she finished, he was coming into the kitchen with his smaller leather case. "Here's your coffee," Gussie said.

To her surprise, he kissed her on the cheek when he took the cup. "My sweetheart, my angel. Thanks. See you in a couple of days." He took a long swig. "Black as night, sweet as love, and hot as hell. Just like I like it."

"Do you really have to go?" She couldn't stop trembling. "Won't you tell me what's wrong?"

"Trust me a little." He drew her close and planted a long, slow kiss on her lips, a kiss tasting of coffee and whiskey and something strange. He drained the cup, grabbed the basket of food, and walked out.

Gussie leaned against the back door, watching him turn the car in the pool of gaslight. The front fender looked odd, bent maybe, and the back fender—was it dented? He shifted gears badly, rasping and grinding, and then he gunned the engine.

She rubbed her cheek, her lips. That kiss. It had held a lingering trace of some French perfume.


When the phone rang at nine o'clock the next morning, Gussie almost jumped out of her skin. After a fitful night for both her and the baby, she'd overslept, and now had just managed to drag herself and Gracie to the kitchen to let Trevania in.

Trevania, inspecting Gussie, frowned. "You look like you seen a ghost. Sit yourself down, Miss Gussie. I'll get that contraption." She laid the morning paper on the kitchen table.

"Wait." Gussie, sighing, handed Gracie to Trevania. "I'd better answer. It might be . . . it might be Ned."

In the dark front hall, her hand hovered over the new telephone on its stand. She snatched it up. "Hello?"

"Mrs. Fletcher? Are you there?"

A woman's voice. Gussie swallowed. "Yes."

"This is Mahala Benedict at Burkett Mills. I'm working in the office with your husband. Is he at home?"

Gussie's heart pounded. "No. You don't know?"

"Know what, dear?"

Gussie caught her breath and a chill crept up her neck. "He left for Savannah last night. He said there was some emergency with a supplier, or a customer—he didn't give me much information."

"I see. I don't know about any such emergency, but he's scheduled to fill in for Mr. Burkett while he's away at a meeting in Atlanta for a couple of days. I need Mr. Fletcher's signature to order some parts, but I'll handle this as best I can. What a time for him to leave!"

The last sentence had been full of feeling. Gussie's stomach turned cold. "Has something happened at the mill? Can you tell me?"

The secretary cleared her throat. "I'm surprised Mr. Fletcher didn't tell you. Our chief mechanic's son got hit by a car. The child will live, we hope, but he's likely to be a cripple for the rest of his life."

Gussie's knees buckled, and she crumpled onto the seat of the phone stand. "I'm so sorry. So very sorry. I'll be sure to have Ned call you the minute I hear from him." She rattled the receiver back onto its cradle and took deep breaths, trying to keep the fog at bay, trying not to faint.

She pushed herself to her feet, gathering her wits. How could she get in touch with Ned? She hurried to Ned's desk in the parlor. Three drawers were locked, but the fourth slid open. She found a few bills and what she was looking for, a letter from Wyckham, something about land prices. She didn't care what it said. The letter had Wyckham's address.

She threw her raincoat over her old cotton house dress to hide the baby spit-up, grabbed her pocketbook, and told Trevania she was going to the telegraph office.

The word he was needed might reach him at Wyckham's, it might not. Her stomach clenched. Right now, she resolved that to keep her sanity she had to keep going, keep to her planned day. That would keep her sane.

When she returned with the receipt in hand, she went upstairs and changed to a nicer day day dress for town. She dusted her pale face with powder, chose a lipstick, and picked up her cologne atomizer.

She'd buy eggs so Trevania could bake a caramel cake for the church bake sale. Something for supper? Tre could fry some chicken, and it might keep until Ned came home. If he came home. Her hands trembled, and the crystal atomizer slipped to the floor. Its netted bulb popped off the stem and rolled across the floor.

Gussie picked it up. She scrubbed the scent off her hands with soap and water, tears running down her face and dripping into the basin. She wanted her mother.

Downstairs, the kitchen had been tidied, the dishes washed, and Trevania was sprinkling a basket of clothes. She looked up, questioning, when Gussie walked in.

Gussie clasped her hands together. "I don't suppose you've heard about the accident to one of the mill children—"

Frowning, Trevania nodded. "Uncle John told me. The po-lice looking to grab one of my folks, but it ain't none of us. Some devil from hell in a fancy car run that child down. Never even stopped."

Gussie's jaw fell. "Did anybody see the car?"

"If they did, they ain't sayin."

Gussie cleared her throat. "Well. Mr. Ned has gone to Savannah and won't be back for a couple of days, so Gracie and I can just eat leftovers from that ham tonight. I'll buy some chicken to fry tomorrow."

Gussie watched Trevania carefully for a reaction, but Tre put on her poker face and turned back to the ironing. "Ain't much ham left. I can make soup from the hambone."

"That'll do. Now I'm going to take Gracie to my mother's and stop at the market. I'd love a caramel cake for the bake sale."

"That's the best idey you had all morning," said Trevania.

Gussie found her mother in the breakfast room clacking on her typewriter, glasses down on her nose, hair in an untidy knot, dressed in a printed cotton frock which had seen better days.

"Mama? Mama!"

Her mother looked up at last, squinting and blinking. "Augusta! Isn't it just awful? I'm writing a letter to the editor. I can't believe not one person saw that car!" She scooted back her chair and held out her arms for the baby.

"What car?" Gussie, chilled, handed Gracie over to her grandmother. Gracie burbled and reached for the shiny oval eyeglasses. Gussie's mother took them off, set them to the side, and the narrow-eyed gaze that met Gussie was that of an outraged social worker.

"Surely Ned must have told you. A car ran over one of the mill children last night and nearly killed him. I went to the hospital to comfort his poor mother. Look!" She pointed to the morning *Clarion*. The headline read:

LOCAL BOY IN HIT-AND-RUN

Car Sought by Police

Gussie read through the article quickly. The boy's distraught father hadn't seen the car, and neither, it seemed, had anyone else. Jack, the brother, had thrown a baseball at the car, but he wasn't sure what kind of car he might have hit. Not a Ford or Chevy, he said. He knew those.

Gussie pretended to study the majestic oak tree outside. "What—what time did it happen?"

"Around eight or so," said Belinda. "Getting dark. The boy's mother had been over visiting the grandmother, down with pleurisy. Oh, it was sad. The father is beside himself."

Gussie sat like a statue. The damaged fenders of the yellow Pierce-Arrow. The hurried trip to Savannah. Ned had said he'd eaten downtown with a customer. Why would he have gone near the mill village?

She swallowed again, went into the kitchen, and came back with a glass of water. Her mother stopped playing patty-cake with Gracie. "I hope Ned's concerned about this. The mill ought to offer some help. Don't tell me he's that callous."

"Well, Mama, I'm sure . . ."

"I'm hoping the police will give this case their full attention. Needle in a haystack, they'll say. Nobody saw anything. Just a poor mill kid. Why, they should be going around and checking every garage."

"Maybe they are." Gussie sipped her water and realized her free hand was clenched, nails biting into her palm. She shook her hand out.

Her mother didn't seem to notice. "Elias Burkett ought to be worried. His workers are already upset about the new work rules. He needs to pay for the boy's medical expenses. Both parents work at that mill. It would be the right thing to do."

Gussie shook her head. "Good luck with Mr. Scrooge."

"Of course he'll balk. I'm going to convince him it'll be good business."

Maybe now wasn't the time to tell Mama about Ned running off to Savannah or to ask her to watch Gracie. "I need to get some eggs and things, Mama. I see you're busy, so guess I'd better be going."

"You just got here, and now you're going again?"

"I was just walking the baby and decided to drop in."

"Really?" her mother's gaze turned searching. "You look strained, honey. Things all right between you and Ned?"

"Of course, Mama." She looked away to hide her blush.

"I'll walk out with you," Belinda said, her voice softer.

Gussie had left the baby carriage by the back door. In the back yard, pecan trees in full leaf towered above azalea beds, now spent of blooms. Other beds sported a color riot of geraniums, petunias, and marigolds, scenting the air. Gussie sighed. She'd never be able to garden like her mother.

Because she'd rather be dancing than digging.

Her mother was saying, "Come to dinner on Sunday after church, you and Ned and my little chickadee. It's the Fourth of July. "

Gussie swallowed and forced a smile. "We'll come." She kissed her mother's cheek.

She set out on the sidewalk as the sun climbed into a cloudless pale sky overhead. Before she'd walked half a block, rivulets of perspiration trickled down her temples and down her neck. Her cotton dress clung to her back and legs. She'd be drenched by the time she got home.

Still, it felt good to be walking, out of the house, where the wretched telephone couldn't ring with bad news. Maybe she'd take Gracie home and go to the town market rather than the corner store. She could go on the trolley and look for early peaches along with the eggs. She and Trevania could put up a few jars for the winter. She could send some to that poor family.

Peaches. Peaches. Peaches. She said it to herself, all the way home. She wasn't going to think about anything else.

At home, Trevania told her there had been no messages.

Oh, God. Where was Ned?

# Chapter 36

On Monday, the fifth of July, a rainy spell had just ended, leaving curls of steam rising from the cobblestones. In the stifling atmosphere indoors, Tenny, assigned to both the men's medical ward and the sterilizing room, gave cool baths and adjusted electric fans and then sterilized instruments, up to her eyes in steam.

After morning duty, she splashed water on her face before she dragged herself outside to watch the Independence Day parade on the front steps of the nurses' quarters with the other girls. High-stepping bands in red and white uniforms, horses and riders in spangled cowboy gear, and bunting-draped automobiles carrying the mayor and the aldermen passed by, followed by girls dressed as Lady Liberty or Betsy Ross on gaily decorated mule-drawn floats.

One of the other interns, Mason, came to join them for a few minutes, but no Pete. Maybe he was eating barbecue and sweet corn with his swell friends. Maybe Enid had cornered him for a party.

"Coming with us to the band concert?" one of the other students asked.

She shook her head. "I've got some letters to write." What if she ran into Arno Shackley? Pa and the kids? Would they see through her disguise? She trudged up the steps to head back inside.

"Tenny!"

She wheeled toward the familiar voice. Ramona, in a wide straw hat, was grinning like a pumpkin and whipping a small flag around.

Tenny bounced down the steps and hugged her.

"Hey girl, you folks did a fine job on Joe," Ramona said. "I was hopin' you'd be able to get loose to go down to the park for the band concert."

"Gosh, I was going to write letters . . ."

"They can wait!" Ramona urged. "We'll stop by the drugstore and get cherry dopes!"

Tenny ached to go and decided to risk it. "Come on up with me. I need to change."

"Twenty-three skiddoo."

In her room, Tenny shut the door. "Ramona, uncover your head. I want to see how you've healed. I didn't have time last week."

Ramona slowly pulled off her hat. "You like the topper? I bought it off Myrtle Mincus. Got tired of that yellow one."

"The hat's okay." A chunk of Ramona's hair was missing, and a ruddy scar snaked its way down her left temple like an angry salamander. Fresh hair, short and frizzed like wool, grew in patches.

"It won't ever come back, will it?" asked Ramona slowly.

Tenny shrugged. "Mostly it will. It might not be the same texture, and it'll take time. Don't worry, you look good in a hat." She needed to change the subject. "Is Joe back at work?"

Ramona half-smiled. "Thank God. He's a supervisor, so they didn't replace him. But he didn't get paid those two weeks. And he still coughs."

"Give him slippery elm tea," Tenny said. The best thing for him to do was to leave the mill.

She buttoned her best cotton dress and pulled on her straw cloche, buckled her T-strap shoes, and then adjusted her new eyeglasses. She'd bought two pairs—one smoked and one clear—at forty-five cents apiece from Woolworth's. "Okay, I'm ready."

"Gosh, look at them cheaters. You don't look like yourself."

"Good." Tenny swung her bag over her shoulder.

Though Ramona seemed in good spirits on the way to the drugstore, Tenny knew something was off, and not just her walking. After they were settled in a booth with icy cherry dopes, Tenny leaned forward. "You can tell me, Ramona. What is it?"

Ramona choked back a sob. "There's a new girl in my place. Durn, Tenny, I know how to do most anything in that plant and told them so. They told me there was more girls where I come from." Her eyes blazed. "If it weren't for Joe Kinley, I'd be in a pickle."

"Joe's too good for the likes of that place."

"It's that Mr. Fletcher makes me so mad," Ramona said. "None of the men on the floor can stand him. And the girls." She swallowed. "He flirts, makes 'em think they're special, and then he moves on. I begged Joe to find another mill that would maybe hire me too, but he don't want to give up his seniority." She lowered her voice. "They've got their group now. All together. No more scared rabbits. A union man's in town to meet with 'em."

Tenny's stomach clenched. "Oh, Ramona. Joe needs to be careful. You too."

She shook her head slowly. "He won't let me come to the meetings anymore. There's going to be a strike, Tenny. This night work's killing people."

"Didn't you say Clete Mincus might be a spy?"

"Maybe I was wrong. Joe says he's been a help."

"I wouldn't trust him worth a lick."

"Look," Ramona said. "We won't do anything right away. We'll lay low for a couple of months and build up our strength. Then, when they least expect it—well, I'd better hush. I'm not supposed to talk. To anybody."

Tenny, afraid they'd been overheard, saw only two old ladies that looked alike, one wearing black, spooning up chocolate sundaes. She glanced up at the wall clock and took a last slurp of her drink. "We'd better go."

They threaded their way through the crowd in the park past women in peach and teal print dresses, damply smelling of powder and cologne. They watched men in pinstriped seersucker jackets arrange chairs smartly in front of the bandstand, while children whooped on the grassy lawn.

Tenny thought she saw the nursing assistants among colored women in bright straw hats who milled and joked under the shade trees with men in Sunday shirts. Some sat and rested against the broad trunks of spreading oaks.

They took a wide arc to avoid the millworkers clumped toward the back of the crowd, the women in flowered rayon dresses, the men in hats and suspenders. A few had brought blankets to spread on the grass.

Tenny noted that the mill men huddled, talking, while the women whispered among themselves. There seemed a difference about these women now, something restless and hard. They'd been good workers, grateful to have a job at all. Young Sam's accident had stirred something beneath the surface and jolted the men out of their belief that they couldn't change anything.

The band members, in red-striped shirts, uncased their shining trumpets and trombones as people found their seats. Tenny bought roasted peanuts from a baseball-capped boy scampering between the chairs, and they settled back.

When the band struck up "The Star-Spangled Banner," Tenny and Ramona rose with the rest of the crowd and sang into the perfect summer day. Tenny, spotting familiar faces, edged Ramona with her elbow. "Ned Fletcher's wife. Two rows ahead, no hat, curly bob that's frizzing."

Ramona leaned forward to see. "H'm," she murmured. "Cute girl, but I'm surprised he picked her."

People shushed them and they were quiet until the music ended.

"Why are you surprised?" Tenny murmured.

"The girls he usually favors are the dark-headed, front-loaded type. Is that her baby?"

Tenny peered at the cottony-haired boy over Gussie's shoulder, and her pulse pounded. Whose child was that? Gussie's sister's? Dizzy, she grabbed the side of her chair.

"What is it?" Ramona asked. "Are you okay?"

"I think it's the heat." A kind stranger passed Tenny a funeral fan. With each flap of the fan, she told herself she couldn't suspect every gray-eyed, fair boy child around two years old of being her son.

After the sing-along of "America," the crowd began to leave, some stopping for newspaper cones of boiled peanuts, juicy red slices of watermelon, and Coca-Cola in bottles.

Tenny noted that Ramona had become pale and unsteady. "You're still not well."

Ramona pouted. "Except for these headaches, I'm fine." She elbowed through a group of girls like she really meant it.

Tenny caught her arm. "Take it easy. It's going to take a year to get your health back."

"Don't worry about me," Ramona said. "We come from tough stock, us Finches and Kinleys." On the outskirts of the crowd, she brightened. "Hey. There's Joe, come to walk me home." She waved and whistled to get his attention, and he whipped off his hat and circled it wildly when he spotted Tenny.

"Come on over and give that old rascal a hug," Ramona said. Tenny took one step forward, and then she spotted Clete Mincus lurking in the knot of people near Joe.

"Kiss Joe for me," she said, waving back at him. "I've got to get back and nap before the night shift. Come see me again."

"Sure I will." Ramona hugged Tenny good-bye, then limped across the lawn to join her husband.

Tenny skirted the crowd and left the park, heading for the nurses' quarters. She hated telling a story to Ramona, but she didn't want Mincus to see her. As sly as he was, he might see through her disguise.

In her school postbox lay a letter from Mrs. Brown, forwarded from the Callahan Home. She ripped open the letter and read it standing. She read the page again, and gave a long, low whistle. "Whoever would have believed it of Pa?" she muttered.

# Chapter 37

After the Independence Day concert, Gussie said good-bye to her sister and mother and watched the Hupmobile depart. Then she gave Trevania her pay and carfare, checked on a sleeping Gracie, and stretched out on the divan on the front porch. She left a front window open so she could hear Gracie if she cried. The overhead fan ruffled the sheer curtains behind her, and she basked in the breeze, feeling a good kind of tired. And then a lump rose in her throat. Perfect day, except for Ned.

The fragile relief that had settled in after he'd returned from Savannah was gone.

On Friday, she and Trevania had put up peaches. All the feverish peeling and sugaring and boiling and packing and sterilizing had kept her busy, had kept her from thinking, while the steam rose and the overhead fan whirred.

After Trevania left, Gussie was storing jars in the pantry when she heard the sound of a motor. She went to the screen door. Ned was unfolding himself from the seat of a Model T roadster covered in dust and insect blotches, fenders caked with mud.

She wiped her hands on her apron and walked down the back steps as if wading through molasses.

Ned stepped out of the car. Gussie silently took in the bandage around his head, the sling cradling his left arm, and the cast on his left ankle. "You drove back from Savannah like that?"

Ned smiled lazily. "Babe, I was lucky to find somebody who needed a ride, and let him do most of the driving. Dropped him off downtown."

"What happened to your Pierce-Arrow?" Each word came slowly, deliberately.

He reached out and touched her face. "No kiss for your loving hubby?"

"Not until you explain all this." She folded her arms.

Ned let out a whoosh of air. "You were right, sweetheart. I shouldn't have gone off half-pickled like that. I smashed up the car, landed in a ditch, got knocked cold. I was kind of out of it for a couple of days, but Wyckham's been looking after me."

Her voice went up an octave. "Wyckham! I sent him a telegram! Why didn't he reply?"

Ned paused, blank-faced, as if this was something he hadn't considered. "I told him not to. I didn't want you to worry."

Gussie shrieked, "Didn't want me to *worry*? When that Mrs. Benedict called me—"

"Calm down, honey. Calm down. It's all right now. Come here and give me a big smooch to show me how much you missed me."

Gussie stood calmly in place, hands folded.

He gave her that melting, little-boy-lost look, and then came to her side, putting his good arm around her. "My sweet Gussie, you have a right to be mad." He nuzzled her neck, and her strength crumbled.

She laid her head on his shoulder. "Oh, Ned—"

"You're trembling, babe. Don't worry. I'm back. I hope you don't mind about our ritzy car."

"Oh, no, Ned," she said into his shirt, inhaling his familiar smell, feeling the comforting rhythm of his heart. "Mama always thought it was too grand, anyhow. I'm just glad you're here." She touched his bandaged arm. "Does it hurt?"

He stroked her cheek. "A little. They gave me some medicine for the pain."

Still shaken, Gussie walked with him into the house, carrying his bag. "Did they tell you that someone ran down one of the mill children? It's upset all of us, especially Mama."

Ned looked down at her, warm concern in his tea-colored eyes. "It's a pity. I'll ask Burkett to see that they get some help."

"Mama said she'd ask him, but if you do too . . ."

"Of course," he said. "I've missed you so." He smoothed her hair from her face with his good hand. "I want to make love to you tonight, long, slow love, touch and taste you everywhere . . ." He kissed her gently. "I want you to touch me, too. You know how I love you."

Gussie relaxed into his arms, warmth deepening and spreading through her body, her lips tingling. He had said he loved her, he loved her. Everything was going to be all right.

And now he was gone. Not even Pete had joined them today. He'd wanted to go to a picnic with some of his crowd, even though *she* would be there. Swanee. Would her fiancé, Russell Vincent, be there too? That would be interesting. The latest gossip was that Russ still played golf with Jean Claire Morgan, the niece of the governor.

Everybody knew that Russ had political ambitions. Maybe the engagement was getting a little strained. After all, Swanee had spent months abroad.

The street was quiet, save for the muffled cracking of distant fireworks. A bicycle swerved around the corner, and she lazily watched it come closer. Henry Benedict! He'd just have to come up and amuse her. She was too tired to move a muscle.

Henry parked the machine and took off his flat cap.

"Good afternoon, Henry!" she called.

He turned the cap thoughtfully. "Can I talk to you for a minute?"

Gussie regarded him through half-closed eyes. "Did my father send you?"

"I'll explain," he said, mounting the porch steps. His serious expression meant this was no casual call.

"You'd better come in." Tiredness suddenly gone, Gussie rose from the divan.

Henry sat in the parlor while she fetched cool drinks. She cut two slices of pound cake and jerked a dish towel off a pitcher of tea. Then she chipped some ice from the block in the icebox. That ice was as cold as she felt inside.

She carried a tray to the parlor and set it on the coffee table. Then she perched on the sofa, clasped her hands around her knees, and waited.

Henry gazed directly at her. "I'm looking into the Latrelle case."

"Have you joined the Pinkertons?" Her voice came out more sharply than she intended. She seized her glass and took a gulp of tea to hide the pounding of her pulse. Ned had nothing to do with it. *Nothing.*

"Listen, Gussie. The police have arrested a black man in a pickup truck. He didn't do it. I know John Woods. He buried my father."

"John Woods? Digger John? That's Trevania's uncle and Velma's husband, and he's a preacher! How could they? Does my father know about this?" *Looking at some of my folks,* Trevania had said.

Henry nodded. "He told me that they'll have to let him go for lack of evidence, but he thinks The Klan is behind the arrest, agitating for blacks or northern labor organizers to blame it on. The judge warned me of their influence with the police, and told me if I wanted to dig further, I had his blessing."

"Are you going to be a lawyer, Henry, or a Pinkerton man?" She gripped the soft velvet arm of the sofa. "Mr. Benedict, exactly what do you want to know?"

"I want the truth," Henry said. "I want justice for that boy." He raised an eyebrow and gave her a lopsided smile. "So I'm 'Mr. Benedict' to you now? Was I 'Mr. Benedict' when I picked you up from your bicycle crash on campus?" He took a big gulp of tea, and then wolfed down a piece of cake.

"I'm very grateful for your help," she said carefully, but Henry had taken a notebook and pencil out of his pocket.

"I'm looking for cars with damage. Where they were that night, where they are now. I take it your husband's not home?"

"Yes. I mean no. You need to talk to him." Gussie folded her hands tightly to stop their trembling.

"I've called at the mill four times this past week," Henry said. "Not available, sorry. And my mother is the secretary! Where is he? I felt sure he'd be home on a holiday."

Gussie, face warming, cleared her throat. "He's supposed to be in conference with Mr. Burkett. There's some kind of labor problem."

"Mother didn't know about it." Henry rubbed his chin. "Maybe I could wait here for him."

"No! I mean—the baby is napping—" She felt Henry's gaze on her.

"Gussie," he said, "let's stop this polite dance. When did Ned get that black Ford he's driving, and what happened to his Pierce-Arrow?"

Gussie bit her lip, then shrugged. "He smashed it up on the way to Savannah, sold it down there, and bought the Ford to drive home."

"When was that?"

Gussie licked her lips and took another sip of coffee. "You know already from your mother, I'm sure. He left for Savannah the night the boy was hurt. It looks bad, I know."

"Who bought it?"

Gussie shook her head. "A man named Curtis Wyckham had something to do with it. That's all I know."

Henry scribbled on his pad.

Gussie felt a rock land in her stomach. The dent. Should she tell him about the dent? She opened her mouth but words wouldn't come.

"Please, Henry." Wrung out as a dishrag, she rose from the sofa, stumbled, and nearly knocked the tray off the coffee table. "I've told you all I can."

Henry, on his feet at once, put out a hand to steady her. "I'm sorry, Gussie."

He strode out to the hall tree and lifted his cap from the hook. He fitted it to his head before the mirror, watching her behind him. "I won't bother you again," he said. "Unless I find that car."

He turned and looked into her eyes, and the concern, the tenderness she saw made her swallow back tears. She looked away.

"You must love him very much," Henry said.

Her lower lip trembled. "Henry, I . . . I think I hear the baby."

Henry gave her a long look. "Good afternoon, Miss Augusta."

She closed the door behind him, hurried upstairs, and looked down on Gracie, still sleeping. "Hush, little baby, don't say a word," she sang softly. "Papa's going to buy you a mockingbird . . . ."

She fled into her own room and burst into tears.

Ned came home around suppertime scowling and silent. Gussie set out barbecued pork and potato salad and sliced tomatoes, along with fresh, hot pole beans and corn bread. She tried to distract him by telling him about the band concert, but he only grunted when he picked up his fork.

They ate for a few minutes in silence. Ned seemed somewhere else entirely, until he looked down at his tomatoes. "Where's the Durkee's, Gussie?"

"Sorry." She fetched the squat bottle and set it beside him. "How was your meeting?"

"All right." He spread the mustardy dressing on his tomatoes, then cut and ate them one by one.

"What's happening, Ned?"

He stared at her. "Those damned agitators have got the hands stirred up," he said. "Bolshie nonsense. Can't reason with lintheads. We need to get ready for trouble."

She didn't like the hard set to his jaw or the strange hunted look in his eyes.

"Lucky to have a job," he said. "No damn gratitude. We ought to lock the bastards out and see how they like it." He cut a bit of the juicy pulled pork. "Hey! This is good! Where'd you get it?"

"Mama bought enough at the park to share."

She babbled about the parade and the band concert. He wasn't listening, but it helped to fill the empty space between them. When she ran out of things to say, she rose and gathered the plates.

Cutting a slice of cake, she felt the same fear she'd felt in Cuba: Max and the gambling and the storm, the hotel. *Venga, venga.* She realized with sickening clarity she hadn't trusted Ned for a long time.

She set the cake in front of him.

Ned snapped his fingers. "Got something for you, doll! Old Burkett asked me to sit at his table at the big Red Cross shindig come September. They're hosting it in their ballroom, and he means for me to buy tickets. Get yourself a new dress."

He pulled a wad of bills out of his pocket and laid them on the table. "I want to take you and Gracie out to see the fireworks tonight." He winked at her. "And maybe later we can have fireworks of our own."

Gussie managed a weak smile. Inside she felt sick.

# Chapter 38

*Dear Mrs. Brown,*

*I was sorry to hear that the church burned down.*

*Thank you for your long letter and I hope you and the Reverend are both well. Do you really think it was Mr. Shackley that did it because he didn't like Brother Jethro's sermon on the evils of hypocrites, against those who hide behind masks and will not make themselves known? I am so glad that he said they do not speak for real Christians who care for the poor in spirit and those who are despised by man.*

*I was surprised to hear that Pa was so upset about the church that he has finally come all the way back to Jesus. Praise be that he is going to help build the church back with his own two hands.*

*And now Mr. Shackley is demanding more of the crop from Pa? How does he think Pa is going to feed the kids? I think Pa is near about to a slave. I wish he would have the guts to just get up and pack all his worldly possessions and hop a freight out of town, but I know he would never do it for fear that Shackley would sick the sheriff on him and drag him back and put him in jail.*

*And then what would happen to Shelley? I sure do miss that sister of mine and I swear I'll come get her one of these days. Lord, I hate that man. I know you don't like for people to talk about hate, but Shackley deserves to be smited by the Lord with a righteous sword.*

*I am glad that the kids are all right. Please tell Merry I saw somebody who looked like Byron, and I am enclosing a clipping with his picture in it to show them.*

*Here are 2 dollars for the brothers and sisters and one dollar for the church and I send everyone lots of love. Please send more news of Shelley. I worry about her all the time.*

*Your friend,*
*Tenny*

Tenny took a pair of scissors and carefully snipped an article out of a week-old *Ashbyville Clarion*.

MILL WORKERS PROTEST NIGHT WORK
*Northern Agitators, Claims Plant Manager*

She added a picture of Ned Fletcher, along with a photo of mill workers carrying picket signs and an article about the strike. Ned Fletcher struck a pose like Byron, or what she remembered of Byron.

Pick of the litter, people always said about Byron, since the rest of them grew up to be skinny little runts like Pa. Must have taken after his mama's side of the family, people said. Ma had been plumb willowy, of a height with Pa.

Tenny folded the article and slipped it in the envelope. Elias Burkett had been ready for the wildcat strike with his detectives ready, as well as the police. He'd claimed the last thing he wanted was bloodshed.

The peaceful strike was over in three days, and it had come to naught. Mr. Burkett wouldn't budge. Instead, he vowed to install new machinery that would be labor-saving and more efficient—in other words, eliminate jobs.

Tenny learned from Ramona that the boss's spies in the plant had leaked word of the strike and he'd known almost as long as they had. He'd fired two strike leaders and hired others in their places, and promoted Clete Mincus. Joe Kinley, as his best worker, was only given a warning.

Tenny ached for Ramona and Joe. For them, the defeat was bitter gall. She stuffed her letter in the envelope, licked it, sealed it, and addressed it to "Mrs. Jethro Brown, Rte. 3, Friendship Baptist Church, Weedy Grove, Ga."

The church wasn't there anymore, but they still had a mailbox, and that hadn't burned down. Their little parsonage was right behind the church, down a lane.

She set out for the post office, enjoying the fine October weather. She was approaching the flight of marble steps when, of all things, Mr. Ned Fletcher himself pulled up in a black Ford. She ducked behind the staircase wall so he wouldn't see her, and she watched him stride up the steps and pull open the heavy door. She waited behind the wall, and was rewarded when not five minutes later he stepped out into the bright sunlight.

He'd grown a beard to go with his mustache. Maybe to hide a scar? She remembered the time Ma had cleaned up Byron's busted chin with moonshine, and he'd sucked up, gritted his teeth, and said, "I'm going to kill that bastard someday." Then he'd apologized to Ma for the language. But he wouldn't tell her what the fight had been about.

Tenny stepped out from the wall, challenging him to ignore her. Ned Fletcher turned and their eyes met for a split second. Her steady gaze met his look of momentary surprise and then his eyes became blank, unknowing, unheeding, unwilling.

He nodded briefly and moved on.

This was not the brother who took up for the girls when Pa threatened to whip them for being sassy. Who'd taught Milton how to plow. Who'd brought Ma arrowheads, wildflowers, pretty rocks. Byron had been a good son, a good brother.

This Ned Fletcher was mean.


Back in her room, she changed into her uniform for her shift. She tidied the room and folded the newspaper on her desk to toss in the trash. The name Godwin under a photo caught her eye. The column Local Doin's by Maxine Withers featured the committee for the upcoming Red Cross Ball: Mrs. Elias Burkett, Miss Ola Stratton, two ladies she didn't know, and Mrs. Emmett Godwin, Senior. Pete Godwin's mother. She squelched the flutter in her belly. This would be Pete's last year of medical school.

She clipped the article about the Red Cross Ball to place in her scrapbook. She'd be as likely to ever go to a Red Cross Ball as buy antiques from Mr. Lyman Stratton's shop.

# Chapter 39

Gussie really didn't want to go to the Red Cross ball. Last year, she would've been over the moon to be wearing a new dress, looking forward to dancing the night away with her handsome husband. She listlessly adjusted her pearls and examined her pout in the mirror.

Dabbing on lip pomade with her little finger, she watched Ned loop his necktie, bearded chin jutted. The relatively short, handsome beard seemed to her like a disguise. Beards were not in fashion unless you were some sort of poet or artist. Who or what was he hiding from?

She gripped Ned's arm as they mounted the steps to the Burkett mansion. A September harvest moon cast a silvery glow on the portico and columns, and the air held just a hint of fall crispness.

The ballroom's tall arched windows blazed with light, and the wail of a jazz trombone reminded her of other balls, other nights—a sparkling social pond she'd just waded into when it turned into mist. The magic of falling in love with Ned seemed a distant memory.

When the butler opened the door, she adjusted the embroidered blue silk stole around her matching dress, a copy of a Mainbocher design, and then stepped forward into the hall.

Ned smiled down at her. "You'll wow 'em, kid."

Gaslights fluttered in sconces, throwing shadows down the long gallery where portraits of Burkett ancestors in dark suits with wing collars, one in a Confederate officer's gray, gazed down on the guests. The house smelled of polish, old wood, and some indefinable perfume: the scent of money, perhaps.

Her eyes were drawn to a portrait of Toby Burkett, a handsome work, executed in a modern style. Toby had been every bit as beautiful as Swanee, his dark hair with a bit of curl. He'd been painted in his tennis togs, his racquet in his hand, the Tennis Club behind him. She gazed at it with sadness. If Toby had not died. . .

"Come on," Ned said irritably. She joined Ned in the doorway to the ballroom, where Swanee, shimmering in peacock blue beaded silk chiffon, fluttered from guest to guest. Her low jeweled headband held a peacock feather, and of course, she wore her long string of pearls. Gussie caught Ned's fleeting look—what was it? *Hunger*, that's what it was. She stifled the urge to pinch his arm, *hard*, and instead touched it gently and smiled at him. He smiled back with a casual fondness.

Swanee glided toward them, languorous as a panther. Ned's face remained a polite, respectful mask. Just as Swanee opened her scarlet lips to speak, Lyman Stratton, aunts Ola and Edith trailing in his wake, burst into the group, grinning. "Hello, darlings! I haven't seen any of you in the longest time."

Swanee kept her smile, sauced with the tiniest bit of a frown, and shouldered away to greet the incoming Professor Moon. Ned's expression remained impassive, but his eyes tracked her.

"Miss Ola!" Gussie exclaimed, too loudly. "Don't you look charming? I love that lavender silk."

"Fabulous, don't you think?" said Lyman. "She finally let me toss that orange and teal Deco horror. But can't do anything with Aunt Edith, can I, darling?" His widowed aunt always wore black, even after her lily complexion had turned sallow. He explained that Aunt Ethel had stayed home with neuralgia and then moved on, eager to circulate. Gussie watched him pose with his aunts as Maxine Withers, society reporter for the *Ashbyville Clarion*, aimed her flash at them.

Gussie laid a hand on Ned's shoulder. "Papa told me that Miss Ola's been walking out with Arno Shackley. Papa thinks he's after her money so he can buy Arcadia. You know Papa swore he'd never sell Grandpa's old place, but it keeps losing money."

Ned's jaw tightened and his eyes narrowed. "That old fool is never going to buy Arcadia, Gussie. I'll see to that."

Gussie stared at him open-mouthed. Did Arcadia mean that much to him? When had he come to know Shackley? The mills didn't buy cotton directly from the growers, and Ned wasn't from around here.

Before she could match any puzzle pieces, the band struck up a Charleston. "Come on, kid," he said, grinning. "Let's dance." The debonair Ned was back.

Five different partners later, Gussie had lost track of Ned, and she was thirsty. She fluttered to the punch bowl, greeting friends, but didn't see him. As she stood sipping from a crystal cup, she noticed Swanee slide though the French doors from the terrace and melt into the crowd.

Just as Gussie accepted a refill, Ned appeared behind her, wrapping one arm around her shoulder. "Hey, babe."

"Your hands are so cold," she murmured.

He shrugged. "I've had a drink."

"But the punch cup has a handle." There. She'd said it.

"Come over here," he said. He led her behind a potted palm and pulled out a silver flask. The rum he splashed into the drink tasted of Cuba, of soft winds. Sipping it gave her the strange sensation of being warm on the inside, icy on the outside.

The band struck up "My Heart Stood Still," and Ned stretched out his arms to her. "It's our song, Gussie."

Ned seemed to dance on air, dipping her low and swirling her, but she felt she'd lost her pep. He dipped her so low, she was gazing at the thousand crystals of the French chandelier. She glimpsed a lanky dancer waltzing by with her sister Jessie. Henry! Jessie! She nearly fell, but Ned caught her just in time.

"Are you feeling delicate, my dear?" he murmured.

"I'm sorry, Ned. I got dizzy. Let's stop." She took a deep breath and excused herself to go to the ladies' room.

Ned told her he was going to get a drink.

When she returned from powdering her nose, she circled the long way around the ballroom, searching for Henry and Jessie. She found him coming back from the refreshments table with two tiny chicken sandwiches, but didn't see her sister.

"Henry!"

"Like a sandwich? I got one for Jess but she went to dance with some old fellow she knows."

Gussie took a sandwich and began to nibble it. "I don't understand. You're escorting my sister?"

Henry shrugged. "The judge bought a couple of extra tickets, and he asked me to bring Jess, thinks she ought to get out more. How could I say no? She's a good egg. Anyhow, it was a good excuse to see you. I wanted to tell you, they managed to trace the Pierce-Arrow."

The blood drained out of Gussie's face.

Henry pivoted to say hello to Miss Ola Stratton. When she was beyond earshot, he continued in a low murmur. "The car was sold to Curtis Wyckham. He took it to a body shop, and it came out all fixed and painted light green. The shop guys can't recall where the dents were. That was odd, don't you think?"

Nausea rose, and her breath turned shallow. "But Ned . . . fell asleep and ran into a ditch on the way to Savannah."

"That's what he told you. You didn't notice any dents before he left?"

"I'm . . . I'm not sure." Had there been dents, or was it a trick of shadows?

"Well, think, girl!" Henry said *sotto voce*. "Everything now depends on Sam Latrelle recalling what happened. The police would love to pin it on Digger John, because some so-called witness said they saw his truck that night, even though the other boys said it was a car. Elias Burkett wants this case solved so the mill folks will simmer down." He rubbed his fingers together. "You get the drift. Hey, here comes Jessie. I'll get her another snack."

"Wait, Henry. How is Sam?"

Henry didn't answer, but his eyes narrowed, and Gussie followed his gaze. Swanee's mother zig-zagged her way across the dance floor, hands flapping dancers aside like Moses parting the Red Sea. Gussie watched, looking confused.

"I'd better find out what's going on." Henry stepped forward and nearly collided with Dr. Emmett Godwin heading for the door as fast as his tuxedo would allow, followed by Dr. Hooper and that bone doctor Henry didn't know well. Dr. Godwin mumbled excuses and kept going. Something was *very* wrong.

Gussie found her father and mother glaring at each other, Mama's mouth set in a stubborn line. "Papa! What's happening? Why are all the doctors plowing out of here like locomotives?"

The judge's grim expression silenced her. "They need all the docs they can round up. There's been a riot down at the mill village between the strikers and the scabs. Bloody battle."

"But I thought the strike was settled."

"Not really," Judge Pemberton said. "The workers came out badly in the negotiations, and the strikers blame the scabs and spies. Where's the King of Siam? Shouldn't he know about this?"

Gussie didn't see Ned in the ballroom. "I'll go look." Her father suggested the library. On the way, she found Jessie and Henry preparing to leave.

"I'm going down there," Henry said.

Jessie nodded. "I'll go with you."

Behind them, the band struck up a tango. The lush, sensuous music seemed discordant, out of place. Beyond these thick stucco walls, the music and flowers, people were fighting, people were hurt. Gussie turned back to the dance floor.

Ned and Swanee were the only dancers. They glided across the floor, eyes locked. Maxine Withers crept forward, camera poised.

Gussie, furious, dug her nails into her palms. Not only were Ned and Swanee dancing with steam practically rising from their bodies, but *someone else was taking pictures*. And Jessie was leaving with Henry!

She just had to be where the fight was happening, camera in hand. She hurried across the dance floor and gripped Ned's arm. "Ned! There's a riot at the mill. You should be there!"

Swanee smiled and patted Gussie's arm. "No need, dearie."

Ned reflected Swanee's smile. "E.B.'s called out his detectives, and the police are there. What could I do?"

Gussie's face flushed. All her life she'd had to look up at people and have them talk down to her. No more. "Ned Fletcher, you're their manager. You could speak to them, calm them down. *Listen* to them."

"Can't reason with 'em, babe," he said evenly. "They need to know we mean business. We provide the jobs, don't we? Don't trouble your little head. Have a good time."

"*A good time? My little head?*" Her parents had left quarreling. Gussie realized that Mama wanted to go and talk to the people, and Papa was putting his foot down for fear of her safety.

"Come on, Gussie, honey. Let's dance," he said, winking at Swanee as she slithered away. Maxine Withers approached, camera in hand.

"Can I get a picture here, Mr. Fletcher, of you and your sweet wife?"

The flash went off in an instant, and Ned, shocked, lunged for the camera. Maxine cleverly dodged him, making for the mayor's table. She followed the mayor out the door.

These pictures, of Ned having a high old time at a ball, would surely come out in the same issue as the pictures from the fight and the arrests of the workers. Ned must have realized that. And no one would be able to bribe the editor not to publish them.

Papa always said that the editor hated Elias Burkett, who had tried to buy him out more than once and was trying to get his pals at the bank to call in the editor's loan.

Ned shrugged, extracted a packet of Sen-Sen from his pocket, and popped one into his mouth. He grabbed Gussie's hand and strode toward the door.

Gussie's heart leaped and her breath came fast. "Can we stop by the house and let me get my camera?"

Ned bellowed, "Are you nuts, Gussie? You're going home."

In the car, she begged, pleaded, and swore. When he pulled up in front of the house, she leapt out almost as soon as he'd stopped the car. She ran in, grabbed her little Kodak, and ran back out, panting, only to see the Ford screeching around the corner.

Camera in hand, she stood in the street and watched the car's exhaust plume float away into the moonlit sky.

# Chapter 40

Henry, shucking his tux jacket at the door, found his mother and young Sam's mother, Mildred, drinking tea in the living room. The judge had dropped him off but was against Jessie going too, and she submitted unwillingly.

Mildred's eyes were red-rimmed, and her springy dishwater hair hung in limp hanks, as if she'd been running her hands through it. Mildred looked up at him with confusion, and he felt like a fool in his fancy clothes. His mother sprang up and hugged him. "You told me you'd be in after midnight, Henry."

"I just wanted to make sure you were all right. What about Emory, Mrs. Latrelle?"

She sighed. "He's down to the hospital seeing to the men. Some of them was hurt pretty bad." She glanced around as if she'd misplaced something. "I'd better get on back. Mama's looking after the young'uns, and it's late. I just needed Mahaly's comfort a bit."

"Let me walk you over," said Henry.

"I know you mean well, Henry, but no," Mildred said. "You stay here with your mama."

"You might not be safe."

She shrugged. "Pshaw. Anybody who wants to make trouble is down at the mill. Thank you kindly for the tea, Mahaly." She rose and went out, and Henry stood on the front porch and watched her, a moonlit figure on a cold dark street, until she disappeared into the shadows.

"What did she tell you?" Henry closed the door behind him so the warmth from the little space heater wouldn't escape.

Mahala sighed. "They said the fight was between the strikers and the scabs, but I think there were some goons in there too, to beat up on the strikers, and I wouldn't be surprised if they happened to be KKK."

Henry lowered himself to his chair. "Doesn't make sense. Those workers got a licking in the negotiations. Why beat up on them now?"

Mahala lifted Henry's jacket from the back of the chair and smoothed it over her arm, picking off a stray hair. "It was to teach them a lesson, I think, and scare them away from that union organizer and that Brother Perry."

"I guess I've had my nose in my law books." Henry rubbed his jaw. "I didn't know that was going on."

"I'm telling you what Emory told me. They tried to keep the union man's visit under wraps."

"Who ratted them out?"

"I'm guessing Clete Mincus. Emory has had trouble with him."

"Clete's a bad piece of work."

Mahala's eyes darkened and she shivered. "I can't stand that man. Like a scorpion, he is, with the women. Even at my age. He measures you up for his purposes." She got up and headed for the kitchen. "Let's have some hot chocolate."

"Sure," said Henry, following her to the kitchen. She pulled out a saucepan and spooned cocoa into it, then tipped in a good measure of sugar. "Mother, I know you're loyal to Mr. Burkett—"

"He's always been fair to me." Mahala poured in enough milk for two cups, lit the gas, and set the pan on the stove. "He's well thought of in the community, and he carries that sorrow about his son. Toby was the nicest boy, a comfort to his mother. Miss Clara was so proud of him. He was a little older than you, Henry, wasn't he?"

"I kind of looked up to him. He used to help me with tennis when we were boys. That was before Father—" He didn't finish. Father had died, and that was the end of the tennis club for Henry.

Henry still didn't believe suicide. Everybody liked Toby, even Jessie Pemberton. A star tennis player and golfer, he was being groomed to take over the family business. Talk was that he'd marry Marjorie Ashby, of very old money. Money they managed to hang onto despite the Late Unpleasantness.

But there was the time Henry had congratulated Toby on his performance in the U.S. Open golf tournament, saying he'd done Ashbyville proud. Toby had shaken his head. "I'd like to leave this town and become a pro. I don't belong here."

"Sure you do," Henry had replied. "You've got it all, Tobe. Family, job, and if you and Marj marry . . ."

"I'll never please Father," Toby shot back, "much less Marjorie." He slung his towel around his neck and walked off the tennis court.

Toby's death had hit old Elias very hard. The old man had gone into seclusion for a month, and that's why people like Mahala Benedict were reluctant to be too critical of him.

"Look, Ma," Henry said. "Burkett's okay as long as nothing affects his bottom line. And he hires people to make sure of that. People like Ned Fletcher." Henry paused. "I have no doubt that Fletcher's the one that ran into Sam."

The cocoa was boiling, and Mahala took a blue potholder, lifted the pan off, and skimmed the film from the top. "Be careful about saying that, Henry. You could get in trouble."

Henry was impatient with that kind of talk. "Mother, I found Fletcher's car. It had been dented, sold, repaired, and sold again."

Mahala poured the cocoa into two mugs. "Your father is dead because he found out things people wanted hidden."

"My father? It was an accident," Henry said. "That's what you told me. That's what everybody said. And now you're telling me it was *murder*?"

"I've always let you believe in the accident," she said. "But now you need to know the truth. Someone tampered with the brakes. Frank always kept the car in perfect condition."

"Mother, why'd you keep it from me?" Henry clenched his fists, his face warming.

Mahala gazed at him sadly. "I didn't want you to grow up knowing your father had enemies."

Henry paced the floor. "Was there an investigation?"

Mahala raised an eyebrow. "If you can call it that. There was no proof of tampering—so they said." She sank into a chair at the tiny wooden table and sipped at her cocoa. "Frank was gathering evidence against that Grand Dragon about those two black people found in the river."

"What was the evidence?"

"Frank didn't say. He thought it was safer if I didn't know."

Henry tried to sound calm. "Who was this Grand Dragon?"

She shook her head and looked out the back window, past the ruffled lace curtain, into the darkness.

"Don't protect me anymore, Mother!" Henry grabbed his mug from the table, and walked into the front room where the space heater hissed. He sat in his chair and stared at the flames. "I'm going to the hospital."

"You'd just be in the way," his mother said from the kitchen, but her voice didn't carry conviction.

"There's some kind of connection between all this, and I'm going to find out what it is."

"Drink your chocolate," Mahala said, like a mother who knew her son was becoming his own man and wanted to mother him anyway.

When she heard the wail of the ambulance, Tenny was sitting at the chart desk of her ward, the patients asleep and the hall quiet. There was always an ambulance on Saturday night, so it didn't really register. Her mind was on the Red Cross Ball. If Pete Godwin had been in town, would he have gone? She pictured herself in a pale green gown and pale green T-strap satin shoes, and Pete wearing one of those tuxedo jackets like in that new movie *The Great Gatsby*, which she'd gone to see last Sunday.

"Hey, Oakes." The voice stabbed her fantasy. She looked up and saw Enid. "Quit smirking and get your fandango down to emergency. We need extra people. Alice here can cover."

Tenny rose deliberately, exchanging glances with Alice, but Enid was already walking away.

Ten men were waiting for help. One, a boy of fifteen, teeth missing in his wide, blood-caked mouth, doubled over with pain, holding his ribs. Tenny headed toward the boy, but the charge nurse stopped her and assigned her to prepare extra beds in the men's casualty ward. All those waiting men, some whom she might know!

Biting her lip, her throat dry, she rolled cots into position, tucked in sheets and blankets, and laid out supplies. She longed to be helping patients. Who was hurt? How badly? She prayed she wouldn't see Ramona's Joe—or Ramona.

When the beds were ready, she was ordered to help with the injured. She rolled up her sleeves and hurried down the corridor, almost colliding with Dr. Emmett Godwin, still wearing his fancy clothes. "Glad you're here, girl." He plunged into the doctors' lounge to change.

She went to scrub, passing orderlies bringing in another man on a stretcher. Pulling on gloves, she was directed to a patient waiting in the corner of the room. She stifled a gasp. Her surgery training hadn't prepared her for this.

The man's mud-covered face was a mass of contusions. One long laceration split his forehead, and blood was congealing around it in dulling, darkening red. One eye was bloody, the cheekbone below it sunken, swelling, apparently smashed.

As she sponged the sticky, matted hair, she found other tumescent areas on his scalp. The man groaned, but was barely conscious. That would make her job easier until the morphine arrived.

She was so concentrated on cleaning the mud and blood she didn't think about the man's features. When she stood back to see if she'd missed any dirt, she froze. Clete Mincus. The thought of her escape from him brought back the sleepy hard eyes, the teakettle steaming, Myrtle's gaping red mouth. She turned aside and retched.

A nurse in white patted her on the shoulder. "Got to you, huh? I'll take over, honey. You take a break."

She nodded thanks, unable to speak. Knees like jelly, she turned away and stepped into the hall. She took long, gulping breaths, silently blessing the angel nurse who'd saved her from committing murder. For two cents she'd have pinched that man's miserable nostrils together and let nature take its course.

She glanced into the waiting room. Worried women sat with men waiting their turn, their injuries wrapped with rags, but Tenny didn't see Ramona or Joe. Relieved, she returned to work.

Her next patient, redheaded and freckled, reminded her of the boy in the hayloft with whom she'd bartered her favors for half a bar of chocolate and a place to sleep. The remembering brought a blush of shame.

And then another patient needed her, and another. It was nearly three-thirty before she was able to take a break. In the nurses' lounge, she bathed her face in water cold enough to hurt her teeth. The temperature must have dropped ten or fifteen degrees during the night.

She poured herself a cup of coffee from the percolator and gazed out the window at the huge round moon. Her mama always said the full moon brought out violent behavior. Some of the nurses agreed, though Dr. Epstein, who'd studied with Freud in Vienna, said that belief was nonsense.

Down in the parking lot she saw Dr. Emmett, dressed once again in his evening clothes, walking out to his automobile. He'd done what he could. Lord, he was a good man. Pete would've relished being able to help tonight.

She finished her coffee. It had been a horrible night, but in another way it had been a good night. She was here, where she was supposed to be, helping people, and the feeling was one she never wanted to lose.

# Chapter 41

*Dear Tenny,*

*I always think about you and pray for you. Emmy Dee come back home, sadder but wiser, and married the Harper boy. God knows she is lucky he come to forgive the days when she was lost to sin. Merry is still keeping house for your Pa. I I don't know what he is gone to do if she ever marries that widower Mr. Haskins and your Pa and Milton has nobody to do for them now. Not even Shelley.*

*That Pa of yours has become one of God's saints if I ever saw one.*

*I didn't want to worry you before but now I have just got to tell you. The county health people come and took Shelley away. It seem she had some problems with the flux and Merry took her in and they said somebody been messing with her.*

Well Merry didn't tell them Shelly been cleaning and such for Mr. Shackley, didn't want to cause trouble. The county people got her sent to Milledgeville afore she got in the family way.

Your Pa takes the mule and wagon to visit her ever once in a while and we all write her regular but you know she can't read, somebody got to read it to her so we don't know how much she hears from us. She misses you something fierce.

I don't believe for one minute it is God's will she got the way she was. Them boys was careless the way they raced horses around, and when Eben Shackley tried to make up for it, he was the one doing God's will, something his daddy never saw the need for.

God's will is something we humans are called to do. I know I am right here doing what the Lord wants, and though it is hard sometimes, there is pleasure in the doing.

Now you asked me about Byron. I couldn't tell from that picture you sent me if that Fletcher man looked like him or not. Byron never had whiskers. But there is something to tell you about Byron. A woman who says she is his lawfully wedded wife come looking for him, claim he stole some money from her. She was thinking he must be dead but somebody seen him in Savannah and she went and hired her a Pinkerton man and he found out Byron came from Weedy Grove but not where he went after he got out of the Army. It was like he plumb fell off the face of the earth.

Your sister sent that woman on her way because nobody heard tell of Byron for years. Byron's wife even came to see Brother Jethro and me. I took her name and address and told her we would let her know if we ever heard from him. I told her Byron didn't have much religion but his sister Tenny did and

*wanted to find him too. I showed Merry the picture you sent
and she said it didn't look much like him but you never know.*

*Thank you for your Christian charity in writing and
thank you so much for the money. The Lord bless you and
keep you.*

*Yours in Jesus's love,*
*Delight Brown (Mrs.)*

Tenny wanted to ball up the letter and throw it at the wall. Shackley
had been messing with Shelly! At last she was out of his clutches. But
why wouldn't Pa get out of that place? Fear. He was afraid of Shackley.
She wished he would just go out and shoot Shackley one day and say
he was aiming at a deer. But that sheriff pal of Shackley's would never
believe the story.

To calm down, she took out her shoebox of newspaper clippings. She
lined up her scrapbook, the box, scissors, a ruler, a pen, a bottle of ink,
and a pot of clean white paste smelling of the schoolroom. The rays of
the slanting afternoon sun fell on the book.

She lifted the clippings out of the box and trimmed them. She laid out
one about the strike, one about the fight, and then a long piece about the
conditions in the mill.

Ramona and Joe Kinley had been interviewed, and they told of
the night work, the stretch-out, the paltry wages, the unfair system of
promotion. Mostly, they minded that the higher-ups didn't care enough
to listen.

Tenny was proud of their courage but afraid for them. Ramona had
finally taken a job behind the counter at Mabel's, the same greasy spoon
where Tenny had first encountered the straw boss. Tenny had urged
her to consider nurse's training. The hospital didn't usually take married
women, but it did happen.

Ramona had shaken her head. We'll see what happens with Joe, she'd said. We're not going to back down. We're not going to sit back and shut up like they want us to.

If Joe got fired, they'd go back to the hills for a time. Maybe take up farming again. Maybe go to a South Carolina mill. Rumor had it that there was plenty of work, with signing bonuses and good management.

Tenny placed the clipping of the interview, the one with their pictures, in the top right-hand corner of the page, and arranged the other clippings on the page before she dipped her brush in the paste pot.

Nothing much had changed at the mill. All that violence, all those broken bodies, for nothing. At least Clete Mincus had gotten what was coming to him. She felt sorry for Myrtle, who had to live with him.

After she finished the page, she shuffled through the clips she'd saved from the society page, the pictures from the Red Cross Ball. She lifted the picture of Ned Fletcher dancing with his wife. Mr. Fletcher was gazing at something or someone in the distance.

She picked up and read Mrs. Brown's letter again, and then she wrote a reply. She put it in the envelope along with the newspaper picture of Ned Fletcher dancing with his wife. Then she sealed it and carefully wrote the address.

The glue in the scrapbook was dry. Tenny closed it, put away all her writing materials, and took the scrapbook to the closet. She spotted the old croker sack on the top shelf. It wasn't useful, and it was taking up room. She pulled it down and unrolled it. Burying her nose in it, she smelled corn and old boots, Bible pages and graveyard dust.

She smelled home.

She rolled the sack tightly, tied it with a piece of twine, and stuffed it back onto the high shelf.

She took off the moonstone necklace that the antique shop man had given her and stroked it before she laid it on the dresser. He was wrong about his prediction. She would never make enough money to walk into his shop, point to something, and say, "Can you have that delivered?" But he had said that necklace would protect her. She believed that. She had to believe that.

And Shelley was in Milledgeville! In the Georgia State Sanitarium.

She had to get Shelley out.

Gussie, having dinner with her parents because Ned was out again, found out from her father that young Sam Latrelle had finally awakened from his coma.

"And the police investigation?" she asked, looking down at her half-eaten catfish, the shreds of coleslaw, the smears of pepper-flecked sauce.

The judge snorted with disgust. "The case is still open, but it's on the back burner, I hear."

"Can't you talk to Mayor Harrison?" Gussie asked.

"Old Barney craves the votes in the mill town, but without any evidence, there's not much a mayor can do. Humph. They tried to take in John Woods! Had a witness say they saw a truck down there about that time, but the kids swore it was a car. Well, I had a few words to say about that. That witness got paid. Wish I could prove it."

"Well," said her mother, "Emmett says young Sam is coming around. He says the boy's going to get his memory back."

"That's wonderful, Mama," Gussie murmured.

"You've hardly eaten a thing, Gussie."

"I'll take the rest home."

"And some of that banana pudding," her mother said.

At home, she'd fallen asleep in bed with her book waiting for Ned to come in, and had awakened to the slamming of the icebox. She'd listened to Ned eating Mama's leftovers in the kitchen. Had he really gone out to dinner?

She pretended to be asleep when he finally crept into bed. She held her breath, afraid he'd put out a hand, want her. She lay still, pretending sleep, listening to his heavy breath. He did not reach for her. He hadn't reached for her since the night of the ball.

When she was certain he was asleep, she got up and opened the window, breathing in the fresh, chill air. The evening was unusually quiet—no motorcars, no ambulances and sirens, no clip-clop of horses' hoofs. She gazed out at the starlit sky, where a sliver of moon sailed.

She shivered. Was Ned really so rotten as to run down a child? What was he hiding? Where had he been this evening? What was her duty?

She gazed down at the garage, at the flickering gaslight. At the garage that held a plain black car.

Early the next morning Gussie, bleary-eyed, sipped coffee while she spooned mashed bananas into Gracie's mouth. She didn't turn when she heard Ned walk into the kitchen. He walked over, placed a kiss on her cheek, and set down his briefcase.

"There's bacon and buttered toast on the stove. I'll fry you a couple of eggs," she said tiredly. She had no appetite herself.

"Don't bother," Ned said. "I'll grab something at the drugstore."

He sounded concerned for her. She looked up in surprise to find him gazing at her with a look of—what was it? Surely not love. She hadn't seen that in a long time.

"I stayed out late last night drinking, it's true," he said. "They were folks I needed to cultivate if I'm going to get anywhere in this town."

She searched his face. He was lying. The baby wailed for more bananas, and she picked up the baby spoon. "All right, Ned," she said. Now just leave. Go to work.

"I have a surprise for you," he said.

Gussie poked another spoonful at Gracie. "You do?"

"Don't you want to know?"

"Yes, of course." She did her best to smile.

He lifted his briefcase onto a chair, unbuckled it, reached into it, and brought out a wad of cash. He plunked it on the table in front of her. "Here, go buy yourself a new dress."

They were barely scraping by! "Have you been gambling?" she blurted.

He smiled infuriatingly. "Just a little poker."

She fought to hold back a tide of angry words. She took the money and pecked his cheek. "Thank you."

"I'm lunching out," he said, halfway out the back door. "I may be late from work."

She nodded. The door closed. Gussie finished feeding the baby just before Trevania came in.

"I'm getting a new dress, Tre." Gussie got up and wet a washcloth for the baby's face.

"Wonder what he done?" Trevania said, hanging up her coat.

Gussie laughed hollowly. "Right now, I'll take the dress."

Up in her room, Gussie stuffed herself into a corset, then into a navy wool dress that had fit her perfectly two years before. Now she looked like a link sausage.

Slipping on her coat, she frowned at the bulges spoiling the sleek line. She wanted her paisley silk scarf to drape for camouflage, but it wasn't in the drawer or the closet. Sighing, she reached for a salmon and lavender silk Art Deco print, a gift from her sister Anna.

She caught the trolley downtown. On the seat beside her, an image from a discarded newspaper caught her eye. She picked the paper up and saw a lifeless body sprawled on a blotchy concrete sidewalk in front of a barber shop. A reporter must've been lucky to get that shot before police cordoned off the area. The caption read *Refused to pay extortion.*

Max had been from Chicago, and he looked like a gangster. Ned had borrowed money from him. Had Ned paid the loan back? He'd never told her how much money he owed and always cut her questions off with "That's my business."

She alit from the trolley in the center of town, the paper folded and tucked into her shoulder bag. She stopped at Woolworth's for sewing notions to mend her ripped clothes and bought extra baby socks for Gracie as well as unmentionables for herself in a larger size. She simply must start riding her bicycle more.

She headed to Stephenson's to look at their styles. Maybe she could afford one really nice dress that fit and even treat herself to lunch at the tearoom next door. She'd just reached for the emporium's door handle when Swanee Burkett strode out, a dress box under her arm. She froze as she saw Gussie. Their eyes locked.

"Why, Swanee! I thought you were at Essie Swift this quarter," Gussie said sweetly.

Swanee covered her discomfort with a huge smile. "How are you, Gussie? It's a study day before midterms, so I decided to take the train down and do some shopping."

Gussie kept her own smile. "You don't have to study?"

"I keep up." The other girl's eyes swept Gussie's thickened figure. "I don't suppose you get out much, do you, these days?"

Gussie's cheeks warmed. "I'm out now. Ned wants to buy me a new dress."

"How nice for you," Swanee said, her voice becoming steely.

Gussie wanted to explore this hostility. "Like to have lunch at the tea room with me? I don't see you much anymore."

The syrupy tone returned. "Forgive me; I've simply got to take care of a few more errands before the train back to school."

"See you, Swanee."

Swanee swished away and Gussie ducked into the store. Swanee had been lying, of course. Gussie knew quite well that the train to Essie Swift didn't leave until 5:30. She stationed herself in a shadow just inside the vestibule, where she could see out but anyone outside couldn't see her.

She watched Swanee cross the street and head toward the parking lot across from the Dunnigan Hotel. She'd driven here in her roadster, of course, although she wasn't allowed to have it at school. It was a ridiculous impulse, but Gussie took a deep breath and slipped out of the door, keeping Swanee in sight.

She was in luck! A taxi was letting out a fare in front of the hotel. She hopped in and spoke to the startled cabbie. "Can you follow somebody for me?"

The cabbie frowned and searched the street. "Sure, ma'am," he said. "Who?"

"That girl." She pointed out Swanee's roadster, now backing out of the parking space. "She mustn't know we're following her."

"I know, I read them dime novels," the cabbie said. He chuckled as though she'd made the biggest joke in the world. "Wait till I tell this to the other guys."

"I'd appreciate it if you wouldn't mention it," said Gussie. "I'll tip well."

"Oh, I see," said the cabbie. "I know what's up."

Gussie was sure he didn't know what was up but didn't say so. Swanee drove the little car as fast as she could, risking a speeding ticket. The cabbie refused to keep up, and Gussie clenched her fists in frustration. "Speed up!"

"It's better this way," he told Gussie. "She don't see me, but I can still see her."

The roadster traveled to the edge of town, veered onto the highway, and turned onto the river road.

Gussie, biting her lip, her heart pounding, watched the car's spare tire bob and weave ahead of her, covering the two familiar miles, and when the roadster took a turn through a thicket of trees, Gussie was not surprised.

"You seen what you want to see?' the cabbie asked.

"You can take me back to town now," Gussie sighed.

The cabbie backed into the road leading to the thicket, turned around, and headed back. As the two miles rolled by, Gussie wasn't sure whether she felt relief or disappointment. Maybe she just felt stupid and embarrassed. It wasn't her business who Swanee risked her reputation with.

Just as they reached the main highway, another car approached the turnoff. A black Ford. Gussie sank in her seat, yanking her cloche down to her nose.

"Hey," said the cabbie. "I seen that guy before."

"Drive on, please," said Gussie, heartsick. She wasn't in the mood to shop for a dress now, she didn't want any lunch, and she didn't want to go home. She asked the cabbie to take her to Lyman Stratton's antique shop.

A sign above the door read Lyman's Hall of Antiques. To compose herself, she stopped to admire the display in the window. A ship-in-a-bottle's sails billowed beside a red cut-glass lamp; antique silver hair combs beckoned on a swath of black velvet. Gussie almost wished she hadn't bobbed her hair.

She stepped to the door and turned the knob, but it didn't budge. She rattled it; then she peered through the lace curtain covering the glass. Lyman, lips set in a thin line, looked back from the other side. He turned the latch and swung the door wide, his face somber. "Gussie, good to see you. Come on in." After a beat, "Nice scarf."

"What is it, Lyman? Why's the door locked?" Then she saw the blue bruise on his forehead. "Goodness! What happened?"

Weariness flickered across her friend's face. He brushed his taffy-colored forelock aside. "Gussie, dear," he said with a sigh, "I had the most awful experience."

"Well, for heaven's sake, tell me."

"Well, it was stupid. I should have run. I'm no Jack Dempsey, you know. I'm barely a featherweight."

"Lyman, you got in a fight? You?"

He slumped. "Last night. I was working late on the inventory, and I heard, out back, the most gruesome sound of crunching metal. I went to see if it was a car crash."

Lyman wiped his face with a handkerchief.

"Then what?"

"I saw this yahoo with a crowbar in his hand! My car! I rushed out like a wild man from Borneo, but he knocked me to the pavement and ran off. I hit my head, Gussie."

He touched the knot gingerly. Gussie made sympathetic noises. "Did you call the police?"

"Police!" Lyman burst out bitterly. "Yes, they came all right. Wrote it up. They treated me as if I was making the whole thing up." He looked over his natty suit and brushed off a smudge of dust. "Nothing will happen."

"You're lucky it wasn't worse. If your skin had broken, you could have bled all over the place."

"Gussie! Ugh. Don't even talk about that possibility. The question is—why?"

Gussie couldn't imagine who would want to harm Lyman.

"Oh, I have enemies, Gus. Elias Burkett's always hated me, but attacking my car would be too subtle for him."

Gussie's brow furrowed. "Did you sell him a fake antique or something?"

"Hardly!" he sniffed. "Much darker, dear. You're such an innocent. He's always blamed me for Toby's death, although he'd never come right out and say it, because that would have been admitting Toby was queer."

"Lyman!" Gussie blushed to the tips of her ears. Nice people didn't talk about such things.

Lyman set his jaw, face flushed. "I loved Toby," he said. "I loved him as a friend, as a troubled human being. We were not lovers, and I did not seduce him into being queer."

Gussie twisted her rings, breathless. Lyman was different, but she'd never speculated why. She'd just accepted him as an eccentric, and that was that.

Lyman fixed her with a baleful glare. "Toby did not commit suicide. He did not fling himself off the bridge out of despair that Marjorie Ashby wouldn't marry him. There are all kinds of tales, but only one truth. Somebody pushed him."

"You can't mean that, Lyman!" Gussie hugged herself to take away the chill she felt. "He was strong and healthy. Why couldn't he save himself?"

"The impact could have knocked him out, or broken his neck—or he could have been drugged."

"Oh, oh!" Gussie could hardly breathe with the weight of what she was hearing. "Why would anyone want to murder Toby?"

"Why would anyone attack my Pierce-Arrow? Gussie, it's time you grew up."

"Wait," Gussie said. "Lyman—you said Pierce-Arrow? What color?"

"The color of newly minted leaves," he said sullenly. "So?"

"The man was bashing your right front fender? What about the back?"

"He was."

"Not the hood—not the windshield," Gussie said with mounting anxiety.

"I don't see what you're getting at," Lyman said.

"The car that struck that mill child would have dents there," Gussie said.

"You mean someone's trying to pin that sordid crime on me?" Lyman said. "Why would I ever go down to the mill?" He furrowed his brows and pursed his mouth. "Wait. Doesn't your husband have a—"

"Yes," Gussie said quietly. "Ned went to Savannah that night. He came back with a Model T, said he'd wrecked his car. Henry Benedict thinks Ned was involved."

"So Ned bashes my fender to implicate me?" Lyman mused. "But it wasn't Ned Fletcher that knocked me down."

"Did you get a look at him?"

"A shabby sort of fellow," Lyman said. "Stocking cap pulled low and a silk scarf tied around his face."

Gussie's heart skipped a beat. "It wasn't paisley, was it?"

Lyman looked at her with astonishment. "Paisley! I was hardly in a position to notice his fashion sense. Everything moved so fast. He was about six feet. The scarf didn't go with those nasty clothes. That I can tell you."

Gussie swallowed, fighting dizziness. It would've been easy for Ned to grab her scarf and then exchange his clothes with a hobo down by the rail yard.

A long moment of silence followed, which Lyman broke at last. "Well, let's change the subject. Can I show you anything today?"

She glanced down at her shoulder bag, then gazed longingly at the stacked rugs in the back of the shop. "I so want a rug for my living room, Lyman, but Ned says money is tight."

Lyman shrugged impatiently. "Well, darling, are you helpless? Can't you make some moolah of your own?"

Gussie stared at him in astonishment. "Doing what? I can't type, and I haven't finished college, so I can't teach. Anyhow, Ned would have a fit."

"You take divine pictures, Gussie. Remember? I've sold a couple of them. Those river scenes--" He walked over and picked up a silvery frame. "This style would be perfect for them."

Gussie laughed. "Oh, Lyman. You've sold two in a year, right? That won't pay for a rug."

Lyman didn't bother to hide his annoyance. "Borrow money from your father for film and chemicals. Set up shop taking portraits."

She wrinkled her nose in disgust. "But I wanted to be an artistic photographer, a photojournalist, like Margaret Bourke-White. Advertising? I could do that, but in Ashbyville? They wouldn't let a girl like me in the old boys' club."

"You mean you want to be a serious photographer? I thought with you it was parties and drinks and boys! Not that there's anything wrong with all that . . . but really, Gussie . . ."

"I'm young," Gussie protested. "I thought there was plenty of time to be serious later."

"There wasn't, was there?" Lyman said. "Lots of us make that mistake."

Gussie looked down in shame and saw a rug.

"So do you still have those dreams? What are you, eighteen?"

"Right now I can't think past something to cover my floor."

Lyman pointed to a very old and fragile china cabinet. Beneath it lay a Turkish rug with a border of black and green and tan figures, startling in their complexity, framing gorgeous red and peach medallions.

"That's it," he said. "That's your rug."

Gussie couldn't speak. Looking at the intricate patterns gave her a funny feeling, way down in the pit of her stomach. She couldn't possibly earn enough . . .

"Clara Burkett had a fit over it," Lyman said.

Gussie stared at him. "What does she need another rug for? Her house is paved with rugs."

Lyman shrugged. "She wants to give some of them to Swanee."

"But Swanee's still in school."

"Clara's thinking of the future. She's anxious for that wild child to marry. If the girl's not careful, Russell Vincent will get away."

"He was her father's choice. Russ wants to stay in good with the old man."

"I think he's already having second thoughts. She ought to marry young Pete Godwin. He's been pining after her for years."

"That's a lost cause," Gussie said, chagrined. Everybody in town must know about Pete's unrequited love.

"Never say never."

The conversation was becoming uncomfortable. This wasn't what she'd come for. Lyman obviously hadn't heard anyone talking about Ned being involved in the accident. Henry had come up with that theory by himself.

"I'm not letting Swanee have my rug, Lyman. Here!" She plunged into her bag and extracted the money Ned had given her. "Can I make a down payment?"

Lyman smiled. "Of course, and I'll give you easy payment terms. If you earn your own money, you'll have the rug quicker. Not have to ask Daddy or hubby."

Gussie nodded thoughtfully.

He walked her to the door, and she heard the lock click behind her. He was more frightened than he'd let on.

She caught the trolley back to her neighborhood. Ned had said he wasn't coming home for dinner. She felt that she'd boarded a train and found it speeding fifty miles an hour toward a brick wall.

# Chapter 42

Mahala Benedict closed the office door after Ned left for lunch. She'd had enough of his furtive phone calls and sly looks and questions about where she was going for lunch. She suspected that his own lunch hour would be good and long. Was he seeing the Burkett girl? That poor wife of his! The young woman seemed so in love with him. Some women just couldn't help loving a bad man.

She pulled a set of keys from her pocket. She had a job to do.

She'd start with the obvious. One drawer of Ned's desk was locked, but she knew that the old desks in the offices used the same keys.

The prophylactics she found in one drawer annoyed her rather than embarrassed her. Doubtless he should have taken them along today. Then there was a silver flask, but that was not her concern. In a zippered pouch she found a surprising amount of cash, and she riffled through it before deciding she didn't want to take the time to count it. She closed the drawer and relocked it.

In the rest of the drawers, she found the usual company forms and letters, company checkbook, bills and receipts, business letters, stationery, pens, pencils, ink, paper clips. In the bottom drawer lay an unopened box of Cuban cigars.

She went through every desk drawer. No papers pertained to the Pierce-Arrow. She wasn't sure what good it would do, anyway, because Henry told her they would've changed the license plates.

In one unsealed envelope she found a picture of a pretty young woman standing in front of a bicycle shop, with the inscription on the back: *Sarah Grady, 1917*. Was this his girl? Where might be a bicycle shop named Grady's Wheels? Henry was the cyclist in the family. She'd ask him. Reluctantly she placed the picture back in the envelope.

The drawers done, she looked among the few books in the bookshelves. In a copy of one of the *Mental Efficiency Series*, she found a slip of paper with feminine handwriting—*darling, I miss you and love you—can't wait to see you again*. The note was signed with a large, graceful letter "S." Sarah? Or did that handwriting seem oddly familiar?

She stared at the note, tempted to ball it up and toss it in the trash. Only the thought that Ned might miss it and suspect she'd been snooping made her replace it.

She hated the thought of going through all the drawers of the tall filing cabinet, which held files going back to Toby Burkett's time. Ned hadn't allowed her to clean them out, saying he'd do it one day.

The boy's death still haunted her. Toby's tenure as manager trainee had been up and down, as he and his father adjusted to working together. He'd done what his father asked with resignation and simmering anger, but in his unguarded moments she'd seen in him a love of life, a hidden joy, a feeling that only came out when he talked about sports. She felt he would've found his way eventually. She never suspected he'd commit suicide.

The enthusiasm that had buoyed her at first began to flag. Going through all these papers would take days, and by the end of the week she'd be back in her own renovated office.

On a hunch, she tested the backs of the file drawers for anything taped there, and found nothing.

Opening each drawer precariously wide, she felt behind the last dividers. Nothing there. Finally, to reach the lowermost drawer, she lowered herself to hands and knees, the cold, gritty floor hard against the knees of her sensible cotton lisle stockings.

She reached back, back—and her hand closed on something that felt very much like a checkbook. Before she could dislodge it, she heard the door open behind her.

Mahala looked up slowly at her employer and suppressed a giggle at his astonished expression. "Oh, Mr. Burkett," she said. "I was trying to retrieve a pencil. It must have rolled under this cabinet here."

"Never mind the pencil," said Elias Burkett. "Order another gross if you need to. Your time's more valuable than a pencil."

Mahala reminded him that she was beginning her lunch hour.

"Yes—ss" said Burkett, stroking his mustache. "As a matter of fact, I'm looking for Fletcher. Where is he?"

"Why, he said he was going to lunch out," she said.

"Damn," said Elias Burkett. "I beg your pardon, Mrs. Benedict. The man I was going to meet missed his train. My wife is at some ladies' luncheon. My daughter's gone God knows where. I don't want to go home to an empty house and a plate of cold cuts."

She said quickly, "Oh dear, Mr. Burkett, what about Mr. Wilkins?"

"Jacob?" Burkett grumbled. "He's got dyspepsia. Never dines out. Eats a sandwich at his desk."

Mahala, who knew the elderly bookkeeper's extreme thriftiness, said nothing. The spark in her employer's eye came alive, much to her dismay. "Mrs. Benedict, get your hat. I'm taking you to the Carriage House. My treat."

Unladylike words flitted through Mahala's mind, but she gave her boss a melting smile. "Just give me a moment to wash up, Mr. Burkett. I'll meet you at your office."

"Very good, my dear. It'll be a working lunch. You can brief Fletcher on anything he needs to know later."

"Yes, Mr. Burkett."

Elias Burkett walked away and Mahala bit her lip. She dared not keep the boss waiting, but she had to investigate the mysterious checkbook. Why was it hidden away?

She ducked in front of the cabinet and lifted the heavy book out. She flipped to the blank checks—from a company named Boston Machine. The name didn't mean anything to her. She slipped the checkbook back into the drawer, took her coat and hat from behind the door, and walked down to Mr. Burkett's office.

She found him smiling, expansive. "Let's go, my dear."

When they arrived at the Carriage House, he insisted on ordering lunch for both of them—"the chicken Marengo is something you must try"—and a very good lunch indeed was set before her. She only wished she had more appetite.

She asked him if he ever did business with a company called Boston Machine, but he said Fletcher took care of those details. She picked at her elaborate dish, trying to do it justice, while Mr. Burkett talked on and on about his daughter, about his hope that she'd marry soon before she did some fool thing to ruin her reputation, about how she might just lose the most eligible bachelor in the state because of sheer pigheadedness, and no doubt that trait had come from her mother.

Mahala stole a glance at her watch, feeling sorry for poor Clara Burkett, who perhaps needed to be pigheaded to contend with a self-centered daughter and overbearing husband.

When Mr. Burkett finally pulled his Cadillac touring car into his personal parking space, Mahala's heart sank to see Ned's Model T in its usual spot. She took a deep breath. Had she fully closed the lower file drawer in her rush to leave?

She entered the office, hung up her coat, and turned around, willing herself not to as much as glance toward the filing cabinet.

Ned, complexion as flushed as if he'd played several sets of tennis, looked up from his desk chair, telephone in hand, and placed his hand over the mouthpiece. Then he murmured a good-bye and hung up.

"Have a nice lunch, Mrs. Benedict?" He smiled at her in that insolent way he had, looking hugely pleased with himself. Mahala wondered if the young lady, whoever she might be, had had a good time.

"Mr. Burkett was kind enough to ask me to come, yes. But he came in here looking for you."

"I'm sorry to have missed the chance," said Ned, his lingering smile reeking of satisfied desire. Mahala hated that she would have to share the office for the rest of the afternoon with this loathsome creature.

She sat down, fed a sheet of paper into her typewriter, and began to pound out another letter. The typewriter clacked away the hours. Ned didn't leave the office again, and still wallowed in his chair at closing time. She gratefully put on her hat, took her coat, and left.

Henry would be so disappointed. He'd hoped she'd find a dated receipt for car repairs and some description of the work, but Mahala feared it had been destroyed, if it had ever existed. Still, young Sam Latrelle had finally remembered bits of that night, and could pick a Pierce-Arrow out of a lineup.

At the exit, she put on her coat, buttoning it tightly for the four blocks home. She didn't want to wait for the trolley, and walking would help her to collect her thoughts.

As she reached the front gate, a woman on a bicycle skidded to a stop and waved at her. "Yoo-hoo!"

Mahala blinked. This young woman resembled the girl in the photograph hidden in Ned's desk. She wore a sturdy set of tweed knickers and a wool jacket, and a cycling cap corralled her wavy hair, crisp and brown as oak leaves.

Wearing a determined expression, the girl wheeled the bicycle over. "Ma'am, can you help me?"

"Perhaps," Mahala said, intrigued.

"Does a Ned Fletcher work at this plant?"

How should she answer? "I believe he's still in the building," Mahala said cautiously. "May I ask how you know him?"

The girl's gaze didn't waver. "Does it matter? I really need to see him."

"It's after closing time." Mahala bit her lip and wished she had Henry's advice. "If you wait here, you'll catch Mr. Fletcher coming out shortly, that is, unless he has more work to do."

"Gosh, it's cold out here," she said. "Maybe I could wait at his house. Does he live far?"

Mahala considered carefully. Was Ned's visitor bold, or desperate? "Before I give you his home address, I need to know why you're looking for him."

The young woman frowned. "I've come a long way to collect a debt." Her hands gripped the bicycle's handlebars. "And that's all I'm going to say."

Mahala nodded, half to herself, half to the girl. Perhaps there was a truth here that Ned's Gussie needed to hear. She told the young woman where Ned lived and gave directions to the house.

"It'll be a haul on this wheel," the girl said, "but I've come this far, and I'd ride to the ends of the earth to see that son-of-a-bitch."

Mahala pressed her lips together in disapproval. Such language! But then, Ned deserved it. "How far have you come?"

"Just from the train station, but that's far enough." The woman brushed a few strands of hair out of her face. "By the way, my name's Sarah."

"Mahala Benedict."

Just then, a black Model T rolled through the gates and shot off down the street.

"Speak of the devil," Mahala said. "There he went. I don't know if he saw us or not."

"I'll be off now. Thanks," said the young woman. She mounted her enameled steed, pushed off, and was pedaling furiously before Mahala could say another word.

"Good-bye, good luck," she called, watching Sarah's legs pump the bicycle into the twilight. Mahala wondered what mischief she'd set in motion. It would be no more than Ned deserved.

"But Ned," Gussie said, "what do you mean you have to go to Savannah? You just got back." She settled the lid on the soup she'd been making and followed him upstairs. Gracie was napping, thank goodness.

"It's the same deal. Just a couple of days." He threw a clean shirt, underwear, and two pairs of socks into his valise.

"Can't it wait until tomorrow? I've been feeling so awful." She was almost sure she was pregnant again.

"Listen, kid, just take it easy." There was an edge to his voice that frightened her. Her back hurt, and she eased down to the bed, flattening out. Staring at the ceiling, she heard the click of the clasp on his case. He leaned over and gave her a kiss, aromatic with the spicy vetiver cologne he always used. It used to make her melt. This time she shrank from it.

"Back soon, sweetheart," he said.

She listened to his footsteps on the stairs and the clatter of a desk drawer in the front parlor. The drawer banged shut; the lock clicked. The back door slammed. Very dimly, the grandfather clock in the hall ticked away the minutes since he left.

Gracie, awakened, began to cry. Gussie heaved herself up and lifted the child out of her crib and changed her. Downstairs, she first fed Gracie, then set her in the downstairs playpen. For her own supper, she dipped the fragrant vegetable soup, brimming with chunks of ham and tomatoes, and sat alone at the kitchen table.

For the past week Ned had looked drawn and strained, the shadows under his eyes deep. At night, more often than not, before he came to bed he stared out at the moonlit street below, window open, no breeze stirring.

And now, this sudden departure. He'd opened the desk before he left and taken something out. She remembered the picture of his sister that she'd found in his valise, the mysterious papers she'd never examined. Ned had secrets.

She was going to have another baby. She needed to know these secrets. Her spoon clattered to the plate.

She headed to the desk in the living room. If the drawers were still locked, she'd try to pick them as Rafael picked the lock at the dilapidated Casa de Recogidas. She reached for the first drawer when the doorbell rang.

Her stomach fell. The police, telling her that Ned had crashed on his way out of town? Henry Benedict with more questions? Or even worse, her father? With Gracie safe in the playpen, she ventured to the door and opened it.

A young woman with curly brown hair, wearing knickers and a wool tweed jacket, eyed her with curiosity. "Excuse me, is this where Ned Fletcher lives?"

Gussie's hand flew to her mouth. "He just left! Has something happened?

"Well, damn. Missed him again! Yes, dearie, something *has* happened." The brown-haired woman's eyes narrowed. "Has he ever spoken to you of Sarah?"

"Sarah? His sister?" Gussie squeaked. She felt the blood leaving her face. This was the girl in the picture.

The girl laughed hollowly. "His sister! Is that what he told you? Oh, that's rich. I mean, really rich. Oh, no, Mrs . . . Fletcher . . . or should I say Mrs. Chance?" She put her finger to her chin. "No, you can't be Mrs. Chance, because *I'm* Mrs. Chance. Sarah Chance. I'm his wife."

The shape in front of her began to blur. The world was turning gray, and the last thing she remembered was the stranger reaching out to catch her.

# Chapter 43

Gussie blinked awake, a cold, wet dishcloth on her face.

"Don't worry, hon," a woman's voice said. "The babe's happy. You got any hooch?"

Hooch? *Hooch?* She struggled to sit up. Who *was* this person? "There's brandy. In the sideboard."

"It'll do. We need to talk."

Within an hour, Gracie was asleep and Gussie was sitting at the kitchen table, Sarah across from her. They fingered glasses of medicinal brandy while Sarah recounted her tale of Byron Chance, the husband who left to make a killing in Florida land and never came back.

"I believe your Ned is my husband, and I'm here to get my money back," she told Gussie. "You can have Byron, if you want him. I've got another fella wants to marry me."

Gussie's questions tumbled out: "How did you meet him? Do you have any children? Did you know him long? Did you ever meet his parents?"

"Whoa, whoa, one at a time," said Sarah. "No kids. God, I'm tired. Rode all day on that train from Savannah, then I pedaled from the station out to the mill on the wheel, and then I had to ride all the way out here. Stopped for a bite to eat on the way at some tea room and that uppity woman told me she didn't want to serve a woman in pants! Can you imagine!"

"Where was—"

"I asked her, what did she want me to do, go to some speakeasy? I'm a respectable businesswoman, not some flapper. Well, some sort of English lady in the tea room stood up for me. 'The poor girl's in proper dress for cycling,' she said. The tea room lady gave in, and I stayed and talked for a while with the English lady."

"Was that lady's name Verity Hapsworth, by any chance?"

"Could have been." Sarah looked around the kitchen. "Can we talk more later? I'm all tuckered out. Maybe in the morning, if I can catch a little sleep here. Where's Byron? I saw him leave the plant. Took off like a bat out of hell."

Gussie sank into a chair. All this was too much. She said slowly, "He came home from work, packed a case, and took off. For Savannah, he said."

Sarah slapped the table with her palm. "Back to the scene of the crime! I might have caught the bastard if I'd just made better time." Gussie colored at the profanity. Sarah was saying, "I'd bolt after him, but I'm bushed. Point me where to bunk, honey."

Gussie didn't see that she had much choice. "You can choose between the sofa in the parlor or the daybed in the baby's room." Not in *her* bed, that was for sure.

Sarah gave a short, sharp laugh. "Maybe not with the kid." Gussie fetched a pillow, her blue wool blanket, and a flannel sheet. Sarah stroked the satin binding of the blanket. "You come from money, don't you?"

Gussie blinked. "Why, I never . . ."

"You never thought about it. I'll give you some advice. Think about it. Regarding Byron. Good night."

Sarah was still asleep on the sofa in red long johns, blanket tucked around her, when Gussie brought Gracie to the kitchen the next morning. The coffee was almost perked and Gracie stoked with oatmeal when Sarah appeared in the doorway wrapped in the blanket, mass of hair springing in all directions.

"Thanks for letting me stay," she said. "If you don't mind, I'd be a lot sweeter with a bath."

Gussie nodded and swallowed. "Upstairs. The bathroom's warm." She turned away, trying to hide her trembling lip. The whole thing still felt like a bad dream. She sat down with a cup of coffee, sipped it, found it was too hot. She pushed it away, sunk in gloom, barely looking up when Trevania let herself in the back door, humming.

"Mornin', Miss Gussie. It's gone be a beautiful day." She turned to the peg by the back door and hung up her coat, then turned back, eyes narrowed. "Now if you tell me nothin's wrong today, I'm gone tell you pigs circlin' overhead."

Gussie cleared her throat and looked up from under her curly bangs. "We have company for breakfast."

Trevania crossed her arms. "Miss Gussie, from the way you look, it like to be a haint."

"No ghost. It's . . . a relative of Ned's," Gussie said. "A woman."

"And I suppose the boss man ain't here?" Trevania didn't hide her disgust.

"No," Gussie said. "He's gone to Savannah. Again."

Trevania shot her another look. "You got to do better than oatmeal for company." She washed her hands at the sink, filled a saucepan with water and put it on to boil for grits, then took a brown bowl of eggs from the refrigerator. Bacon was sizzling in the pan and baking biscuits perfuming the kitchen when Sarah walked in, damp-haired, dressed in wool knickers and sweater.

"Hey there," she said to Trevania, and sidled over to a chair. She plunked herself down. "Got any coffee? I'm about to have a Java fit."

Trevania, poker-faced, picked up a cup, filled it, and set it on the table in front of the visitor.

"Sarah, Trevania." Gussie figured last names didn't matter. Trevania nodded, then turned back to breakfast, cracking eggs and stirring grits. She checked on the biscuits and set a jar of syrup on the table.

"Lord, you have a nice house," Sarah said. "And the food smells *divine*. Byron's done all right for himself." She turned to the bassinet. "Let me take another look at his little one."

Gussie tensed, but Sarah made no move to pick the baby up. She gazed at the child with wistful sadness. "We never had a baby," she said. "Just didn't happen."

Gussie got up and sidled over to the stove, catching Trevania's eye. "I'll finish breakfast. Would you take Gracie and change her?"

Trevania, with a sideways peek at Sarah, nodded. She washed her hands, dried them on a towel, and lifted Gracie out of the bassinet. "Call me if you need me."

Gussie, glad to be busy, forked bacon out of the pan and drained it on brown paper. "You were going to tell me how you met Ned, I mean—Byron?"

Sarah grimaced. "Yep. Let's eat first."

Gussie scrambled the eggs, then whisked the biscuits out of the oven, almost burning her arm. She scooped dollops of creamy grits onto Blue Willow plates, and set a loaded plate in front of Sarah, who dug in without even blessing the food, unless you counted "Lord, this is good."

She ate as though she'd been out in the woods for a month living on nuts and berries. Then she wiped her mouth. "I could kill for some orange juice."

"I'm afraid we don't have any," said Gussie. "Ned won't drink that canned stuff. Said living in Florida spoiled him."

Sarah buttered another biscuit, ate it, and washed it down with coffee. "Yep, he always wanted fresh squeezed. More coffee?"

Gussie picked up the pot. "Sarah. You promised to tell." She filled cups for her visitor and herself, sat down, and waited.

Sarah leaned back, sighed, and folded her hands around her coffee cup. "My father had a bicycle shop. I never had any brothers, just some older sisters, and Mama had already passed. Dad made me his flunky.

"I met a lot of boys in that job and got engaged to one. Guess what. He's buried somewhere in France. So what could I do but keep working for Dad?

"I was fixing a bicycle one day, grease all over my face, and one of the best-looking men I'd ever seen came into the shop and wanted to rent a bike. I told him the only one his size was the one I was fixing.

"Byron leaned over and lifted that wrench out of my hand. I just stood there like a fool while he finished the bike twice as fast as I could've done it. Then he rode away. When he came back he paid me double and asked me to go dancing."

A month later they'd been married. She'd been twenty-six to his twenty. When her father retired because of heart problems, he'd turned the shop over to them. They'd made good money: the business had plenty of customers because of Byron's charm and Sarah's business ability, and they were building a good nest egg to provide a house big enough for them and her daddy too.

"I won't say life was perfect. Byron liked to go to beer halls with the other fellas and he met a shark named Curtis Wyckham who kept telling him he needed to buy real estate if he wanted real cabbage. Showed him brochures about Florida. I told him he wasn't touching that nest egg. I was tired of living behind the shop."

"Wyckham!" Gussie exclaimed.

Sara nodded. "So you know him too." She went on to say that with those brochures and Wyckham's encouragement, Ned talked her into letting him take the nest egg to Florida to buy a lot or two on the beach. "Lord, he was excited!" Sarah said. "He told me we'd sell the land later for four times our money and then we could buy one of those fine houses on one of the squares, like the swells."

Here Sarah stopped.

"And he never came back," Gussie said slowly.

"Daddy and I had a hard time after that," Sarah said. "Cars were getting more affordable, and I won't bore you with the rest. Now, just when I've caught up with him, he's slipped away again. Like an eel, he is. Like a snake."

"How did you find out he was here?" Gussie raked a fork through the grits on her plate.

"It's a long story. Sure you want to hear it?"

"Sure."

"First, my aunt thought she saw Byron in Savannah and told me. I hired a Pinkerton to see if he could find him. Found his family in Weedy Grove. He'd told me he was from Florida.

"I went up there and met Meredith, his sister, who hadn't heard from him in years. Later on she sent me a picture of this Ned Fletcher. Said her sister Tenny sent it. You know anybody named Tenny Chance?"

Ned. Spinning stories. With everybody. "Tenny? I don't think so." Gussie racked her brain. Then she remembered the old lady on the streetcar hollering at Ned, something about France. *No. She was calling him Chance.*

She felt the blood drain from her face. Her last shred of hope that Sarah had the wrong man was gone.

"I decided to check this Ned Fletcher out," Sarah said. "All I want is my hard-earned money! If he'd just repay me, I'd let him go." She looked around. "Oh yeah, I need a divorce too, so I can marry my fella. Solid citizen."

Gussie looked at Sarah curiously. "Why didn't you go to the police?"

Sarah got a far-off, tender look. "I know he was bad, but I can't hate him. We had some great times." Then she frowned. "Anyhow, it's my word against his. He could say I agreed to let him invest the money, and the courts usually take the man's side."

Gussie wrapped her arms tightly around herself, cold though the kitchen was warm. She'd heard enough. "I don't know when he'll be back. Did you ask Wyckham?"

Sarah sniffed. "First place I went. That praying mantis gave me the runaround. Well, sure. He hasn't seen *Byron Chance*, he hasn't, just your Ned, so he wasn't telling a lie. I swear, Byron's the luckiest cuss ever walked the earth. If that lyin' s.o.b turns up you know where to find me. Grady's Wheels, Savannah."

Byron's wife mopped the last of her breakfast with a piece of biscuit, then she got up, washed and dried her hands at the sink, and breezed out. She reappeared a few minutes later wearing her jacket, cap, and scarf, carrying her knapsack. She stuck out her hand.

"Good-bye, Gussie girl. Thanks for the hospitality. Good luck. And I guess your Ned handled the money, didn't he? Better find out if there's any left."

Gussie shook Sarah's hand, warm and sweaty, and said good-bye to the woman who'd turned her world on its end. Standing on the porch in the cool November mist, she watched Sarah pedal away, scarf flying, until the young woman turned the corner out of sight.

And then, like a sleepwalker, she drifted over to Ned's desk in the living room.

In the top drawer were pencils, pens, envelopes, and scraps of paper with scribbled addresses. She tugged on the other drawers and found they opened easily now. He'd cleaned it out, leaving only paid bills, receipts, and a few unpaid bills. The lowest drawer held only an empty whiskey bottle.

At a noise on the porch, she leapt up, heart racing. Had he come back? In the dim glow of the porch light she could make out the wagging tail of a roving dog. She returned to the desk and spread out the bills. From Rosenberg's, the drugstore, the grocer: all reminded Mr. Fletcher that payment was past due. Angry, she slammed the drawer shut, but it wouldn't go in.

She drew it out all the way, and saw a letter wedged against the back corner of the frame. She reached in, caught a corner, and slipped it out. She read the letter with growing astonishment.

Max Herbert wrote that he'd consider the house in payment of the debt. Until Ned could arrange it, Max wanted the checks to keep coming. He'd drop by to sign the house papers on his next trip to Miami.

It was dated just two weeks before.

Ned had offered to settle what he owed to Max with their *house*? But she owned the house! Was Ned planning to forge her signature? Tie her up and force her to sign?

The phone shrilled and she raced for it. Out of breath, she told Mrs. Mahala Benedict that Ned wasn't home. He'd left for Savannah the night before.

"My dear," said Mrs. Benedict, "I'm afraid I have some very bad news for you."

# Chapter 44

Gussie, instead of telling Papa, asked him to read the letter from Max.

"Damn," said the judge, reviewing the scribbled sheet of hotel stationery. "Excuse me, dear. Who is this Max character? Can't spell worth a hoot."

"Oh, Papa! He's a sleazy character from Chicago we met in Cuba." She wished the pounding headache she'd developed in the past hour would go away. She really felt awful. And her back was killing her again.

The judge clamped down on his pipe. "So how did Ned get involved with a crook?"

"Max lent him money to gamble, and—"

The judge studied her. "Augusta, you've been white as that letter paper ever since you got here. So your Ned's a gambler, a bigamist, and a swindler. Anything else?"

She told her father about the call from Mahala Benedict.

Her father puffed on his pipe for a minute or two. "An embezzler as well. To pay off this Max. Wonder how much he borrowed?"

"He never would tell me." Hot and nauseated, she took a step back from her father. Could she feel this sick from fear and dread?

"H'm," said the judge. "It's a good thing I didn't put that bungalow in his name, like he wanted. If he forges your name, a sale won't be legal."

Gussie gnawed her lip.

"All these debts," he father was saying. "They have to be paid. First thing is to pay back the mill, and maybe the court won't be so hard on him, assuming we find him. I'd give you the money if I had it."

"Oh, Papa. I know money has been tight."

The judge snorted. "I don't want you dealing with any hoodlums. Maybe I can talk your aunt into selling Arcadia. You know Shackley wants to buy it. Last week he came to see me again. Made a generous offer. Miss Ola Stratton's money, I'll wager."

Gussie straightened, heart hammering. "Sell Arcadia? Papa, anything but that! And to Shackley?" Her throat caught, and she coughed and croaked.

The judge picked up the cutlass letter opener, the gift from Cuba, and tapped it on the desk. "Can't spend sentiment. The land's used up, cotton's been killed by the boll weevil, and the house needs repairs. The tax man's happy to collect anyhow. I can't abide Shackley, but he's made me a good offer."

Gussie's body felt wooden. Arcadia was the last remnant, the most beautiful remnant, the most romantic remnant of her childhood.

The judge mused, "Maybe I could sell some of the timber, if I could get a decent price."

"Papa." Gussie leaned forward. "I'll get a job."

The judge pulled his mustache. "You? Work? Not much money in taking pictures, Gussie-belle."

"If only I could have gone to New York." She had flubbed the dub for sure with another baby coming. She felt odd, with the tugging in her belly and the awful back pain.

"I think you wanted to go to New York to kick up your heels." He stopped. "You feeling all right?"

"Papa, I'm just a little wrung out. I'll figure out a way to earn money. Lyman Stratton has an idea for me. And we might find Ned." She began to shiver.

"He'll most likely go to jail." Her father peered at her closely. "Honey, you're looking awfully pale. I'm going to tell your mama to put you to bed. You're overwrought."

"No! I'll get some money, somehow!" Gussie tried to get up from the chair, but the room began to spin. She stumbled, sank down, and lost her breakfast.

When she opened her eyes again, she was lying in her old bed and an electric fan was whirring.

Her mother's faint voice rose from downstairs. "She's hot as a firecracker, Emmett. Can you come right away?"

Gussie struggled through a yellow fog to a bright white consciousness, her skin hot and tender where the sheets rubbed. She swallowed, wincing at the pain in her throat; with each breath her chest ached and her head throbbed. She was going to die. She'd never see Gracie again, and they would bury her next to her grandmother Augusta, and *then* Ned would be sorry.

Her mother's voice, soft and soothing, dispelled the last of the mist. "Hush, chickadee. You're going to be all right. I'd better not beat around the bush. You've had a miscarriage. You never told us you were expecting again."

Gussie blinked. Her mother's face appeared over her, haloed, in the brilliant sunlit room.

"I'd been hoping it wasn't true. And my eyes hurt."

Her mother got up and closed the blinds. Gussie took in the pale tan walls and medicinal smell. "The hospital? I'm in the *hospital?*"

"You've been feverish for two days, Gussie. Influenza. It might have brought on the miscarriage. I'm taking no chances with you, and I don't want Jessie or little Gracie catching it."

Now she remembered. She'd collapsed while talking to Papa.

"Where *is* Gracie?"

"Trevania's looking after her. Your sisters cut some sasanquas for you. They would've come to see you, but you're still contagious, and they're around children every day."

She reached over and touched the rosy pink petals. "Any word of Ned?"

Mama shook her head. "Hush. You need to get well." She rose to answer the soft knock at the door.

"Hello, dear!"

A bright feather bobbed around the edge of the door, followed by the hat of Miss Ola Stratton. She walked in wearing a rose silk gown and carrying a vase of pink and yellow florist roses. Gussie's headache began to pound.

The good lady smiled. "How are you today, Augusta? These posies are from Lyman and the rest of us. He wishes he could come to see you, but he's afraid of germs."

"But Miss Ola," Gussie's mother said firmly, "She's not supposed to have visitors. There's a sign on the door."

"Oh, pshaw, I'm immune to everything," Miss Ola said.

"Thank you for the flowers, thank Miss Ethel and Miss Edith, and Lyman," Gussie said, hoping she would leave.

Miss Ola cast a sideways glance at Gussie's mother, who'd taken the flowers and set them on the broad window shelf. "Have you seen my ring?" Miss Ola held out her hand so Belinda Pemberton could inspect it.

"Very pretty. When is the happy occasion?"

"February, on Valentine's day, at First Baptist," Miss Ola said with barely-concealed pride.

Gussie cast a pleading look at her mother, who gave her a sly wink. "What does Lyman think about your engagement, Miss Ola?"

Miss Ola opened her mouth, closed it, and then opened it again. "He's getting used to the idea," she said uncomfortably.

"Is he all right now from his . . . accident?" Gussie said.

"Oh. Fine. Still a few headaches, but fine. Silly for him to fall in his shop like that. Always with his head in the clouds, I say."

So he hadn't told his aunts what really had happened.

"Well, I'm sure you have lots of people to visit, Miss Ola, and Gussie needs to rest, so we'll let you get on with your rounds." Her mother's tone didn't leave room for disagreement, and she shepherded the lady toward the door.

Miss Ola nodded. "You get well soon, young lady, hear?"

Gussie sighed with relief when the door closed. "How on earth can she marry that horrible man, Mama? I think Miss Rose died to get away from him."

Her mother straightened Gussie's cover and tucked in the blanket at the foot of the bed. "Love is a mystery. Who knows what draws two human beings together. Maybe Miss Ola can overlook his failings."

Gussie's cheeks flamed. "Mama, overlooking Ned's failings is what got me into this mess!"

Her mother wisely said nothing.

"Okay, okay, say you told me so."

"I'd never do that, chickadee." Her mother smoothed Gussie's hair off her forehead. "Miss Ola may well find herself in a mess too."

A brief rap sounded at the door, and the young nurse, Miss Oakes, came in rolling a cart with a basin, a bottle of alcohol, and some folded cloths. "Time for a rub, miss. Brings down the fever."

"I really have to be going," her mother said. "I'll be back later. Would you like some magazines? Lemon drops?"

"Bring me a murder mystery," Gussie said. "Bloody and vile."

Her mother smiled. "That's the spirit. I like a fighter."

Tenny silently rubbed the alcohol over her patient's back, trying not to be rough on her sore muscles. She longed to talk to Miss Gussie about her husband when her patient was feeling better. She needed more evidence that Ned was her brother Byron.

But how could she question this poor woman, sick, and just lost a baby? What could she ask that wouldn't be hurtful or rude? And what if she was wrong? People do have doubles. She had read it in *Ripley's Believe It or Not.*

Sharp, cold alcohol fumes filled the room as Tenny rubbed. The patient wasn't talking; she seemed floppy as a wet mop. Tenny finished the rub and capped her alcohol. To her surprise, Mrs. Fletcher rolled over and gazed up at her. "I've met you before, haven't I? When I had Gracie?"

Tenny smiled. "Yes, I'm Nurse Oakes. Time to get your temp and pulse." She slid the thermometer firmly under Gussie's tongue. "One hundred and one." Tenny noted it on the chart. "You came in with a hundred and four."

Noticing Miss Ola's gift, Tenny seized the opening. "What beautiful roses. Did your husband bring them to you?"

Gussie made a choking sound and then spasmed with coughing. Tenny insisted she take a sip of water, and then settled her in bed, lifting her feet. "All right now?" Gussie nodded, and Tenny smoothed the covers over her. "You'll be back at home with him before you know it."

"Those flowers were not from him." Gussie sank back into the pillow. "He's left me."

"He's left you?" Tenny blurted, stepping back from the bed. She backed into the side chair and sat down with a thump. "Like he left us too? And Sarah?" *Oh gosh—what had she said?*

"How do you know about Sarah?" Gussie's eyes widened. "What do you mean he left you? Did he marry you too? Or worse?"

Tenny reddened. She squeezed out a cloth with cold water and smoothed it over Gussie's brow. "No, ma'am. He was not my husband or my sweetheart. I think . . . I think he might be my brother."

"Your *brother*?" Gussie struggled to sit up. "Sarah came to see me. She said her husband's name was Byron Chance. And she asked me if I knew a Tenny. Is that your Christian name?"

"Yes, ma'am." Tenny buried her face in her hands. "Tenny Chance is my real name, not Oakes. Please don't tell anybody." Her breath came in gulps.

Gussie stared down at the sheets. "So what Sarah said was true. I had a tiny hope she was mistaken."

Tenny straightened and pulled herself together. "I wanted to ask you some questions, and I'm sure you have some for me. I don't want to upset you. You need to be calm to get well." She went over to the sink and washed her hands, then she picked up the glass and filled it. "You need plenty of water to bring down that fever."

Gussie took the glass, sipped, and regarded Tenny for a long time. "You might be my baby's aunt."

"I thought of that." Tenny looked down, embarrassed.

"You came from Weedy Grove, didn't you?"

"Please don't ask me about that. I don't want to be judged by where I came from."

Gussie was quiet for a minute. "I don't do that," she said. "I just wanted to know if there's any chance Ned could have gone to your people."

Tenny shook her head. "He'd never go back to Pa, unless it was to kill him."

Gussie sat back, blinking. "Oh."

Tenny bit her lip. "I'm supposed to make you feel better, not worse." She paused. "You won't report me, will you?"

"Of course not."

"All right," Tenny said. "I'm going to give you medicine for your cough. It'll relax you." She took a bottle of brown liquid from her tray.

"What's in it?" Gussie looked dubiously at the thick brown syrup.

"Just a little opium and extract of licorice," Tenny said, filling the spoon. "And then I'll give you aspirin. Now be sure to drink that water."

Gussie choked down two spoonfuls of the bitter cough mixture and two aspirin tablets, drank half a glass of water, and then lay back and closed her eyes.

Tenny said a silent prayer that Mrs. Fletcher would sleep a long time and forget about her troubles. She set the flowers outside the door for the night and rolled her rubber-tired cart down the hall, footsteps muffled by her thick-soled shoes. Byron! Once upon a time he'd been her hero.

That was before he took to brooding. Then he'd had that fight with Pa, and then Ma had died and he'd left to join the Army. The fight was the key to the puzzle. What had it been about?

She shook her head. She had to concentrate on her patients. The next one was groggy, not up to talking, but the next patient, an older lady recovering from the flu rampaging through town, appeared bright and alert.

Tenny took her vitals while she chattered. "Dr. Emmett was in to see me, and he said I was about ready to go home," the bird-like lady said. "He was bragging on that son of his. You know, I taught that boy in school. Smart as a whip he was. Have you met him?"

"Yes, ma'am," Tenny said, her cheeks warming. "He's nice."

"Well! I like to see a smiling nurse!" said the lady.

"It means you're going to be just fine," Tenny replied.

She stopped to look out the window at the bare November trees, the oaks stubbornly holding on. Christmas wasn't far away. Would Pete be back?

Last summer. Oh, last summer.

After the injured boy had recovered enough to leave the hospital, Pete had invited her to a car race out at the new dirt track. He'd found a rare Sunday afternoon when they'd both be off duty. He knew it was against hospital rules, but he was so sweet, saying he'd make sure to fix it if they got caught.

She'd said *No* then.

And then, almost at the end of summer, she was halfway to the drugstore to buy more hair dye when he came running down the sidewalk after her.

"I thought I saw you!" He grinned, huffing a little. "Going anywhere special?"

"Just to the drugstore."

"Oh, can't that errand wait? Come driving with me, right now. Who knows when we might have the same day off again? Who knows when we might have such perfect weather?"

"Same answer. Against the rules," Tenny said.

"I could get Pop to square it. Tell you what. You go on to the drugstore, and I'll pick you up there in half an hour."

Tenny thrilled from her toes through her sweaty blouse to the cloche that was pulled way, way down. She pulled out her dark glasses and put them on.

His car pulled up to the curb at Walgreen's, where Tenny waited with the dye packet tucked in her shoulder bag. She hopped in fast and closed the door. "Where are we going?"

"I thought we'd drive out by the river. I used to take my cousin out there on photography junkets. You know her. She was a patient of yours, Gussie Fletcher."

"I know her." Tenny sobered.

"What's that serious face for?" Pete asked. "I'm not taking you out there for immoral purposes, or even to drink hooch. It's a beautiful spot I want to share with you."

The river. The river she'd bathed in on the way to Ashbyville. The river that washed away all her past. Funny how that past kept washing up on shore, like dead leaves. Or dead people.

The leaves above them bore a hint of yellow, and it hadn't rained lately. The river ran deep and green and clear, and a few fishermen on the banks had cast their lines.

They motored along with the windows open, the breeze carrying sweet fall scents of muscadine. Pete proclaimed that one day he'd have an open roadster. Too bad he had to drive his dad's doctor-mobile, stodgy as it was.

"I think it's grand." Tenny admired the sunny roadside edges where purple-blue asters grew. When they came to a rise, Pete stopped. "There's a good view here."

They climbed atop a rock overlooking the river, and the dapples of the sun on the currents of the water, the earthy scent of the riverine banks, the clay, the sweet woodland smells, awoke a shiver deep in both body and soul, and she slipped her arm through his.

Pete's cheek touched hers, and then he kissed her, more deeply than before, and he ended the kiss slowly, as if he were afraid of breaking a spell. She wanted him to kiss her again, but she was afraid. Afraid of what might come next, even though he had promised. She knew that men did not always keep their promises.

"Tenny . . ." he said. "Would you do one thing for me?"

Her heart thumped wildly. "What?" When she saw his mischievous look, she smiled. He was going to tease her.

"What?"

"Would you let your hair grow into its real color?"

Her spirits plummeted. How could he ask that? He didn't know why she used dye, and she wasn't about to tell him.

"I can't." She swallowed tears. It had been such a perfect afternoon, that kiss had been so wonderful, and now this. "Maybe we'd better go back now. I have to get my uniform to the laundry and pick up the clean one, and I have studying . . ."

"Can't we do this again?" Pete asked. "I apologize if I was out of line."

"No, you weren't," she said, gazing at him, and then she looked away. It was life that was out of line.

She asked him to drop her at the drugstore, and she'd walk back from there.

The next week the hospital became so busy, everyone worked extra hours. There were accidents from falling tree limbs, near-drownings, and mysterious fevers, and no one had time to go for a drive. And then the summer was over and he'd gone back to Emory, leaving her a note that he'd looked for her to say good-bye.

Because he had asked her to go again, because he had kissed her by the river, those moments became a flower near her heart, a secret flower she could cup in her hands when work became drudgery or Enid was mean to her.

And he had sent her a postcard, a lovely postcard of a railroad bridge over the Chattahoochee River with a train on it, signed "Your Friend" so the other nurses wouldn't know. *See you at Christmas* was all he wrote.

# Chapter 45

You'd think they could let sick people rest. Gussie bit her lip at the knock and hoped it wasn't some detective looking for Ned. "Come in," she said wearily.

She blinked when Henry Benedict stuck his head around the door. "Can I talk to you?"

"Henry, I'm not supposed to have visitors." Gussie yanked the covers higher, wishing she'd asked her mother to bring her best robe and some face powder.

Henry had the grace to look sheepish. "That Nurse Oakes looked after me when I had appendicitis. A little chocolate does wonders with her." He slid a small purple box onto her side table. "Here're some bonbons for you. May I sit down?"

"You might as well, you're here," she said. "You could catch this flu, you know."

Henry took the visitor's chair, hat in hand. "I'll take my chances and get right to the point. It's about your husband."

Gussie fidgeted, took a sip of water. "Your mother called me. I know about the trouble at the mill."

Henry turned his hat around and around. "She didn't tell you all of it. Your husband was diverting mill funds to a private account, which he was using to pay one Max Herbert of Chicago. Tidy sums. Blackmail?"

There was no point in keeping anything back. "He owed Max money. Gambling. I found a letter he'd missed in the desk when he cleared it out. A threatening letter."

"So you knew this Herbert character?"

"We met him in Cuba. He took us to the Casino and encouraged Ned to gamble."

Henry nodded. "The police want to question you, but your father's kept them away until you were better. He didn't want to be the one to tell you, so he sent me."

Gussie turned her face, tears stinging her eyes. "Papa didn't want to say he told me so."

Henry leaned over and gave her his handkerchief. "Let's not make this a habit. I'm running out of clean linen."

Gussie sniffed, blew into the handkerchief, and then smiled. "I'm glad you know what to do when a woman cries, Henry."

"Well, it helps if I'm not the cause of it."

Gussie thanked him and picked up the box of chocolates. She opened it and bit into one with a creamy center. "Yum. You're not the heart-breaker type, Henry. Thank goodness." She was grateful for Henry's steadiness, and she wished he'd quit looking at her like that. "Chocolate?" She held out the box.

Henry shook his head and cleared his throat. "The next thing I have to tell you is a little harder."

Gussie set the chocolates carefully on the side table. "I can take it." She tightened her grip on Henry's handkerchief.

Henry took a deep breath. "Your father sent me to Savannah as a courier. Said the documents were sensitive and he didn't want them in the mail. That errand didn't take long, and I had time to visit repair shops before I caught the train back."

The door opened, and a nurse with an expression like she smelled used diapers stuck her head in the door. "No visitors. You'll have to leave, sir."

Henry turned to the nurse. "Well, hello, Enid Barlow, fancy meeting you here."

"Henry Benedict! I could say the same for you." The expression softened a little.

Henry winked at her. "You're just as pretty as ever. Be a good nurse and let me have some time here. It's not just a social call."

The nurse called Enid sniffed. "We have to observe the rules."

"I happen to know of a few rules you haven't observed, Enid." He smiled at her as if it was a huge joke.

She glared at him. "Five more minutes."

The door closed, too hard.

"What did you find?" asked Gussie. Her headache was returning.

"One of the mechanics acted nervous, like he had something to hide. I told the judge, and he passed the cops the information. This time, since Fletcher had run, they decided to look into his sudden trip to Savannah.

"They got the mechanic to admit that dents were taken out of the fenders of a Pierce-Arrow and the car was painted green."

Gussie, dizzy and sick, reached for her water glass and gulped, coughing a little. She wiped away tears. "Can they prove it's the same Pierce-Arrow?"

"Well, the identification number's been tampered with, and the license plate on it belongs to a wrecked car." Henry looked at his feet and swung his hat.

Gussie lay back on the pillow and an icy calm came over her. "That's not all, is it, Henry?"

He looked up at her. "Can you stand more?"

She nodded. "I need to hear it all."

"Well, then. Young Sam Latrelle's memory is coming back. His dad told me that when the police came to talk to Sam, he picked a Pierce-Arrow out of a photo lineup as the kind of car that hit him. Since it was twilight, he wasn't sure about the yellow." He paused. "There aren't many Pierce-Arrows in Ashbyville. His and Lyman Stratton's."

Gussie took a deep breath. "Oh."

Henry must have seen the change in her face. "What do you know, Gussie? Have you been talking with Lyman? You know somebody bashed his car?"

"Lyman told me Toby was murdered!" Gussie blurted. "Did you know that?"

"Toby? Murdered?" Henry clenched his jaw.

"Let's not talk about Toby," Gussie said. "We don't have time. I've got to tell you—I did see a dent in Ned's car when he came home that night. I didn't want to believe it. And I think he took a scarf of mine to . . ."

"To do what?"

"To hide his face when he bashed Lyman's car." Gussie twisted her wedding ring back and forth. She finally slid it off and set it on the table. "Have you talked this over with Papa?"

Henry glanced at the ring, a circlet of tiny diamonds, and paused before he nodded. "Of course. He'll come and prepare you to talk to the police. They'll ask you if you have any idea where Ned went. If you were covering for him."

Gussie licked her dry lips. Did the police need to know that Nurse Oakes might be Ned's sister? The young nurse had been so certain that Ned would not have gone to her people in Weedy Grove, and Gussie had promised not to reveal Tenny's origins.

She cleared her throat. "I can only tell what I know. He said he was going to Savannah, but he could be in Florida, still trying to sell that land."

Henry nodded. "Maybe I'll go to see Curtis Wyckham."

"But Henry," Gussie implored, "I'm sure the police will get to Wyckham since he had such close ties with Ned. Why do you care so much?"

"Do you have to ask, Gussie?" Henry's green eyes gazed into her own sea-colored ones, and the moment hung between them like a shimmering curtain.

Slow heat crept into Gussie's cheeks. This was no time for Henry to declare his love. She yearned to bury herself in his arms and let herself be comforted. But she couldn't. She sniffled into Henry's handkerchief.

A knock sounded at the door. "Five minutes are up."

Henry stood, hat in hand. "There's another reason I want to bring Ned Fletcher to justice. Emory Latrelle and his wife helped Mother and me a lot after we moved across the street from him. That is, after my father was killed. I owe them a great deal."

"Your father was killed?" Gussie sat up straight. "Was he in the war, then?"

"My father was murdered," Henry said.

The door opened and Enid stood there.

"I'd better be going," Henry said.

"You'll tell me more?"

"Anything you want to hear. I'll come see you when you get home."

Gussie saw the pain and anger in his eyes. "Oh, Henry."

He walked over and clasped her hand. "To hell with germs. I'm sorry about everything, Gussie. You don't deserve any of this."

They gazed at each other, still holding hands. He didn't move, and neither did she, weighted down by unspoken words. "Gussie . . ."

Anguished, she gripped his hand. "Henry. You've been so good to me, such a good friend. But please don't ask me for more now. My life's like a jigsaw puzzle with half the pieces missing."

Henry nodded. "The picture will one day be complete, Gussie. I promise."

And then he was gone. Gussie sank back, exhausted, and sank into a long sleep. She dreamed of a hedge maze, so tall she couldn't see over it, and every corner led to a blind alley.

# Chapter 46

DECEMBER 1926

Rumors drifted among the nurses that Mr. Burkett's daughter Swanee had broken her engagement to Mr. Russell Vincent and was going to marry somebody else.

Tenny didn't really care who the girl married, as long as it wasn't Pete Godwin. The routine days of medications and baths and scrubbing—the endless, endless scrubbing—gave her too much time to think about Pete's postcards.

Her hands grew chapped and raw and then hard with calluses, just as the soles of her feet had hardened in the days when she had walked the long, dusty rows of cotton. She bought a bottle of glycerin and rosewater so her hands would be pretty for him.

She marked off the days on the calendar, remembering Ma's scrumptious Christmas cake from sorghum and their own hens' eggs, and sent Mrs. Brown money for oranges and candy for Pa and the others. She met Ramona one Sunday for a Christmas concert in the Methodist church, and found that Ramona and Joe were going back home for Christmas, as the mill was giving the employees one day extra off.

As the holiday approached, she watched the halls and listened for Pete's voice, anticipating that he'd soon pop around the corner in his white jacket, stethoscope around his neck.

But he did not appear, and she dared not ask his father.

On Christmas Eve, downhearted, she was returning to the desk from her rounds, hoping she'd stay awake through the double shift, when she heard, "Miss Oakes?"

Bubbling with happiness, she turned, and he was walking toward her. She longed to rush into his arms, but she waited.

Eyes soft, he clutched her arm. "I thought it was you, Nurse Tennyson."

"Dr. Pete. It's good to see you." She spoke normally, even casually. She didn't say *I had almost given you up.* She didn't say *where have you been?*

They regarded each other for a long minute and the delight in his eyes faded into seriousness. "Girl, you're a sight for sore eyes," he said. "Dad sings your praises. Says nothing fazes you."

What was wrong? Why the solemn face? But she said, "Anybody who grew up in a family like mine can handle just about anything." She'd broken her taboo. She'd talked about her family.

Pete raised an eyebrow. "I want to hear about your family. I'm on my way to check one of Dad's patients. An emergency."

"Accident?" Was that why he seemed so somber?

"No, she was admitted with an acute headache that developed during a Christmas party." He looked as if he wanted to say more, but a blue-striper walked by. A machine hummed and radiator pipes clanked. A draft chilled the hall, and the smell of disinfectant rose from the floor.

"What do they think it might be?" Tenny finally said.

Pete frowned. "Not sure. Hope it's not meningitis or a brain tumor, or some infection Miss Ola picked up here on her Sunday visits. You know her, don't you?"

"Yes, the flower lady," Tenny said. *The one who wants to marry Arno Shackley.*

Pete laid a hand on her shoulder. "I'll see you later." And he was gone.

Around midnight, all was quiet. She'd found Miss Ola a private room and discovered she was with her nephew Lyman Stratton, the antique dealer who'd given her that moonstone pendant. He'd given her a smile of recognition.

The doctor in charge had ordered a strong dose of phenacetin and close observation, and Lyman stood by as Tenny administered the medicine. After Miss Ola had dropped off to sleep, Lyman told her he was still expecting her to shop with him one day. She pulled the pendant from beneath her apron and stroked the glowing stone. "I'm wearing it. So far, so good," she said.

"Good girl. I see you took my advice about the hair dye."

"Some people wish I hadn't."

"Oh? Is that why you're so radiant tonight?" He winked.

"Hush, Mr. Stratton," she said, blushing. "Is . . . anyone else coming to sit with her?"

Lyman shook his head. "No, thank goodness."

After making rounds once more, Tenny was free to take a break. She rode the creaky elevator to the top floor, walked to the lounge, and opened a frosted-glass window to get a breath of the still, cold air. A rising star glowed, seeming to grow brighter as she gazed. She closed her eyes and made a wish.

She poured herself a cup of coffee, wondering if he'd look for her. A probationer walked in, got coffee, and asked if she could carry the cup to her desk. Tenny nodded, and the student walked out. Tenny flipped aimlessly through a copy of *Physical Culture* magazine. The room became chilly.

Closing the window, she heard the door close behind her. Something in the air changed. "And here you are," Pete said.

She smiled, her heart in her throat. "I have ten more minutes." She forced her voice to be light, though her heart was racing.

"Is anyone checking your time?"

She grimaced. "I think Enid's around. I have no idea why she's here."

"Then we'll talk fast." Pete walked over to the percolator, poured himself a cupful of the black brew, and sank onto the hard sofa. He patted the seat beside him. "Come sit beside me."

She perched gingerly on the edge.

"Back, back," he said. She leaned back and took the weight off her feet, feeling awkward. "Now spill the beans, Nurse Tennyson. What about that family?"

"It's very boring." She tried to keep her voice light.

"Oh, come on. *You're* interesting, so they can't all be dopes."

"Not dopes exactly," she said. She might as well let it all out. He was acting tonight as if he'd never kissed her, and she might as well tell him. He could go ahead and disappear from her life.

She told him about the sharecroppers' shack, the brothers and the sisters, the cotton, the blistered hands from gripping the hoe, the sun pounding her head and the sweat rolling down her neck, the smells and the washing and the sickness, and about Ma dying.

What she did not say were words about Weedy Grove or Arno Shackley or the mill. Or the baby.

"You've come a long way, kid," he said, nodding. "I admire that."

"Thank you." She wished he wouldn't smile at her that way. Tenderly. She glanced down at her watch. "Seven minutes and I've been talking the whole time. Now it's your turn. Are you going to help out here until you go back to school?" She sipped coffee to hide her hopefulness.

A shadow passed across his face. "I won't be working holidays this year. Tonight was the exception."

"I guess you need a break?" To hide her disappointment, she took her cup to the sink, washed it out, and hung it on a peg. The stars outside seemed to dim. She waited for him to say something—*anything*—about what he'd be doing instead, and when he didn't, she glanced back at him. At his vague and perplexed expression.

"Was I too nosy?" she asked, a catch in her throat.

He shook his head. "Of course not. I've . . . got some social duties this year, that's all. Parties and whatnot. Family."

Tenny's blush rose. There it was, the difference between her world and his, and she'd made it painfully obvious with her story.

Pete, apparently lost in his own concerns, didn't seem to notice her discomfort. Well, his social and family duties were not her business.

"I've got to go," she said. "Merry Christmas, Dr. Pete."

Pete unfolded himself from the sofa and rose. "Thanks for the chat. Merry Christmas, Nurse Tennyson." He leaned over and kissed her on the cheek. Her heart thundered in her ears. His body radiated warmth as he moved closer and a scent of sandalwood and musk. His hand touched her glasses. With a horrid squeak, the door to the lounge swung open.

Pete dropped his hand and they stepped apart as a nurse entered. Pete, eyes never leaving Tenny's, smiled, abashed. Then Tenny plunged out into the hall. She'd welcome a cotton-picking tan right now to disguise her rosy cheeks!

She realized the nurse she'd passed was Enid Smith Barlow. What had Enid noticed? Tenny didn't care.

Pete took her arm. "Wait, Tenny." She turned and gazed into his earnest, perplexed, dear face.

"Don't ever be ashamed of where you came from," he said. "Look how far you've come, and where you're going. I wish I could see more of you. You don't know how much I wish that."

Why couldn't he? Before she could ask, Dr. Huff came charging down the hall like a man on a mission, and quick as a sneeze, he'd taken Pete away.

There was nothing to do but go back to work.

She'd bide her time until June, when Pete would be back. In the fall she'd begin her last year. The year 1927 might be a very good one.

# Chapter 47

T he year 1927 started out well enough.

Miss Ola had left the hospital. Dr. Emmett Godwin had diagnosed her with an inflammation of the arteries and had sent her home with instructions to rest and take phenacetin. Tenny, relieved to have morning hours again, had glimpsed Pete standing outside the hospital beside his father's car, dressed in tweed jacket and tie. Waiting for Dr. Emmett, she guessed, to take him to the station for the train to school.

He'd caught her at the window and waved at her, with a look of—what was it? Regret? She tentatively waved back.

Social duties.

He'd never bothered about social duties in summer. Five more months until summer, and if the dining room chatter was right, he'd planned to intern at this very hospital. Did she dare to dream?

On the second week of January, on a wickedly cold day when windows were feathered with frost, the first blow fell with two letters.

One was addressed in Ramona's laborious, curvy script. The second was a man's printing. She tore open Ramona's first.

> *Dear Tenny,*
>
> *I am sorry to say we wont be coming back to Ashbyville. Once we got home everbody cried and carried on so about my head and all and about the trouble Joe got mixed up in and they all begged us to stay and said the mill here was gone to be hiring when they get that new section built and the new boss is good to the workers.*
>
> *My Mam said it was lonely for her with all us younguns gone out to work, just her and Pappy and the cow and the mule, and she sure could use my help around the house. Well what could I do what with the smell of pine and cinnamon and Mam's best pound cake tugging at my ole heart.*
>
> *As for me I am still having trouble with my balantsing and spells like to being drunk so it don't seem they will hire me but you never can tell. When the summer comes I'm gone make preserves and such to sell the folks what come up here for the air. Leastways you can breathe here when you come out of the mill.*
>
> *Be sure and write me and tell me the news at the hospital and the mill.*
>
> *Your friend,*
> *Ramona*

And then she opened the second envelope. Joe Kinley wrote that Ramona was gone. She'd stepped outside to take the letter to Tenny to the mailbox, and halfway there, sank to the ground. She'd never woken up.

Tenny crumpled and broke out in sobs. It wasn't fair, it wasn't fair! Ramona didn't deserve to die, all for wanting a little better treatment at work. Tenny would never see her old friend again.

She spent a week grieving, and then Alice tried to cheer her up with some gossip she'd heard: Enid had worked extra hours over the holidays because her smoking and canoodling with interns had been discovered, and her uncle, the doctor on the Board of Directors, had talked Miss Wells into giving her extra duty instead of kicking her out.

Tenny found nothing good in that. Enid would take out her spite on a junior nurse, and Tenny was a prime target. Tenny trod carefully for two weeks, waiting for the axe to fall.

It happened on the coldest, blusteriest day of the winter, when the wind slapped sleet against the panes and a tracery of black limbs swayed against a leaden sky.

The hospital bulged with respiratory ailments and fevers and patients who'd wanted to live for one more Christmas, now losing the will to fight through the bleak and fickle winter.

Tired and hungry after a grueling morning, Tenny was glad of the blissfully warm nurses' dining room, where steam rose from the serving line and the homey smell of beef stew percolated through the air. She was ready for stew, English peas, yeast rolls, and apple pie.

Alice beckoned her to a far table. Weaving her way through the packed room, Tenny had to pass by Enid's stronghold. The senior student glanced up with a wicked gleam of triumph. "Thought you had a chance, did you? Swell fellows like him don't marry girls like you."

"What are you talking about?" Tenny fought her racing pulse.

Enid grinned maliciously. "Don't tell me you're the last to know."

Now Tenny noticed that the whole cafeteria was buzzing. Whispering students glanced her way. She tossed her head and walked on.

At Alice's table, she slid her tray into place and wedged into a chair. "What's going on? Why are they acting like I turned green?"

"Oh, Tenny, you'll never believe–" Alice leaned her way and whispered.

Tenny sat in stunned silence for a full minute. Pete Godwin had eloped with Swanee Burkett. He'd given her an engagement ring for Christmas, and then she'd followed him back to school on the next train. They'd been married by a justice of the peace in Atlanta. Her parents, who'd been planning to announce the engagement the following week and have a fancy wedding in June in the First Baptist Church, were fit to be tied.

The wedding announcement had appeared in today's *Ashbyville Clarion.*

"My, my," Tenny finally said. Then she slowly and methodically cut up her stew, as if she might be fixing a plate for a young patient or a man with a broken arm. She was not going to waste perfectly good, nourishing food on something as trifling as a broken heart.

# BOOK III

~~~~~~~~

## Chapter 48

The day that Swanee had her baby had been a still July day full of the dry-hay scent of scorched Bermuda grass, where even in the densest shadows the air hung thick as clabber.

Gussie knew she'd gone to the hospital, and Gussie was waiting for Mama to call with any news. She put Gracie down for a nap and took a bowl of ice cream to the front porch under the ceiling fan, flailing at the sticky air in vain. She finished the treat and picked up her book. Elinor Glyn's stories had helped her forget her heartache. Not only the books, but the portrait studio she'd opened in the front parlor.

She had customers! Mama, of course, was steering brides and graduates her way, but Gussie didn't mind at all. Anything to keep from moving back home and becoming a child again.

To earn more, she helped Lyman Stratton at his shop two days a week. Lyman had sold two of her artistic photographs, and he'd even proposed mounting a show of her work. He'd suggested showing the river nymph, but she disagreed. Lyman liked controversy and scandal, but Gussie had had quite enough, thank you.

She'd thought her life was over, and now she had another chance. She was still young and improving her craft. Someday she'd take a portfolio to the Big Apple. So Pete didn't think she could make it? Ha!

A passing ambulance screamed by, and Gussie shuddered. The sound always brought back the thought of young Sam Latrelle, healing well, but he'd always wear a brace. He'd never grow up to follow in Ty Cobb's footsteps.

The wail faded off into the evening. The grandfather clock ticked away the silence, and the sun sank into reds and purples over the rooftops. Seven o'clock chimed. "Mama!" Gracie called, whimpering. Gussie closed her book. Why hadn't she heard anything? It must be an awfully long labor.

After Gracie had been fed, bathed, and tucked in for the night, Gussie made herself a ham sandwich and listlessly ate it in the empty kitchen while shadows fell.

Was Pete happy? He worked so hard now she never saw him.

She'd taken a basket of her peach preserves to welcome the couple home after they'd settled in after Pete's graduation. No one had told her Swanee was pregnant. Smiling through her shock, Gussie merely congratulated them on the blessed event, now understanding the elopement. But when had Pete had time to court her?

That day, Pete had showed Gussie around the house like any proud husband, but his pride, his gaiety, seemed forced. Maybe he hadn't planned on being a father so soon. Maybe he was unhappy that the house was one he couldn't afford but a gift from Swanee's father.

She took her own bath and washed her hair, and with a pumice stone scrubbed black silver nitrate stains from her hands.

Fresh and wrapped in a flowered kimono, she walked down to the parlor and studied her nature prints to see if any might be good enough for Lyman's shop, but her mind drifted. Why hadn't her mother called with any news? Should she call her? No.

Gussie picked up her romance novel and nestled herself on the sofa. *The number of beautiful things he would want to say to her about it all—the oceans of love he would desire to pour upon her—the tender care which should be his hourly joy . . .* The words swam on the page. She closed her eyes and was out by the river with her camera, in the sunlight with the dragonflies. She fell into a doze.

A soft rap on the door jerked her awake. Her heart leapt to her throat. *Ned? Henry?* She stiffly rose, pulled back the curtain, and peered out.

Pete!

She flung the door open. His pale, haggard face shocked her. "What is it, Pete?" Her hand went to her chest. "What's happened?"

"Swanee had the baby." Hoarse, his head low, he choked out the words. "A little girl, seven pounds, three ounces."

"The baby . . ."

"Healthy."

Gussie reached for his hand, clasped it. "Swanee? She didn't . . ."

He shook his head. "She made it through. She had an ischemic attack during the birth."

"A what?"

"A stroke. Apoplexy."

Gussie dropped his hand, stunned. "But that only happens to old folks."

"Not always."

She shepherded him in and led him to the sofa, still warm from her nap. "Let me be the doctor, Pete." She fetched the medicinal brandy and two crystal glasses from the dining room cabinet. She filled both and handed him one. He held it, not moving, not speaking.

"Tell me, Pete," she urged. "Tell me everything."

He sighed. "There are different kinds of strokes. This one was caused by a hematoma—a broken blood vessel—in the brain. The vessel might have been weak since birth. Pregnancy and birth put a strain on the circulatory system."

Gussie leaned forward. "How can I help?"

Pete downed a slug of his brandy and gazed at her. "She's young, with a good chance of recovery. She'll need friends. Be a friend to her, Gus, while she fights this battle."

Gussie took a sip of brandy, choking a little on the liquid heat. "How? She's hated me ever since I married Ned."

Pete's face twisted and grew stony. She'd said the wrong thing.

"I know about that fling she had with Ned," he spat. "She was wild. Rebelling against her father. There were more men than Ned. If I knew who got her pregnant, I'd kill him with my bare hands."

Gussie's mouth fell open in astonishment. "It wasn't you?"

Pete shook his head. "This baby is full-term, Gussie."

Gussie set down her glass so hard it sloshed. "Pete Godwin, do you mean to tell me she took advantage of you? Didn't tell you she was pregnant?"

He looked out the window, chin high. "I knew the circumstances."

Gussie wanted to shake him. "How *could* you, Pete, after she was so cruel to you?"

Pete sipped brandy, as if collecting the right words. He finally spoke. "She called me in tears last fall, begging me to arrange an abortion for her. She said she had no one to turn to. She didn't want anything more to do with the baby's father."

"Did she tell . . ."

Pete shook his head. "I didn't ask who, or why. I told her I didn't know anyone who would perform such an operation. She called me a liar and swore she'd find some back-alley granny woman with a knitting needle. She couldn't have her father know. It would kill him, after Toby. Well, I *have* seen the results of those back-alley operations, and, well . . ."

"And what?"

He swiped at his eyes with the back of his hand. "Suppose she died? I couldn't let her risk bleeding to death or infection in a filthy, stinking shack somewhere. You know how I've always loved her. I asked her to marry me instead. That's what I could do for her."

Gussie closed her eyes in disbelief. "She accepted you at last. Small comfort, Pete."

"Don't be unkind, Gussie."

Gussie trembled with anger. And Pete wanted her to be *friends* with this girl? She took a gulp of the amber liquid. She forced herself to speak evenly. "I'm sorry. You have no idea of the father?"

He shook his head slowly. "She refused to tell me. She claimed she'd been drunk at a party. Somebody she'd never marry." At that, Pete blushed. "Anyhow, I felt I could make her happy, and what's one kid? I'd like a houseful."

Good Lord, he was still a fool. Didn't he see Swanee had the wife and mother instinct of a black widow spider? But Gussie held her tongue. Pete was hurting enough.

He reached for her hand. "You're the nearest thing I have to a sister. I need someone I trust to help me, as well as Swanee, through this. Her mother has never been the same after Toby's death. She's barely holding herself together."

"Surely Swanee has friends . . ." Gussie began, and then she remembered that Swanee's childhood friends had melted away, one by one, as Swanee had charmed, mesmerized, and stolen their beaux. Gussie gazed into Pete's face, so troubled, and tenderness washed over her. "Of course I'll help."

He enveloped her in a hug, and then a wail from Gracie shattered the silence. "Mama!"

"Go to your little one," Pete said. "I'm off to the hospital to catch a few winks before I'm on duty." He kissed her on the cheek. "You're the greatest."

As she closed the door behind him, she tried to make sense of her foreboding about this marriage. Maybe she was just a good-time flapper, but she'd been to church and learned that you couldn't build a house on sand. And desperation was about as sandy as you could get.

Maybe she was selling Swanee short. Maybe she'd learn to love him as he ought to be loved. Maybe he'd deeply forgive her wild ways.

Gussie wished she could be sure.

The simple garden daisies Gussie brought to the hospital looked like bedraggled waifs among the buxom florists' sprays in Swanee's hospital room. She edged her offering between roses and lilies on the broad windowsill, trying not to stare at the one-sided droop of Swanee's face.

"The baby's so pretty," Gussie offered.

Swanee shook her head *No* and pursed her mouth as best she could.

Maybe she needed a light touch. "Mama says new babies all look like monkeys until they grow into their faces."

The sour expression didn't change. Pete had warned her Swanee didn't like trying to talk, so Gussie rattled on about how much fun she was having watching Gracie grow, and Swanee had that to look forward to.

Swanee responded about as much as a corpse. Well, Gussie wasn't about to stay where she wasn't wanted. How could she tactfully leave? Luckily, a young nurse stuck her head in the door. "Bath time. Visitors are excused."

Gussie brightened. "Miss Oakes! How nice to see you again." Their eyes met, the silent secret knowledge about Ned a bond between them.

"Mrs. Fletcher." The young nurse, now in a blue uniform with white cap and apron, smiled. "You're looking very well."

Swanee interrupted with a garbled demand, and the nurse walked over to fluff her pillows. "There, ma'am." She tucked an extra pillow under her patient's shoulder. "Keep this side supported."

Gussie rose and slung her bag over her shoulder, noting that Miss Oakes seemed under a strain today. Well, Miss Apple Cider Vinegar here would strain anybody. "Good to see you, Miss Oakes. I'll come again, Swanee." For Pete, of course. She reached for the door.

Swanee called out something that might have been her name.

"Did you call me?" Gussie rested her hand on the doorknob.

The patient spoke. Gussie didn't understand, so she turned around to face her.

"She says thank you for coming," Miss Oakes offered. Swanee glared at the nurse.

"You're welcome."

But she was still leaving. She closed the door behind her.

She made her way down the hall and the elevator. What had Swanee really said? It could have been "go chase yourself, flat tire," for all she knew. She'd almost made it through the lobby when she heard "Got a minute?"

"For you, Pete, always," she responded. One quick hug, and then she tweaked the collar of his white jacket. "You're a real doctor now. Even got a new stethoscope."

He led her to a front window looking out on the street and the park beyond, out of earshot of a weary-looking man hunched on a dark brown sofa. "I'm worried about her prognosis," he murmured. "Pop has called in one of my profs from Emory."

Gussie searched his face. "But you were so hopeful."

"She's angry and depressed."

"And how about you, Pete? How are you managing?"

He chose to take the question literally. "I've hired Ida Blackstone to help with the baby, and my mother sends Nola over to cook and clean three days a week. We need to get somebody permanent, but money—you know."

"I know. What's Aunt Amelia going to do without her help every day?"

Pete shrugged. "She'll make do. Pop's not home that much."

Gussie smiled. "Aunt Amelia's a trooper, Nola's a rock, and I'm glad Swanee's got Miss Oakes here. She's very grown-up to be so young."

Pete fiddled with his stethoscope and Gussie found it hard to read his expression. "Absolutely nothing fazes her. She's got a special way with patients."

Gussie watched two children run across the front lawn, pursued by a frantic, haggard mother. "My mama would say girls like Miss Oakes ought to be doctors."

"It's tough on women doctors." Pete's brows furrowed. "I wouldn't want it for a daughter of mine."

Gussie stared at him. "Pete, how can you be such a troglodyte? Don't you believe in woman's equality? What if that little daughter of yours wanted to follow in your footsteps?"

Pete stared at her. "Where did all that come from? I didn't mean I was against women's rights, Gus. It's that they have such a struggle to get accepted. It might mean heartache."

Gussie touched his collar. "Women are tougher than you think. We want to take our own risks. Pete, I . . ." She bit back what she was about to say. "Pete, you're the best thing Swanee's got going for her." She kissed his cheek, then headed for the door so he wouldn't see the tears stinging her eyes.

Tenny, knees a little unsteady, edged into the second floor lounge and headed for the coffee pot. It had taken all her effort to be kind to Pete Godwin's wife. She felt compassion for her as a human being, but caring for her was torture. Still, jealousy was a luxury Tenny couldn't allow herself. She was a professional, a year away from being a graduate nurse.

In the long months before Pete had come back to Ashbyville, Tenny had plunged herself into work as if the Devil himself was cracking a whip at her back, heedless of foot-aching hours, slopping-full bedpans, endless demands from patients, and doctors who expected to be obeyed at once, even when they were wrong.

The lounge door opened, and Alice hustled in. She went for a tin of oatmeal cookies, wrestled it open, and held it out. Tenny reached for a cookie and sighed. Alice frowned. "What's the matter, kid?"

Before Tenny could answer, Enid Smith Barlow strode in, glared at them, and poured her coffee. She stalked out, ignoring the open cookie tin, which she usually raided.

"She's still trying to find out who told about her and that intern Mason Dawes," Alice murmured. "Her uncle's got her on a short leash."

"Everybody knew," Tenny said.

"But she thinks it's you." Alice munched her cookie.

"I don't know why she's always had it in for me."

"She's jealous of you."

"*Me?*" Tenny curled her lip in disbelief. "Why, for heaven's sake?"

Alice dusted crumbs off her hands and ticked off the reasons on her fingers. "You're pretty, she's not quite. You're smart, she's not quite. You keep the rules, she can't catch you breaking them. The patients like you, and so does Pete Godwin, whom she wanted to marry in the worst way."

"I'm not pretty," Tenny said.

"Are you kidding? A little paint and powder, bob that hair and quit dyeing it, and you'd have them falling out of the beds," Alice said. "And do you really need those eyeglasses? I've seen you read without them."

"I don't have time for bobbed hair and paint and all that foolishness." Tenny felt her pale cheeks warming and turned away. "She wanted to marry Pete Godwin?" her voice caught a little, and she cleared her throat. "Why should that have anything to do with me?" Her voice cracked a little. "He married somebody else."

"He likes you a lot," Alice said. "Maybe more than he ought to, because he's been sweet on that rich girl for a long time. She wouldn't give him the time of day. She was engaged to that senator's son. Enid was scheming to pick up the pieces of Pete's heart after the wedding. What a surprise!"

"I've just been with that rich girl," Tenny said. "You know what happened to her."

"I'm sorry, Tenny," Alice said, and from her sympathetic look, Tenny realized that Alice had known all along how Tenny felt about Pete, what her impossible hopes had been.

"I've got to go." Tenny left to scrub down the medication room. She was glad for the duty. At least she wouldn't have to go back to the wards and be *sweet*.

# Chapter 49

Be a friend, Pete had asked. Be a friend to the woman Ned had had a fling with, the woman who had married Pete for advantage. Why not? It would be nice to see Swanee humbled.

A Red Riding Hood-style basket on her arm, Gussie walked up to a small two-story Victorian house, its gingerbread trim bright with new green paint, summer petunias in purple and pink beginning to fade.

Ida Blackstone, plump and matronly with salt-and-pepper hair, opened the door. "Why, Miss Gussie! It's good to see you! How's that sweet young'un?"

"Wonderful. How've you been, Mrs. Blackstone?" Gussie smiled broadly, delighted to see the nurse again. Why, she must be over sixty and still going strong.

Ida Blackstone pressed her lips together. "Tolerable, just tolerable."

"What's the matter?"

A bell's angry clatter erupted above their heads, and Mrs. Blackstone's bushy brows contracted. "Oh, Lordy. That's Her. I'd better go see what she wants before she wakes up Baby. Come on in and I'll call you up when I think it's safe."

"Safe? But . . ." Humble Swanee? She had badly miscalculated.

Ida Blackstone's ample body was already halfway up the staircase, heading toward muffled screeches. Gussie gazed up at the balusters as the screeching came to a stop.

Nola Washington emerged from the dining room, broom in hand. "Goodness me, Miss Gussie," she said, "Didn't that Mis' Blackstone invite you to sit in the parlor?"

Gussie shook her head. "She didn't have time. What's going on here?"

Nola shook her head. "When Miss Swanee gets het up, it take a while to jolly her," she said. "Come on back to the kitchen. Coffee's still hot on the stove."

Gussie liked the idea of fortification and followed Nola back to the kitchen and set her basket on a new kitchen table of swirly oak.

Nola poured coffee into a delicate china cup. "Help yo'self." She pointed to the cream jug and sugar bowl on the table. Gussie stirred sugar and cream into her coffee and, waiting for it to cool, gazed out at the back garden, where a grassy lawn edged with flower beds and camellias indicated that Swanee's father had probably sent his gardener over.

A garage with a room above stood to the left of the lawn, a toolshed built against one side. A shovel and rake leaned against the shed.

Nola followed her gaze and nodded. "Dr. Pete says he's gone have the back yard in full bloom by the time Miss Swanee can walk again. A yard man comes in ever' once in a while."

Mrs. Blackstone, mouth pursed, plunged into the kitchen. She rolled her eyes. "You can go on up, honey."

Nola turned to the laundry and picked up a shirt. Gussie deposited two jars from her basket on the kitchen table, then carried the basket upstairs. Swanee was sitting up in bed, a green satin coverlet folded across her lap. Her dark hair, freshly cut in a side-parted straight bob, fell in a silky curtain over the affected side of her face.

"So, Gussie. Pete ask' you to come?" Swanee smoothed the lapels of her white bed jacket with her right hand, nails lacquered bright red. Her face, or at least the part not hidden by the curtain of hair, was as beautiful as ever.

"I came here because I wanted to," Gussie said, which was true, in a way. She'd told Mama she was doing her Christian duty. She no longer envied Swanee, not one bit, even though her own nails were ragged from childcare, she packed extra pounds, and her hair was about as easy to style as a Brillo pad.

"I've left some of Trevania's blackberry jam and vegetable soup in the kitchen, and here's something special." She reached into the basket and laid a book on the bed beside her.

"A *book*?" Swanee's gaze swept past the book to the pile of opened boxes on a dainty upholstered chair. Nightgowns, robes, and slippers spilled from crisp crinkly tissue. Roses and lilies and dahlias in vases reposed on the dresser and vanity, and a box of chocolates, half gone, lay open on the bedside table.

Gussie smiled. "Look at all these gifts! How wonderful that people care so much."

Swanee's lower lip jutted as much as it was able. "Po' pi'ful Swanee. God Works in Mysterious Ways. I'm Praying for You. To *debil* with them."

Gussie had been trying, but this was too much. "I'm here to help you, Swanee Burkett. If you're going to be nasty, I'll leave right now." She grabbed the book and jammed it into her basket, then turned to go.

Swanee's voice rose. "Waaay, Gussie. What book?"

The haughty expression wavered and Swanee's eyes betrayed a trace of fear. So the suit of armor had developed a crack? Gussie's shoulders relaxed. "An Elinor Glyn romance. I was planning to read to you. I know you can't hold a book."

Swanee held out her good hand as if asking for candy. "Sorry, Gussie. Please read. Blackstone hate me."

"What? That kind, motherly woman?"

"She on'y like babies." Swanee's half-lipped pout made Gussie want to smile, but she kept her poker face. Swanee entreated, "C'mon. Read. So bored."

Gussie surveyed the green satin, the white lace, the tissue paper, the pile of nightgowns. The book she had chosen featured a young doctor as hero, someone like Pete. She'd hoped that Swanee would realize how fortunate she was.

"All right." Gussie looked for somewhere to sit. In her flighty flapper days, she'd have slid the pile of gifts from the dainty bedside chair onto the floor. Now she folded the gowns and put them away in a dresser drawer, set the slippers on the closet floor, and hung the robes on clothes hangers without comment. She found a Chinese lap writing box, lacquered red, still in the last gift box.

She lifted it out, admiring the embossed willows and flowers. "How beautiful! You can write in bed."

"Neber write," Swanee pouted. "Read. Please."

Gussie made room for the box on a chest of drawers, sat down, and opened the book. "Chapter One."

At the end of the second chapter, hoarse, she was glad to close the book when Nurse Blackstone stuck her head in the door. "Need anything?"

Swanee's good eyelid fluttered. "White pill. Please."

The nurse's lips compressed. "Doctor says you're not supposed to have 'em except at night." A scowl settled across Swanee's face.

"Pete knows best, Swanee," Gussie said.

"He want me to be comfy," Swanee murmured, tearing up. "Don't be mean, Mis' B."

Mrs. Blackstone's face settled into granite. "I'll try to reach him and get permission." She turned and walked out.

Gussie rose and laid the book on the bedside table. "That's all for now. I need to let Trevania go home."

"Already?"

"Maybe Mrs. Blackstone will read to you," she said.

"No, won't. Come back and read t'morrow, Gussie?" Now her voice was sweet as peach cobbler.

"I'll try." Gussie picked up her basket, said good-bye, and walked downstairs to the kitchen, where bottles rattled in the sterilizing kettle and Nola's iron hissed on damp shirts. The kitchen smelled of warm cotton.

"Is she always like this?" Gussie asked the baby nurse, batting away clouds.

"Honey, you don't know the half of it." Mrs. Blackstone grasped tongs and lifted a bottle from the pot. "I've cared for the afflicted a good deal. I've seen lionhearted folks and chickenhearted folks, but this one's missing a heart." She settled the bottle on a cooling rack. "My husband retired this year from carrying the mail, and now he wants me to quit. He wants us to get a little place down at Tybee, where he can fish the livelong day."

"Well, I—"

Mrs. Blackstone went on. "I only came here because of Dr. Pete. And I tell you, that baby's sweet as can be but I've just about had all I can take of that one." She rolled her eyes towards the upstairs. "He's given me strict orders about them pills. Told me not to call him. If I tell her that, she throws a fit."

"She'll settle down after a while," said Gussie. "She's had a terrible shock."

Mrs. Blackstone placed another bottle on the rack. "Huh. Carries on like she's the Queen of Sheba. Got to have it done and done right now, have a rub, change the sheets, bring me this, bring me that, hollering bloody murder and that little baby needing so much too."

"Please, Mrs. Blackstone. Dr. Pete needs you."

"Hmph," she shrugged her shoulders. "I don't know I'd stay if Jesus himself asked me."

Gussie smiled. "You're a good Christian, aren't you?"

Mrs. Blackstone sighed. "I'm going back upstairs and take up my cross."

# Chapter 50

Tenny had avoided Pete all summer, and she'd almost made it to the lab with her specimens when he walked out of a ward. He saw her, brightened, and hurried her way. She waited, on her guard, face serene, heart hammering like Gene Krupa's drumsticks. "Good morning, Doctor."

He took her elbow. "How about having a cup of coffee with me? Can you take a quick break?"

What *was* this? She kept her calm. "Sorry, Doctor, but I've got to drop these specimens off and see three patients."

"Later, then?"

"I don't think—" Her knees weren't cooperating. Neither was her belly.

He caught her gaze. "It's important."

She looked away. "I'm off at four."

"See you in the cafeteria."

After he walked off, she took deep breaths to calm herself, as Miss Verity had taught them at the Home, saying she'd learned that trick in India when her father was in the civil service. In and out, count to eight. When Tenny felt calm again she delivered her specimens and went to her patients, the new mothers.

She concentrated on giving them baths and rubs to soothe their bodies, smiles and encouragement to feed their souls. She worked so hard that the floor nurse gave her a rare compliment. And then she entered the room of her last patient, Abbie Clendon, a skinny teenaged wife who'd had her first baby two days before.

Pete was at the patient's side.

Tenny's stomach clenched, and she turned all her attention on the young woman, whose breath was coming in ragged gasps. She turned her flushed face toward Tenny. "It hurts so bad."

"The episiotomy," Pete said.

"I should have had the baby at Big Mama's house like she wanted," Abbie Clendon wailed. "All her girls popped 'em out in the front bedroom with none of this cuttin'."

Pete's hands framed an imaginary narrow pelvis. "Look here, Mrs. Clendon. You're not built for popping, and you would've torn for sure—or worse. Here's Nurse Oakes. Let's have a look at you."

"What's the pain like?" he asked. Tenny, spreading a light cotton drape over the woman's belly, frowned at his abrupt manner. Couldn't he see that the girl was terrified?

"It stings and burns like fire."

Tenny instructed Abbie to bend her knees and scoot down, then she lifted the blanket. Tenny winced to see the puffy-red, angry-looking episiotomy, a sign that infection had set in. She exchanged glances with Pete.

Pete observed the surgical site, and then nodded for Tenny to settle the patient in bed again. He jerked his head, meaning he'd talk to her out in the hall.

Tenny gave the patient a cup of water and three aspirin tablets before meeting Pete in the hall, closing the door behind her. Miss Nightingale's book commanded that patients should never overhear conversations between doctors and nurses. She walked a little way down the hall, and he followed impatiently.

"Were you responsible for this patient?" he said, when they'd stopped.

"Yes." Tenny kept her eyes on his.

"You should have noticed this infection sooner."

Tenny fought to keep her temper. This week, all the babies seemed to have arrived at the same hour and the nurses had been run ragged. "Doctor, you know infection happens despite our best efforts." Once again she thought the female body, though a marvel of God's creation, could have used a little better engineering.

"Not on my watch."

"What would you have me do?" Tenny snapped.

"Are you using iodine?" Pete's eyes were cold.

"Saline compresses and hydrogen peroxide. It's less painful."

"My orders are iodine. Twice a day. And have a word with the night nurse to continue the treatment."

Tenny clenched her fists. "This girl is young and healthy, Doctor. I'm sure she'll fight this off. And it would be helpful to be kind to her. She'll have it rough at home."

"Telling me my business, Nurse?" He looked more amused than angry, and this made her more furious.

"You're just out of school yourself, Doctor." She knew she shouldn't talk back, but she was right, and she'd rather die than go over his head to Dr. Emmett Godwin or Dr. Golightly, the obstetrician.

"And you're out of line, Nurse. I ought to report you to Miss Wells."

"Go ahead." She bit back tears. "Are we finished here? I have a few other patients to see."

"I'll talk to you later." He strode off.

She did not go to meet him for coffee at four o'clock. She put on her straw hat and went to the drugstore. She bought more hair dye and sat at the counter and drank a vanilla milkshake and wondered if women could become pharmacists.

Three days later, when Pete slid into the chair beside her in the cafeteria, she stiffened and clutched her spoon like a cudgel. For once, she sat at a table alone, late for lunch. She'd almost finished her cheese sandwich and bowl of vegetable soup.

He lowered his voice. "You didn't keep our appointment."

She gazed at him a long moment and laid her spoon down. "Should I have?"

"Maybe I was a little hard on you." He had the good grace to sport red ears.

"Maybe you were." In fact, Dr. Golightly had countermanded Pete's order that evening.

"I'm trying to apologize."

"There's no need, Doctor. You were doing what you thought was best. I had my own opinion of what was best."

Pete looked as if he was going to say something, and then stopped and gazed at her with a wordless plea that struck her to the heart. The muffled chatter around them, the clank of knives and forks, the smell of soup and turnips faded away.

"You didn't come only to apologize," she said. "Why did you ask me to meet you in the first place?"

Pete clasped his hands in front of him and leaned forward, his eyes earnest. "You know, some of the girls here are allowed to go on private duty cases. It's part of the training."

Tenny shook her head. "I know. It doesn't interest me."

"You aren't making this easy." He gave her a weak smile.

What? Was he trying to get her out of the hospital? Did he feel that guilty? "Are you proposing I should take a case?"

"Wouldn't you like to try it?" Here was that puppy-wants-a-treat look again. "The going rate is ten dollars a week. In another week you'll finish with the OB rotation anyhow."

She shook her head slowly. "I know that the hospital gets most of that money. We're just cash cows."

"Sometimes," he said carefully, "the patient's family can add a little extra, if you know what I mean."

Tenny knew what he meant. "More often they don't, so I hear. This case must be important to you, Doctor. Why should I leave my education here, and for how long? Give me a good reason."

Pete shifted uncomfortably, but he didn't evade her eyes. "I need someone to work for me. In my house."

She sat back stunned. Of course. He needed someone to look after his baby. And his wife. Tenny looked down at her hands, then at the remains of the cheese sandwich on her plate. Her appetite was gone. "I heard Ida Blackstone was working for you."

Pete nodded. "Yes. She's good, but she wants to retire. She's given me a couple of weeks to find someone else, and I've almost run out of time. What do you say, Tenny? You're excellent with babies."

Tenny shook her head slowly. "I'm still a student, and Lord knows there are plenty of graduate nurses like Mrs. Blackstone that need jobs. Nurses with experience."

Pete leaned forward and lowered his voice. "I'll level with you, Tenny. Word's gotten around the nursing community. No one wants the job. My wife, well, she's not taking her infirmity well."

"But I haven't yet nursed a stroke patient."

Pete broke in, urgency in his voice. "Then it's part of your education. I'd make it worth your while."

She folded her hands in her lap. "It's not a question of money."

He held out his hand in a plea. "I don't understand. Is it that—that difference of opinion we had? I thought we were friends."

"Yes," she said. "We're friends." She sat as still as one of Mr. Lyman's figurines. She couldn't betray in any way what she'd once imagined about that friendship. It had been stupid, a whim of a silly girl. She had taken his attention, his kisses, his trip to the river, his stupid postcards from school, to mean something.

"Tenny," he said, giving her the smile that once had melted her, "will you promise to think about it?"

She tilted her head toward Enid Smith Barlow, three tables over. "Why not ask Barlow? She'd jump at the chance." Of course, Tenny thought cynically, Barlow would probably try to poison the patient.

"Maybe I will."

Tenny, secretly pleased at the anger in his voice, rose from her seat and said she had to get back to work. He barely muttered his good-bye. She walked over and handed her tray to the white-garbed kitchen worker.

When she turned to leave, her heart sank when she found herself facing Enid. "What were you and Dr. Pete talking about so cozily?" Enid handed her own tray over.

"A patient." Tenny bit back the urge to tell her it was none of her damned business.

Enid nudged her with an elbow. "Too bad for us the boy wonder got married. And now too bad for him."

Tenny glared at the other nurse and her fingernails dug into her own palms. She opened her mouth for a retort when she realized she'd be playing into Enid's hands. She closed it.

"I've seen the way you look at him," Enid said.

Tenny turned on her heel and left, face hot, conscious of Enid's eyes on her back. Why did that girl hate her so?

In the nurses' lounge, Tenny let her hair down, then combed it smooth before pulling it back up into a tight knot. She covered the knot with her cap, securing the cap firmly with hairpins. She knew she wasn't fashionable, but she *didn't* want to bob her silky hair.

Her hair was a link to the time people thought she was pretty, a link to her twin sister, a link to that boy at the gas station, the way he'd stared. That boy that was now a doctor. And at one time he'd asked her to let her hair grow out.

Bitter gall. She scrubbed her hands and went back to work.

All afternoon, while she fed babies, rocked them, instructed mothers how to breast-feed, argued with those who wanted to bottle-feed, Pete's offer hovered as a possibility. Caring for just one baby plus an invalid. Easy, right? Hard work and hustle was her bread and butter, her jam, and her coffee. It kept her from thinking about what might have been.

On the other hand, if she took the offer, she'd have extra money to put aside for Shelley, and she'd have private-case experience when she looked for a job after graduation. Hospital administrative jobs weren't plentiful, and why should they hire graduate nurses for everyday duty when they had a ready-made source of cheap labor?

She hoped Pete *would* ask Enid. She smiled into her sleeve at the thought of Enid and Swanee in the same house. Then she'd feel sorry for Pete, but only a little.

She'd be glad of a new rotation assignment. When she tended the babies, she was reminded of the boy child she'd held in her arms for only minutes before they took him away. Only the consideration of his possible father kept sadness at bay.

The next afternoon, she was running her finger down the list of assignments when she heard Enid Barlow's voice behind her. "Well, Oakey, looks like we're switching duty. Have fun in Cardiac and try not to kill anybody."

"Try not to become your own patient, Enid." Tenny walked away while Enid was trying to figure out what she meant. So Pete hadn't asked Enid to help him. Maybe he'd found a graduate nurse who'd take the case.

Cardiac was mostly men, she knew. Not much you could do for them, except for the digitalis. Most wouldn't stick to the low-sodium diet or the prescribed rest. There were the new treatments, the mercury diuretics—Merbaphen, Mersalyl——but those were hard on the kidneys.

She knew how to get along with the male patients by now. Their privates held no interest or terror for her now, and she was so brisk and formal, so correct-looking in her round eyeglasses and tight bun, that they hardly ever looked at her as someone to flirt with.

This would be an easy quarter.

# Chapter 51

O n her second day with the three cardiac patients, Tenny stood at the nurses' station going over Mr. Wilson's chart, fretting over his elevated temperature. Infection was always a possibility, but since she'd had the kerfuffle with Pete she'd been extra careful about bacteria. Still, they couldn't police every visitor for infections, and Mr. Wilson's wife looked after a passel of children and grandchildren.

"Oakes," the head nurse interrupted her, "they're bringing in a new patient. He's to go to room 438." Tenny put Mr. Wilson's chart aside and went down to 438, a private room, to make sure the bed had fresh sheets.

When they wheeled him in, Tenny stood rooted to the spot as two orderlies transferred the big, heavy man to the bed.

It was his breath that struck her first, the breath that came in labored, fearsome wheezes, bringing back the memory of that night when he had covered her with his body and kissed her with that foul tobacco mouth. Now, in his pale, ugly, sweat-covered face, that mouth was working like a fish on a riverbank. She felt as if she couldn't breathe, as if she'd been injected with the paralytic drug curare. Mouth dry, she licked her lips.

Dr. Emmett Godwin strode in and gave her instructions. The chart's numbers told her Arno Shackley was a very sick man.

*Good.*

But what if he recognized her? He hadn't known her in the hall that day, brown hair tucked under her cap, her skin pale. He'd known her as a towhaired, suntanned girl-child in the fields. Up close, could he detect the cropper kid under the nurse's uniform? At least she had her glasses.

Still. How could she endure it? Sponging his body, collecting his specimens, taking his vital signs—suppose she had to touch him *there*. Maybe—maybe she could ask for a different assignment! Gloom overcame her. Miss Wells would never agree. And then she'd want to know why.

Tenny asked anyhow.

"You're good with difficult patients, and you've never shied away before." Miss Wells' eyes bore into hers. "Why this one?"

Tenny licked her lips. "It's a . . . personal matter."

"I'm inclined to let you do your duty," Miss Wells replied crisply. "You need to put aside your emotions while you work. In my opinion, you should nurse this patient at least a week. If problems arise, I'll consider a change."

"Yes, ma'am." Tenny swallowed hard.

The next morning, she tied on a surgical mask, as she did for contagious patients, before she came in to check Shackley's vital signs. If she could see him just as a body to nurse, a body unattached to an evil soul, perhaps she could get through the day. Weak and sleeping much of the time, he gave her no trouble at first.

The second day, his pig eyes brightened when she opened the door. She met them in spite of herself.

"Hey, girlie, when can I get out of here and go home?"

"When the doctor says you're well enough." She used the diction Professor Moon had taught her, hiding traces of her country speech. She prepared her patient's sponge bath. She was careful to drape the sheets to preserve the patient's modesty and to distance herself. Nevertheless, when she had worked her way down to his lower belly, she stiffened at the sight of sagging flesh and fatty folds, and carefully kept the area she dreaded covered with a towel.

She ignored his malicious grin and handed him the washcloth. "Please finish your bath." She turned her back and busied herself with tidying the bedside table, feeling his eyes on her.

"I'm done," he said, entirely too soon.

She picked up the basin and asked him to drop the cloth in, feeling her face pinkening beneath the mask.

"You scared o'me?" His voice, grating and rumbling, sent chills down her spine.

"I'm following rules." She let no expression crack her composed face.

He just grunted, a snide chuckle that raised the hair on the back of her neck.

Her last duty was administering his digitalis preparation and mercury diuretic.

In the medication room, she gazed at the syringe for the digitalis preparation. The digitalis had to be precise; an excessive dose might kill him. She paused. No one would know if she administered more than prescribed. The doctors might conclude he had some condition that they hadn't yet discovered, or he'd manifested an adverse reaction to the drug.

Maybe she could just not give him the medication at all and substitute saline. She shuddered at her murderous thoughts. But then again, maybe she'd just be helping God along? Maybe she'd be doing the world a big favor. What about all the cruelties she had heard about and witnessed from this man? What about the missing black people? What about Shelley?

The voice of Miss Wells in her head reverberated like a gong. *You girls are in a position of trust. The physician depends on you to procure the right medication, measure the correct dosage, administer it at the proper time and in the proper manner, and make an accurate record.*

Her mission was to relieve suffering. Yet it was the Devil on her shoulder telling her that the suffering of many would be relieved if this man died.

She was glad that Pa, now a born-again Christian, had given up whisky. Maybe Shackley's moonshine habit had caused him to have this heart condition, made worse by anger at Pa for not making his moonshine any longer.

She took the medicine tray to Shackley's room. He'd dropped off to sleep, looking about as vulnerable as a sleeping boar. When she woke him for the dose, he grunted and complained, but she checked his pulse—above sixty, as it was supposed to be. Then she gave him his injection and the mercury tablet with water.

As she was leaving the room, she glanced down the hall and spotted Miss Ola Stratton, no, Mrs. Ola Shackley, approaching. Perhaps Miss Ola would talk him to death. She quickly removed her mask when the older woman approached.

Unfortunately, the head nurse had noticed her removing the mask. When Tenny arrived at the nurses' station Miss Burridge asked, "Do you have a cold, Miss Oakes?"

"Ah—I have a scratchy throat," she found herself saying.

"A scratchy throat. Any fever?" the other nurse looked at her keenly, and Tenny flushed.

"No, not really. It's just a precaution."

"Well, it looks odd, Miss Oakes. The patients on this floor aren't contagious, and I don't want them thinking you have some kind of infection. Maybe it would be best to leave the mask off."

"Yes, Miss Burridge."

Oh, double humiliation. She spotted Enid Smith Barlow grinning wickedly before she disappeared into a stairwell.

The next day, Tenny, bare-faced, headed with fresh linen toward Shackley's room, praying he'd be asleep. At the door, she heard Miss Ola's melodious chirping about new kitchen appliances, repairing the tenants' shacks, and maybe cleaning out the old well.

Tenny strode into the room, all business, and noticed Shackley's face had turned dangerously red. "Time to change the sheets, Mr. Shackley. I'll need your cooperation."

"Just get me out from behind these damn bars," he grumbled.

"Please, dear, your language." Miss Ola smiled, picked up a Japanese fan, and fanned vigorously.

"No, sir, it's flat on your back for another week or so."

Tenny changed the pillowcase as fast as she'd ever done. Then she covered her patient with a folded fresh sheet, turned him to one side and coiled up the used sheet flush with his back. She put the fresh sheet halfway on, rolling it up to lie next to the old one. She then logrolled him over the hump of sheets to his other side and whisked out the used sheet from underneath.

The warmth of his flesh when she'd touched him repelled her, and she wished it would have been cold and rubbery. She didn't like to think of him as being human.

She untucked and rolled the used bottom sheet to the middle. Tenny then spread a fresh top sheet over the wrinkled one, and instructed Shackley to hold tightly to the clean sheet while she eased the dirty cover down to the foot, leaving no chance of exposing him. She added a white cotton blanket and tucked in both, mitering the corners.

Fortunately, Miss Ola burbled like a creek with chatter, but Tenny nearly dropped a pillow when Miss Ola said, clear out of the blue, "Miss Oakes, where are you from, dear?"

Tenny breathed in, breathed out. Eight breaths. "Nowhere, really. We traveled around." The lie was second nature to her now.

"There are some Oakeses down *our* way, aren't there, Mr. Shackley?"

Tenny caught her breath. Instantly she regretted taking the name from the storekeeper's sign. She should have made something up.

Shackley was appraising her with that keen pig eye. "Miss Ola, this girl sure does favor some folks down there."

"They say everybody has a twin somewhere." Tenny kept her voice casual, but her heart pounded so hard, she was sure he could hear it. She bundled the soiled sheets, bustled out of the room, and tossed the sheets into a cart. Two more hours until her shift ended. She prayed he wouldn't press the call button.

Thank God he didn't.

When she saw Dr. Emmett in the hall the next morning, it seemed only natural to ask, "When is Mr. Shackley going to be dismissed?"

Dr. Emmett peered at her from over his glasses. "Think we'll keep him the full two weeks, though he's rarin' to go. Why?"

Tenny shrugged. "He keeps asking."

Dr. Emmett nodded absently. "Yup. He's an impatient old cuss. Tell him he stays. My orders."

She nodded and continued on her rounds, biting her lip in frustration. The longer Shackley stayed, the more likely he'd figure out where he'd seen her. And then what? Would he come after her? Would he turn her in for stealing the Bible? For stealing the money? His words against hers. He might discover the Inez Callahan Home, the baby. God help her, he might think the baby was his. And what if he wanted to claim the little boy?

Shackley was getting old, and his only child, Eben, had been killed in the Great War. There was no one to inherit his acres when he died, unless you counted Miss Ola. The possibility of Tenny's own little boy being snatched from his adoptive home and forced to live with Shackley made her gag. At least her sister Shelley was away from him. But in the sanitarium!

That night, reading in her room, Tenny couldn't concentrate on the words, though the Elinor Glyn romance was one she loved and the potted narcissus she'd brought from a vacated room smelled heavenly. Her mind kept going back to Shackley.

She would not think of him. She would *not*. She imagined herself in a garden, a garden she'd seen in the pages of one of Miss Verity's books, a garden in England. She closed her eyes and imagined walking between high hedges, alongside beds of fragrant pinks and phlox and daffodils, hollyhocks and nodding foxgloves . . .

*Digitalis*. It was made from foxgloves, she had learned in class.

She pulled down her Materia Medica book from the shelf and reviewed the recommended dosages again. Could she go through with it? The heart condition would be blamed, and then she'd be safe from him evermore. So would her baby, her little boy. Wherever he was.

She hardly slept that night. She made her rounds the next morning thinking of nothing else but her plan. She was so nervous that she dropped a bedpan, sloshing urine all over the floor, earning her a bawling-out from the floor nurse.

When it came time for Shackley's digitalis, her hands were steady. Twice the normal dose would be enough. "Looks like a storm outside, Mr. Shackley. It's dark and those clouds are moving fast," she said.

She picked up the hypodermic, filled with a double dose.

Outside the room, a man being wheeled down the hall groaned in pain. Alice's voice said, "Don't worry, we'll do our best to make you comfortable. Won't we, Dr. Emmett?" Reality slammed Tenny. Her hand trembled.

Shackley stared at her. His pig eyes held a shadow of recognition; he focused on her low cap. "Girlie, I think I know you. What's behind them glasses?"

His hand lunged for her spectacles, knocking her hand, and she dropped the syringe. It clattered to the floor and shattered. Tenny jolted backward out of Shackley's reach and knelt to wipe up the mess.

"Nearly got you, haw-haw."

Her face flushed. She felt faint at what she'd almost done. She took the towel with glass shards and scrambled to her feet. She slipped out the door and hurried to the medicine room.

As the door of the dispensary closed behind her, she broke down in tears, shivering and shaking.

She gasped in shock when she felt a hand on her shoulder.

"I wondered who was in here boo-hooing, and I find it's you," Pete Godwin said. "What's the matter? Drop another bedpan?"

Tenny turned to him, mortified that he'd heard about that episode. His joking manner faded when he saw her face. Another nurse walked in, glancing curiously at the two of them. "You're trembling," Pete said, and took her arm. "Tell me about it. Not here."

She nodded, wiped her face clean, and followed him down to a small spare room that served as a chapel where doctors and clergymen talked to families. "I can't go on," Tenny said. "I can't nurse Mr. Shackley."

"Why not?"

All her reserve melted away. She wouldn't lie to Pete. "He's the reason I left home," she said. "At first he didn't know me. Now I think he recognizes me."

"What did he do?"

Tenny turned away. "I asked Miss Wells to change my assignment, but she wouldn't."

"You didn't tell her the truth."

Tenny shook her head.

"I'll take care of it," Pete said.

Tenny didn't want him to go over Miss Wells' head. She'd be angry, and she'd demand all the details.

Pete hesitated. "You could leave here for a while. The position at my house is still open."

A glimmer of dawn touched her dark world. A way out. But would Pete want a would-be murderess in his house?

"Look," Pete was saying, "I'll square it with Dad and Miss Wells. We have a garage apartment where you could stay. It's meant for live-in help, but I can't afford a maid and nurse both. Our cook's borrowed."

She glanced down at her interlaced hands. She'd be away from the hospital, and Shackley wouldn't know how to find her. "How long would you need me?"

Pete's face relaxed. "Until Swanee regains some of her functions and the baby's a bit older. How about three or four months? You could come back to the hospital in January and resume your cardiac training."

Tenny chewed her lip. The money was tempting. But what if Swanee *didn't* recover her functions? What then? Could Tenny bear being so close to Pete? On the other hand, maybe seeing him every day would take away some of the magic. After all, she didn't really know him.

"If you'll talk with Miss Wells, I can be at your house tomorrow morning," she said and swallowed. "I can't go back in that room, and Mr. Shackley needs his digitalis. He grabbed for my eyeglasses, and I dropped the hypodermic. He didn't get his mercury."

"Of course. I'll ask Barlow to give him the medication."

"Please," she said, suppressing a smile. "Don't let him know where I've gone."

"Of course not."

Tenny wanted to hug him, but she held out her hand. Pete Godwin was a decent man.

# Chapter 52

G ussie ought to go to Pete's house and meet the new nurse. She'd been putting it off, with work at the antique shop, as well as two family portraits, a wedding, and an assignment to photograph the judge for a civic publication. Okay, it *was* Papa's idea, but still . . .

No excuses today. Trevania and the baby had left for the park. She put away the camera and light meter and pushed the floodlights back against the wall. She rolled the carpet sweeper with a flourish over the new Turkish rug from Lyman Stratton's shop, the rug she'd finally paid for by selling Ned's desk and Morris chair and the books and clothes he'd left behind.

She stored the props, the kimono and fan and paper lanterns, in the hall closet. She didn't understand why girls wanted to be photographed as Japanese maidens or Greek goddesses, but she was happy to oblige. She liked the artistic pictures much better than silly, happy brides who didn't know what they were getting into.

She washed her hands and face, touched up her lips, and then chose another book for Swanee from her shelf, *The Lost Heir of Linlithgow* by Mrs. Southworth, and then added a Mary Roberts Rinehart mystery.

Enjoying the unseasonable burst of cool air, she lagged along the sidewalk under overhanging dogwoods whose leaves were beginning to turn, their tips a rich burgundy that would clothe the entire tree in another month. In grass and dirt front yards, children hooted and played, while yard men clacked mowers across plots of green. Drifting scents of sweet grass raised her spirits as she approached Pete's house.

Bo Paul Hunter greeted her with "Mornin', ma'am." She greeted him in return, and he went back to watering Swanee's marigolds and snapdragons.

Trevania and Bo Paul were keeping company now. Trevania had told her, "Bo Paul gon' go to Cincinnati one of these days, get him a railroad job, just you wait and see. Only thing keeping him back is me. I don't want to leave my mama and my Uncle John."

Gussie rang the front doorbell. Pete, to her surprise, opened the door. "Come in, come in." Behind him, a slight, white-aproned figure in blue crossed the hall with a tray. Pete nodded toward the young woman. "You remember Nurse Oakes, don't you?"

"Of course," Gussie said happily. "How are you, Tenny?"

The girl smiled shyly. "Fine, thank you, Mrs. Fletcher."

"I don't mean to keep you." Pete touched Tenny's arm and the girl slid away, mounting the stairs as soundlessly as a wraith.

"She looks more filled out, healthier," Gussie remarked. "How on earth did you arrange for her?"

"They let them do outside work for experience," Pete said. "She's in charge of Swanee and the baby both. I've told Nola to feed her up." Pete looked Gussie up and down, smirking the way he used to, just to provoke her. "Your figure is pretty good. Can I get you a snack?"

"Hush your mouth, jelly bean. You know I'm trying to lose this baby fat." Gussie's teal dress was taut across her stomach, and she patted it.

"Really, you look wonderful," Pete said. "Come in my study for a minute and let's talk."

Pete's study had once been a small glassed-in sun porch off the living room, but he'd put up siding, bought a good desk, and installed some bookshelves.

The picture of the river girl hung on the wall opposite the desk. The nude girl in the river hunched as if cold, her hair piled on her head, her arm positions saving the picture from an obscenity charge.

Gussie whooped. "What does Swanee think about that?"

"She hasn't seen it," Pete said, a little abashed. "I've just hung it."

Gussie gazed at the picture and tapped her chin. "Did you notice she looks a little like your Miss Oakes?"

"Bushwah." Embarrassment flickered across his face, and he turned away to square up the medical journals on his desk.

"So Ida Blackstone's retired for good?" Gussie said diplomatically.

Pete sighed, and his face relaxed. "So she says. I was lucky to get Oakes. She's a heck of a good nurse." He motioned to Gussie to have a seat, and he took his desk chair.

"Tell me how Swanee's doing." Gussie perched in a small straight chair.

Pete hesitated as if he was deciding what to tell her. When the phone rang in the hall, he hurried out to answer it, obviously relieved.

She studied the picture. It did look like Tenny Oakes.

"Hey, Gus!" He returned and grabbed a jacket off the back of his chair. "Pop has a visitor who can school me on new stroke treatments. Wants me to come right now. Thanks so much for coming."

Gussie saw him out and gazed at the upstairs landing. *Was* Miss Oakes the girl in the picture? Hard to tell, in profile. Yet Gussie's experience with posing and angles made her conscious of the way people moved, the way they carried themselves.

And here came Miss Oakes gliding downstairs with her light footstep. She smiled and raised her eyebrows. "She's ready for you now."

The unspoken words were: *Are you ready for her?* Watching her, Gussie felt certain that Tenny Oakes was the river nymph. Well, well.

Pete, driving home an hour past dusk in his father's old Buick, felt hope for the first time since they'd brought Swanee home. His father's colleague had given him reasons to believe that she would make a complete recovery with time and care. The only fly in that balm was that the patient needed to put forth effort.

Swanee had never been one for effort.

Indulged from the cradle, she'd never felt the need to exert herself and didn't see why she should do so now. She was sure that some medication would put her right.

He hated to tell her that physical therapy was what she needed. The stroke had happened in the right hemisphere. Her reason and thought were unaffected, but her left side was extremely weak. He'd ordered a brace for her left leg, and he dreaded asking for cooperation.

He drove into the garage and cut the motor. It had been a rotten afternoon. After he'd left his father, he'd reported at the hospital and been smacked by a bargeload of typhoid cases.

He sat in the car and composed himself. He needed to be calm and cheerful when he proposed the new treatment to Swanee.

He entered a quiet house. Was Miss Oakes still on duty? Though her day supposedly ended at six, her twelve-hour duty never really ended. He shed his jacket and walked directly up to Swanee's room, where he found Miss Oakes helping Swanee out of bed.

"Allow me." He walked over and took Swanee's other arm.

"Thank you, Doctor."

"Where to?"

"I want bath," said Swanee. "No more sponge."

The water was already drawn, steam curling from the open door. "You were going to do this by yourself?" He frowned at Tenny.

"It's what I'm trained to do." Something in her tone led Pete to glance at his wife's face. It remained impassive.

"I'll help."

Pete rolled up his sleeves. He held his wife steady while Miss Oakes unbuttoned the satin gown and slipped it off, unveiling the creamy skin that had seemed a soft miracle when he'd first touched it.

Together, they lifted Swanee into the tub, and together they lifted her out when the bath was done. Pete found himself not looking at his wife's nude body, but at the flushed face opposite him, and the spark that coursed through him made him turn away in shame. He'd splashed water on his shirt by his clumsiness, and he left them both. He went to the spare bedroom, his bedroom now, to change into dry clothes.

He met Tenny in the hall when she was coming up with a supper tray and told her that he'd take over now. She nodded and left them. Now he sat beside Swanee while she picked at chicken pot pie and butterscotch pudding. He stifled the urge to help her eat. It might set off one of her tantrums.

After she'd eaten all she would, he set the tray aside and wiped her hands with a warm cloth. He remembered the way her skin had felt when he lowered her into the water, he remembered his shameful spark. He took her weak hand, massaging it, stroking her fingers, desire hovering like a crazy, dipping moth. "I've missed you," he said. "I've missed you so much."

She narrowed her eyes, then looked away. He should have taken the warning, but he leaned forward and kissed her throat. "Swanee—"

"Don't," she said, turning rigid.

"Can't I just touch you, hold you—"

"No." She wouldn't look at him.

Pete got to his feet stiffly. He walked to the door with the supper tray and looked back at her. She was gazing out the window at the gray fall of night.

He returned the supper tray to the kitchen, and was surprised to find Miss Oakes with an empty soup bowl and a novel in front of her. "You should be off now," he said briskly.

"I thought you might need me a little longer."

He shook his head. "The baby's asleep, the house is quiet, and she's thrown me out."

Tenny got up to go, and her eyes met Pete's with a look of—what was it—pity? Tenderness? The melting look disappeared quickly, but it had transformed her. She was strangely beautiful, with not so much physical beauty as an intense presence, as if an aura surrounded her.

There was something between them, something that was meant to be. Now it was too late. She turned back to him, her hand on the doorknob. "How are things at the hospital?"

He understood what she was asking. "Shackley's long gone, sent home with instructions he may or may not follow. We're seeing too many typhoid cases. I'm meeting with the public health people tomorrow."

"I'm sorry. Wish I could be there to help."

"I'm glad you're here. Good night, Tenny." Her Christian name—it had just slipped out. "Sorry. Miss Oakes."

She smiled uncertainly. "Tenny's fine." And then she edged out the back door.

Pete watched her walk across the grass to the apartment over the garage. When he saw that she was safely in, he latched his own door. He heated up the vegetable soup Nola had left, and unwrapped the waxed paper from a thick ham sandwich. He ate the soup and sandwich at the kitchen table, then washed the bowl and spoon, left them to drain dry, and walked back to his study and his easy chair. He picked up the evening paper.

The words danced on the page like so many hieroglyphs, and his gaze strayed to the river nymph on the wall. He imagined Tenny as she had appeared that day, with her hair unbound, flowing around her shoulders, face glowing and bronzed from the sun. Another image superimposed itself upon that scene: the girl in front of the livery stable, the girl in the washed-out dress and workboots, and then another image flowed into the other two: a towhaired waif from the Inez Callahan home, bare feet in childbirth stirrups.

Like a butterfly, floating in and out of his life. To shut her out, he buried himself in his newspaper, where Charles Lindbergh's childhood was the latest offering about the aviator hero, three weeks past the famous flight.

Flying over the Atlantic solo? How about solving the typhoid problem? Privies and wells, sewer lines and clean water—not the stuff of legend, but the stuff of survival.

Sanitation wasn't as romantic as flying, for sure. He put the newspaper aside and went to his desk. There he covered lined paper with notes for the meeting with the county health people until his head pounded. He slipped the pages into a compartment in his doctor's bag and went up to bed. He looked in on Swanee, but in the dim light from the hall she appeared to be sleeping, as did the baby. He went to bed and slept badly.

The typhoid outbreak kept him from dwelling on either Swanee or Miss Oakes for almost a week. The public health people were trying to find whether the river had become contaminated, from mill sewage or elsewhere. A popular recreation pond might be the source.

He'd been only a boy during the Typhoid Mary outbreaks, but he remembered his father's outrage. The woman adamantly refused to believe she was a carrier, kept on working as a cook even though families kept coming down with the disease. She didn't even think she needed to wash her hands. Eventually she had to be quarantined.

On Friday of that exhausting week, Pete got away around two o'clock, arriving home wrung out and hungry, hoping for a late lunch and a couple of hours of peace and quiet before he had to go back.

In the kitchen, Nola was folding towels. The fragrance of soap and sun-dried cotton filled the sunny room, along with the sweet smell of baking.

"Nola, I could eat a tough old goat."

"Don't have none of that, Dr. Pete, but I'll fix some sandwiches." Nola set the stack of towels in a basket and walked to the counter. Humming, she slid a loaf out of the breadbox. "We still got some of that roast beef and fresh pimento cheese."

"Sounds good. One of each." He sank into a chair while she chinked ice from a block into a glass and poured sweet tea. He drained the glass. Tenny walked in, empty baby bottle in hand, and he felt his spirits revive.

"How's Her Highness?" he asked.

"Which one?" Tenny smiled. "Baby's dropped off to sleep and Miss Swanee wants something sweet."

"What about it, Nola?" Pete winked at the nurse. "Do we have some cake? Some for Miss Oakes too, so we can fatten her up."

"Mr. Lyman brought over some of Miss Ethel's fresh scuppernong pie yesterday," Nola said. "This pound cake in the oven is gone take a while."

Pete grinned. "The famous pie. How about cutting three slices? I'll have some with my lovely wife and her intrepid nurse."

"I'll fix a tray for the two of you," Tenny said firmly. "I'll have mine later."

A piercing infant wail interrupted Pete's reply. "Let me see to Baby," he said. "I've hardly laid eyes on her this week."

He hurried upstairs, pausing at the hall bath to scrub his hands. He found the baby dry and her diaper well-pinned, so he considered colic.

When he gently massaged the baby's tummy, she let out a fresh wail. Maybe he'd give her paregoric, maybe something gentle like chamomile tea. He draped a clean towel across his shoulder and laid the baby there, patting her. She hiccupped once, twice, gave a huge belch, and then stopped crying.

"Want to see Mommy?" He coaxed a smile and a burble from her, and then he brought her to Swanee. His wife didn't object when he settled the little girl into the crook of her good arm. Maybe he'd ask Gussie to take a portrait of the two, mother and child.

When the baby instinctively nuzzled into the ample curve of Swanee's bosom, Pete grinned. "It's too bad you couldn't breastfeed her."

"I'm no cow." Swanee glared at him and pulled her robe closed.

Pete shook his head. Modern women liked to pretend breasts didn't exist, and bound them flat against the body with corsets. Breastfeeding was considered fit only for peasants. Thank Providence for Aunt Belinda, who encouraged natural feeding for every type of woman.

He sat with Swanee awkwardly, the room silent except for the clacking of a lawn mower outside. Finally Tenny appeared with tea, sandwiches, and pie.

"Take her." Swanee indicated the baby with a nod.

"Of course." The folding table was covered with tissues, pots of face cream, and magazines, so Tenny set the tray on the end of the bed and took the child.

Pete watched them leave, uncomfortably aware of the trim waist and curving haunches beneath Tenny's crisp blue uniform.

After he settled the tray across Swanee's lap, she insisted on feeding herself and drank her iced tea left-handed, not spilling too much. Pete mopped it up and ate his sandwiches and pie.

The room fell silent. Pete had nothing to say that would interest her; certainly not typhoid cases. From outdoors drifted the sounds of a sleepy afternoon: the calls of towhees, the hum of motorcars, Bo Paul Hunter's hoe on weeds. He was about to nod off from weariness when Swanee's fork hit the plate with a clatter.

"Finished." She settled back and closed her eyes.

He wet a cloth and wiped the crumbs from her gown, then he picked up the tray and walked out. He paused at the door of the nursery. Tenny was rocking the baby in the white wicker chair, humming a cradle song. Pete set his jaw: why couldn't it be Swanee singing to her baby—*their* baby—like that?

The slanted afternoon light backlit Tenny's elfin face, and in the aura he saw the girl whose path in life had wandered across his like a drunken bee in a field of clover. Bemused, he took the tray to the kitchen and left it on the table. He went straight to his study and gazed at the picture again. He lifted it from the nail. Perhaps he should put it in the drawer. No. He carefully hung it again.

He riffled through a stack of medical journals his father had given him, marked with articles on stroke. He opened one and began to study a piece about advances in physical therapy. Before he'd finished the third paragraph, the phone rang.

"I'm sorry to bother you, sugar," his mother said. "I know you're tired, but your father can't get away. Miss Edith called. She said Miss Ola came back from Weedy Grove all of a sudden, plumb hysterical, out of her mind. They think she's having a nervous breakdown. Can you go over and see about her? Lyman's out of town, and the others can't drive."

"Don't worry, Mother, I'll take care of it." He hung up the phone, went back to his study, and stacked the journals on his desk. He had until six before he had to be back on duty, and was glad for an excuse to leave the house.

He pushed the Buick as fast as he dared along the streets of the old neighborhood where Lyman and his aunts lived. The last time he'd seen Miss Ola was when Shackley had been discharged from the hospital. She'd seemed in good spirits then. Did the old bastard drop dead all of a sudden? That would make Tenny happy. Pete smiled grimly. Lyman too.

Lyman despised Shackley, and Shackley, he figured, returned the feeling. Lyman was not the marrying kind, as his mother put it. Rumors had surfaced after Toby Burkett's death that Toby and Lyman had been more than friends, and it was whispered that the relationship had had something to do with his suicide.

That was absurd. Toby liked sports, hanging out with the guys. Certainly not antiques. And strangely enough, the only time Pete had seen Toby depressed was after he came home from the war.

The big Victorian house with its wraparound porch loomed ahead of him. He pulled up to the curb behind a vehicle marked POLICE and jerked the handbrake with a screech. So the law had been called? Why? He grabbed the new black leather bag his father had given him for graduation.

An officer in a too-tight uniform, a former schoolmate, sat in a rocker on the porch. Pete walked up the front steps and hailed him. "What's wrong, C.B.?"

C.B. Potts scratched his head. The policeman said, "I think the old girl's gone plumb off her rocker, Pete. Hy-steerical, if you ask me."

"What do you mean?"

"She said Shackley was trying to kill her and wanted me to go out and arrest him. For one thing, his place is out in the sheriff's territory. I'd kind of hoped you could calm her down so I could get a statement that makes sense."

The front door was unlocked. Pete strode into the house. "Hello? Miss Edith?" The sound echoed in the hall, dark with oiled wood and Oriental carpets, its Tiffany fixture glowing with dim greenish squares of light. Miss Edith appeared in rustling black silk and sensible shoes, wringing her hands.

"Well, you're not your father, but thank goodness you're here," she said. "In there." She indicated a doorway to the left. Beneath the front parlor's heavily draped windows, Miss Ola reclined on a wine velvet fainting couch, yanking at her disheveled hair. Pete entered the velvet and mahogany cave, made his way to the couch, and lowered himself to one knee. "Miss Ola? It's Pete Godwin. The doctor."

Miss Ola's eyes, wide and wild, roved in her head. "He's a monster! Going to murder me!" She reached for Pete's tie. "You have to believe me."

Pete intercepted her hand before she choked him. "Exactly what did your husband do, Miss Ola?" He lowered her hand to her side and patted it as though it were a nervous dog.

"He tried to *kill* me," she repeated. "He's a monster." Miss Ethel continued to wring her hands. Miss Edith nudged Pete's arm, holding out a glass of brandy. "Here, son. This might help."

Pete wanted to glug the brandy himself. Instead, he took the glass and held it to Miss Ola's lips. She took a sip. "The Devil's poison!" she cried, whacking it out of Pete's hand and splashing the alcohol over herself, the sofa, and his coat.

"Look what you've done, Ola," scolded Miss Edith. "It's prescribed medicine." She scurried off and returned with a damp cloth. She attended to Pete's jacket, then removed Miss Ola's brandy-soaked blouse, covering her with an afghan, and she mopped up the remaining drops.

"Let me examine you, Miss Ola." Pete, using his calmest voice, opened the bag. When the agitated woman saw the stethoscope, she settled down and let him do his job. He searched for marks or bruises, and found no evidence of a beating. Her pulse was racing, but she didn't show evidence of poisoning: no nausea, vomiting, skin pallor, no trouble breathing. Her pupils appeared normal. Her hair carried an odor of wood smoke, perhaps from a smoky chimney.

Pete delved into his bag and took out a syringe and a vial of sodium amytal, while Miss Ethel and Miss Edith hovered anxiously. "I'm giving something to rest her," Pete said. "She ought to sleep for a good long time. I'll come back tomorrow, and maybe she'll be clear-headed enough to tell me what actually happened."

As he looked at the sisters' anxious faces, he reminded himself that Miss Ola was not used to the marital state. It might well be nothing but a domestic argument. He was here to heal, not to judge, and he wanted facts. He picked up his bag, took his leave of the sisters, and walked out to the porch. The policeman, C.B., rose from the rocker and tapped ash from his cigar. "What's the verdict, Pete?"

Pete shrugged. "I couldn't get much out of her. She was too distraught. I've given her a sleeping drug. I didn't find a reason to involve the law right now."

"I hope not," said C.B. "The Sheriff always counts on Mr. Shackley to give big in his re-election campaigns."

"We'll see," said Pete, an edge to his voice. "If Arno Shackley *did* try to kill her, I won't stand still for politicians trying to hush it up."

"You know I was just funnin'," said C.B., stubbing out his cigar in a seashell, almost knocking it off the end table.

"I know, C.B., I know." *Some fun.*

Ten minutes later, in his own kitchen, he found Tenny at the table, once again reading one of Swanee's books, while baby bottles rattled in the sterilizer. She looked up. "How is Miss Ola?"

Pete raised an eyebrow. "How'd you know where I'd gone?"

"I overheard you on the telephone."

"She's all right," he said neutrally. Besides patient confidentiality, it wouldn't help Tenny to hear Miss Ola's story. The girl was frightened enough of Shackley. He clenched his jaw at what he imagined the bastard had done.

"These bottles are ready." She rose, crossed to the stove, and dipped them out with tongs. She lined them up on a folded towel.

"Tenny." Pete cleared his throat. "Is there anything you want to tell me about Arno Shackley?"

She turned pale and stared at the row of bottles. "He is an evil man. That is what I can tell you." She turned off the stove and dried her hands. "I'll go now. Good night, Dr. Pete."

"Wait—"

She slipped out the back door and was gone.

# Chapter 53

Miss Ola was filing for divorce as soon as possible, Dr. Emmett Godwin told his son a few days later. She'd returned to the Victorian house with her relatives for good.

After the lady had recovered from her nervous episode, Dr. Emmett's medical work-up had found that she was in remarkable shape for a woman her age. She'd declared to the doctor that marital relations were not all they were cracked up to be, and she didn't see why people made such a fuss over the whole thing. As for the accusations that her husband had tried to kill her, she'd changed her mind. She was sure the fire was an accident.

It was a blessing that one of the black farm hands had heard her hollering from the upstairs room where she was trapped, and he'd hauled over the barn ladder for her to clamber down. Nobody knew why the cook had been sent home and the outside doors were jammed. After she'd gotten out, coughing but alive, the whole house had collapsed in a fiery whoosh. Shackley had claimed he was out at the camp house when it happened.

Across country store checkerboards, farmers speculated that Shackley, losing money on cotton like everyone else, had burned his house for the insurance money and more. Whispers went around that Shackley had persuaded Miss Ola to change her will in his favor, cutting out Lyman. Nobody knew this for gospel, though, because Miss Ola's lawyer's secretary was the most close-mouthed biddy in town.

Pop had said the whole thing was a foolish woman's imagination, but Pop hadn't seen Miss Ola frightened out of her mind, literally raving. Miss Ola's rescuer must have had reason to be frightened too, for when the sheriff and insurance people went looking to get the farm hand's story, he'd cleared out along with his family and mule, leaving behind a perfectly good nanny goat.

The typhoid outbreak finally was ebbing. Pete left the hospital that evening on time, desperately hoping to bring a smile to Swanee's face. He'd talked Pop out of a bottle of the French wine stored away before Prohibition. Dr. Emmett had gone to France in 1903 to study surgical techniques, his taste for fine wines increasing along with his knowledge of surgery.

Arriving home, Pete was disappointed to find that Swanee had already eaten her dinner; Tenny told him that a plate for him was waiting on the stove covered by a cloth. She placed the last of Swanee's clean cutlery in a drawer and told him she'd heat his dinner if he wished. Shaking his head, he shooed her out, saying she'd already stayed past quitting time.

He lifted down two glasses from the china cabinet in the dining room, opened the wine, and carried a tray with glasses upstairs.

Swanee lay back on the clean embroidered sheets, a soft cream-colored blanket over her legs. The red Chinese writing box Lyman Stratton had sent her from the antique shop lay on top of the covers, and he was glad to see that she was taking an interest in the outside world.

"Have you been writing letters?"

"Nurse does it." She never referred to Tenny by name. When she looked up and spotted the glasses and the wine, her eyes gleamed. "Darling," she said, "nice." She tilted her cheek to be kissed.

Pete's spirits rose. "Pop sends his best to you, my love. This is the last of his Saint-Emilion." He set the wine and glasses on the dresser, kissed her, and then he palpated the jaw muscles on the slack side of her face, hoping for a response. He felt a small twitch of movement, not as much as he'd like.

He lifted the writing box off the bed and set it on a side table. Nice of Lyman to send this to her so she could keep her pen, paper, envelopes, and stamps handy.

Smiling, he poured two glasses of the Bordeaux. "Here's to a complete recovery and to the rest of our lives together." She accepted the glass with a shrug. He ached for her. Did she not believe she would recover?

He liked seeing her enjoy her wine. He wanted so badly to hold her in his arms; there was no medical reason not to. It was too soon after childbirth for complete intimacy, but they could be close. After that first rejection, he'd been waiting for her signal.

She drained her glass. "So good." She licked the last drops from her lips and, dimpling, held her glass out for more. "Please?"

One more wouldn't hurt, and he hadn't seen her this happy in weeks. He filled her glass, sat in the bedside chair, and set his own glass on the floor.

He palpated her limp hand and thrilled at the response of her fingers. Then he leaned over and kissed her pale throat, her beating pulse. His hand dusted softly over the silken gown, tracing her curves, which had grown more lush and womanly from her forced rest.

His forefinger pushed under the lace edge of her gown and traced the blue veins on her pale breast.

"Don't," she said.

He looked up, drunk with longing. "Please."

She looked away from him. He withdrew his hand and kissed her again, tracing her ear with his fingers.

"No more, Pete."

Pete's hand dropped to the blanket. "I can wait a little longer."

The animated side of her face flickered and darkened, like a will-o-the-wisp in the night. "Never." Her voice held a knife edge.

Pete took a deep breath. "Sweetheart, you can't mean that. You're upset about something. After you're better . . ."

"No more babies."

Pete felt his stomach drop, then anger surged. *This baby wasn't even his.* He forced himself to speak gently. "You're still recovering," he murmured. Her mind, her emotions weren't yet normal. "I have no objection to birth control."

Swanee stuck her lip out. "Tried that."

*Who was it?* "I won't rush you. But don't say never."

Obstinately, she turned aside. Frustration building, Pete snatched a pillow off the bed and squeezed it until his hands ached. He set it gently on the bed, calmer. Swanee had not moved, watching him.

"My darling." He kissed her then, and instead of the one-sided lips he knew, her whole mouth felt dead. He pulled back and looked at her questioningly.

"Can't talk. HATE IT!" She scowled and held out her glass for more wine.

He sighed and filled her glass halfway. He filled his own to the rim. They sipped the Bordeaux quietly; the electric fan whirred and a car passed, and then an ambulance screamed in the distance. Pete thought of the hospital, of Tenny. Of the river. Wine warmed his empty stomach and he felt lightheaded, far away.

Swanee handed him her empty glass, and then she turned on her side, her back to him. The glass was warm from the heat of her hand, and he held it for a long moment before he set it on the tray.

He pulled up the sheet to cover her and walked out, closing the door softly behind him. He looked in on the sleeping infant who was his daughter and yet not his daughter, and then walked slowly downstairs to his study.

He sat at the desk and gazed at the river nymph on the wall. What faraway days those were, the days when he had gone to the river with Gussie and her camera, the days when Swanee had lain in his arms, sweet, hot, urging him on . . .

He banged the desk with his fist, knocking off the medical journals.

He picked them up and went to the telephone to call his father. An elderly cousin had been pestering him for advice. After he'd rattled on for a few minutes, his father interrupted, "You didn't call me to talk about Mittie's constipation. You and I both know she's got a habit of taking Brown's Syrup."

"So do you think she's a dope addict?"

"She refuses to admit she's taking it, and that's why she's calling you. I'll handle it. Now what's really on your mind?"

Pete hesitated. He'd never told his father the real reason he'd married Swanee, and he wasn't ready to spill his guts now. "Swanee's not in good spirits, Pop."

"I know. What's changed?"

"She gets angry that she can't talk well. She takes it out on me, to put it bluntly. How can I calm her down while she recovers?"

Emmett Godwin cleared his throat. "Not Brown's Syrup, for sure. Those ornery types tend to take more than they need. So it's the speech that bothers her? Why not call that Moon fellow?"

"Professor Moon? No thanks."

"Listen, son. Remember that Lackland child with the cleft palate? After the surgery, Moon taught the boy to talk pretty well."

"I don't like Moon."

"You won't be working with him. Think of what's best for your wife."

Pete sighed. "She's contrary. She'll say no."

A bell clanged upstairs.

"She's calling for me now. Talk to you later, Pop."

Swanee, her mask of indifference firmly in place, asked if there was any more wine. He said, "No more wine today, my love. But here's news. Pop thinks I ought to call Professor Moon to work with you."

She narrowed her eyes. "Why?"

Pete shrugged. "Pop says he can have you talking like a Broadway actress, so I hear."

She gave him a blank stare for a long moment. "Waste time."

"Swanee, don't give up. Don't you want to get out and about? You can have your old self back. Really."

She scowled. "Phooey."

"All you have to do is try. Please."

She shrugged. "Why not? So boring here."

Pete went straight to the telephone. Mr. Moon had had a cancellation and could come the day after tomorrow. Pete still didn't like him, and it wasn't from the memory of him searching out unruly teenagers at parties. The man seemed to be always putting on an act.

Two days later, Tenny greeted the Professor at the door. Would he remember her from the Home? She'd given up her eyeglasses, and her hair was growing into its natural color underneath her cap.

He still wore the brown double-breasted suit, his dark hair escaping its pomade and falling over his forehead, and gazed with all-seeing heavy-lidded eyes, underscored by dark half-moons and rimmed by wire glasses.

"Ah, an old pupil," he said. "We never finished your lesson. You're doing quite well, I see."

"Yes, sir. I enjoyed your classes."

"I look forward to working with Mrs. Godwin. She has an excellent tone, if I recall."

She asked him to wait while she made sure Mrs. Godwin was ready.

A plush divan with a scrolled side had been brought into Swanee's room, and she reclined there like an Egyptian queen, an afghan across her legs, a novel propped beside her. Cookie crumbs surrounded a sweating glass of iced tea on a side table. More crumbs lay on the floor among a heap of magazines. "Let me tidy up for Mr. Moon," Tenny said. "He's waiting." She collected the magazines.

Swanee cast a disgusted glance at the red nails on her left hand, the nails that Tenny had lacquered the day before. "No."

Tenny jerked her head up. "But you have an appointment."

"Changed my mind."

"He might not ever come back if you cancel," Tenny said. "If you want to get better, you need to work at it."

"Pete always saying. No use."

Tenny straightened, set the magazines in a basket, and dug in her apron pocket. "Would you like your letters now?" She held up four envelopes. She dreaded going back downstairs and telling Mr. Moon that Swanee had backed out.

"Open." Swanee indicated a silver letter opener. Tenny slit the tops of the envelopes, took out the letters, and placed them on the table beside Swanee.

Then she took a small whisk and pan from the closet and swept up the crumbs. Then she'd go face Professor Moon with the news he wasn't wanted. She stole a glance at her patient, who was staring at one of the notes as if it held the secret of eternal life. Suddenly, Swanee's scowl lifted away. She tapped the note card against her lip and looked up at Tenny. "Send Mr. Moon. Now."

# Chapter 54

W as it a miracle? Three weeks with Professor Moon, and Swanee
had undergone a sea change. Now she simpered and beguiled;
she laced sweetness and light into her requests. The eccentric Professor
had changed the very atmosphere of the house. Dr. Pete's haunted,
miserable look had faded away, and Nola's grimness was a receding tide.
Tenny still caught a frown every now and then. "She ain't gonna change,"
Nola said. "Wait and see."

On Professor Moon's next visit, Pete, off work for a couple of hours,
was reading in his study while Moon worked with Swanee in her room.

Tenny hefted a laundry bag and tiptoed out of the sleeping infant's
room next door, smiling when she heard the professor's hearty encouragement down the hall. Once downstairs, she dumped the laundry into
the big basket. She'd just begun to sort the tiny garments when she heard
Pete call her.

"Yes, Dr. Pete?"

"Would you please bring me a cup of coffee?"

He didn't usually ask her to wait on him. She hated the way her heart thumped every time he called her, hated the way she had to hide it. She poured the coffee and walked back to the converted sunroom.

"Here you are." He was looking at her so oddly. Did she have spit-up on her apron? Was a button undone? She placed the coffee on his desk with and smiled uncertainly. "Is there anything else?"

"I thought you might like this picture." He pointed to the wall across from his desk.

She turned, expecting a painting, but it was a photograph, an image of a girl. Nude. Wading ankle-deep into the river, looking down at the water, her pale hair piled on her head. A flush raced to her cheeks. Why was he showing her this?

"Doctor!" She turned away.

"Tenny, I'm so sorry. I didn't mean to embarrass you."

"What did you think?" Fierce and hot, she clenched her fists.

Pete rubbed the back of his neck, face fallen. "The picture is beautiful. It's a work of art. A river nymph. I hoped you'd like it."

"What would your wife think?"

He shrugged. "She's never entered this room."

She knew. She knew that the river nymph was herself. It was her hair, her body, and the river, the bank, the twisted tree roots of the Ocmulgee. She choked out, "How did you come by that picture?"

Pete studied his desk. "My cousin took it at the river by accident, while she was trying to shoot some ducks. With a camera . . ."

"Miss Gussie took that? Oh, my God." She choked, and tears spilled over her cheeks. "What about my reputation?" She swiped the tears with the bank of her hand and reached for her handkerchief.

Pete looked up at her with repentant eyes. "No one knows who the model is. Except me."

Tenny could hardly breathe. She licked her dry lips. The muffled upstairs lessons, Nola's singing while she hung the laundry, the cars racketing on the streets, all faded into the buzzing of bees.

"It's the first time I ever saw you," Pete said. "I hoped . . ."

Upstairs, Baby let out a wail. Tenny seized the excuse and fled.

She stumbled up the stairs and scooped up the infant, nuzzling the fine down on her small head. Baby on her shoulder, she walked down to heat a bottle. *Why* had he wanted her to see that picture? The first time he'd seen her? What had he hoped?

She'd come a long way from that dip in the river. That day, she had stretched her arms to the sun and washed off all the remains of her old life. She'd vowed then that she would become someone worthy of respect. She'd almost forgotten her vow with Shackley at the hospital, and only grace had saved her. She had no place in her life for disturbing emotions, no place in her life for a scandalous entanglement.

Sin was for people with nothing to lose.

Maybe he was sorry he'd shown her the picture. Maybe it was just admiration of the photograph. She suspected something more, and she couldn't let him have such hopes. She had adored him. That would not have been too strong a word.

It was too late now.

Tenny would see this job through. Just another two months. She would keep her relationship with Doctor Pete strictly professional.


During the next weeks, as Swanee worked with Professor Moon, her speaking became clearer. Rather than dictate her letters to Tenny, she worked out a way to print her words, the red Chinese writing box propped against her leg. She practiced folding paper and stuffing envelopes with one hand propped against the other until she could do it alone.

Dr. Pete was happy that she was corresponding with friends, and Tenny wasn't sure if she should tell him that his wife was becoming secretive about her letters. If she was working at her box when Tenny came in, she'd stow her paper and click the box shut. "Private," she said, in no uncertain terms. Tenny didn't really care. She just chalked it down to Swanee's natural orneriness.

And then, one morning, when Tenny was helping Swanee with her daily exercises, she noticed a smoky smell. "Miss Swanee, have you been smoking? You know Dr. Pete's strictly forbidden it."

"Phoo!" Swanee waved her hand dismissively, "It's just paper. Professor Moon said to write down my bad thoughts and burn them. He said it would help my frustrations."

"But not up here by yourself!" Tenny insisted. "Nola will be glad to burn any papers in the back yard, where it's safer."

Swanee's face took on its petulant, wide-eyed look. "I flush the ashes down the toilet. Please don't tell Pete."

Tenny struggled with this request. She ought to tell, but she didn't really want to confront him, not after the picture. "If you promise not to do it again, I won't mention it."

"I promise," Swanee said. "Now help me get up. I want to read on my lounge." She was now able to turn a book's pages with the right setup.

After that day, Tenny didn't detect any more smoke. Still, the toilet overflowed once and they had to call a plumber, who grumbled about finding a wad of torn-up stationery in the pipes.

Tenny kept her secret, and tension hovered between the couple like the unreported smoke. Once, Tenny glimpsed Pete touching his wife's shoulder, and Swanee stiffened and shuddered.

Dr. Pete seemed so lonely. Despite her impulse to comfort him, she hardened her heart. She must finish this job and walk away toward her future, toward respectability. She called the Inez Callahan home, hoping to talk with Verity Hapsworth, hoping for words that would keep her strong.

But Verity had been summoned back to England to look after her ailing mother, and the good-hearted but overworked assistant was managing the Home in her absence. Letitia didn't know when Verity would be back: three to six months was her estimate.

The very next day Mr. Moon called on the telephone, saying that he had a horrific case of laryngitis and would have to miss two lessons. When the laryngitis turned into bronchitis, he missed another week. Swanee reverted to her old foul humor, quarreling with Nola, tormenting Tenny, and harassing Pete.

On Friday of that week Tenny dreaded the day ahead, even though the morning was crisp and cool, even though, below the steps from her garage apartment, the bronze chrysanthemums Bo Paul Hunter had planted were blooming gloriously.

She let out a breath of relief when she saw a note on the kitchen table meant for her and Nola. Gussie Fletcher was coming to lunch with Swanee today. She headed back outside to cut a few of the flowers for the luncheon trays.

Miss Gussie arrived in a rust-colored wool coat and hat with a book under her arm.

"Go on up, she's waiting for you." Tenny took the soft coat and hung it in the hall closet. "New romance?" she nodded at the book.

Gussie raised her eyebrows. "Mary Roberts Rinehart. A mystery. I brought her a classic last time and she hated it."

"I remember," Tenny said. "She threw it across the room." Tenny had picked up the book off the floor, spine cracked, pages loose. She reassembled *Anna Karenina* and read it with great pleasure.

Pleasant chatter tumbled from overhead as she and Nola placed chicken à la king, pickled peaches, and fresh rolls on dainty china plates, and then on japanned trays with lacy mats and silverware. Two more trays would hold glasses of iced tea and the dessert, ice cream and devil's food cake.

Tenny smiled when she opened the door with the first tray and the flowers. "Your lunches, ladies."

"Well," said Swanee, "about time you got here. We're about to *starve.*"

Tenny, flushing, set the tray on a folding table next to the fainting couch. Gussie met Tenny's eyes and gave a little shrug.

"Let me adjust your cushions." Tenny, knowing she had an ally, calmly pushed the table in front of the fainting couch and settled Swanee. Gussie pulled her own chair to the table.

Tenny went back downstairs for the second tray. She'd just asked Nola to bring the iced tea and dessert when the back door opened and Pete walked in. "Is there enough lunch for me? I'm sick of eating on the run."

"Do you want to eat with the ladies?" Tenny asked.

"If they'd like to have me. I've got an hour."

Swanee shook her head. "We're talking. You can have him to yourself." She picked up a silver spoon and studied her upside-down reflection.

Stiffly, icily, Tenny took a deep breath. "May I get you anything else?"

Swanee lifted a fork and jabbed a slice of peach. "I've seen the way you look at him."

"I can't imagine what you mean." Tenny felt her blood drain from her face. Enid Smith Barlow had said something like that.

"Oh, spare me. And take these stinking mums away."

"Stop embarrassing Miss Oakes, Swanee." Gussie lifted the vase of chrysanthemums and handed it to Tenny. "I'll be happy to take these home."

Tenny fled downstairs, vase in hand, and almost collided with Pete, standing at the foot of the steps with a flyer in his hand.

She ran sobbing past him into the kitchen. She slid the flowers onto the table, sloshing water. She knuckled her tears away and Nola brought a towel for the table. "Goodness, child."

She felt Pete's hand on her shoulder. "I don't know what she said to upset you, but she'll apologize."

"Please don't say anything," Tenny gulped. "I'm all right."

"You are not all right," said Pete. "I need to see her anyway." He showed Tenny the flyer he held.

Tenny gazed at the advertisement. "You're going to buy a rolling chair?"

"She needs to get out of that bed," Pete said. His jaw set, he stalked upstairs. "Out of this house."

Tenny couldn't stop trembling. She sat at the kitchen table, her face in her hands, Nola murmuring words of sympathy, when Pete returned. He squeezed Tenny's shoulder.

"I just want you to know," he said, "that I'm grateful for all you do for my wife and baby. Why don't you get some fresh air? Take Baby for a walk."

Nola agreed. "I'll take care of the ladies upstairs," she said. "And you need your lunch, Dr. Pete."

It was useless to argue with either of them. Nola busied herself with a plate for Pete while Tenny went up to dress Baby for an afternoon stroll. When they passed the dining room on the way out, Tenny carrying the infant in a blue blanket and bonnet, Pete glanced up, brightening. "Let me hold her." Tenny placed Baby in his arms. The look of love he gave the child was almost too much to bear.

Gussie walked home, a jar of chrysanthemums in her basket, mulling over the unsuccessful luncheon visit. Swanee's illness had made her more volatile, but there was something brittle and desperate about her now. Why was she so despondent over Moon's two-week absence? Why had she lashed out at that poor nurse, accusing her of having a crush on Pete? Surely Swanee didn't have a crush on the professor!

Both ideas were absurd. The girl was a professional and did her job well. She worked hard with Swanee on the physical exercises, and ran her feet off looking after both Swanee and the baby. And Pete was as faithful as they came. Look what he'd done for that ungrateful Swanee and her unwanted child.

Gussie picked up her pace when she heard the trolley coming. She had clients coming in an hour for engagement portraits. She raced to the stop, swung on, and bought her ticket. She settled in her seat, eager to get back to work. The business was growing, but she wasn't independent by a long shot. She needed both Papa's help and her salary from Lyman to make ends meet. There was no question of letting Trevania go; she needed her too much. Mama, busy with her social work, had little time for baby-sitting.

Papa had suggested Gussie might move back home and set up a studio in the girls' former playhouse. That move would be a last resort. Jessie was still living at home and she'd have three bossy people calling the shots. She'd never be her own woman.

Alighting from the trolley, she walked the hexagonal paving stones through scattered leaves. She squinted into the sun. Was that a car parked in front of her house? A car that looked like a thousand other black Fords?

Ned? Heart beating wildly, she quickened her steps.

When she neared her front walkway, the car door opened. A compact bulldog of a man in a tan double-breasted suit leaped out and grinned at her. "Hiya, little lady."

# Chapter 55

Max beamed at her, his stained canine teeth like the kind that chomped down and held on. A bony man with chilling, pale eyes and thinning blond hair climbed out the other side.

Gussie knew why they had come.

She folded her hands, forcing herself to be calm. "Hello, Max. I haven't seen or heard from Ned in months. He didn't leave any money behind."

"Oh, no, no," said Max, raising his palms outward. "That ain't it at all." Taking Gussie's elbow, he guided her up the walkway toward the porch. "Good man, your Ned. Good man to do business with. I was passing through on my way to Miami and I thought I'd hop off the train and pay a little call. He was supposed to give me some papers."

Gussie stopped in her tracks. "I don't know anything about that. Did you try his office?"

Max scowled. "Yeah. And I was just wondering why that secretary says he ain't with the firm no longer."

She held her gaze steady. "He's left town. He's deserted me." She willed herself not to glance at the house. Max didn't know about the baby, thank God. Out of the corner of her eye she saw a curtain at the front window move ever so slightly, and prayed that Trevania was watching, knowing a client was due to arrive. Max gave her a polite sneer. "Maybe you just forgot where he's at. Maybe you could use a reminder."

"I'm telling you the truth." Gussie's fingers curled into clammy palms. "He didn't tell anyone where he was going. He might even be in Cuba." She glanced over to the thug, who'd opened a penknife and was cleaning his nails with it. She dredged up a charming smile. "Please excuse me. It's been nice to see you again. Please give my regards to Sylvia."

She turned to go, but Max clamped her elbow in a vise-like hold. "Speaking of Cuba, pretty lady, one night he was pretty happy and let me know about a spread called Arcadia. How he was gonna buy it, and he was gonna buy a place down the road too, some guy name Shickle, or something like that. He ain't out there, is he?"

"No!" Gussie said. "My father owns Arcadia. And are you talking about Shackley? I don't know anything about him."

"Your Ned got some kind of itch about this Shackley. Thinks he owes him something."

Gussie shook her head. Had Ned been gambling with Shackley? She didn't know that Ned had ever met the man. Wait! That afternoon at the garden party, the afternoon she'd left with him, he'd been asking Lyman Stratton about Shackley.

"Let me go!" She tugged, trying to loosen Max's grip on her arm. She couldn't make a break for the house. They might force their way in behind her.

Max chewed on his cigar and eyed the door. "Maybe we oughta search this place first." Gussie clenched her jaw and took a deep breath. They'd go in that house over her dead body. Max, smelling of tobacco, hair oil, and sweat, twisted her arm behind her back and pushed her forward. She resisted, stumbling. "Get going," Max growled.

"No!" She let out a high-pitched scream, loud as an ambulance, hoping to alert the neighbors. She kicked out, connected with his shin with her heel. He let her go and went for his gun. She whirled and hit him with her basket. The jar of flowers sailed out, splattering him with water, and landed on the dry grass. He yelled and reached inside his coat again. So did the thug.

"Hey!"

Gussie whirled to see her father's Hupmobile roll to a stop behind the black Ford. Henry Benedict leaped out. "What's going on here?"

Max's eyes narrowed.

Henry advanced, never taking his eyes off the dark-jawed men in shiny suits with bulges under their coats. Gussie looked frantically back at the house. Trevania was standing in the door, holding her biggest cast iron frying pan.

Henry's smile was friendly. "Miss Gussie, the judge sent me over. Don't believe I've met these gentlemen." He turned to Max and thrust out his hand. "Henry Benedict from the judge's office."

The men looked at each other. Max gave Henry a limp-fish handshake. "Max Herbert. We're, ah, businessmen from Chicago. Business with Mr. Fletcher."

Gussie edged over beside Henry, relief flooding her. "They didn't believe me when I said Ned had left town."

Henry slipped a protective arm around her waist. She relaxed against him, trembling. Thank God. Trevania must have called the courthouse. Papa would have sent the police, wouldn't he? Why weren't they here?

"A cop's on his way over," Henry said, reading her mind. Henry looked from Max to the pasty-faced man, both now sweating. "Everybody's looking for Ned, including the police."

"The bulls after him?" Max grunted.

Henry nodded.

Max glared at his accomplice. "Let's go."

"You weren't threatening Mrs. Fletcher, were you?"

"It's okay, Henry," Gussie insisted. She just wanted them gone.

Max was edging away. "We was just having a friendly chat." Neighbors were peering from behind curtains by the time a police car turned the corner and pulled up.

C.B. Potts yelled out the window, "Everything okay, Henry?"

"Come on, Sly," Max said to his accomplice. "We got a boat to catch."

Max and the other man stiff-legged back to the curb and got into the car. Henry strode over to talk to C.B. while the car pulled away. Now Gussie saw it was one of Abner Jones's rentals.

"What's going on?" asked C.B. "Do I need to tail those guys?"

Henry shook his head. "They're on their way out of town."

"I didn't like their looks," grumbled C.B. "I think I'll keep an eye on them, make sure they get on the train."

Gussie waited until C.B. was out of sight, and then collapsed in Henry's arms. He patted her back gingerly, and she nestled closer to him. It felt good being warm against his tweed jacket. She closed her eyes. "Henry, I'm so glad you came. How . . ."

"I was in the law library working on a paper and your father sent a runner to find me. He couldn't leave."

Gussie murmured, "They were about to force me to go in the house. To look for Ned. I was afraid they'd take Gracie."

"Who were these guys, anyhow?"

Gussie looked up then, and shook her head. "We met him and his wife in Cuba. Ned gambled with him. When he'd lost all the money we'd brought, he borrowed from Max and lost more. I had to wire Papa for cash to pay the hotel bill."

Henry smiled ruefully. "So that's why he sent me to Savannah to check on you."

Gussie nodded, sniffing away a tear. "I'd cabled Papa that I'd made a terrible mistake. Ned knew how to sweet-talk me, though, and I wired Papa that all was forgiven."

Henry nodded. "Yep, your old pater was suspicious. Wanted to make sure Ned wasn't holding a gun to your head, and if things turned nasty, I'd be there to escort you home." He dabbed at Gussie's face with his handkerchief.

"May I?" Embarrassed by the intimacy, Gussie took the square from him and blotted.

She folded the handkerchief, turning it over and over in her hands. She glanced back and saw that Trevania had gone inside. "Papa never liked Ned. Not since that first day he came by and sounded Papa out about Arcadia."

Henry smoothed a damp tendril of hair off Gussie's cheek. "Did he marry you for Arcadia?"

"Let's not talk about him." Warmth lingered on her skin where Henry had touched her. She'd never tell him why Papa consented.

"You've come to my rescue again," she said, handing back the square of cotton lawn. "Please come in. I want to hold my baby close, and I'm sure you could use a cold drink."

Trevania, who'd substituted the baby for the frying pan, held the door open wide for them. "Thank you, Jesus!" she cried out, jiggling the baby on her hip. "And thank you, Mr. Henry!"

"Thanks to you, Tre," Gussie said, "for calling Papa."

"The judge, he'd know the best thing to do."

Henry winked at Gussie, and she held out her arms for Gracie. She hugged the child close and murmured words of love into the russet hair.

"What happened in Cuba? I want the whole story." Henry, sur-rounded by camera equipment and backdrops, leaned forward on the wine velvet parlor sofa and took a long swallow from a glass of iced tea.

Gussie rattled her ice, stalling. She owed him some answers, because he had this insane habit of coming to her rescue. "My client will be here in fifteen minutes."

"I'll be brief. The more we know about Ned's involvements, the easier it will be to find him."

She picked up a Japanese fan from the coffee table and unfolded it. "Even Papa doesn't know the whole story." She whipped the fan, refresh-ing her hot cheeks. "You don't need to worry, Henry. Let the police handle Ned."

Henry leaned forward. "Let me help you. I know you want to do it all, and you're doing well. But this is over your head."

Gussie swallowed. Why couldn't she accept help? She told him about meeting Max and Sylvia on the beach. The hot day, the cigar, Sylvia's jewels.

Then everything spilled out: getting lost, meeting Rafael, the old padre, the casino, the hurricane. "That's all," she said, leaving out the lazy fan and the tropical languor and way the rum had made her feel, the billowing curtains and the sweet moments, the dream that had turned to a nightmare.

Henry met her eyes. "You doubted him, even then."

Gussie looked away and bit her lip. Her fingers went to her ring and touched bare skin. "So much I refused to see. I had to defend him to Papa all the time, and I've learned that when you defend something, you become much fonder of it."

"Good observation," Henry said. He picked up her hand. "Did he take your rings?"

"They're safe." Gussie pressed her lips together. They were in her jewelry box.

"When you met Ned, was it love at first sight?"

"Stop it, Henry. No more personal questions." She sat up straight and squared her shoulders.

Henry had the good grace to look abashed. "Sorry. What else can you tell me about Ned? Anything."

She hesitated. "I met a nurse at the hospital, Miss Oakes. She thinks Ned is her long-lost brother. At first I felt her story was farfetched, but now I'm not so sure. She wouldn't tell me where she was from and begged me not to ask her again. I'm not even supposed to be telling you this, but today has changed things for me."

"So that means Ned Fletcher wasn't his real name. What was it?"

Gussie bit her lip. "She said her brother's name was Byron, and that's the name Sarah Grady gave me. Byron Chance."

"I think I know Miss Oakes," Henry said. "Looked after me when I had my appendix out. But who the heck is Sarah Grady?"

"Ned's other wife. Sarah Chance." Gussie took a big gulp of tea to hide her shakiness.

"Holy cow!" Henry's eyes shone.

"Humph," she said. "Don't look so pleased. Sarah came to see me. She's looking for him too, for the money he stole from their savings. I don't suppose Papa has told you any of this?"

Henry shook his head. "He wouldn't."

Gussie inspected her ringless hands and rubbed the spot where the symbol of her former happiness had shone. "Sarah wants to remarry. Papa has advised her to file for divorce at once, but she's afraid if she divorces Ned now, it'll be harder for her to get her money."

Henry snorted. "If he's found."

Gussie told Henry that their bank account had been looted. She barely had enough for groceries. She smoothed her skirt. "I'll bet he went to Cuba and gambled his escape money away." The doorbell rang. "That's my client, Henry."

"Your father will want a report." Henry stood up. She rose too, and he took both her hands in his. "I'll call you after I talk to the judge. And Miss Oakes."

"She's working for Pete temporarily. You can find her there." Gussie saw him out, graciously ushered her client into the parlor, and then hurried the empty tea glasses back to the kitchen.

"That man sure sweet on you." Trevania took the glasses from her and set them in the sink.

Gussie closed her eyes. "That's what scares me."

# Chapter 56

W hen Henry Benedict called Tenny, she was surprised to hear from the witty, quiet fellow, the appendix case, who'd given her a box of chocolates. But wanting to talk to her about "a member of her family?" He wouldn't say more. Was Pa in trouble? Backslid out of Jesus' embrace, arrested for moonshining?

She'd hear him out, if only for Pa's sake.

He met her by the garage at Dr. Pete's house the next Sunday afternoon and gallantly opened the car door for her. "I see they've got company," he said, nodding toward two other cars parked in the driveway.

"My patient's mother usually spends Sunday afternoon with her," Tenny said, settling into the seat of the gleaming black Hupmobile. She stroked the leather seat. "Nice car."

"It's borrowed." Henry smiled. "I'm kind of a gofer for Judge Pemberton, and he lets me use this buggy sometimes."

"Judge Pemberton? Mrs. Fletcher's father?"

"Yup," Henry said. "He's great to work for. In fact, I imagine Pete would be great to work for, right?"

"Of course," Tenny said, smoothing her white blouse. "I'm learning a lot."

"Pete was a couple of years ahead of me in school," Henry said. "Of course, Miss Swanee Burkett, debutante of the year, was famous. Lots of men drowned their sorrows in bootleg hooch when she married him."

"Let's talk about something else," Tenny said. "I can't talk about my patient, and it's not right to talk about my employer."

Henry shrugged. "Sorry. I'm just making conversation. I didn't ask you here to gossip." He pulled up in front of the Rexall drugstore. "Best sodas in town," he said.

He escorted her past displays of patent medicine, soap, toothpaste, and cologne until they arrived at the soda fountain, its silver counter fronted with tall blue-cushioned stools. They took the last vacant booth in the back, ordering ice cream sodas in tall glasses, strawberry for him, chocolate for her, served up by a soda jerk in a white paper hat.

Tenny took a sip, smiled, and twiddled her straw. "So why did you ask me here? Is it about my father?"

Henry's eyebrows shot up. "Your father? No." He lowered his voice. "It's about Ned Fletcher."

Tenny's smiled faded. "You mean, is he my brother? I asked Miss Gussie not to mention what I said to anyone!"

"She wanted to keep your secret," Henry said, a muscle in his temple twitching. "But he's in big trouble. Some gangsters are looking for him, as well as the police. If I can find him first and convince him to turn himself in, it might save his life."

She gazed down at her drink, pondering what to say. "I'm afraid I can't help you. Byron left us when I was eight."

"Hasn't been in contact with your family?"

Tenny shook her head. "He sent a picture when he joined the Army, but after that, nothing." She met Henry's eyes. "I saw Ned Fletcher at the mill where I worked. He looked right through me, like he didn't know me. He favored Byron a lot, but the Byron I remember loved me. In fact, I think this Ned Fletcher got me fired."

Henry leaned forward and his voice lowered. "He was afraid you'd identify him. Did you know a woman came to see Mrs. Fletcher claiming to be Byron's wife?"

Tenny's mouth fell open. "She did?"

"She claimed he'd left her and stolen all their money. All she wanted was the money back and a divorce. She wasn't interested in prosecuting."

Tenny sat quietly for a minute, debating. Henry had the kind of open, earnest face a woman could trust, and she went with her gut. "Look, Mr. Benedict. This is real crazy. Mrs. Delight Brown, our pastor's wife, wrote me that a woman named Sarah came to the farm looking for Byron."

"So she knew where he came from? Why didn't she come earlier?"

"All I know is that I sent Mrs. Brown a newspaper clipping of Ned Fletcher, asking her if she thought he looked like Byron. She sent it on to this Sarah. Said Sarah left her address in Savannah, asking her to write if he showed up."

Henry's eyes gleamed. "And Sarah recognized Ned as Byron and came to Ashbyville to get her money!"

Tenny twisted her hands, shaking her head. "That man can't be the brother I remember! My brother would take me riding on the mule. He'd hunt and fish with Pa, knew every bit of those woods, and taught me how to clean a fish. In the fields he'd always pick more cotton than anybody. Oh, he liked to brag about how he was going to have his own place someday. Even said he'd have the landlord's place. We just laughed at him."

Henry regarded her thoughtfully. "So you were brought up on a farm? Sharecropping cotton?"

"What of it?" Without meaning to, Tenny had just given herself away. She glared at Henry.

"You don't talk like a country girl."

"I've done my best to educate myself."

Henry nodded. "I admire you for that. Where was the farm?"

"I don't see that makes much of a difference, but south of here, about twenty miles."

"Would Byron have gone back there to hide out?"

"What? Where would he hide? Pa would kick him out. There's a camp house in the woods, but the old man would find him."

"Why wouldn't your father help Byron?" Henry asked. "And what old man?"

Tenny ignored the last question. "Pa and Byron fell out before he left. Anyhow, Pa's been born again in the church. He wouldn't hide a lawbreaker."

"Not even his own son?"

"Ned Fletcher cannot be my brother, Mr. Benedict." Heart thumping, she slurped the last of her soda, trying to quell the lump in her throat. Silence blanketed the table.

"Is there a reason you left the hospital?" Henry asked casually.

She felt blood drain from her cheeks. "Dr. Pete wanted me to work for him."

"No other reason?"

She looked up angrily. "Why all these questions? I'm not in a courtroom, and you're not a lawyer, not yet. You wanted to know about Byron, not me. He left the farm when I was eight, and I haven't seen him since."

Henry's clasped hands rested on the table. "Sorry. But can you tell me more about why he left home?"

Yes, this Henry Benedict would make a good lawyer. He was like a dog with a bone. She shrugged. "Nope. It would be just guessing." She glanced at the watch pinned to her dress. "Look, Mr. Benedict, I'd just as soon not spend my free afternoon talking about my brother. I'll bet he got killed in France and somebody wanted to disappear and switched dog tags. I've heard of things like that."

"Well, yes, but—"

Tenny sat up straight, adjusted her cloche, and picked up her handbag. "Can we go? I do appreciate the ice cream soda."

"Wait," Henry said. "Just a minute."

He sat, two fingers pressed to his forehead and staring into a void. Dr. Pete did that sometimes. Tenny shifted in her chair and cleared her throat. He brought his gaze up to hers and smiled. "Sorry. Something came to me."

She waited.

"Just an idea about Ned," he said. "I'll have to think on it. Will you come have another soda next Sunday and talk about it?"

"I've already told you all I know," she said. "Anyhow, I can't. I've already promised Dr. Pete I'd go with them to the Cotton Festival. He's been anxious to get Miss Swanee out of the house, and it's the first time she's agreed to go out in public since . . . well, since the baby."

"On your day off?"

"I'm getting paid extra. If it's your business."

Henry grimaced. "Sorry. I'd forgotten about that festival. Could I at least telephone you?" He rose and stood while she slid out of the booth.

"Better not," she said. "Our phone is in the hall where everybody can listen."

Henry nodded in resignation, but Tenny sensed he wasn't about to give up.

Thankfully, he seemed too preoccupied to make conversation on the way back. Tenny enjoyed riding in an automobile, watching trees and houses fly by, feeling the wind on her face. It sure beat transport by mule and wagon.

Henry squealed to a stop at the Godwin residence. He got out and opened the door for Tenny, then looked around. "My mother would love this yard," he said.

"Bo Paul Hunter does all that," Tenny said.

"Who?"

"Their yard man, comes twice a week. Really good at all sorts of things. You know what? He's been teaching me how to drive a little in case I need to drive Miss Swanee someplace."

"H'm," Henry said. "My mother never learned to drive."

Tenny gave him a sideways look. "Well then, teach her!" She was ready to go but he seemed to be on the verge of asking another question. "Thanks for the soda," she said.

"Thanks for helping."

"I didn't help all that much."

"You may have helped more than you know. I'll stay in touch."

She walked back to the garage apartment without a backward glance. The afternoon wind ruffled her hair, and the sun felt warm on her shoulders. She should have been out at the park enjoying herself instead of talking to that Henry Benedict.

She didn't want Ned Fletcher to be her brother. She wanted her brother to be alive, but not a fugitive, not a lawbreaker. Still, if Ned was Byron, he *might* be hiding back in that camp house, or in a tent in the piney woods.

But that dandy she'd seen wearing expensive suits, sporting manicured nails? That man had never chopped cotton. He wouldn't hide out in a cabin and shoot rabbits and squirrels for his food. And risk Arno Shackley's shotgun?

All she wanted was to forget about it all.

She stretched out on her bed and opened the Elinor Glyn novel she'd borrowed. She'd barely finished a chapter when a car's engine started and then stopped outside. Several minutes later water was running.

Holding her place with a finger, she carried the book to the window. Dressed in dungarees and an old shirt, Pete was uncoiling the hose by the faucet. A bucket with rags rested on the grass beside his Buick.

She laid the book on the dresser and, leaning on the windowsill, watched him dip the rag in the bucket and soap the car. When he turned on the water for rinsing, he raised his eyes to her window. She ducked. Had he seen her watching him?

She grabbed her book, flopped on her bed, and tried to read, but the words swam like so many tadpoles. When she read the same paragraph for the third time, she closed the book. The room had been her retreat, her sanctuary, the only private place she'd ever had. Now it felt like a cage.

# Chapter 57

Gussie stared at the letter beside her plate. She'd put off opening it since it arrived the day before. She drank her coffee and spread some blackberry jelly on her toast and gazed out at the foggy morning, listening to Gracie babble and coo upstairs in her crib.

She finished her toast, sighed, and slit open the letter with a clean knife.

*I'm still looking for Ned,* Sarah wrote. *Have you heard anything? Will you let me know if you do?* Of course, Sarah had no idea the police were looking for him. Her next words jarred Gussie to the bottoms of her slippers. *Do you suppose he might be in Cuba? He always talked about going there to gamble.*

Gussie finished the letter, folded it carefully, and slid it back into its envelope. She took another sip of coffee. The mobsters would surely go there too.

She laid Sarah's letter on the hall table, walked upstairs, and pulled a pleated skirt and cotton middy blouse out of the closet. She was due at Lyman's shop this morning to dust and help unpack a new shipment, a chore Lyman hated with all his heart.

The back door closed with a firm click. *Yoo–hoo*, Trevania called. Gracie squealed in return, and Gussie went to pick her up. She gazed down on the baby, at her rosy complexion and pale, reddish curls. Beautiful, heartbreaking, little bastard.

In the kitchen, Trevania bustled about with a Mona Lisa smile, humming to herself. "What is it, Trevania?" Gussie lowered Gracie onto the soft blue blanket covering the floor of the playpen. "Are you and Bo Paul getting married?"

"I'm disappointed in you, Miss Gussie." Trevania, speaking in singsong, scraped the few breakfast dishes into a pail. "Looks like you could figure it out better than that."

"Come on, Trevania. Have you heard something?"

"You won't tell on me?" Trevania gave her a worried look.

"Bo Paul told you something." Gussie remembered the unhappy lunch party at Pete's house.

"It's this Professor Moon coming over all the time when Dr. Pete ain't home." Trevania shook her head in disapproval.

"Professor Moon?" Gussie laughed. "He's helping Swanee with some speech therapy."

Trevania's face hardened. "Bo Paul say he look like somebody trying to hide something. Carrying in a big satchel."

"Well, for heaven's sakes. It's books and papers he needs."

Trevania picked up the baby, who'd begun to whimper. "Bo Paul, he have a bad feeling about that man. And you know, Bo Paul have the second sight. His mama come from the islands."

Gussie was quiet for a moment. She didn't believe in all that African superstition, but she knew she had a lot to learn.

"You wait and see. Something going to happen."

"Nothing is going to happen," Gussie said, but it was hard to sound convincing.

Trevania gave her a pitying look, put the quieted baby back in the playpen, and set to sweeping crumbs from under the table.

Unsettled, Gussie pulled on a camel-colored cardigan, slung her good leather bag over her shoulder, and set out for the trolley stop. The cool, snappy air, the first foretaste of fall, refreshed her cheeks. Summer had officially ended two weeks before, but real fall weather wouldn't set in until after Halloween.

At the shop, she found Lyman in the back, boxing up the ship in a bottle she'd admired. "Sold it at last," Lyman crowed.

A ship in a bottle was a beautiful thing, a remarkable piece of craftsmanship, encased to keep it protected, safe from greasy fingers. And it would never sail, unlike the ship that had taken her home from Cuba. "Who bought it?"

"Conventioneer in town for a meeting. I'll deliver it to the Dunnigan Hotel this morning, because he's leaving soon. You can keep an eye on the shop, and when that no-good delivery boy I hired shows up, tell him to start uncrating." Lyman gestured to some wooden packing boxes stacked by the rear door. "Can you help with those too?"

"Sure." Chasing after Gracie and long walks kept her in shape. After Lyman left, she donned a pair of work gloves, picked up a hammer, and clawed the top boards loose from the crate.

She couldn't stop thinking about her young Cuban friend, Rafael, and the red bananas, and the peel she'd thrown into the harbor. What had become of the boy?

If Ned had run to Cuba—maybe he knew someone there. She pulled one exquisite Japanese vase out of its packing excelsior and wiped it clean. The Cuban images, the photographs she'd never looked at again, stood out sharply in her mind. There had been one of Rafael standing by the church with the old padre.

Maybe she could write to the priest and Rafael and ask them to send any word of Ned. On the streets of Havana all the time, as Rafael was, he might spot him somewhere. It was a long shot, but the boy knew English, and he'd seen Ned the day they'd left.

What had been the old priest's name? It came to her, shimmering, like the candles in the church that gloomy day. Father Vasquez. That was it. She'd write to Father Vasquez.

The hulking delivery boy came in and she handed him the crowbar. She walked into the shop floor, unlocked the door, and set the sign to OPEN. She straightened the flyer Lyman had posted about the Cotton Festival. She was looking forward to it. Would Henry Benedict be there? She hadn't seen him for a while. Had he found out anything he wasn't telling her?

# Chapter 58

How could the festival not go well on such a beautiful afternoon? Sunny, with just enough of a cool breeze to offset the bright November sky. Tenny hoped she wouldn't see Henry Benedict, with all his questions about Ned Fletcher and Byron.

She'd just finished packing the diaper bag when Pete stuck his head in the door. "I'll help Swanee down the stairs if you'll go ahead and get Baby settled." His voice was clipped, strained.

"Is anything wrong?"

He ran his hand down his face. "She wants to back out. Says she's not ready."

Tenny closed the bag, unsurprised. Swanee had agreed to the outing only when Pete and his mother bribed her with a new persimmon wool dress and a matching wide-brimmed cloche from Stephenson's. They'd told her she owed it to her admirers to be seen looking gorgeous, like her old self.

Now she was balking. Saying she wasn't her old self. Pete edged to Tenny's side and lowered his voice. "Damn, she was speaking so well, gaining motion in her limbs. I don't understand this slowdown."

"I know." Tenny took out the prettiest crocheted blanket, made by Miss Ethel, to wrap the baby in.

"Pop says to be patient. Still, going backward doesn't make sense."

Tenny expertly fastened the tiny buttons of Baby's dress. "Some things we have to leave to God."

He half-smiled. "You really believe that?"

"I believe we can't be God," she said.

Pete shook his head. "I don't know what to think anymore." He gave her a long, searching look and ducked out.

Tenny, flushed, tied Baby's lace-trimmed bonnet and wrapped her in the blanket. Balancing both baby and diaper bag, she headed downstairs. She'd reached the bottom step when she heard voices above.

"Come on, sweetheart."

"No."

"Do you enjoy shutting yourself away?"

"Embarrassing. Can't walk."

"Tenny's coming with us. We have the new rolling chair. I told you that. You'll be greeted like a queen!"

Tenny froze, waiting for an outburst, but the door to Swanee's room swung shut with a loud bang. The voices became muffled. Were they arguing about her? Maybe she should quit now. But the baby in her arms cooed and reached one tiny starfish hand up to her, and she took the chubby fingers and kissed them.

Something about the baby reminded her of her sister Merry. Her eyes, the shape of her pretty face? But why should this baby look anything like Merry? Her imagination, her longing for home, was working overtime.

The door upstairs creaked open. "Miss Oakes!" Pete called.

Rocking the infant gently in her arms, she stood at the foot of the stairs and gazed up at him. The air swam between them, and the words seemed to come from far away.

"Miss Swanee says she doesn't want to go to the park, Tenny." Pete's voice remained emotionless, matter-of-fact.

"Oh." Tenny stroked the baby's back. Well, that would be a relief. Maybe she could take her day off, after all, and go to the festival by herself. Too bad Ramona and Joe wouldn't be there. Maybe she'd see some of the other girls or Alice and her beau.

"I've decided that you and I and Baby will go," Pete said. Tenny snapped to attention. "I think my wife is able to stay alone until we get back. I'm not going to remain indoors on this beautiful day."

"You wouldn't dare go off and leave me!" Swanee shrilled.

Pete called, "You want me here? That's a change. Too bad." He started down the stairs.

Pete's uncharacteristic sarcasm stung Tenny, and the baby in her arms whimpered.

"I think there's a wet diaper." Tenny charged upstairs, edging past Pete to the safety of the baby's room, not meeting his gaze. The diaper wasn't wet, and she re-tied the lacy bonnet. Pete Godwin was acting very differently today, and it both frightened and thrilled her.

They set out in the Buick: Glacial-faced Swanee in front with Pete, Tenny and Baby in back. The new reed chair from Sears and Roebuck and the baby go-cart, a folding stroller, were strapped to the trunk. Swanee's soft persimmon dress dramatized her raven hair and pale skin, and the chic broad-brimmed hat shadowed any remaining sag in her face. Her kohl-rimmed eyes looked enormous.

At the park, they waded through festival-goers in cottons and corduroys, Tenny's excitement mounting at the hubbub and the delicious aromas from the crowded canvas tents selling hickory-smoked barbecue and fried pies. Churchwomen in kerchiefs waited behind tables of luscious coconut and caramel cakes, fragrant pecan and sweet potato pies, and glistening blackberry and plum jellies, all displayed in home-woven baskets. Tenny gazed hungrily at the spread, as she'd been too excited to eat much breakfast.

Pete unstrapped the rolling chair and set it up, while Tenny unfolded the baby go-cart and settled the child in. They bumped along dirt paths to the bandstand. Friends, well-wishers, even strangers, flocked to speak to them.

Tenny, her uniform making her invisible to the smiling, curious faces, held her breath, waiting for an outburst. But Swanee received the well-wishers' compliments like a queen among her subjects, and she bloomed. Oddly, her glance darted into the crowd again and again, as if she were searching for someone.

She watched politicians in string ties shake grimy hands and kiss messy babies. She watched children scampering around the bandstand and eating frozen custard, which dripped on their smocked gingham dresses and neatly pressed shirts. Her gaze also lingered on the black folk, smart-looking in pressed plaid shirts and flowered straw hats.

Pete was watching her carefully.

Tenny lifted her gaze from a pile of peach fried pies and spotted a little red-haired girl in lavender gingham bobbing on someone's shoulders. When they grew closer, she saw that the "someone" was Henry Benedict. Mrs. Gussie Fletcher strolled alongside him, and before Tenny could blink, Gussie had spotted them and headed their way.

Hugs were swapped all around, Swanee bestowing favor in her throne-chair. Tenny stepped away so the family could talk. Henry shot Tenny a quizzical look; she gave him a slight shrug. She had nothing to tell him.

She fingered the magical moonstone that Lyman Stratton had given her on that awful day. Searching the crowd for him, she spotted instead the evangelist, Brother Perry, who'd saved her in the park after she'd left the mill. He was standing on a stump, preaching to a gathering crowd. "Brothers and sisters, lay up not treasure for yourselves on this earth, for doth not the thief break though and steal? Doth not the worm corrupt?"

"Yeah, brother!" Tenny heard. "Amen!" and then a small voice, "I could use some treasure."

More people stopped by to speak to Swanee: Mrs. Belinda Pemberton and Miss Jessie Pemberton, the schoolteacher; Dr. Emmett Godwin and his wife Mrs. Amelia; and a lady she remembered from the hospital visits as Miss Gussie's other sister, Anna; and the lady's little boy, a toddler with hair like cotton.

Her stomach plunged, the way it always did when she saw a towhaired child of two. She wheeled Baby down the path away from them. A sharp whistle from Dr. Pete called her back. It was time to take their seats for the program.

The band on the pavilion, uniforms sharp and brass glinting, began with "The Stars and Stripes Forever." Surrounded by rhythm, by toe taps and claps, Tenny thought of another concert, the day she and Ramona had come to the park, the time before the rioting at the mill. So long ago, and nothing had changed.

After three numbers, the band left the platform, and in the lull before the first dignitary took the stage, Swanee demanded to hold her own baby so that passers-by could stop and admire her.

Miss Gussie's little red-haired girl clambered down from her seat and toddled over. Forefinger in her mouth, she stood gazing at the baby in her fancy bonnet.

"Do you like babies, sweetheart?" Swanee said.

Except it didn't come out quite like that. In the excitement, Swanee garbled her words, lessons forgotten. The child looked from the baby to Swanee's face and ran back to her mother, burying her face in her mother's skirt.

Swanee stiffened and glared at Tenny. "Take her." Tenny lifted the baby off her lap and Pete took Swanee's hand, whispering.

When the mayor stepped up to the podium, Swanee jerked her hand from Pete's grasp. Pete's mouth tightened. Her folded his arms and settled back into his seat. The speech began: "My fellow Americans, today we gather to celebrate our agricultural bounty. For many years we have prospered from King Cotton. Our city and our countryside have profited from growth and they have suffered from the weevil. And now we are diversifying our crops and our manufacturing. We are a marketplace for the area. As your mayor, I pledge to do all I can to promote commerce and ensure the safety of all our citizens. I pledge to pave the streets for the safe passage of our motorized trucks bringing crops to market . . ."

As the mayor droned on, Tenny raised an eyebrow and glanced at Swanee, who stared straight ahead, eyes glassy. The smoke from the barbecue tent drifted over, the aroma reminding Tenny of the time Byron had been working at a pig roast and had brought home three quart jars of pulled pork in tangy, dark red sauce. How they'd feasted!

The state representative stepped up, and she hoped he'd be quick, so they could eat. He was a better orator than the mayor, and he whipped the crowds into a frenzy, jerking back and forth in the manner of a hellfire preacher, his forelock flapping.

Tenny was enjoying the excitement, the people goading the speaker on with shouts of "You tell 'em, Gene!" Pete was grinning hugely. Swanee wasn't smiling, though, and suddenly she tapped her husband smartly on the arm. "I want to go home."

Tenny settled Swanee into bed with a glass of iced tea, her writing box within easy reach. Then, after she'd fed Baby and put her down for a nap, Tenny went to ask Pete if her job was done. Should she mention the promised bonus?

He'd retreated into his study and closed the door. Reluctant to knock, she drank some tea in the kitchen, and then washed the tea glass and baby bottle.

She was just wringing out the dishcloth when Pete, shoulders slumping, wandered into the kitchen and picked up a juicy-looking apple from the dish on the table. He bit into it with a crunch, and her mouth watered.

"Are you hungry?" He must have seen her staring. "Please, have one. They come from my friend in Dahlonega."

She took the largest from the bowl and sank her teeth into it. Sweet, delicious, juicy.

"The weather is good and I'm too restless to sit inside," Pete said. "How about playing a round of badminton with me while they're napping? That'll make up your full day. Don't worry, you'll get the bonus I promised."

Her cheek full of apple, she almost choked. "Badminton? I don't know how."

"I'll teach you."

"But—" She couldn't play in uniform and she didn't have any tennis shoes. Playing with him? Full of risks. But he'd already had one disappointment today.

"I'll go change," she said. Heck, she'd play barefooted. She'd spent plenty of her life without shoes. She'd wear an old cotton skirt and a cotton blouse she'd brought from the Callahan Home. She ate the rest of the apple.

"You're a natural at this," Pete called.

Tenny, running, leaping, chasing the shuttlecock, felt a surge of freedom she hadn't known since her childhood, when she wandered the woods and creeks with Shelley on Sunday afternoons, the one day Pa would let them off farm work. It was the Sabbath, and Ma scolded him if he insisted on the children working.

Tenny had hated that work—the sun and the bugs, the aches in her back and shoulders and blisters on her hands—but work at the hospital wasn't a whole lot better. Footsore and wrung out, she spent days between crisis and boredom. But there, at least, she felt fulfilled. She was helping people.

Working indoors, she'd missed the birds and trees and clouds, the feel of the open sky. And here, the fragrance of damp leaves and fall, the darting of yellow jackets among fallen crabapples. There was something of God about it.

"Atta girl!" Pete called out. She'd smacked a return of his serve.

Tenny smiled. She wasn't *that* good, but she was having great fun. Pete brought out talents she didn't know she possessed. Exhilarated, she swatted a feathered cork against an azure sky. A good shot brought a shriek of glee, a bad one a wail of horror. She was truly living into her soul.

Giddy, she didn't notice the pins working loose from her hair. After a high leap, the pins scattered, her light brown hair with its pale crown falling about her shoulders.

She called a halt and knelt to pick up her pins. As she scrabbled in the clover and grass, a yellow jacket settled on her sweaty hand. When she tried to brush it away, it jabbed her fiercely. She yelped, cramming her fist to her mouth.

Pete knelt and lifted her damp hand. Their eyes met, and her pulse leaped in her throat. The sun beat white-hot between the drifting clouds, and the buzzing in the clover grew louder. He brought the hand up to his own mouth and covered the swelling welt with his lips. His tongue explored the soft webbing between her thumb and forefinger, and he sucked the stinger out.

She gasped at the surge that shot through her. He let go of her hand, and his fingers came to rest on her throat. Her pulse rushed and he leaned down and kissed her just there, and helplessly, she turned her head toward him, and her lips met his.

The kiss was long and the air seemed to thicken with the humming of bees, and her toes gripped the prickly grass, and the wind swam like cool nectar on her skin, and the sun warmed her hair and filled her senses with honey.

She knew this was wrong, but the voice telling her this was far away, far beyond the bright clouds. With a sigh, she pulled back, but he held her tight, and her resistance ebbed away.

"My naiad." He kissed her forehead, her eyes, then her lips, and ran his hands through her hair. "Barefoot . . ." he said. "You, coming out of the water with your hair streaming . . ."

"Please. Don't . . ."

He pressed himself against her, and she felt him, and she flushed with shame at the memory of those men she had not loved, who had forced her and bartered with her, and those memories faded in a rush of thrilling brilliance, the sun in her eyes and in her blood.

She could hardly speak. She opened her eyes to dark branches against a blue autumn sky. This was her idol, the man she trusted. And they were in his back yard, with his wife and baby in the house, who were her charges, and all her being wanted to hold him close, and this was *all wrong.*

She struggled, broke away, and fled into the house. She rushed to the pantry where her shaking fingers closed on a yellow box of baking soda. It slipped out of her trembling fingers onto the table, where it landed on its side, spilling the powder. She leaned on the table, out of breath.

Pete slammed into the kitchen behind her. He wet his fingers, made a baking-soda paste, and spread it over the swelling.

Stricken, she glanced at the white-topped welt and studied his face. She saw only confusion like her own. Maybe she should pretend nothing had happened. She dropped her gaze to her hand.

"Am I off duty now?"

"I'd like you to stay till six." His voice was dogged, thick with longing, unrepentant.

"I'd rather not." Her knees threatened to buckle. She turned to go.

"I want to talk to you. Please." His voice was soft, but he grasped her arm.

She broke away, fled out the door, and ran up the narrow flight of wooden steps to her room, where she collapsed onto the narrow bed, sobbing. She half expected him to pound on the door. When no pounding came and the crying had spent itself, she heaved herself up, walked over to the washbasin, and splashed her eyes and face. She picked up a comb and drew it through the long, silky strands of hair. The pale color had grown out almost two inches.

She closed her eyes and remembered what Miss Verity had said. Breathe in, breathe out. Count to ten. Pray. At last she felt stronger, and her mind was clear. She had to tell him this was madness, that there was nowhere to go. It must stop. *Now*. She walked down the wooden steps and found him stowing the badminton rackets and net in the garden shed.

"Doctor," she began formally, but her voice broke. He held out his hand, and it was trembling.

She let him take her fingers in his and he led her into the shed, where this time she returned his kiss, laid low by the wonder and sweetness of it all: the rich odor of their bodies, the earthy smell of dried manure, the high dirt-smeared window where sun filtered through.

Pete pulled the middy blouse over her head and gazed on her bare breasts with their pale points of pink, and leaned down and kissed them, and he touched her softly, gently, a world apart from the rude fumbling of the other men she'd known.

A sob escaped her lips.

"Are you afraid?" whispered Pete.

She shook her head *No*, a sweet and terrible lie. They knelt, as if praying, on the hard-packed dirt floor and collapsed onto a pile of croker sacks, sinking into the ropy smell.

Pete whispered God knew what soft words. She didn't want to hear them, so she focused on the dirt-spattered window, and everything faded into a rocking blur of green branches, green branches that danced in the sunlight, danced for the very first time.

She opened her eyes afterwards and saw rakes and hoes and baskets and hoses, and the window which glowed with sundust. She stirred on the rough sacks, feeling their scratchiness and the earth beneath her so solid, yet this whole scene was like a lantern slide; it had happened a long time ago to somebody else, and she, Tenny, was barefoot and on the road to Ashbyville with a croker sack slung over her shoulder.

And her tears flowed then, for all that was, and all that was not, in this place of weathered wood and gold.

What would happen to her now?

# Chapter 59

How much time had passed before they realized a world lay outside the garden shed, a world to which they had to return? Pete, touching her chin lightly, broke the spell. "I'd better get back. Of course, I won't expect you . . . that is, I can see to Baby." His gaze, soft, filled with concern for her, took her breath away. She nodded mutely, a lump in her throat, as the wooden door swung shut behind him and stuck ajar on the warped floorboards. A thin sliver of sunlight pierced the dust.

Tenny huddled atop the jumbled sacks until she was sure he'd reached the house, then she rose. She jerked her clothes over her damp body and fled, the door banging on its hinges. She dashed up to her room above the garage.

She soaped and scrubbed as she did at the hospital, hands up to the elbows, sure that her hands must give her away, that they would always smell of love and sin. She would never be able to wash herself clean of the guilt. She bathed in the sputtering shower and then wrapped her nakedness in her old robe and threw herself on her bed, a lump rising in her throat.

She would give notice tomorrow.

She barely heard the faint rap at the door. The rap grew sharper, and she struggled to force her limp limbs out of their torpor. She unfolded herself, slid her body off the bed, and fought through molasses air to the door.

Ridiculous how his troubled face warmed her when she saw it, ridiculous how her treacherous body yearned for his touch, nerves alight. She squeezed her eyelids together.

Pete touched her cheek, his voice husky. "Look at me, Tenny."

Her eyes fluttered open, but she dropped her gaze to the gray boards beneath her feet. "Why are you here?"

He slid his finger under her chin and tilted her face upward to meet his. "There's an emergency at the hospital. Will you—"

"Of course." Tenny's shattered world reassembled itself and turned, wobbling, on its axis. This was real life. The spell was broken.

She struggled into her uniform, fumbling with the buttons, smoothing the skirt. She grimaced in the mirror, embarrassed at the love glow of her cheeks. She splashed her face with cold water, then toweled it dry. She knotted her hair atop her head, pinned on her cap, and, this time, set her eyeglasses on her nose.

The baking soda box still lay on the table in the empty and quiet kitchen. She cleaned away the spilled powder and tucked the box back in the pantry. Then she took a breath and headed for the stairs. Pete, carrying Baby, was walking down, and she waited for him at the bottom.

"I don't know how long I'll be," he apologized, handing her the child. He squeezed her arm, his touch sizzling through the starched cotton. And then he was gone, closing the screen door behind him, leaving a ghostly handprint on her sleeve.

She stood very still. Then she bent and placed the baby in her playpen and turned to wash an emptied bottle.

Swanee's bell rang.

She hefted the baby onto her shoulder and trudged up the steps, heart in her throat. Standing in Swanee's doorway, watching Pete's wife lounging in lace, she simulated a smile. "What can I do for you, Miss Swanee?"

Swanee inspected her nails. "Who won the game?"

"The game?" Tenny swallowed.

"The ba-minton game."

Tenny shifted from one foot to the other, rocking the baby in her arms. "I got stung by a yellow jacket. We didn't finish."

"Stung."

"Didn't he tell you?" She could not bring herself to say his name.

"I dint ask." Swanee formed her words softly, sibilant and snakelike. Her eyes gauged Tenny's reaction. She sighed. "He likes his ex'cise."

"Is there anything you need?" She forced herself into nurse mode. No emotion.

"My ex'cise." Swanee sat straighter in bed. "I feel better."

Tenny patted Baby's back. "I'll get the bassinet so she can stay while we work."

"On the bed. Right here." Swanee rolled over and pulled back the covers.

Tenny hesitated. "We wouldn't want her to roll off."

Swanee shot Tenny an irritated glance. "I won't let her."

She risked Swanee's ill humor. "I'm sure you wouldn't, but she'll be safer in the bassinet." She didn't wait for an argument, but took Baby to the nursery and settled her into the wheeled wicker basket. She could see Swanee's features in the baby's face, in the dark fluff on her head, but her eyes were turning Mildred. Pete's eyes were green. Maybe those Mildred eyes were his. She rolled the bassinet into Swanee's room and settled it beside the bed.

As the little one gurgled and played with her toes, Tenny pulled and forced the affected arm and leg through a range of motion, and then massaged each limb. She hustled and heaved, sweat running down her face, her uniform becoming a damp, wrinkled mess. She forced Swanee to sit, then stand, holding on to a chair with her good hand. At the end of a half hour Swanee said she'd had enough.

Tenny helped Swanee back to bed, and wiped her face and hands with a damp cloth. "I'm hungry," Swanee said. "Bring something warm."

Tenny glanced at the baby, content in the bassinet by her mother's bed, cooing and kicking and reaching for the built-in wooden beads.

"Leave her here," Swanee said.

"Of course." Tenny chided herself for worrying. The baby would be fine with her mother. No need to be overprotective.

Downstairs, Tenny gazed out the front window at the shadows lengthening over the lawn, the shadows growing larger as she felt smaller. How had Swanee known about the badminton game?

Surely Pete must have told her he was going to play. Or had Swanee managed to walk downstairs when nobody came in answer to her bell? Did Swanee know what had happened after the game? Tenny didn't want to think of the consequences.

She took out a frying pan.


When Tenny was halfway up the stairs with a tray of scrambled eggs and toast and canned peaches, the baby shrieked—long, breathless, terrified shrieks. Oh, dear God, what now?

She stumbled up the last few steps, plopped the tray onto the floor, and burst into Swanee's room. The baby was gone! Her heart constricted. And then the baby shrieked again. Following the shriek, Tenny found the red-faced baby on the carpet behind the bed, bassinet overturned. Swanee, half out of bed, was reaching for the infant.

Tenny blinked, not sure what she was seeing. Was Swanee reaching with the weak arm? The child's mother pulled back and looked up appealingly. "Thank God you're here."

Tenny kneeled beside the baby, shaken up but unhurt. The cushions in the bassinet had tumbled out, breaking the fall. She picked the tiny girl up, massaging her limbs, wheedling and singing.

"What about me? I'm twisted like pretzel," Swanee complained.

"You shouldn't have tried to pick her up," Tenny struggled to pick up the bassinet.

"I'm her mother, not you! I pick her up when I want to."

Tenny silently laid the squalling infant back in the bassinet while she straightened Swanee in the bed and propped her with pillows. Then she picked up the fretful baby, rocking her in her arms until she calmed.

Tenny finally returned to the tray on the landing. The plate of food was stone cold.

Some time later, when Swanee was settled with fresh hot food, Tenny took Baby to the pink and white nursery for a nap.

Clean diapers lay ready in a stack, a tin of baby powder and a jar of cotton balls stood by the changing table. In the folding basket-dresser lay a princess's wardrobe of soft blankets and garments embroidered with flowers and love knots and tiny swimming ducks.

Tenny would be going back to the hospital, to the reality of hard life. For just a few minutes longer of this peace, Tenny settled into the rocking chair with Baby. The gentle motion lulled her defenses, and the afternoon flooded back, leaving her dizzy and breathless, her body aching with longing for the dark honey of the dusty shed.

She caught her breath. She could have become pregnant. Tears swelled in her throat. How could she have been so careless? How could she have forgotten all she'd learned at the Home? She'd be kicked out of nursing school! All the more reason to leave this house as soon as possible. There was no place for her here.

Baby had fallen asleep at last, and Tenny lowered her gently to her place among the teddy bears. Outside, twilight was falling, and the gnawing in Tenny's belly reminded her of the missed lunch, the lone apple.

In the kitchen, she made herself a peanut butter and jelly sandwich and poured a glass of milk. She'd almost finished when the telephone rang. She walked into the front hall and picked up the receiver. "Godwin residence, Miss Oakes."

She recognized the liquid voice at once. "Rolfe Moon speaking. Would you give Mrs. Godwin a message?"

"Of course."

"The visit to my studio has been arranged for the day after tomorrow. Tuesday."

Tenny drew in a sharp breath. "Oh, she didn't tell me."

"Ah, an oversight, I'm sure," the voice purred. "We've been planning it. I have a marvel of technology, a Dictaphone, in my office; she can hear herself on playback. It is too inconvenient to transport, alas, or I would bring it to her. It will accelerate her progress. I will call for her at 3:30 p.m. precisely."

"I'll tell her, Mr. Moon. Will I be needed as well?"

He cleared his throat. "No, no, that's quite all right. I can manage my pupil quite well. I have a rolling chair at my studio."

Tenny set down the receiver unsteadily. Why hadn't Swanee told her about this outing? Maybe it was just her general obstinacy. But something seemed off.

She found a piece of the scrap paper that Nola used for shopping lists. Sitting at the table, she wrote the telephone message for Dr. Pete. She had just risen from the chair when the door scraped open behind her.

Pete walked in, haggard, his coat slung over his shoulder, shirt stained with sweat.

Their eyes met for just a moment before Tenny looked away, touching her throat. "What's that?" He walked over and laid a hand on her shoulder, then picked up the slip of paper.

She couldn't shrink from his touch. She explained about the call from Rolfe Moon.

Pete laid the paper back on the table. "I don't know what's going on between her and Moon. When I come in, they shut up. I asked him to let me watch the lesson, and he refused. He said it would make her self-conscious." He began to stroke Tenny's back.

"Please don't." Tenny stood, slipping away from Pete. "He didn't want me to come with her to the Dictaphone session."

Pete looked thoughtful. "Something funny's going on."

"Is it?" Drowning in love and terrified, Tenny couldn't think straight.

"I think she's been writing to some man," Pete said. "I think she was looking for him at the festival."

"Oh, surely not," Tenny said. "I used to write letters for her. She just wrote to people who'd sent her cards and gifts. Relatives, old school chums." But then . . . "Did you know she's writing to Enid Smith Barlow?"

Pete frowned. "They were friends once, and then Swanee dropped her. I didn't want to hire her, and I still don't. I hope that's not what Swanee has in mind."

"She's writing by herself now," Tenny said. "They're still corresponding."

"Maybe she needs friends now more than she used to," Pete said. "I'm glad she's getting stronger."

Should she tell him about the arm reaching for the baby, the arm that pulled back suddenly? She might have been mistaken. Was jealousy making her imagine things?

He still cared for Swanee, despite what had happened in the toolshed. What had Nola told her once? "Whole town knowed how that boy carried a torch for Miss Swanee."

She retrieved the rest of her sandwich, wrapped it in waxed paper, washed her plate and glass, and set them on a rack to dry. She picked up her bag to leave, taking the half sandwich.

"Don't go." He stretched out his hand, but she stepped back, holding her bag to her chest.

"I have to."

She left by the back door, crossed the grass, and raced up the stairs to her room. She would not cry. She would not.

# Chapter 60

Tenny shivered in the early dawn light as she fastened the last button of her fresh, crisp uniform. She was strapping on armor, a barrier between her and the man who had overcome all her resistance. Could she really go back to the hospital, where she'd have to see him almost every day?

What choice did she have? She needed the money she was putting away for Shelley and the few dollars to send to her brother and sisters. Could she find another nursing school? Without a diploma, could she get a private nursing job? Maybe, but it wouldn't pay as well, and she'd never win one of the coveted hospital supervisory positions.

If she asked Miss Wells about other schools, Miss Wells would ask her why she wanted to leave. She was at the top of her class! Oh, why did Verity Hapsworth have to be in England right now?

One day at a time. With this day behind her, she could plan her future. First, clean clothes. The uniform she'd worn the day before needed washing, along with the skirt and middy blouse that had landed in a heap on the floor of the garden shed. She picked the garments off a chair, dirty and sweaty, sweetly rank. She folded them inside the uniform, tucked the bundle under her arm, and walked to the house.

She let herself in the back door and closed it quietly. The morning sun flooded the empty kitchen, sparking off the copper kettle Nola kept scoured and polished. Overhead, pipes gurgled and floorboards creaked with morning activity.

She found the wicker basket full; she pushed aside Pete's shirts and Swanee's nightgowns and sorted out towels and dishcloths to mix with her serviceable garments. She stuffed all the laundry into the tub of the new automatic washing machine, filled it with hot water from the sink hose, and added soap flakes. This new invention was sure different from Weedy Grove, where they'd been obliged to scrub clothes in a washtub with water heated on the wood-burning stove. She was glad to flip the machine's switch and hear it hum to life.

Since she couldn't hear Baby over the chug of the machine, she went to the stairs. She froze. Swanee, on the hall landing, was scuttling like a crab, *without her cane.*

What did this mean? The door softly closed in Swanee's room just as Pete appeared, shaved and dressed, hair slicked down. When he caught her eye she couldn't move. Step by step he moved toward her, tightening the invisible ropes he'd cast.

And then he stood inches away, so close she could smell the morning scent of sandalwood.

"You're in early." A flush crept up his neck and his eyes softened.

She became unmoored, a raft swirling on the river. "I thought I'd start a load of wash. There's so much to do today with all the diapers." She heard herself speaking from far away.

Pete nodded and lowered his voice. "Baby and Swanee are both asleep."

Tenny bit her lip. She'd tell the truth. "I saw her in the hall. Walking without help."

Pete was quiet for a long moment. "Are you sure?"

"I saw her, Pete." Tenny miserably wished she hadn't seen Swanee or called him by his nickname.

He gestured for her to follow him to the kitchen, where his wife couldn't overhear. "That makes no sense," he said. "Why would she hide the fact that she can walk?"

Tenny glanced down at her shoes. "Miss Wells says that sometimes patients malinger because they enjoy the attention."

"I don't buy that," Pete said. "She's always had plenty of attention, and she wants to be well."

"Maybe she just wanted to practice before she told you." Tenny hoped that was true. If the patient could walk, her nurse wouldn't feel so guilty about leaving.

A kaleidoscope of emotions flickered across Pete's face: hope, despair, longing, anger. Then the back door closed with a thump. Nola came in humming the gospel song she always hummed in the morning, *Precious Lord, lead me on . . .*

Now the baby began to wail.

"I'll go," Tenny said. "Please. Have breakfast and don't worry." She edged past him and mounted the stairs. Did she see the door of Swanee's room move?

# Chapter 61

"So you think Ned might be in Cuba?" Henry, rucksack on his back, scuffled leaves underfoot along the path into the park. They headed toward the park's picnic area with its wooden tables and barbecue pit.

"It's the perfect place to hide," Gussie said. "No extradition treaty. But Max is already there, I'll bet. What's going to happen when he finds him?"

Henry pointed a forefinger at an imaginary Ned. "Trial by gangster."

"That's not funny, Henry. What about Sarah and all the money he took? What about Gracie?"

"What if he's gambled all the rest of the money away?"

"If I went after him, maybe I could beg him to come back for Gracie's sake, beg him to turn himself in." She met his gaze and didn't waver. "Would you go with me to Cuba?"

"Certainly not."

"Not very nice of you." Gussie tossed her head and glanced around the swept-dirt walkway. Most of the gossips in town knew that Ned had deserted her, but they didn't know she wasn't ever really married. Let them talk.

"I want to keep you safe." He gently picked a leaf out of her hair, his fingers brushing her neck. The tenderness of his eyes left no doubt of his feeling. She turned away, confused. Henry was so good. He was a rock for her. He was comforting. But where was the passion Ned had stirred?

Passing picnic benches filling with office girls and clerks, Gussie followed Henry to an unoccupied table away from them, a table dappled with sun. He unpacked ham sandwiches and apples, extracted two enameled tin mugs, and poured cups of coffee from a Thermos. He even produced tiny jars of sugar and cream, remembering how she liked her coffee.

She sipped the brew, warming her hands. It felt good to be with Henry in the cool and misty weather while the tall elms slipped slender yellow leaves to the ground. She picked up a leaf and studied it. "We need to find Ned before Max does."

"And how do you propose we do that?" His eyes searched hers carefully. "Go to the Cuban police? Would they be interested? Go to the casino and ask questions? Wouldn't Max go there first?"

"I've thought about it. There's the old padre, and Rafael."

She told him about getting lost, and the rescue, and the church. She told him about writing to the old padre and waiting for a response. Henry looked skeptical. "A kid can be useful, but you need some better connections," he said. "And if Ned did go there, and if he won at the tables, he's probably on his way to South America right now."

"Oh."

"We've come to a dead end. We can't play Pinkerton detectives with real ones on the job. He's trying to get away from Max, the cops, and his lawfully wedded wife."

She glared at him. "You're making fun of me." She wrapped the wax paper and the apple cores in newspaper, and placed the parcel in the rucksack. "Thank you for the lunch, Mr. Benedict."

She allowed Henry to walk her home before he went back to class. All she wanted was to see Ned one more time. She hoped she'd find her love in ashes.


Who could she talk to about Henry, about her feelings? Mama or her sisters just wouldn't do. Certainly not Papa. Pete, maybe. She'd helped him often enough, but he'd be at work now and she had a client coming. Another bride.

That evening she had a hurried dinner of vegetable soup and cornbread and tried to comfort Gracie, howling with teething pain. Finally she managed to settle the child with a crust of zwieback, took a deep breath, and went to the telephone.

Pete sounded awful, croaking as if he'd been up all night. She'd hoped things would amooth out for him. Definitely the wrong time to talk about Henry. "Is anything wrong? I can spare an hour tomorrow for Swanee, if you need me."

He cleared his throat. "Thanks for offering, Gus," he finally said, "but tomorrow Moon wants her to talk into some kind of recording device. He says listening to herself will help her speech."

"Sounds like the bee's knees, cuz."

"She wants to go to his studio alone. Not take her nurse."

Gussie snorted. "Swanee's not having a fling with Moon, Pete. She's rarin' to get out without a chaperone. Want me to borrow Papa's car and drive her?"

"Moon is coming to pick her up. Something's not right," Pete insisted. "They shut the door and won't let anybody watch the lessons."

Pete obviously had a jealous streak. "Get serious. Moon is temperamental. He thinks it'd distract Swanee."

"I know, I know. But something's off."

"Pete," she said firmly. "You're working too hard."

"Goes with the territory. I'm fine."

He wasn't fine, she knew. Something was off, sure, but something he didn't want to tell her. She told him to call if he needed her. She hung up the phone emptier than before.

She couldn't decide about Henry because Ned wouldn't come into focus. Was he the mythical Ned in Havana, in the ice-cream suit, her handsome, confident, charming lover? Was he the crippler of a child, the embezzler, the gambler, the bigamist?

Had she fallen for a made-up person she'd only imagined, an actor against a flimsy painted backdrop that would wash away in the rain?

A scream shattered her thoughts. Gracie and that tooth. She retrieved the teething ring she kept in the icebox, hoping Gracie would sleep tonight. Neverland was far away, that Neverland where Mama had dinner on the table and Ned was on his way home.

Gracie's wails woke her at five-thirty the next morning, nudging her out of a troubled dream. She padded over to the crib she'd moved into their bedroom and found a drooling Gracie, finger in her mouth. As she bent to pick her up, a car's engine came to a stop near her house. She shrugged it off. A neighbor.

She retrieved the teething ring from the floor, settled the baby over her shoulder, and carried her downstairs for a piece of ice. She chipped a chunk from the block in the icebox, tied it into a clean handkerchief, and slipped it into Gracie's mouth. Walking the infant up and down the hall, she glanced out the front window of the dining room. Early fog drifted along the sidewalk, haloing the gas lamp by the walkway.

She blinked twice to make sure what she was seeing. A man stood just beyond the cone of light, a bearded man in a trench coat, his hat pulled low over his forehead. He was gazing at her lighted upstairs windows, and then his gaze traveled to her front door.

Not Max. This man was taller than Max. And Max didn't wear a trench coat.

Heart thumping, she made sure the front door was bolted, then she checked the back. Satisfied, she slipped into the dark living room and peered out from behind the curtain. A motorcar coughed, roared, and then faded into the distance.

Ned had owned a trench coat. From overseas, he'd said.

She didn't sleep again. When the first glimmers of dawn broke through the fog, she dressed and made some coffee. She tried to read the newspaper. She fed Gracie. It seemed forever until she heard Digger John's truck in the driveway. She couldn't wait to tell Trevania about what she'd seen that night and hear what she had to say.

Gussie flung the door open, only to see Digger John, battered hat in hand. He told her that Trevania had eloped with Bo Paul Hunter.

They were heading to Cincinnati so he could get a job with the railroad. Bo Paul had one of his sights, one he couldn't ignore, that the police were about to arrest him on some trumped-up charge, just because somebody had seen him teaching that nurse at young Dr. Godwin's how to drive.

The day passed somehow. She managed two portrait sittings, and her mother came over with more zwieback as well as paregoric to rub on the baby's gums. She didn't tell Mama about the man in the fog, and it seemed like a silly thing to tell Henry.

Henry would want to know details. She couldn't be sure she didn't dream the whole thing, and, anyhow, she didn't know how to get in touch with him without involving Papa or his mother.

When the phone rang at six o'clock, she snatched it up, sure it must be him. "Henry?"

"It's Pete." His voice sounded even worse than it had this morning. "Did Swanee come to your house, by any chance?"

"But why would she have come here? Didn't you say she was going to Professor Moon's today?" Something very strange was going on. Pete paused long enough for an ambulance to wail by. "Moon claims he sent her home in a taxi two hours ago. She never got here. I hoped she might have stopped in at your place for some reason."

"She hasn't been here, Pete. What can I do? I'm stuck at home with Gracie, but I can call people." Pete must be out of his mind with worry. Her problem seemed petty now.

"No," Pete said. "You were the last on my list. Now I'm calling the law."

# Chapter 62

C.B. Potts, the officer, was sitting opposite Pete and Tenny in the parlor. Half-empty cups of cold coffee remained on the mahogany table, along with a plate that still held a few of Nola's tea cakes.

"Strictly speaking," C.B. said, "she's got to be gone forty-eight hours before we can call her a missing person."

"Good God," Pete exploded. "She's got medical problems."

"She's still a competent adult." C.B. Potts reached for another tea cake. "Calm down, old buddy. Maybe she took a notion to go to one of them picture shows."

A picture show! Nola was humming her gospel song in the kitchen with the baby. Swanee's parents, Elias and Clara Burkett, had come and gone. Her father had said he'd pull some strings and get the authorities looking for her, along with his Pinkerton men. Pete had called everyone in her address book, including her dressmaker and her dentist, before he'd tried Gussie.

"She took a *taxi!*" Pete looked around the room as if there might be a clue somewhere. "Moon should have brought her back. I ought to wring his scrawny neck. He says he had another pupil and she insisted on calling the cab rather than waiting."

"What cab company?" asked C.B.

"Ashby Taxi, but they claim they picked her up and dropped her in front of Stephenson's Department Store." Pete ran his hands though his hair. "The salesclerks there said they hadn't seen her."

"I'll look into it, old buddy." C.B. jotted a few notes on a pad and slowly got to his feet.

Pete, white-faced, saw C.B. out.

Tenny waited, hands folded, her blue nurse's uniform stained with sweat, tendrils of her hair escaping from her cap. Pete met her eyes, and saw concern for him. And love. And fear.

The first time he'd seen her, she'd been a will-o-the-wisp who enchanted him. And when he'd met the real, warm, flesh-and-blood girl, enchantment had turned to love. She'd made him forget his long dream of possessing the girl that everyone wanted. And then that girl, Swanee, had come to him, begging for help. He couldn't say no. Be careful what you wish for . . .

Was Swanee trying to make him suffer?

Tenny's hand hovered over Pete's back and finally the tips of her fingers stroked his shoulder. "I'm sure she's all right," she said. "She can do more than you think. Remember when I saw her walking? And you said it must have been a mistake? I know what I saw."

Tenny's face was a study in misery. If only he could hold her, comfort her, take comfort from her. But now he needed to be calm. He needed facts.

"Please go over it all again, Tenny. Please tell me everything you saw. I need to know. We might have missed something important."

Tenny repeated what she'd seen that morning: Swanee, skittering across the hall with only a slight limp, without her crutch. Breathlessly, she added, "The other day. After you'd left for the emergency, I left Baby in the bassinet beside her while I went to make supper. When I came back, the bassinet had overturned and she was reaching for the baby with her weak arm. When she saw me, that arm dropped."

Adrenaline coursed through Pete. "Why didn't you tell me all this sooner?"

A flush bloomed on Tenny's cheek. "I didn't want to seem jealous." Tears glistened in her eyes.

Pete stepped closer, longing to embrace her, but the absence of Swanee and the presence of Nola wedged itself firmly between them. He dropped his hands to his sides.

"Did *we* make her do this?" Tenny wavered, dabbing her face with a handkerchief. "Is she hiding out, playing a trick?"

"I doubt it," Pete said. "She doesn't care enough to make me suffer."

Tenny shook her head. "You mustn't say things like that. It'll just make it harder. I'm going to leave here after she's found."

Pete snapped upright. "No! I won't let you."

"Be realistic, Pete."

"My feelings for you are real." Nola or no Nola, he placed both hands on her shoulders and met her eyes.

She stared at the floor. "I'll wait until you find another nurse."

"Tenny, you can't leave me." He lifted her chin and made her look at him with her brimming eyes. A great gulping sob, and the tears coursed down her cheeks.

He leaned forward and took her face in his hands. "Tenny. I love you. I have loved you since you walked into that river and made me fall in the dirt."

She laughed then, laughed and choked and cried as the words slammed her, shattered her, a thousand tiny crack lines skittering through the walls she had built. She loved him so much, and she had to be strong, or she would never go. She caught her breath and swiped at her eyes with her sodden bit of cotton lawn.

He handed her his dry handkerchief, and it smelled of soap and his skin. "Pete, you'll forget me. Men do . . ."

Pete leaned forward, eyes angry. "Some men. Not me. Do you think it was only physical?"

"Your wife was sick . . ."

"How could you think that of me?" He spoke through his teeth, and he gripped her arm, hard. She winced, and he dropped his hand.

There was a charged silence as each searched the other's face. Pete spoke first. "All I could think of was saving her life. I thought she'd love me for that, and I was wrong. I think she has no love in her, except for herself. I wonder if she felt anything for the father of her child."

Tenny's eyes grew wide. "You're not Baby's father?"

"No." Pete's voice dropped to a whisper.

Tenny, stunned, sat quietly, waiting for more.

He began hesitantly, and then it all came spilling out. "We were in high school. Summertime, fooling around after a dance, down by the river, drinking hooch. She had too much to drink and I was going to walk her sober before she went home. We walked and walked and she got tired and we sat down on the riverbank all away from everybody. And she asked me to kiss her, and then . . ."

He shook his head. "She told me I was the first. I don't think so, looking back on it."

"What happened then?"

"Nothing. After that night she gave me the runaround, played the field. I was one of her admirers, a handy escort when she wanted one. I asked her to marry me. She turned me down."

"Oh, Pete."

"I never thought I'd see you again. When I met you for real, it was an awful situation, wasn't it? The delivery room."

Tenny had to smile. "I threw you out."

"And then you came to the hospital. Just when I thought you and I had a chance, she came to me in trouble and needed help. I stepped up to the plate. It was my big chance to be a hero. I thought she'd be so grateful she'd love me in return. I'd possess the girl I'd longed for. The girl all the other men wanted."

Tenny shook her head sadly. "You were good to her. She'll come back."

"She despises me," he said. "I can't live with that."

"But what if she comes back hurt? Sick? Would you turn her out?"

"She can go back to her parents. They can keep on spoiling her."

Tenny got up from her chair and went over to the window. She slid aside the curtain and looked out at the twilight, at the pale moon rising, at shadowy leaves floating down. In his anguish, Pete may have dismissed Swanee, but what if she came back sweet and loving? Divorce was a scandal.

And if Swanee didn't want a divorce? The girl she knew wouldn't leave without a fight. Tenny would be blamed. Would Miss Wells kick her out of school? Miss Verity would be so disappointed in her! And then what would happen to Shelley?

Without thinking, she blurted, "There's my sister—I swore I'd look after her—"

"Your sister? In Weedy Grove?" Pete raised his head.

"I haven't told you everything. But not now. I'll go back to the hospital to finish my training when all this is over. I can't stay here."

He met her eyes. "Finding Swanee doesn't mean you have to leave me. If we're patient . . ."

She looked away. She dared not risk not only heartbreak but her whole future. Being with Pete would mean the end of all her plans. Even if there was a divorce, would Pete really marry her when he saw the shack where she'd lived? When he knew she had a twin sister in the sanitarium in Milledgeville?

Men like him did not marry girls like her. That's what Enid had said.

"I'll stay two weeks." She walked out of the living room. Nola had made them some fried chicken and pole beans, but she had no appetite. She gathered an apple and some cheese and slipped out the back door.

Pete followed her out and called to her. Something in his tone made her stop. Half his face was in shadow, half lit by the porch light and the rising moon. "I'm sorry, but I have to leave for the hospital early, make up time I was home today. Can you come at six?"

She closed her eyes. She could.

Next morning, she fielded endless phone calls from people asking whether Swanee had come home, even Maxine Withers from the *Ashbyville Clarion*. She told Miss Withers to please call Mr. Elias Burkett for any comments. Nola came in, though it was not her regular day, saying that Miss 'Melia thought they could use a little extra help.

The baby fussed, fretful and out of sorts. Tenny wanted to leave the phone off the hook, but it might be someone calling with information about Swanee. The police did not call.

Tenny set about tidying Swanee's room. Surely she was just playing a wicked trick on Pete, maybe gone to see some friend at Essie Swift College.

Yesterday's nightgown and towels were already in the hamper, but Tenny found a slipper under a chair and went to place it in the closet. But why was the closet half empty? What had happened to her summer things and the new persimmon wool? Had her mother taken some for charity? She placed the slipper in the closet and searched for its mate.

Stooping to look under the bed, she picked up Swanee's Chinese letter box from the floor. Nothing was inside. No letters, no pens, no paper. She noticed a bit of crumpled paper under the dresser, along with the missing slipper. She pulled the slipper and the paper out and smoothed a half sheet of stationery. On it was written *My darling—*

The beginning of a love letter? A good-bye note? A suicide note? And who was Swanee's darling? She needed some air.

She stumbled down to the kitchen, smelling of starch and warm cotton. Baby happily babbled in the playpen while Nola swished the flatiron back and forth across Pete's white hospital jacket. Tenny reached down for the little girl. "We're going for a walk, Nola."

"Time you did somethin' besides stew," Nola said. "What they say about Miss Swanee?"

She shook her head, settling the baby on her hip. "Dr. Pete thinks she may be hiding out somewhere to aggravate him. He says her father's afraid she's gone mad and leaped in the river like her poor brother."

"That boy never done no such thing," Nola said to the ironing board. "Them white fellas throwed him in."

Shock raced through Tenny. "How do you know?"

Nola shook her head, not willing to say more. She gave the jacket underneath her hand an extra sprinkle. "Something mighty strange been going on here about Miss Swanee's clothes."

"What do you mean?"

"Some of them clothes been disappearing."

"Clothes *disappearing?*"

"That's just what I say, Miss Tenny." Nola repeated patiently. "Don't you think I know every stitch she wear? One dress gone every week, and shimmy too, and hose, and shoes, and . . ."

"Why didn't you say something?"

Nola shook her head. "She ain't complained. For all I know she giving them away. She keep saying she never gone rise from her bed again."

Her new dress gone, her summer clothes. Had Swanee been plotting all along to disappear? How could any mother go off and leave her baby?

"Nola, I really ought to tell Dr. Pete." Yet she hated to try to reach him at the hospital.

"You tell him when he come back," said Nola soothingly. "Let him have a bit of peace, and get your walk." She hung up the ironed jacket and straightened it, satisfied with her work.

Tenny took the wicker buggy to the back porch and bumped it down the back steps, then went back for her precious cargo. The warm morning had cooled, a breeze had blown in, and she tucked a blanket around the little one.

She rolled the buggy briskly down the sidewalk, noting the darkening sky and the clouds building to the northwest. She dismissed the weather. She needed to think about the disappearing clothes, Swanee's deceptions about her ability, a note that had begun *My Darling*. If her patient had been smuggling clothes out, she had to have had an accomplice.

Her mother? No. Miss Clara thought Pete was good for Swanee. Miss Gussie? Impossible. That left none other than Mr. Moon. Surely not.

Who else had disappeared? Ned Fletcher, for one. He had plenty of reasons to disappear.

She waited at the corner for the trolley and three cars to pass, then crossed the street, bumping over the trolley rails, heading toward the park. Her brother Byron had disappeared.

She remembered the fight between Pa and Byron.

They'd been out in the dirt yard under the noonday sun, grappling and whacking at each other, and Byron yelling, "You're not my father! You're not my father!"

This was right after Ma died.

She remembered Byron afterward, sitting in a kitchen chair weeping, while Merry cleaned his bruised and bloody face. Pa, though half a foot shorter than Byron, was muscular and strong and had had quite a fist on him, and was mean-tempered when he'd been drinking. She did not know men cried.

She shook her head to clear it. Mr. Moon carried a large carpetbag everywhere he went, supposedly for books and papers. He could have carried out items of Swanee's clothing over weeks. But *he* had not disappeared.

Thunder rumbled in the distance, and she smelled rain right before a fat drop hit her nose. She wheeled the buggy around for home. She broke into a jog as the drops fell faster, and she felt the moonstone from Lyman Stratton bouncing against her chest. She needed its protection more than ever. She grasped it.

The puzzle pieces that had been jumbled now fit together. She knew who Baby's father was. And why Swanee had gone.

But how could she tell Pete?

# Chapter 63

Behind the closed door of his room at the Dunnigan Hotel, taken in the name of Mr. Curtis Wyckham, Swanee threw herself into Ned's arms. "It's been so long. Ned. It's been so long."

Ned closed his eyes and inhaled her sweet scent, the Black Narcissus perfume of the Swanee he remembered. Her body molded to him, what he could feel of it through the damn costume. He opened his eyes and found himself kissing an old lady. He pulled himself away from the woman he'd dreamed about every sodden, sticky, booze-soaked night they'd been apart.

"Can't you take off that get-up?"

She stared at him and tugged at the gray wig. "I almost got caught changing in the ladies' room at the train station."

He closed his hand over hers. "Forget it. I appreciate the effort."

"Just for you, love." She shimmied out of her baggy dress and un-strapped the padding around her middle. Then she fluffed her hair and, wearing only her peach teddy, struck a pose like a calendar girl. "Is that better? Come to Peaches."

Ned was tempted. Oh, how he longed for her body. But there was something he'd been meaning to do ever since the night he'd tried to save Eben Shackley's life out there in France.

He tilted Swanee's chin and gave her a long, slow kiss. "There's a score I have to settle before our train leaves for Tampa. Here's something to keep you happy." Grinning wickedly, he set a pack of cigarettes and a bottle of bootleg Scotch on the bedside table. "I'll bet you're tired of the tea and toast the good doctor gives you."

"Ned—"

"I'll be back, doll. Shouldn't be long. Wear something pretty for me."

He strode out of the room wearing his duster. He'd risked his freedom for the woman he loved, and now she looked ridiculous. Sure, she needed the disguise, but it gave him the willies. Pretending to be Curtis and his old mama checking in! When he came back, she'd look like she was supposed to, and they'd have a real hot roll before they got out of town on the straight shot to Tampa.

He wanted to get out to Weedy Grove where he could catch the old man in the fields. He didn't want to confront him in the house, where there might be some women to mess things up. He wanted him outside, where God could listen in.


Ned looked for the old plantation house at the end of the long drive, remembering the big front porch and a swing, where he and Eben Shackley, when Eben was nine and he was eight, had tried to see how high they could go, and the rope had broken and they'd crashed. Unhurt, they'd run off and filled up on plums from the sweet plum trees in the yard.

Good buddies, they'd been, before old Shackley sent Eben away to boarding school at twelve. They'd met again in France and picked up the easy camaraderie. Eben had told him a secret when he was dying, after Ned had told his own secret to him. Brothers in war and brothers in blood.

Ned parked the car in front of the plantation house, jumped out, and goggled at the sight. Where the white-columned structure had stood, there was nothing but a burnt-out ruin.

"Who the hell are you?"

Ned froze at the voice. He hadn't heard the footsteps behind him.

When he turned, smiling bitterly, he faced a shotgun.

He put up his hands. "You don't know who I am—Pops?"

Shackley scowled. "Pops? You better show some respect, asshole. Who are you?"

Ned felt his own Smith & Wesson beneath his trenchcoat, nudging his ribs. Sweat snaked down his side. He'd won the .38 Special in a poker game.

"Pops." He sneered. "It's the name you call your father, right?"

Shackley hesitated for only a minute, but the minute was enough to let Ned know his mother had told him the truth. "My son's dead," Shackley snarled.

Ned took a step forward. "One of your sons is dead. The other one you didn't claim, the other one you let another man raise. And now the other one is back for a piece of the action."

"Jesus," the old man said, sweat breaking out on his forehead. "You ain't Em's boy."

"Oh, yes. Em's boy," Ned said. "Byron Chance. Or is it Byron Shackley? How does that sound? All I want is a fair share. How about the gold coins, Pop?"

"What gold coins?"

"The ones Eben told me about. The ones you stole from your wife because you didn't want her to have any money. The ones you told the law were stolen, and all our cabins got searched, our back yards dug up. They were in a cabin, all right. Your camp house."

Shackley raised the shotgun, face dangerously red. "You just get right on outta here, boy, and don't bother me with them lies. Who knows how many men Em took up with? You ain't none of mine."

Ned clenched his fists. "My ma was faithful as they come. She told me on her deathbed how you surprised her one night after they'd come here, after our mule got out and Pa left her home alone to track him down. You let that mule out, didn't you? You came over and forced yourself on her. She was a good woman and you tainted her."

"She was a lying bitch, was Emily."

Gritting his teeth in rage, Ned kicked upward with his right foot and sent Shackley's gun flying. He drew his pistol.

"I'm here to get what you cheated my folks out of," he said, scrambling to get between Shackley and the gun. He looked around to see if anyone was coming to help, but the yard was empty.

Shackley glared at him. "Damn Negroes runned off."

Ned shrugged. "Looks like it's just you and me, old man."

Shackley burst out laughing. "Holy shit, boy! That damn gold is long gone. This place been losing money ever since '19."

The laughter was forced, Ned knew. The old man was scared. "Cut the bullshit."

Shackley bolted, but Ned sprang after him, caught him, and wrestled him to the ground. He sat on Shackley's back, twisting his arms behind him. "I think I'll just beat you senseless," he said, cracking the butt of the gun against Shackley's head. He raised the pistol again.

A field hand in dirty overalls appeared out of nowhere, taking in the scene. He was unarmed and looked frightened. Ned wasn't worried. "Get out of here, if you know what's good for you."

"Pick," Shackley yelled, struggling. "Get me Ace and Lulu. Now."

"Shut up!" Ned fired into the ground once, not far from the field hand, and the man took off running. "What the hell was that about, Shackley?"

That got him a sneer. "Oh, I ain't your Poppa anymore?"

"You ought to claim me," Ned said. "I've got all your good points."

"I told him to get the horses ready," Shackley said. "You want the gold, we got to get there. Ain't no road to speak of."

Ned considered. He could shoot him here, but the cabin was a good way from the house. He'd be better off shooting him at the cabin. It would take longer for anyone to find him. At least this way he had a chance at getting the gold.

Ned glanced toward the barn, some fifty feet away, behind the pump house and a wagon shed. He kept his .38 aimed at Shackley's head. "Don't be a wise guy," he said. "I was the best shot in the Army."

The hand named Pick led out two animals, saddled—a big side-stepping black horse, not the white one Ned remembered from years before, and a small brown filly that tossed her head, chafing at the bit.

"Well, son," Shackley said with emphasis on the last word, "I'll ride Ace, and by God, you'll take—"

"I'll take the big horse," Ned interrupted.

Shackley rubbed his chin "Ace's a one-man horse. Hard to handle. Lulu's a steady mount."

"You got no more horses?"

"Sold 'em when I sold the cows."

Shackley could spew hate all he wanted, but Ned still had the gun. He forced Shackley to take Lulu, and he mounted the big black. "Hee-ya!" Shackley cried, and Lulu took off as though the Devil himself was chasing her.

Ace kicked and reared, trying to shake Ned off. Ned realized that Shackley had planned it this way. What Shackley didn't know was that Ned knew horses. Learned them in Florida, at the ranch where he'd stayed.

He managed to get the big horse calmed down, but by this time Shackley was long gone, heading for the camp house, where he'd either grab the coins and melt deep into the woods or stand and defend them with another gun. It was a crapshoot.

Or he might ride on, hide, and wait for Ned to search the house and then ambush him. Ned didn't think Shackley was that smart.

# Chapter 64

Ned cut through the swamp. Shackley wouldn't have risked his horse falling in a hole or getting snakebit; no, he was traveling fast and he'd go the long way around.

He led the unwilling horse across the high ground, pushing beards of Spanish moss aside, dodging a cottonmouth. Cold, green-brown water that smelled of rotten leaves seeped into his boots. He cursed and swore with every squelch that he'd buy a pair of the finest leather boots in Florida. That gold was his revenge, and he intended to spend every last bit.

With luck, no one would find Shackley's body until Ned was safely out of the country.

The ground rose out of the marsh. Through the trees he saw a clearing and then the cabin, and the little mare tied outside. He had to stay cool and work fast. He crept up to a side window, keeping below the sight line. He peered in and saw the wallboard pried away.

Ned darted around to the front of the cabin and, pistol drawn, met Shackley when he stepped out onto the porch with a cloth bag tucked under his arm.

Shackley froze and Ned fired at his chest. The older man crumpled with a groan, tried to rise. Ned walked up to fire again. The old man snarled. "Had your pretty little sister too, I did. Hot little piece of—"

Ned, raging, fired a bullet into his head. Blood gushed across the boards of the porch. Damn. Damn. Damn. Was it Tenny? Was that why she'd come to Ashbyville? Had she run away?

Ned grabbed the bag, unwrapped the strings, and picked out a twenty-dollar Double Eagle. He re-tied the bag and headed toward Shackley's horse, money bag tied to his belt.

Lulu was as bad as Ace. She bared her teeth when Ned tried to mount her, and Ned lowered his voice and gentled the horse. He still needed to get back to the hotel, shed the duster, change clothes, don a wig, shave his beard, and then catch the train out of Ashbyville, heading to Tampa, where he'd catch a steamer to South America. It would make a stop at Cuba. Couldn't be helped.

Back and forth they went, the horse's eyes rolling. Finally, tightening the reins painfully, Ned swung himself up on the mare, which squealed in protest.

"Hey!" A voice rang out from the woods.

Ned stared at a scrawny little man, rifle in hand, emerging from the path leading to the still. *Oh God.* Jubal Chance, his Pa, who didn't know him in this get-up.

"Who the devil are you? What are you doin' on that horse? Where's Shackley?"

Ned grabbed his pistol and fired in Jubal's direction, over the old man's head. Jubal had taught him to shoot. Taught him a lot. And that old man had loved his mama. For a moment Ned's throat welled, and then he gave the mare a vicious kick.

The horse bolted ahead. A moment later a shot cracked behind him. His left arm stung like fire, but the horse was tearing ahead, hoofs throwing up clods of dirt. Three rifle shots rang out, fading as the horse gained speed.

The horse fought him when they neared the barn, wanting to go home, but Ned spurred her past it, right up to his waiting car. Lulu took the bit in her teeth, almost bucking him off before he could slide down. Freed, the bay mare streaked away.

The burned-out house mocked him with its charred beams, its smoke-streaked columns. The house he'd one day intended to own was a devastation. The yard and fields were deserted. No one tried to stop him; no one called out, no one challenged him. But Jubal might be going after the law.

Gripping his bleeding arm, Ned had one thought: get on that train. Over the rutty road, each jounce of the car shot pain through his arm. He gritted his teeth. There was whisky back at the hotel.

He parked in the alley behind the hotel. He made it to the rear entrance without notice, but a bellhop, with a double-take, asked if he needed assistance. Ned mumbled and pretended to be drunk, staying near the wall to hide the bloody arm. He ducked into a stairwell and stumbled up four flights of steps to the floor where Swanee waited.

He banged on the door. "Sugar, quick!"

The dark door swung away. "Good God, what's happened?"

"Whisky." He lurched into the room, closed the door behind him, and sank onto a chair.

His blurry gaze followed Swanee and she seemed to dip and sway on her way to fetch the whisky; her peach velvet dressing gown caressed her pale breasts. She had meant to please him. But damn, she was so slow!

With a trembling hand, she brought him a glass filled with amber liquid, her features swimming behind it. Where was Gussie? Gussie would look after him.

"What should I do?" Swanee's face blurred.

"Haven't you seen anybody shot before?" His mouth felt thick, unable to form words.

"Of course not. You need a doctor."

He was cold, shivering and shaking. "Get me a blanket and some rags. Got to stop this bleeding." He began to struggle out of the trenchcoat.

She silently held the coat while he edged himself out of it, sweat beading his cold forehead.

Still moving too slowly, she brought towels and tucked them under his arm. The blood trickled from his wound, soaking the towels. Red drops spattered the thin carpet.

He pointed to the glass. "More."

She handed him another glass and he gulped it down, burning in his gullet. Damn, if only he could stop shivering.

He had to stop shivering and bleeding so they could make that train. His mind felt like oatmeal and the woman wouldn't come into focus. He needed a clean shirt and he needed a wash, yes, he needed a wash, and damn, he remembered what she needed to do.

"Tear up some of my undershirts and wind them around my arm. Tight." He would do it himself but only one arm worked right. He could find a doc in Tampa, but they had to make that train. He told her what to do as slowly as possible so she would understand.

She stared at him in horror, as if just realizing what trouble they were in, and then she began to cry. It was the only time in his life he'd ever seen her cry.

"Get the damn undershirt."

"I can't." She stared at her hand. Why was she staring at her hand? "I don't know how."

"For the love of God, Swanee. Give it to me."

She handed him one and he held it in his teeth and tore. She wound it round and round, and by this time sweat was running down his forehead in fat rivulets. The bullet must be still lodged in his arm.

Swanee's voice trembled, desperate. "I need to call Pete. He'll know what to do."

"It's all over if you do, girl," Ned said, his breath coming in shallow rasps.

"You're going to bleed to death."

"No—hell—I'm not," he said. "We're going to get out of here."

She stared at him for a moment and grabbed the telephone.

He tried to get up, to stop her, but his legs did not obey him, and he fell back. He cursed and asked for more whiskey. She spoke into the mouthpiece before she gave him the whiskey.

"Help's coming," Swanee whispered, eyes large, chest heaving.

The useless bitch was going to ruin everything. Ned lurched from bed to dresser. "Can't stay. Got to leave."

"It's all over, Ned."

"Got to rest a minute, then I'm going." He crashed to the bed again, panting.

Swanee stood back as Ned, groggy from the whiskey and pain, tried to get up. He heaved himself from the bed and fell thickly to the floor, twitching. He took a gulp of air, trying to clear his head. Maybe she could be useful after all. "I've got a plan," he said. "Come close and listen."

Tenny felt she had no choice but to go with Pete to the Dunnigan Hotel to meet the ambulance.

He'd asked her to come, and since Nola was there, she didn't have the excuse of staying with the baby.

When they arrived, rather than wait for the elevator, he charged up the stairs, pounded on the door of room 439, tried the knob, and then rattled it.

"Swanee! Are you in there?" Pete yelled. "Open up!"

In answer, Pete heard the crack of a gun. He gave a yell and shouldered into the door, but it was heavy and locked fast.

While life-saving seconds melted away, Tenny scurried downstairs to get the manager with keys. When the door was finally opened, Pete rushed over to the blood-soaked man on the floor and knelt by him. The gun lay near his fingers, and flakes of plaster floated down from the ceiling.

"I'd just as soon not call the cops if he's not dead," the manager said. "Bad publicity. I won't charge extra to clean up the mess."

Pete looked up. "He's not dead."

The manager looked relieved until Pete said, "The police will need to know, but I'll call them after we get this man to the hospital. Please leave the room like it is for the time being."

He applied a tourniquet and managed to stop the bleeding. He gave him an injection of morphine and dressed the gunshot wound. Tenny brought blankets to warm the patient, and then took a damp cloth and wiped away the sweat and blood and dirt from his face.

Her heart, already racing, took another thump when she saw the black-purple stain on the cloth. Hair dye. She looked closely at Ned's face. She traced the outlines of his features with her fingers, slowly, tentatively. And then she saw her brother.

"Byron," she whispered.

His eyes fluttered open. "Tenny?" he murmured. "Need a nap . . . and then I'll take you and Shelley to the creek . . ."

"Byron, why'd you do it?" Her voice was hoarse, breaking. The questions she'd been holding for months, for years, tumbled out. "Why'd you leave us? Why'd you pretend you didn't know me at the mill?" Pete laid a hand on her shoulder. She looked back at him and shook her head, silently asking him not to speak, and he stepped back.

Ned blinked again, seeming to come into the moment. "I had to be somebody else," he said. "I'm only half y' brother. Ma was dead. Would have stayed for her. Pa . . . not my father."

"But who . . ." A cold chill crept over her. "Shackley," she said dully.

"He won't bother you anymore," Ned said.

Tenny sat back in shock. "You know what he did to me? How?"

Ned nodded.

She began to weep then, and laid her warm cheek close to his cold one. "You were going to kill yourself—I might never have seen you, talked to you—"

He sounded as if he was trying to laugh. "Better than watching me go to the chair."

The hall outside echoed with the clattering of a rolling bed and the voice of the hotel manager. The door opened and an ambulance crew entered with the stretcher on wheels.

Tenny grasped his fingers, not seeing "Ned" any more. "Byron. You did what I couldn't do. I wanted to kill that monster."

He blinked, tried to smile. "You're better than me, little sister. You were always my conscience."

She choked back a sob. "Don't die, Byron, just when I've found you."

"Not up to me." One eye closed in a slow wink, then he closed both eyes, and then they took him away.

Was she really a better person? If she hadn't hesitated back at the hospital? No. She knew she was meant to save, not to kill.

Pete circled her waist, held her close in a sideways hug. "Are you all right?"

She nodded, longing for him to take her in his arms. She knew he wouldn't. Not here. The room door was still open and he looked distracted. "Did you ever see Swanee?" he asked. "Was she here?"

Tenny walked around the room. There was a faint smell of perfume in the bathroom, away from the gunshot smell and the blood and the disinfectant. She leaned over and picked up a curled white feather from the floor. "She had a hat trimmed with this kind of feather," Tenny said.

"She was gone before we got here. You were focused on saving . . . Ned."

"So she's run out on him, too," Pete said bitterly. "If I thought she really loved him, I could have forgiven her. But she cut and ran when he needed her."

"Maybe she panicked," Tenny said. "Maybe she'll come back when she knows he's alive. Maybe they made a plan."

Pete shook his head. "They did make a plan, and it went wrong. Where would she go without him? And she left that gun here. Why?"

"To shoot his way out?"

Pete shook his head. "No. I think she wanted him to kill himself. She locked the door behind her." He knelt and packed up his medical bag and used a hotel towel to wrap Ned's bloody shirt and the blood-soaked rags that Ned had used to bind his arm.

He glanced up at the hole in the ceiling. "I think we came just in time. He was too shaky to hold the gun steady."

"I know," Tenny said, burying her face against Pete's chest, against sandalwood and sweat and blood. They held each other close, and she wondered at her resolution to part from him. She did not see how she could do it, and she did not see how they could stay together.

They walked down the back steps to Pete's car, not wanting to parade through the lobby in bloody clothes. Pete would have to change his shirt and Tenny her apron before they went to the hospital.

On the way out, Pete stopped by a phone booth and made a call.

Gussie hung up the phone. So Ned had been shot, and he'd been taken to the hospital. He'd lost a good deal of blood, but Pete thought his vital signs were good. All she knew is that she had to go see Ned, speak to him one last time. Was Pete telling the whole truth? If Ned was going to die, she had to say good-bye. She wanted to believe he had loved her. She didn't want to give that up.

Pete had said he killed Shackley and was shot in turn by a sharecrop-per who was out hunting rabbits. He'd told her Ned hadn't been able to talk much, except to Tenny, and then he lost consciousness. And Swanee had eluded them again.

Gussie didn't care about Swanee. She hoped she would disappear for good. Poor Pete. There was something between him and that little nurse, something ever since that day on the river. Strange that she had not put all those pieces together until now.

Surely she'd be allowed to see Ned at the hospital. Why not? She was his wife, as far as Ashbyville was concerned. No one outside the family knew about Sarah, and no one was telling.

But there was Gracie, and she'd have to find someone to keep her, now that Trevania had gone. She had appointments for two Christmas family portraits and one glowing bride-to-be. She began calling clients, rescheduling.

She told Lyman she wouldn't be available to help him in the shop for a day or so. When she revealed what had happened, he told her to take as many days as she needed. And then he'd whooped to hear that Arno Shackley was dead.

And Ned had confessed to being Byron Chance. Officially, she was no longer married. Still, she had to see him.

"No," her mother said. "I won't mind Gracie for you to go now. He's probably in surgery. I'll talk to Emmett and find out when you can see him."

Gussie had walked to her mother's in the chilly weather with Gracie in the baby carriage, needing to do something, anything, to get out of those four walls.

"But that's the main reason I need to be there!" Gussie wailed. "He's my husband! Any good wife would be at her husband's side at a time like this!"

She didn't like her mother's calm reply. "Augusta, was he ever at your side when you needed him?"

Gussie looked down at Gracie, who had stopped her contented playing and was looking up at the two adults with a block in her hand, her tiny face squinched up as if trying to understand the raised voices.

"Mama, don't be mean."

Her mother adjusted her glasses, then took them off and wiped them. "I'm just trying to make you see things as they are, and not what you want them to be." She put them back on her nose and reached out to smooth Gussie's curls. "He's not a good man, child. When he recovers, he'll go to jail, and then to trial, and then to prison, if he's lucky. If he's not lucky, those gangsters or the electric chair will get him."

"Oh, Mama! Don't say that!" Ned had read poetry to her, given her flowers and pearls, taken her on flights among the stars.

"He ran down that boy," her mother said.

Gussie broke down and sobbed.

Her mother fetched her a cup of chamomile tea. "Now, go lie down in your room. I have phone calls to make."

Gussie, who hadn't slept well ever since Ned had deserted her, finished the tea while her mother talked on the telephone. Then she went upstairs, changed into a robe, and lay atop the covers. She closed her eyes because they were gritty and tired.

Her mother's call jolted her out of a dreamless sleep. She rose, splashed her face with water, and combed her hair as best she could. Somehow, she was not surprised to find Henry Benedict waiting in the parlor.

"How can I help?" he asked.

"I'm not sure." She felt secretly comforted.

Gussie's mother bustled in with coffee on a tray and set it down. "I brought a cup for you too, dear. She nodded to Gussie. "Everyone's out looking for Swanee. Nobody at the hotel has seen her. They say the person who signed for the room was with an older woman."

Gussie gratefully took a cup of the hot coffee and doctored it with sugar and cream. "Did you hear from Uncle Mac?"

"You can go to the hospital tomorrow," her mother said. "The police are trying to question him. He's called that man in Savannah to get Ned a lawyer."

"Wyckham," Gussie mumbled.

"Swanee," her mother sighed. "I don't know what Elias is going to do if he finds her."

Henry set his mug on the tray. "Let's go search. Anybody have any ideas where she might be hiding? I know the police are checking the trains, as well as hotels and cafes. Burkett's people are checking her friends."

"Let's go to the river," Gussie said. "Lots of places to hide there. Maybe she found a boat."

"Somebody would have seen her at a bridge," Henry said. "Anyhow, how'd she get around? Is she on foot? Strong enough to drive? Does she have a car? Is that Moon still helping her?"

"They're watching him, for sure," Gussie said.

Henry and Gussie took Papa's Hupmobile to the river. The river road yielded nothing but regrets.

Gussie sighed in frustration. "She made elaborate plans to leave, Henry. Pete said she'd been smuggling out her clothes for weeks, and she and Ned must have worked it all out by letters that Moon mailed for her." Her voice turned bitter. "She went to a lot of trouble to make this escape. She was determined, I tell you. She wouldn't have left Ned to die."

"They said he'd tried to shoot himself."

"That's what he'd have you believe." At the thought of his many deceptions, her chest constricted in pain. Were all the sweet things he'd told her lies? She shivered, and Henry draped his arm around her shoulder. It felt comforting.

"Gussie, did you see any of this coming?"

"I put the blindfold on myself. There was always something that crackled in the air between them. It made me horribly jealous. *I'd* never had that kind of effect on Ned."

Henry was silent, and a flicker of awareness passed across his features.

"What is it, Henry?"

"I saw them together in a café, down near my neighborhood, before she married Pete Godwin. They were pretty thick."

"Why didn't you tell me?" Gussie's voice went up an octave.

He cleared his throat. "I didn't know you that well then, and I didn't want to hurt you. It wasn't my business anyway."

Gussie sniffed back tears. Why had she been such a fool? Ned had been so mysterious—like the man who comes out of a shadow in a dream laced with rushing rivers and singing rocks, a dream of dark woods and the smell of earth. A dream not civilized or tame and now forever lost to her. Ned, an earthquake that heaved and buckled the road to her destination.

Henry—oh, dear Henry. He took his handkerchief and blotted her eyes and drew her to him. She laid her head on his chest. "Hush, Gussie," he said. "It's going to be all right."

She took one last glance at the river before they pulled away.

# Chapter 65

No one paid much attention to the old lady in the train depot checking a carpetbag into a locker. Swanee hobbled out past a uniformed guard and caught a trolley to a street from which she walked to a once-proud Victorian house, not too far from where she'd made a rendezvous with Ned at his boarding house.

This once-elegant Victorian with its gingerbread trim had been carved up into four apartments, and in one of those apartments lived Enid Smith Barlow's mother. It hadn't been too hard to convince them with a little ready cash to shelter her for a while. Father would never think of looking in Enid's mother's humble apartment.

Of course, that meant letting them in on the plan. She could be sure that they'd keep their mouths shut until she and Ned got safely away. She'd promised them more money when she got to South America. She had their address, but they'd have to reach her through Professor Moon. Only he would know their whereabouts, except possibly that Wyckham man.

Ned would recover; they'd make the contacts he'd promised. They'd prosper. They'd have a wonderful social life there. She'd already learned Spanish in school. Life in Buenos Aires wouldn't be hard at all.

Now for the next problem: the Ashbyville station would be watched. They'd take the risk of driving to another station on the line, but they'd need a car. Ned's was in the hotel's parking garage. The polic would most likely be watching it. Even if she could sneak her own roadster away from her house, it was too conspicuous.

There was one other option. Enid and her mother had hung on to Dr. Satterfield Barlow's old Ford, despite having to sell their house and most of its contents to support themselves after the money had run out. Swanee would rent the car from them. She'd pay enough to cover tickets for the two women to take the train to Irwinton and bring the borrowed car home.

Surprisingly, when she made the offer, they balked. Maybe they were afraid they wouldn't get the car back. Swanee doubled her offer. She wondered if Enid would finish nursing school.

Outside the hospital, the stars shone faintly against a new-moon stark black sky, punctuated only by light spilling from a few windows of the upper stories.

Swanee huddled in the chill shadows wearing her old lady disguise, a gray wool cocoon coat with tatty fur trim that reached up to her gray cloche hat with white feathers pulled low about her face.

She clenched her jaws and willed herself to be patient, shivering whenever she reckoned their chances of success. An ambulance pulling up to the door would be the end of everything.

It was nearly two o'clock in the morning. At this hour the halls, Enid had assured her, would be virtually deserted. Enid would wheel Ned down the hall, descend by the creaky service elevator, and use the ramp where Swanee waited nearby with the old Model T.

She flinched when she heard cracking in the shrubbery and shrank closer to the side of the building. It must have been an animal, for the big hospital doors swung open.

Swanee went weak with relief when she saw the rolling chair silhouetted against the light. As they came closer, Ned appeared to be unconscious or dozing, head lolling to one side.

"What's wrong?" Swanee whispered hoarsely, heart in her throat.

"Gave him an extra dose of morphine," Enid said. "Wanted to make sure he'd be in no pain for a while." She smoothed the hair off his forehead. "He'll be able to walk when he comes to."

Swanee glared in jealousy, but Enid didn't notice or didn't care. She gave Swanee a package containing morphine pills, a bottle of saline solution, and a roll of gauze, along with instructions on how and when to change the dressings.

Enid helped to settle Ned in the car and hurried back in as they drove away. Swanee headed out past the river, past the city limits of Ashbyville, onto the dark and rutty dirt road that would take them to Irwinton, where they'd leave the car and catch the night train to Savannah. Fresh, cold air whistled through the window gaps, and Ned snored in the seat beside her. The sky above was black as marble with sharp pinpoints of stars.

Wyckham would find them a place where Ned could fully recover, and then they'd be on their way to freedom. Surely Ned had not done all those things they said he'd done. Not *her* Ned. While she and Ned were making their fortune abroad, the lawmen would find the real culprits, and then she and Ned would return to Ashbyville and the mill, and Ned could see his star rise with Swanee alongside him.

They'd left a mess, but other people could clean it up. They always had.

# Chapter 66

When Tenny came to work that morning, she heard Baby cooing and hurried up to her, surprised to find Pete wasn't up. His bedroom door was ajar. She peeked in and saw that he was asleep, his glasses on the bedside table. She ached to touch him. She resolutely went to the baby.

The little one dressed and fed, Tenny retrieved the morning paper from the front porch and scanned the front page.

MAN ARRESTED IN SHACKLEY MURDER. Her heart leapt to her throat. But Ned was in the hospital. Could you arrest someone in the hospital?

*Jubal Chance, a farmer*, it said. They had arrested Pa!

She waited until Nola came before she changed clothes and took the trolley to the courthouse. She found that Pa was in the county jail and she couldn't see him until tomorrow. She swore she'd get him a lawyer; she knew he hadn't killed Arno Shackley.

She told the deputies that lots of people had reasons to kill the plantation owner and Pa was born again. She didn't want to tell the sheriff that

Byron had done the killing, but how to get Pa off the hook? Maybe Miss Gussie's father could help.

Back at work, once again in her uniform, she joined Nola in the kitchen to cap baby bottles. In the hall, Pete shouted at the phone, hung up, went to his study, and slammed the door.

Her heart sank. Now was not the time to ask favors, but she walked to the study door and knocked. A long moment passed while cars went by and bottles clinked as Nola put them away in the icebox.

A chair scraped. Pete opened the door, gazing at her with red-rimmed, puffy eyes. Reeking of sweat and whiskey, he stroked the stubble on his chin, and his eyes drank her in agonizingly.

She swallowed. "I need a favor."

He reached out an unsteady hand and tucked a strand of hair behind her ear. "Anything. But first you need to know what's happened."

She caught her breath and went cold. "They found her?"

Pete rubbed his forehead. "Ned Fletcher escaped from the hospital during the night. He'd have needed help, and she's my best guess."

"Wasn't there a guard?"

Pete shrugged. "He hasn't been charged with anything yet, and he's not in any condition to leave."

"There must've been somebody on the inside," Tenny said. "He couldn't walk." She immediately thought of Enid. Swanee's friend from the past, a friend she'd been corresponding with.

"Let me do the worrying," Pete said, and reached for her hand. "What do you need?"

Tenny's face warmed and she stepped back. "I need to get my father out of jail. Do you think Judge Pemberton would help me? The sheriff thinks Pa killed Shackley, but I know Ned killed him. Nobody'd believe me, because the man they arrested is my father."

"Your *father*?" Pete blinked in astonishment.

She smiled sadly. "Jubal Chance is my father." She held out the newspaper to him.

Pete took it and scanned the article. "Well, I'll be damned," he said. "It says your father claims he found the body?"

"Yes. He's the one that shot at Ned trying to escape after he killed Shackley."

Pete shook his head. "Did you believe your father wanted to kill Ned?"

"I believe Pa put that bullet in Ned right where he wanted it."

She pointed to the photograph of the river nymph on the wall. "I was on the way to Ashbyville after I ran away from a sharecropper's shack Arno Shackley owned. He owned us too."

There was a moment of awkward silence as Pete took in what that meant.

"I'll do whatever I can to help," he finally said. "I need to keep busy to keep from going crazy." He lowered his voice to be sure Nola wouldn't overhead. "You know I love you."

"I'd better go," Tenny said, choking. "Thank you for helping."


At that moment, Gussie was lying on her mother's best velvet sofa breathing a horrible smell. She coughed, and then she opened her eyes to her sister Jessie's voice. "How very Southern of you to faint, Gussie dear."

"Hush," said Mama, waving the bottle of smelling salts.

"Aren't you glad he's gone?" asked Jessie. "Wasn't that rich, escaping from the hospital?"

"I wanted to talk to him," Gussie wailed through her gasps. She batted away the salts. "I was ready to go to the hospital when the phone rang!"

She looked up at Mama, Jessie, and Velma, who'd made her a cup of hot black tea with plenty of sugar and milk. Now Velma told her in no uncertain terms to drink it down. Gussie complied. The steaming, sweet brew soothed her.

When the dizzy spell had passed, she sat up, her fiery energy seeping back. "I'll chase him down. I'll go after him. I'll bet he went to Cuba! He was there before."

"Cuba? Why? That Max character will look for him there, won't he?" Jessie said.

"There's no extradition treaty, and he knows his way around."

"Calm down, Gussie," her mother urged. "The police will find him. They can find steamship records, passenger lists. No doubt they're checking all his old haunts."

"Or they might just say good riddance to bad rubbish, why bother?" Gussie said bitterly.

Gussie's mother laid a hand on Gussie's shoulder. "I think Elias Burkett didn't like it that Ned took both his money and his daughter. He'll be furious with Swanee, but he'll find her."

"So Swanee's with him?" Oh, more horrors!

"So we think. He had help to leave the hospital. In his condition, he couldn't have done it by himself. That's what Pete says."

"Where's Gracie?" she asked, cold to the bone. Had they kidnapped her too?

Gussie's mother smiled. "She's fine, in the kitchen with Velma. I ought to have little Baby come over too. Pete's in a state, and he might like some peace and quiet."

It came to Gussie, then, that the two girls were both Ned's daughters, half-sisters. They might as well get to know one another as cousins. It had been Ned that night in the fog, looking up at her window. He wanted to say good-bye to them, because he knew he might never come back. As wrong-headed as he was, he still had a ghost of a feeling for her and their precious child.

And she didn't want him dead.

The next day, Tenny's spirits soared. Ballistics tests had proved it was Ned's gun and not Jubal Chance's gun that had killed Shackley. Tenny would be able to collect him from the jail and take him home—if she could find a car.

And so she asked another favor.

"Are you sure you can drive the car?" Pete asked.

She nodded. "Bo Paul Hunter taught me. I was afraid I might need to drive—" She didn't say *drive Swanee*.

Pete nodded, and a shadow crossed his face.

"I'll let Pa drive it to Weedy Grove," Tenny said. "He'll like that. If Nola can look after Baby, I'll be back by evening."

Poor Baby, growing up without a mother. Should Tenny find a way to stay for the sake of the child? No, it was impossible.

"My mother really needs Nola today, but Aunt Belinda's offered to keep Baby," Pete said. "I can get a ride somewhere if I need one." Now he gave her a half-smile. "Does your father know what you've done with your life?" he asked. "Have you kept in touch?"

Tenny shook her head. "I've been writing letters to Mrs. Brown, the pastor's wife. She and Brother Jethro have been good to my family."

"So now you want to take your old man home? Why?"

"I want to see my folks. I want to tell them what's happened. I don't know what they're going to do now, what's going to happen with Shackley's place. I want them to know I'm here and that I'll try to help."

"Maybe I can help too," Pete said mysteriously.

Over her protests, he cleaned up and drove her to the courthouse, where he collected Jubal Chance from the jail and brought him out to the car.

Her father craned into the Buick. "I don't need no nurse. Where's my daughter? He turned to Pete. "You said she was here."

"Pa, I'm your daughter. I'm Tenny, and we're taking you home." She looked down at the blue uniform and laughed.

"Lord preserve us," he said, blinking his old eyes. "You ain't my little Tenny." Disbelief crossed his crusty old features.

"Yeah, Pa, it's me." She took off her cap and unpinned her bun and her half-pale, half-brown hair dropped past her shoulders.

The old man blinked and nodded. "Still pretty as your ma, even with that funny-lookin' hair."

His eyes narrowed. "Whose car is this?"

"It's mine," Pete said. "I'm her boss, and I'm driving."

Pa climbed in and scanned Tenny keenly. "Why'd you run off like you did? We needed you, girl."

"I had a reason to go, Pa." Her voice cracked. Shackley was dead, but the memory choked her.

"You hear I found Jesus?" Pa asked. Tenny told him about Mrs. Brown's letters, and they they rode in silence until they were out in the country.

"I'm sorry I took the Bible, Pa," she said. "I didn't know it had money in it. I spent it getting educated, but I'll pay you back. But how'd you come by it? Why'd you and Shackley chase me?"

Her father chuckled. "Oh, Lord, girl. That were money he give me to buy sugar and copper for another still. He set me up, I'd make the shine. If I got caught, he'd get me out of jail. He had his Klan buddies in the right places."

He turned sorrowful eyes to her. "In that Bible were the onliest picture of that boy I ever had."

Tenny felt ashamed that she'd imagined Pa had sold her. But now she needed to know if Byron had told her the truth.

"Pa, you just called Byron 'that boy.' What was the quarrel about between you and him? Was that the reason he left home?" She knew she was treading on dangerous ground.

Pa glanced over at the driver.

"You can talk in front of Dr. Pete," she said. It didn't matter anymore what he knew. They had gone beyond hiding things.

The car purred down the road and the mist rose from the roadway, hazing the morning sunlight. The smell of woodsmoke drifted from cabins across a field. Pa waited a long moment, the way he used to do when he was thinking about what to say.

"Your Ma told Byron on her deathbed that I warn't his Pa. That Arno Shackley come here and had his way with her soon after we moved in. Said he was taking his rights as landlord. He swore to her he'd kill me if she ever told. So she never did.

"She told Byron because she figured that since Eben Shackley died in the war, Shackley might own up and claim Byron, ease his way in life. But when Byron went to see him, Shackley claimed Em'ly had made the whole thing up. Byron was so mad he came and told me, though his ma had begged him not to. I didn't want to hear it and clobbered him."

"Did you ever suspect it, Pa?"

Pa shook his head. "I did wonder for a long time about why he was so much bigger than me or your ma, but your ma always said her pa was a big man. I told Byron he was a fool for going to Shackley and a bigger fool for telling me. I was sick to heart that day I run him off. I didn't mean to do it.

"He told me, girl, that one day he'd come back and get even with me and Shackley both. Looks like he done it."

"When did you realize that this Ned was Byron, Pa?"

"Not right at first. But when he fired at me, I got a good look at him, and I knew. I raised that boy, you know, taught him all he knew. Liked to broke my heart to raise my gun to him. But girl, when I shoot, I shoot to kill, and I didn't want to kill that boy. He had some good in him. He just lost his way, like I did."

Tenny's heart raced when Pete turned onto the country dirt road to Weedy Grove. It smelled of leaf smoke, the sky was blue as could be, the chinaberry trees lined the fields, and the fields still held the tags of cotton, and there were shacks—

The shack where she had been born. The others—Merry and Emmy Dee and Milton—ran out to greet them, and Mrs. Brown was there too. Tenny flung open the door of the car. ne.

"I can't stay too long," she said, hugging each in turn. "Dr. Pete needs to get back."

"Well, you all just come in and set a spell," said Mrs. Brown. "I've brought cake. We've been waiting since you rang up the parsonage."

Tenny opened the trunk, reached in, and brought out the Bible. When she placed it in Pa's hands, she strode briskly up the weathered gray steps, so she wouldn't have to see his tears.

On the way back home, Pete caught her hand whenever he could, and she didn't pull away.

# Chapter 67

The fog was rising on the river toward evening when Gussie sat with Henry in her father's car, looking out at the river. She'd just wanted to get away from everybody and try to make sense of the past few days.

"I know you wanted to find Ned," Henry was saying. "I wanted to help you. But your father's dead-set against your getting involved. Says to let law enforcement do their job. Let Burkett's detectives do their job."

"I can at least write letters," Gussie insisted. "Write to the old padre. Ask him to have Rafael report if he sees Ned in Havana."

"It's a long shot. He could be holed up in Savannah, but they haven't been able to get anything out of Wyckham," Henry said.

Gussie stared out at the migrating geese which stopped by, honking and ruffling their feathers. "I feel so helpless."

"You know," said Henry. "We could travel together if we were married."

"Married? Oh, Henry!"

"You're not really married to Ned," Henry pointed out. "Not legally."

Gussie squirmed in her seat. She wanted to get out, walk away, anything but face facts. "But Henry, I never wanted a life in Ashbyville. If I'm really free, I could leave town, take Gracie with me . . . my little bastard! In New York no one would know. I could say I was a war widow." Tears welled in her eyes.

Henry drew out his handkerchief and dabbed at her wet cheeks. "Don't use that bad word about your daughter. If you married me, I'd adopt her, of course. Here in Ashbyville, you have your mom and dad, your sisters, Pete, your aunt and uncle. They're all rooting for you. Who's going to look after Gracie in New York?"

Gussie crossed her arms and stared out at the river. A chill wind gusted from the north, ruffling the river, and Henry reached over to roll up Gussie's window. His arm lingered and she unfolded herself and let him kiss her, a long, slow kiss, a kiss that went on and on and stirred something in Gussie she hadn't felt since those first months with Ned.

"Maybe we'll go there together some day. New York," he murmured.

"You're still in school, Henry."

He lifted her chin and made her look at him, made her meet his gaze. "You're a modern woman, I'm a modern man. You keep on with your photography, with your job with Lyman Stratton. I'm thinking about quitting law school and joining the Pinkertons to learn the business. Then I'll hang out my shingle as a private eye."

Gussie had to smile then. "Henry, you'll do nothing of the sort. Papa thinks you'll be a brilliant lawyer. Don't change your life's plan for me." She was still dizzy from that kiss. Henry had metamorphosed somehow from a lanky student into a man worthy of her attention, all while she'd been preoccupied elsewhere.

"It isn't just you," Henry said. "I'm going to find out who killed my father and who killed Toby Burkett."

"You suspect who it is, don't you?"

"Yes, and he's dead. But there may be more people involved. I suspect Ned knows something, just a gut feeling. Another reason I want to find him."

Gussie stopped then, watching the river flow, carrying things away, carrying away fallen leaves and litter and fish and dead bodies, and the river flowed in, carrying floating flowers and ducks and reflections of blue sky and glittering sun and leaping fish.

She still had her talent, and she felt good about making her own way. That bright life, the jazz and cocktails, the lovers and the wild parties, didn't seem to fit this Gussie that she had become.

She laid her head on Henry's shoulder. "It'll take time," she said.

"We've got all the time in the world," Henry said. "Time, and the river."

Gussie glanced up when she heard a car, and then sank back into Henry's arms when it continued on down the road.

Pete parked as closely as he could to the spot, the sprawling flat rock where he had stood with Gussie and her camera that day. He'd had Nola pack a hamper carefully, with hot coffee in a Thermos and ham sandwiches and freshly made apple tarts.

A chill was falling, but Pete and Tenny sat atop a blanket and ate the sandwiches and drank the coffee and savored the apple tarts as well as a few squares of chocolate Pete had tucked in.

Wisps of fog rose from the river, a fish splashed, and the moon peeped over the treetops. Finally Pete spoke. "I brought you here so we could talk, and you've hardly said a word."

Tenny hugged her shoulders, looking straight ahead. "I have to go. Miss Wells told me I have to come back."

"I know," Pete said, his throat thick.

"So what is there to say but good-bye?"

He swallowed and spoke softly. "I wanted to show you where I first saw you and knew from the very beginning that we were supposed to be together."

"Forgot it awfully quick, didn't you?" she said, her voice hardly more than a whisper.

"That's not fair, Tenny." He took her cold hand, warming it, and told her how he'd come to marry Swanee: what she'd asked him to do, how he'd refused. What he had done instead.

"And Baby is Ned's, isn't she?" She found it hard to call him Byron. He wasn't her Byron, not the Byron that had showed her how to bait a hook and feed baby goats and taken her with a zinc pail to where all the blackberries hung ripe and low over the roadside.

"I'm her legal father. Ned and Swanee deserted her."

There was a long pause. She let go of his hand.

"What if they turn up? What if they change their minds?"

"Tenny." He caressed her cheek. "Somebody will kill Ned or he'll go to jail, and Swanee can't come back to Ashbyville. She'll be disgraced and might even be charged with aiding a fugitive."

"What if that happened?" She looked up at him stubbornly. How much did he still care for his runaway wife?

He took both her hands, then, and gazed into her eyes. "Swanee was always a woman in disguise. You're real, and I want you by my side, now and always. It isn't going to be an easy road. I believe that you love your niece, and I know that you love me. Will you marry me once I'm free?"

A lonely whippoorwill called, and then they heard the too-whooing of an owl, and he leaned over and kissed her, and they were lying on the blanket, the picnic things spread all around, and the moon poured stippled light along the rippling river. The rock was hard but the blanket was soft, and their bodies were warm.

They clung together in hunger and thirst, overflowing with grief and their love. Afterward she wept.

"Pete," she said through her tears, "I can't be your mistress. There's no way we can keep that kind of secret in Ashbyville. And I do want to finish school, become a trained nurse. I need respectability."

"Hush," he said and kissed the salty tears off her face, "I won't take that away from you, though it'll be hard. You don't know how hard."

She bowed her head. "I know, Pete. Yes, I do."

He tipped her face up towards his. "Look at the river," he said. "It took the life of my friend, but it brought you to me. You came out of that water like a newborn babe, facing a new life with courage. I hardly deserve you, my river nymph. My own struggles and trials are just beginning, but if you're there, I can survive."

Tenny gazed out at the rippling water, glimmering with points of light from the moon and stars. She rose, then, and walked to the edge, stepping carefully. She kneeled and dipped her hand in the water, and he did the same. She laid her head against his heart and twined her hand, which had touched life, in his.

# Notes and Acknowledgments

~~~~~~~~~~~~~~~~~~~~~~~~

First of all I'd like to thank my husband Joe, even though his proposal of marriage—one day after I'd finished the second draft of *The River Nymph*—delayed the book for more time than I'd like to admit. But he kept after me until I resumed work on it, and since then he's been my greatest supporter and reader.

A raftload of thanks to the Midtown Writers' Group for listening to drafts and redrafts and challenging me to prove my historical facts. Special thanks to Anne Webster, R.N., for keeping me straight about nursing procedures.

I owe a great debt of gratitude to those nurses of the 1910s and 1920s who committed their experiences to the page, and to all the "cotton mill girls" who wrote or recorded oral history of their work experiences. And to Steve Archer, who told me first-hand what mill work was like.

I so appreciate Nanette Littlestone's and Alicia Dean's editing, Peter Hildebrandt's fine layout and his willingness to bear with me until we got the lovely cover right. Namaste.

The town of Ashbyville is fictitious, of course, but it was loosely based on the town of Macon, Georgia, about fifty miles from my home town. Thanks to the Washington Library there for its excellent books on Macon history and hospitals. I did not base my cotton mill on the actual cotton mill that was once in Macon, but I assembled my mill and its mill village from various accounts of mills in Georgia and South Carolina, both fictional and historical.

A reading list of books for those interested can be found on my website, www.annelovett.com.

# More by Anne Lovett

www.annelovett.com

## RUBIES FROM BURMA

Can a young girl find the courage to save the sister she hates?

In a rural Georgia town in 1941, young Mae Lee Willis feels invisible next to her glamorous, sultry older sister, engaged to Lt. Duke Radford, son of a wealthy industrialist. But when Ava dumps Duke for another while he's on an undercover mission in Burma, Mae Lee, who loves him from afar, fights to make sure he comes back to them. Her actions cause unintended consequences... and she eventually must make a choice that will change her life forever.

"Exceptionally satisfying—Lovett is the real deal."
—Kirkus reviews

## SAVING MISS LILLIAN

An unspoiled island's fate stands in the balance as a nurse fends off a plot to kill the island's owner.

Single mother Sunny Iles, after a romantic disaster, impulsively quits her nursing job to take another in the next state. To fill the six weeks between jobs, she signs on to look after an elderly grande dame who just happens to own an island. The catch is that somebody is trying to kill the lady to get control of the island, and Sunny finds that not only is she now a bodyguard, but definitely doesn't need to fall in love with the hunky island naturalist.

"A closely woven tale of greed and deceit—a winner for sure!"
—Fran Stewart, author of the *ScotShop* and the *Biscuit McKee* mystery series